On
Her
Own

On Her Own

A NOVEL

Lihi Lapid

Translated from the Hebrew by Sondra Silverston

HARPERVIA

An Imprint of HarperCollins*Publishers*

ON HER OWN. Copyright © 2021 by Lihi Lapid. All rights reserved. Printed in the United States of America. No part of this book may be used or reproduced in any manner whatsoever without written permission except in the case of brief quotations embodied in critical articles and reviews. For information, address HarperCollins Publishers, 195 Broadway, New York, NY 10007.

HarperCollins books may be purchased for educational, business, or sales promotional use. For information, please email the Special Markets Department at SPsales@harpercollins.com.

Originally published as זרות in Israel in 2021 by כתר

FIRST HARPERVIA EDITION PUBLISHED IN 2024

Designed by Yvonne Chan

Library of Congress Cataloging-in-Publication Data has been applied for.

ISBN 978-0-06-330976-0

24 25 26 27 28 LBC 5 4 3 2 1

Deddy, my brother,
I missed you for so long, now I will miss you forever.

The sound of footsteps wakes her. She has no idea where she is, but she knows she shouldn't move. Her senses sharpen. The smell is unfamiliar. Carefully, she opens one eye to a narrow slit and sees soft red slippers, a nightgown hanging above them, moving down the steps toward her. Soundlessly, she curls up in a corner and tries to remember how she ended up in this stairwell. Her flashy minidress is scratchy and she realizes she has no panties, so she presses her thighs together. She has no idea how many hours she's been here. She tries to open her eyes, but the glare of the fluorescent light is blinding. She closes them again. She wants to sleep some more, a lot more, to rest her head on the step again. To be oblivious. But that won't get her anywhere. And then she remembers: a place, that's what she needs. A place to be for the time being.

◆ ◆ ◆

He didn't believe that was what she'd do. And he told her so. "You can't be without me. You'll come crawling back," he said and laughed loudly with his friends, peeling away the last vestiges of her dignity. "But you promised me," she pleaded, and he just sat there in the front seat, made the music louder and lit a cigarette while the men in the back seat with her touched her, stroked her. "I believed you," she whispered through her exhaustion even though she knew he didn't hear, and pleaded again, "Stop, please." He lowered the volume of the raucous music and told her not to insult them. "They're not nice enough for you? They didn't act nice tonight?" he snickered, then turning serious, he rebuked her, "What is it with you?"

The too-much-aftershave guy who always devoured her with his eyes said to him, "Relax, Shmueli, it's okay, I've had tougher bitches than her," unzipped his fly, and pushed her head down while the other one pulled off her panties. She tried to resist. He tore them. They stopped at a light. She felt like she was going to vomit.

◆ ◆ ◆

The light in the stairwell goes out. "Is someone here?" she hears the woman shuffling in the red slippers say in that old lady's voice that has amassed many years and memories. The light will go on again in a minute so she takes advantage of the brief darkness to open her eyes and calculate the danger. She listens to the old lady dragging her feet to the light switch and tries to hold her breath. She needs more time to decide what to do, to understand where she is and where she'll go from here. She won't go back, no matter what. There's no place to go back to anyway. Definitely not to him, and not back home either. She needs to think quickly about where she *can* go.

"Is someone here?" the old lady asks again after she switches on the light, dazzling Nina, forcing her to cover her eyes, blinded to everything but the tattered red slippers of the sleepless old lady, and if only she'd go back to her apartment already, back to bed. She feels around for her evening bag or her phone and realizes that she didn't take anything when she ran away. Stupid idiot, she says to herself. As her eyes begin to adjust to the light, she takes a deep breath and tenses her body. She'll dash out to the street. And from there, it doesn't matter where. Just as long as that annoying old lady disappears and lets her wake up and think and decide what to do. But what annoys her most is that her mom was right. "Shit," she curses.

The light goes out again.

The first rays of sun shatter on the glass door of the building, bathing the silhouette of the old lady in yellow. Now it's clear that the old lady sees her.

She's trying to think of something to say when the old lady calls out to her happily, "Dana! What are you doing here?! My *mamushka*!"

Though Nina evades the sunbeams, she realizes that that's it, she's really screwed, now it's not just the old lady but also some Dana who'll turn up in another minute. She looks around, trying to figure out where this Dana is supposed to be coming from before the old lady sees she's not anyone's Dana and calls the police and she gets even more screwed. She has to get away from here.

But before she can figure out what's going on and do something, the old lady comes over and throws her arms around her. "Dana," she says joyfully, and then moves Nina's face away to examine it close up.

"Dana. My Dana," she says. "You're here. You came back to me."

Nina lowers her head, trying to hide her face with her disheveled hair. Just don't let this old lady turn on the light again, she wishes silently, her head is exploding.

◆　◆　◆

"It'll be the end of you," Shmueli shouted at her back as she ran away. "You think you'll manage here without me? And who will you call, eh? Who'll help you? Just wait, you'll beg me." And that was it, she didn't hear any more. She doesn't know what hurts her more now, her heart or her cheekbone where he slapped her when she said she didn't want to sit in the back with them and he told her she didn't understand how much that disrespected his friends. She'd already seen many slaps in her life, in movies and also in reality. Some of her girl-friends got slapped more than once by their parents. She just never imagined it hurt so much. Soon, when she looks in the mirror, she'll see the black-and-blue mark on her forehead as well and won't even remember how she got it, whether someone else hit her or maybe she banged her head on the door trying to get away from them. She curses the day they met. The day she thought was the luckiest day in her life, until now.

She always knew she was beautiful. It was something she grew up with. The way some kids have a blanket or a ball or a dad. Like all girls, when she got to be a teenager, she began to see her flaws and thought all the other girls were more than her. More beautiful or more clever, or their hair was always perfect or their breasts were bigger than her very small ones, but with time, she couldn't help but feel what happened to people when they looked at her. The older women, the ones who had always hugged her and pinched her cheek when she was a child, or handed her a piece of candy and spit three times against the evil eye, *tfu tfu tfu*—they stopped touching her, didn't go near her anymore. The warmth in their gazes and the smiles on their faces disappeared too. And the more distant they grew, those older women, the closer the girls in her class came, trying to understand, to touch, to feel it close up, to learn how to acquire a bit of that breath-taking thing for themselves. Then the boys came closer, as if she were a bowl of honey, and then the older guys began to buzz around her, at first with puffed-out chests, then with motorcycles, and then the men who got out of cars some kid had polished for a few pennies began to look at her, trying to steal her attention. Some of them attempted to trap her in their shiny, humming webs, to tie her up with their ropes and, for a moment, hold on to the feeling that they could possess that rare thing, and she saw the sweat of their efforts on them.

There were also the men who only looked at her but didn't try to possess her or get close to her, knowing they didn't stand a chance. The same way she looked at the expensive brand names displayed in the shop windows at the mall. They looked at her with the knowledge that she would never be theirs. It wouldn't happen to them. The kind of man who had already suffered enough blows in life and knew his place, who walked behind his wife in the shopping center, sometimes holding her small handbag on his arm. The kind of man who, looking at her, recalled his youth with a sense of having missed out, mostly because of some girl to whom he hadn't dared tell his feelings a long time ago. They were the men who had the look in their eyes that saw what she tried so hard to hide, the child in her, a look that peeled away the thorns and exposed the vulnerability. The male look that always prompted her mother to use the expression Nina hated so much, "He's a good man." Who needs a good man, she would say, laughing at her silently, sometimes out loud, as they sat at the greenish Formica table in the narrow kitchenette that could hold only the two of them, and even that was a tight squeeze. And her mother would say, "I do."

A good man isn't so important, Mom, you don't understand anything, she told her. What you need is a strong man. A man with power. She didn't tell her how much she dreamed about that man who would come to take her away from here, who would start his car and whisk her away to another place. No, he wouldn't be a good man, she knew. She had no illusions about that. But she was smart, she already knew something about this world, and she thought she'd use him no less than he would use her. Use him to fly far away from here. And look, he came. She only had to touch him sometimes, and that was okay. Shmueli, whose friends called him Johnny, was so excited that it was over quickly. And she was excited by the intense feeling that she had power over him. How addicted he was to her hands. To her touch. He followed her to school. He would pick her up in the morning to take her there just to have those five minutes with her. He would leave Ofra in front of the TV in the evening and drive over for a quick visit, just come down to the car for a minute, he'd say. At first he didn't need a lot. Just her hand, sometimes her mouth a little. Then he began to touch her under her clothes and it took him longer. That's why he wanted to have her for a whole night.

Her mother sat across from her, rubbing the table with the rough tips of her fingers, cleaning away more and more invisible crumbs. Then she reached up to her head, took out the clips, and let her beautiful, full head of hair land gently on her shoulders. And for the first time, Nina saw how much gray streaked her hair and how much the original wheat color had faded.

It needed to be washed. They both knew.

"It's not a good idea," Irina told her in despair, trying to stop a train that had left the station a long time ago.

When Irina was Nina's age, she too thought she knew better. Better than anyone. In the end, she turned out to be an idiot. Now she's here, alone with her daughter who thinks she knows better and doesn't understand that she doesn't. She only just turned eighteen, and she's smart, it's not that she isn't, but not as smart as she thinks, and for a while now, from afar, you could see the word *trouble* engraved on her. A large warning sign written on her beauty. Because Nina was much more beautiful than she had been at her age, when she was an idiot.

She'd been a good-looking idiot. Her Nina was more beautiful than her. Too beautiful.

Nina had fought it for years. As a child, she tried so hard to keep people from seeing only that, tried to hide it, to cover her face with her hair. "Let me see you," Shmueli said, holding her face after he'd pushed away her hair, coming a bit too close. A lot too close. "You promised you wouldn't touch," she said.

"Right," he replied, "and I always keep my promises, so I won't touch, but maybe you will," and he pulled her hand toward his groin. "Only if you want to," he said with a laugh. "You don't have to." But in the end, she had to. Not that day, but two days later, when it was almost dawn and she was so tired and she knew she had an exam that morning and was eager to go home and take a shower. She touched his pants there and he pressed her hand down with his own, really, really hard, and she heard his breathing in her ear, and the panting, and the groaning, and she didn't want to see his face contorting. He told her that now he was dirty because of her. That he had a better idea for the next time. One that would leave him clean.

❖　❖　❖

"You don't understand, you just don't understand," her mother said angrily during that conversation, after Shoshi at the day-care center told her the name of the person she was running around with. "You're a child. What business do you have with that man?"

"He loves me."

"Loves you? Wants you maybe, not loves you."

"He loves me."

"Do you love him?

"He loves me."

"That's not what I asked."

"Yes. I do."

"You don't. And he doesn't love you either. You're nothing to him. He's just using you. He'll toss you away, like an old rag he'll toss you away. What do you need that for? You know what kind of reputation you'll have?"

"You don't understand," Nina shouted, clutching her mother's wrists, forcing her to look at her wrinkled hands with their short nails she'd painted with gel polish for the bar mitzvah their neighbor Michal had made for her son, which now was chipped and peeling. "I won't be like you," she said, "I won't destroy my life, my body, my hands, for just enough money to pay the bills in this shithole. Forget it. I won't be like you. I'm leaving this place."

"Don't talk to me like that," Irina raised her voice, her anger causing all the letters to explode in that accent she couldn't shed, that hadn't softened with the years. Then she switched to Russian, *Yob tvoyu mat syka blyat'*, she hissed the string of curses, and Nina stopped talking. She wanted to shout, but realized that she'd already gone too far. I'll show her, she said to herself, I'll show her yet.

There was a long silence, and Irina got up and walked out of the room, as tall and proud as usual, only her shoulders showing how tired she was. She'd been bearing this burden alone for eighteen years and this was the first time she'd ever felt that she had no more strength. That she wanted someone to take care of her for once. She remembered that birthday of hers, when Nina was five, and how she'd come home from work to a house full of hearts, candles, flowers, things that Nina had collected and cut and arranged for her, how they'd sat together, she and Babushka and Ninotchka, and how she'd blown out the candles with one breath.

"What did you wish for?" Nina had asked.

"You're not supposed to tell because then it won't come true," she'd replied even though she wanted so much to share the joy with her. To tell her that there, in that small kitchen, was everything she wanted. There they were, finally together, the three of them together, and they didn't need anyone else. Later on, Babushka wasn't with them anymore, and how hard it was without her, how much Nina tried to make up for that absence. But as the years slowly passed, they were okay, and she didn't need anything more. The two of them was fine. It was good. And although she knew that in no time at all, Nina would be grown up, she didn't think it would happen so fast, and not like that. A month earlier, she'd put some money into a small savings plan for students so that her little Nina, her beautiful Nina, would have what she'd never had. She didn't want anything for herself, only for her little one to soar as high as she could. But not at this cost, not with a man who would take her and harm her.

◆ ◆ ◆

Irina goes into the bathroom and washes her face, looks at herself, remembers how she, like Nina, thought she was so smart, and how she too thought she'd twist them, the men, around her little finger, and she really did. Especially Nina's father. He loved her so much, but it burned out quickly, so quickly, when she had a belly and wasn't as happy or beautiful anymore. In the end she found herself somewhere in the middle of a blazing desert, on the second floor, alone with a baby girl. Without a language, without a profession, with a sackful of promises that he took with him to his next woman. And to this day, she's paying the price for it with her loneliness. Because one day, the beauty betrays you, fades, slowly falls away, and men no longer look at you, and women's glances no longer linger for that extra second that caresses your body and your face. A battle lost from the outset, its end foretold. Sometimes there's one galloping horse that might slow down during one of its turns around the track, and for a moment, you'll feel as if you've won, and you'll believe it'll stop, but no. And the beauty continues to tire, to erode, in the end collapsing under the weight of the years. And with beautiful women—the years pile on the weight with greater cruelty.

◆ ◆ ◆

For the first time, she's working in one place, not running from house to house to accumulate more and more hours, battling her body's exhaustion in the face of the need, the necessity. It'll soon be a year since she started there. And she actually likes it. Finally she's not alone, but with other people, women. How scared she'd been to work with women and be part of a group, because as a young girl, she didn't get along with the other girls, with the gossip, with their closed circles and the jealousy and the internal wars, but now there was no longer a reason to be jealous of her, she thought sadly. Over the years, she got used to working alone as a cleaner, going from a four-hour job to a five-hour job, and most of the time, there wasn't even anyone there to see her. Her body hurt, but she loved being alone, being the one to decide with no one there to mix in. But now she's discovered how nice it actually is that they see her, that they see what she does, how much she invests in her job, how hard she works. And no matter how hard she works, it's not as hard as shaking out heavy living room rugs and moving the beds because the women of the house always check behind them. From the first minute on her new job, she made the decision to get along with everyone, to keep out of the assistants' quarrels and the tension between the staff and the management. She didn't care. She was in charge of the cooking and cleaning. She's still surprised at how much she now enjoys the things that once put her off, responsibility and teamwork. She has a job with vacation days and holidays and things she never thought she'd have, like a pay slip and sick days and pension payments, and she's not sacrificing her health for more income. Now she wants to become a permanent employee. When that happens, she'll have peace of mind. Slowly she's taken on more responsibility, expanding her duties, and it seems as if no one in the day-care center remembers how it was without her. "You put the Lego in the dishwasher?" Shoshi the manager asked in surprise, and Irina said, "When all the pieces are smeared with ketchup and macaroni—then yes," and Shoshi laughed and said that made sense and she never would have thought of it. And she loves being with the children. They're happy around her, happy to see her, and their presence brings out a softness in her that she never knew she possessed. She feels confident around them, doesn't need to worry about what they'll think or say, doesn't have to defend herself against those little ones who haven't been ruined yet, soft and sweet as cactus fruit that still haven't grown thorns. And she basks in their love. The love of the little boy who runs to her in tears, of the little girl who asks her to put her hair in a ponytail. And how adorable they were yesterday when they checked every inch of the day-care center for leavened food, *chametz*, before Passover, using the traditional feathers and candles in their search. "Helping Irina making the center kosher for Passover," they called it.

◆ ◆ ◆

She's sitting at the stop, waiting for the bus to come. Tomorrow's the Seder night and she's on her way home from Haviva's. "Please come help me before the holiday," Haviva asked. "How can I prepare the Seder without you?" Irina has helped her with the Seder for so many years, and every year Haviva tried to persuade her to stay until after the main course, but Irina wouldn't do it. It didn't matter how much money she offered her. She told her she'd be happy to come the next morning. And she did go a few times, but after Haviva's sons got married, the daughters-in-law helped her. "I really lucked out with them," Haviva told her.

"Stay to help me tomorrow night and I'll pay you." Haviva tried this year too, maybe because it had already become a tradition between them. But Irina knew in advance that she'd want to come home to her Nina, to be with her. And now that the day has arrived, Nina isn't here. Who would have believed two weeks ago that something like this would happen? Now, of all times, when she can finally give them the life they wanted, Nina's not here. She'll come back in another few days for sure, she reassures herself. There'll be a lot of tears and it'll hurt, but they'll get past it. If only the manager makes her job permanent like she promised. And maybe, she dares to hope as she looks down the street, maybe Nina is home now. It's been ten days already, enough. Maybe she's come back and is waiting for her. And suddenly, she feels too impatient to wait for the bus.

Since she met him, Nina has been speaking to her in a way she never dared to before. It never used to be like that between them. She herself never had the nerve to speak to Babushka that way. Chutzpah was never an option. "No culture," she used to mutter and tighten her grip on little Nina's hand whenever she saw a girl on the street or in the supermarket yelling at her mother, "No culture." She also checked the community center ads and if something interesting was coming, she was the first to buy them tickets, even if that woman in the community center gave them a puzzled look, why bring a little girl to a play for adults. Irina couldn't care less about that, and she would save up more and more money for it, for culture. Twice they traveled to the big city of Beersheba to hear a concert and once to see a performance of the Israeli Russian Theater, Gesher, which they had to leave before the end so they wouldn't miss the last bus. They sat in the last row, the cheapest seats, but that didn't bother her, and at the second concert, Irina spoke to the usher, and during intermission, the woman called them over and moved them to the fourth row. "The fourth row is the best," the usher said with a heavy Russian accent, adding angrily, "Who doesn't come when they have fourth-row seats? No culture there." Irina has never forgotten that. Now, thanks to her new job, she's ordered tickets to the performance of a symphony orchestra conducted by some Israeli everyone loves, two really good seats in the third row on the side. Because she has a new job now. And because she deserves it. But Nina isn't here. And she's angry. Angry about the lack of culture, about her Nina talking in the ugly, disrespectful way those sabras talk. It's a good thing Babushka isn't alive to hear it. To see it. Her weak heart would have broken. That heart was already cracked from years of cold weather and small apartments, and all she wanted in the last years of her life was the sun. I don't want a hospital, she said, please, just the sea. The sea. And more than anything, she wanted an orange.

Something else enters, unannounced, into her sadness and anger. It comes like a punch to the chest. Maybe something is wrong with Nina. That's something she hasn't thought about until now, that maybe something bad is happening to her. She should have stopped her from going, she definitely shouldn't have carried on about decency and education. What does decency matter now if her Nina is in danger? And that train is racing through her heart now.

The bus arrives and she replays that day in her mind, how she sat and listened to Nina skip down the steps in her high heels, down the two floors that Irina had climbed wearily so many times. And all she did was go to the window and peer through the shutters to see her daughter get into the car, and that man didn't even get out to open the door for her. Don't you see? she wanted to scream at her, don't you see it's not love? And when she finally did shout those words, it was too late. And she'll never know whether it would have helped if she had shouted them long before then.

◆ ◆ ◆

"Dana'le," the old lady says, takes Nina's hand, places it on her heart, and begins pulling her along to the stairs. Nina finds the unfamiliar touch strange and unpleasant and she wants to jerk her hand away. Get away from here, she says to herself, get away, but that night with all the running, the drinking, the fear, the way that asshole yelled at her, everything that happened there and what she saw has destroyed all her strength. And she doesn't have shoes either. She won't be able to walk far barefoot, definitely not in that short cocktail dress with the plunging neckline.

"Put on some nice clothes, some makeup," he told her before they left, explaining that this is how it is in the big city and she should get used to it.

She hadn't been out of the apartment for a few days, she just sat there in front of the TV. Punishment. He even took her phone away after his friend groped her and she fought him off. She tried to tell him that he hurt her, but that didn't interest Shmueli, nothing about her interested him anymore. "Be a good girl for a week and you'll get it back," he said. "And don't insult my friends anymore."

He used to show up at the apartment with his friends, unannounced. Suddenly they would all breeze in, sometimes in the morning, sometimes in the evening, to watch soccer, to play cards. "Enough with the rags," he said one day, tossing a short dress at her, and since then, whenever he came in, he would ask, Why aren't you wearing the dress I brought you? So every night she washed and dried it, and except for that, never took it off. She ate and cleaned and waited in it, never knowing when they would arrive, and in that dress she made them coffee and put the snacks he bought on plates, and she could barely bend over, that's how short it was. "So they'll get a little peek, babe, what's the big deal?" he said, and they laughed. Then he sat her on his lap and she felt his excitement and he closed his eyes and everyone watched and he panted, and she wanted to die of shame, and he took her into the bedroom and she heard them laughing. Later, he just left her there, then yelled at her to come out because they wanted coffee, and when they all got up to leave, he said, "You're starting to act nice, this is how I love you," and she replied that she didn't feel like he loved her anymore, and he asked in a whisper, "Why, baby?" and she said, I just don't. Then he took her into the bedroom and shouted for his friends to get going, he'd be there in a minute. He closed the door, hugged her, and said, "How can you say that? I never loved anyone like I love you."

She told him that she was closed up in the apartment all the time.

"You want to come with us?" he asked.

Yes, she said.

And to this day, she regrets it. That was her biggest mistake. Going out that evening.

"Put on a little more makeup," he told her, and she didn't argue. "And don't act stupid," he whispered, "or else you won't go out again for a long time."

❖ ❖ ❖

Thank God, the old lady doesn't switch on the glaring light in the stairwell again, and only the glowing rays of the morning sun spill inside and are caught in the thick, tangled gray hair. "Dana, why didn't they tell me you were coming?" she says in a soft, pleasant voice. "I've been waiting so long for you."

Nina knows she should say something. It would be better just to take off, but the tiredness prevails and she simply stands there, knowing that now she'll certainly ask her why she's barefoot, and what will

15

she tell her? But the old lady doesn't ask anything, just strokes Nina's hands with her scrawny fingers and keeps mumbling how good it is that Dana has come, here she is, Dana is here. The old lady starts climbing the steps and Nina follows. Slowly, as slowly as possible. On the first floor, the old lady walks from door to door, peers around, looking for something familiar. Then another floor, and Nina has the feeling that this search will never end, but look, there's an open door. Second floor, apartment number five. Ben Zion. Remember, Nina says to herself. Memorize.

"Are you tired?" the sweet old lady asks with a smile, ignoring the fact that she's barefoot and wearing a short, torn, glittery mini.

"Very," she says, as they walk through the small, messy apartment, the sour smell of mildew and neglect hovering in the air, crying out for someone to open a window. "Here's your room, waiting for you, sweetheart," the old lady says, opening the door of the bathroom with a flourish, then laughing, and opening the second door. A soft light floods the room, which is completely pink. Like in a little girl's dream, a little angel's room with dolls and curtains imprinted with tiny fairies and even wallpaper with glittering stars.

"I haven't touched it," the old lady says, "since you left, I haven't touched it. Here are your pajamas," she says, pulling something suitable for a little girl out of the closet, and then she suddenly walks over to Nina, hugs her, and says, "I've been waiting so long for you. So long. I knew you'd come back to me. I knew you wouldn't forget me."

The old lady breaks away and looks at her face, and for a moment, something in her expression changes. Nina lowers her head, expecting a shout of alarm, and the old lady gives her a slightly different look, not as soft, but then her smile returns and she asks warmly, "You want to take a shower? I can see you had a rough flight. Go take a shower."

Nina goes into the bathroom and locks the door behind her, glad to be alone for a moment to try to think about what to do next. Everything is so weird. Through the closed door, she hears the old lady making a cup of coffee for herself in the kitchen against the background of the deep, flirty voice of a radio announcer. Quiet songs ease the transition from night to morning.

She looks at herself in the bathroom mirror. She pulls her hair back and peers at her swollen left cheek, and there's a black-and-blue mark on her forehead. Her makeup has run, staining her face with black mascara tears, and her pink bra is showing through her torn dress. She doesn't understand why that old lady didn't say anything, didn't react at all to the mess that's supposed to be her face, and maybe that's why, for a fraction of a second, there was something distant, something frightened in her expression. And who the hell is that Dana, who must be on her way here.

She knows this isn't the time to analyze a weird old lady's behavior, she has a few hours of grace and she has to use them to get some sleep in this safe haven. The worst thing for her now would be to wander around outside. There's no way of knowing whether he's looking for her. He or his people. She has to take advantage of the time to sleep so she can get her strength back. She can barely stand on her feet. She remembers running so much last night that her breath was gone and she didn't know whether they might suddenly appear, so she tried to get into a building to at least hide. She ran from one door to another, and one after the other was locked. Luckily she found this one, which was open, and then that creepy old lady, who wanders around the building at five or six in the morning as if it were noontime, throwing out garbage, picking up newspapers and taking a filthy young girl into her apartment. Most people would have looked away and kept walking, at best, or driven her out with a broom or called the police, at worst. But that old lady looked at her, ignored all the black-and-blue warning signs on her face, took her into the pink room, and called her Dana'le. As if they knew each other.

Nina has a lot of questions, but they'll wait until later. Now she just wants to take a hot shower. And put her head down for a few hours. She starts peeling off her dress and is immediately struck by the disgusting mixture of odors coming off her body, a combination of cigarette smoke in her hair, of too-strong aftershave mixed with the stench of the sweat of the men who had pressed up against her, along with the too-sweet perfume she'd sprayed on herself in the apartment, but even that couldn't cover the smell of her fear. The images of that terrible evening make her want to vomit.

An idiot, that's what I am, she thinks, and, as if seized by a sudden fit of madness, she rips off the rest of her dress and turns on the hot water. The mirror is immediately covered with steam, preventing her from looking at herself. Her battered, smeared, pathetic self.

The water washes the night off her body, along with the night before it and the two weeks that had stunned her, shaken her, taken her from her home, from her mother, from everything she knew, and in the end had spit her out at the threshold of this nice or not nice old lady's home, a suffocating Tel Aviv apartment filled with notes. An endless number of notes. Large, small, pasted, pinned, thrown around.

Tomorrow she'll read them. After she gets some sleep. She's curious about what's written on them.

The soothing water embraces her like a protective blanket. Her cheek hurts at the touch of it, but the rest of her body is grateful. She wraps the soft towel around herself and goes to the closet in the other room, where she finds a pile of pink winter and summer pajamas with hearts and teddy bears, stripes and flowers, in a variety of sizes, all with the price tags still on them and all too small for her, a crazy little shop of girls' pajamas.

She squeezes into a pair probably meant for a twelve-year-old, but the soft fabric stretches and feels good, and besides, that's all there is. She has just sat down on the edge of the soft bed when she hears a knock at the door and the old lady on the other side of it asks hesitantly, "Dana, you're okay?"

Nina doesn't say anything, she's so tired and confused. If only the old lady doesn't throw her out, not now, she only wants to put her head on the pillow and get under the covers, a short rest for her aching body, to figure out what's next, where she'll go. She's on the verge of tears. Again.

"You're okay?" the old lady asks, this time in English.

"Yes," Nina replies.

"What?"

"I'm okay," she says in English, thinking it must be all right to pepper the conversation with a different language. She has to grab on to every clue, everything that will keep her here for another day or two, until the swelling goes down and her face looks normal again.

"Wonderful," the old lady says.

Nina opens the door and the old lady is standing there, so she reaches out and switches off the light, darkness is better. Safer. She gets into bed, the feel of the blanket that envelops her is so pleasant and the soft mattress seems to gather her into it. It's comforting. Even pleasurable.

The old lady, who has walked over to the bed with her, says, "Good night."

"Good night," Nina replies in English and feels the old lady taking hold of her hands. Usually she doesn't like to be touched, she's not one of those girls who enjoys holding hands, giggling and hugging, but something in that touch reminds her of her babushka, who she misses so much, who never managed to learn even a little Hebrew. And here she is, clean now, lying in the dark room, light threatening to infiltrate through the shutters and the door that has been left slightly open, in a bed with clean white sheets and two unfamiliar hands holding hers with a grandmother's warmth and love, and for a moment, she's filled with longing for a hug after the sea of aloneness that almost drowned her during those stormy two weeks. And even though she doesn't want to cry, the teardrops fall and are soaked up by the pillow.

And she falls asleep.

◆　◆　◆

Carmela goes out of the room and closes the door, almost forgotten feelings rising within her. She has been waiting for this visit for so long, and Itamar had an excuse every time. Once it was because Dana was too little and the flight would be hard, and then because she was too big and had important exams at school, and she couldn't miss school in the middle of the year when he came for the memorial service, and she had summer camp with her girlfriends during vacation, and things were a mess at work, and each time, she hoped that this time she would come with him. On the days when her mind was sharp and clear, she admitted to herself that she didn't know what would happen first, Dana would come or she would stop caring.

"Itamar dear," she told him during their last conversation, "if she doesn't come with you, she can at least come on her own in the summer. I'll pay. Don't worry."

"Ask Itamar to let Dana come on her own!!!" was written on several of the notes scattered around the house, the ones that were almost everywhere, especially near the phone and also near the switched-off computer and beside her bed.

The first time she said it, he was angry that she mentioned money. "Mom," he said, "it isn't about money."

But she'd been saving, she explained, and Itzik had been saving too, and she had the money. It's okay. Itamar remembered how, as a child, he had been apprehensive on the days before the fifteenth of the month, when his parents, Itzik and Carmela, began to worry. At night, Itzik would make columns with a ruler on a piece of paper, sit with the invoices, receipts, and check stubs, and tap on the calculator. He remembered how the house filled with a tense silence, no TV, no radio. And how she would also remain silent, just sit there and wait for the final verdict about whether the month had been good or not. And how much sales tax they had to pay. And would they be scrimping or celebrating. Then Itzik would suddenly call out, "Carmela," and she already knew from the tone of his voice, and Itamar, even as a child, knew as well. Already then, he told himself that he had to succeed. He had to. So he wouldn't need to live with that anxiety every month.

"This summer is problematic for me, for us, to come on vacation," he told his mother that year, and also the next. Once he explained that those were the final days before the merger, and the following year—that it was the merger, and he had to be there to transfer all the data on the operation. He used all sorts of words to explain product and management, things Carmela didn't understand, and he knew she didn't understand, and the longer she remained silent, the more he spoke, and she felt the air being squeezed out of her.

She waited the entire year for summer, all those unnecessary months flew by in her life until they would come to visit. And again they disappointed her, another year. He and his kibbutznik wife, whose control over Itamar Carmela hadn't liked from the beginning. She also told him that when he and his Naama had fought and separated for almost two weeks and he tried to grow a backbone, but in the end, gave in and drove to her kibbutz with flowers and a ring that he and Itzik had bought for a ton of money from Karashi. When Carmela heard about that ring, she asked Itzik worriedly what would happen if Naama said no, what would they do with such an expensive ring? Itzik laughed and said that he'd given Karashi a security check, but they had agreed that he wouldn't cash it, and only if it worked out, Itzik would bring him cash and get a discount. She didn't like the fact that Itzik always tried to slip small amounts past the Income Tax Department. Here one hundred shekels he didn't put into the cash register, there a discount for cash payments. She'd lost so many nights' sleep because of that monkey business of his, afraid they'd be audited. And they would fight about it every time. Now even the great Karashi was doing the same thing.

But that was such a long time ago. Later on, she decided to accept Naama in the nicest way possible, like the daughter she never had. But then it didn't matter anymore because they brought Dana into the world. Little Dana, that small miracle, that creature who lit up her heart. From the moment she was born and made her a grandmother, Dana had captivated her with a force that surprised her, and a bond was formed that she never thought she would have. It was the same for Itzik.

They lived nearby at the time and Carmela was happy to go every day to help, to be there when the kibbutznik couldn't manage and, in desperation, handed her that screaming thing, and in Carmela's arms, that thing calmed down, smiled, became her Dana. She'd never felt such pleasure, such contentment with the boys, she thought. Like Naama, she had been an anxious mother too. And she hadn't had a mother beside her to help. Now it was different. She was calm, everything came naturally to her. Or perhaps it was because of Dana, who was the sweetest thing she'd ever seen, or maybe it was because she was a grandmother this time, not a mother.

Then Itamar said he could help them out a bit now. It was after the picture of him and his friends was published in the newspaper, and Itzik laughed and said, "Who would have believed that with the Bermuda shorts and the flip-flops they were about to sell their company to that large corporation with roman initials instead of a name."

Itamar explained that he would instruct them there on the product and the project, and also it was a good opportunity, a great opportunity that would be a shame to pass up. A little bit of America wouldn't hurt. Another experience, a year at most, to discover and learn, he said as he sat across from Carmela and Itzik, explaining why he was going abroad, and if you want to succeed in the world of high tech today, you need experience in a large international company, preferably in America, and he would never have such an opportunity again. It's not often that you get an offer like this, along with a work permit. And Dana's still small and Naama hasn't found work, so why not?

They looked at him with sad eyes he tried to ignore. It's just a year, he kept saying. At the time, he really believed that it was only for a year, and even though he knew it was crazy to move for only a year, he wasn't ready to give it up. He was curious to see how things worked in the big world, to find out how he measured up against the big boys.

At first, the plan was for him to go alone for a few months. "It's only for a short time," he told Naama in a conversation he'd spent a week planning, "I'll come to visit every month." She looked at him as if he'd gone mad. When he and his partners had talked about it in the office, it sounded logical, and now, talking to her as she sat on the rug with Dana playing with her dollhouse, it really did seem a bit off the wall. And stupid. Go to America alone? Naama said in English, so Dana wouldn't understand. She had no reason to be here alone with their daughter and she would go even if she had to pay for it herself, which were empty words because they had a joint bank account. He knew it was also because her business was going under, and this way she had a reason to let it go. Close it up. Slowly, he had begun to realize that she always looked for reasons to move on to the next thing. She'd had plenty of dreams, but never saw them through. She said she'd go back to designing Internet sites, something she could do anywhere in the world.

The next day he told his partners that Naama was coming with him. And his daughter too. They were surprised and tried to tell him that the company couldn't pay for the family now. That no one knew whether the deal would really go through and it was too great an expense. Hanoch was the angriest. He'd wanted to go too, but he hadn't suggested it because his kids were little and it was clear that they were sending only one person, not a family. True, Itamar was the best fit—his English was excellent and he knew how to speak to people— and Hanoch was just a techie. But now he was angry at himself for having missed out on the opportunity.

Itamar saw they were upset and told them not to worry, he would pay for Naama's ticket, he was sure it would work out, the American company would buy them and merge them and it would all pay off, he wouldn't let this opportunity go to waste. We'll laugh about the money later, he told them.

They started packing. Not like two people going on their post-army trip, but like two people who are moving forever, and they even rented a storeroom for all their things even though Carmela offered her place.

Little Dana wandered around the boxes, repeating the word *America*, and Carmela said that maybe she should stay with her. Dana laughed, darling Dana with her round cheeks and hair that fell into her eyes, and the way she pushed it away like a little lady made Carmela melt. She thought about the documentary she'd seen with Simone de Beauvoir, who said that one isn't born a woman, one becomes a woman, and this little one had become such a woman, too quickly. And maybe that de Beauvoir was wrong.

"Who do you love the most?" she asked her, and Dana would come over and curl into her arms. "I love gamah," she would say in English. Carmela hugged her, unable to believe that this was happening to her, that they were leaving. That they were taking her happy pill away from her. She pleaded with Itzik to tell Itamar to stay, that without them she wouldn't survive. Itzik wanted to know why she was asking him. After all, over the years, he had been her child, her little Itamar, who she pampered. He always told her she was spoiling him. And look, this is what's happening. He wanted to tell her that, but he knew it would break her. So he kept quiet.

"You never tell Itamar what to do," she said, "so if you tell him, they'll realize that they can't go, that it's not done. Nobody leaves two old people alone."

Itzik told her that children don't live for their parents, it doesn't work that way. Children have their lives, and they have to do what's good for them. They're only going for a year, he said, and you don't really want Itamar to remember you later for not supporting him with your whole heart. Wouldn't that be a shame? he asked, hugging her. "You gave him everything, don't stop him now. Let him do what's good for him. Think of him," and she hardened her body and he caressed her slowly until she softened. But a painful disquiet remained in her heart, suffocating her.

"And isn't it a shame that the child won't be with me?" she asked him.

How long she had waited for a girl. All the miscarriages before Uri, and then between Uri and Itamar, and each time she hoped that this time it would be a girl. That she'd have a daughter of her own. To sew clothes for her and be a friend to her.

"You still have me to take care of," Itzik said, smiling that big smile of his. He didn't know that, later on, it wouldn't be funny, and he laughed so rarely after that.

Itamar, Naama, and Dana left, and the house grew silent. And the silence was painful. Especially at Friday-night dinners, the two of them alone, the only sounds coming from the knives and forks.

When they left, there were two pictures on the sideboard. One of Uri in his uniform, and one of Itamar, Naama, and Dana in America. Later, Itamar gave her a picture of everyone at the brit after Ariel was born. And now there were three pictures.

And what about me? Isn't it a shame about me? she wanted to say to Itzik then, and later she mumbled it that night when he didn't wake up and she no longer had Itzik and she stroked his lifeless hand. Itamar called when he was on the way, and by the time he arrived, they had already set the date for the funeral, no one knew who set the date, but there was a time and place and a death notice and a funeral. Luckily, Itamar arrived in time. And standing at the fresh grave, she wanted to ask Itzik, What about what's good for me? Later, she screamed those words night after night. Maybe soundlessly, but with a breaking heart. What about what's good for me?

◆　◆　◆

"It's too bad you rented a storage unit. Seriously. It's really okay to leave the boxes with us," Carmela told him then, surrounded by their packed possessions. "Go, see what the place is like, and if it's really good, I'll send them to you, or you'll come here and take them. After all, you'll come to visit."

He looked at her, her sweet Itamar with his honey eyes, and stopped packing. "Go to Mommy," he said to Dana in English because they'd started getting her used to the language, and sat down beside his mother, took her hand, looked at her beautiful face and those eyes that had watched over him wherever he went. He had felt that gaze so many times, knew she was there. When he kissed a girl on a bench outside, when he scored a goal, she was there, behind a fence, peering out at him from the apartment window, his mom. Once Doron from the eighth grade laughed at him, laughed at her when he saw her behind a bush, and Itamar beat the living daylights out of him. In the principal's office, they asked him what happened. Such a good boy, never hit anyone, what did Doron do to you? What? his teacher and the principal and his parents asked him, but he said nothing. He didn't open his mouth.

◆ ◆ ◆

"I only have one child," he'd heard her crying back then, and he remembered not understanding what that really meant, thinking only that it was a good thing it happened after his bar mitzvah because otherwise, they would certainly have canceled it. Later on, he understood and always felt guilty for thinking about his bar mitzvah.

Ever since, the days between Passover and Memorial Day had become a time of mourning in their home. In the deafening silence, it seemed as if all the glasses would shatter from the tension in the air. And he would withdraw into himself, unable to contain their pain, sick of hearing the "be strong for them" that people said at the shiva and would say over and over again at every anniversary of Uri's death, and he was barely capable of being strong for himself. "Only one child," she would cry to Itzik, the silent father, every time Itamar worried her, when he came home too late, or reported for his first draft call. She cried and said, "And if something happens to him? I'll die if something happens to him, I'll drop dead right then and there."

"Listen, Mom," he said, hugging her, comforting her, "we're going for a year, tops, and then we'll be back. My whole life is here, you and Dad, and our business, which will always remain here. It's very important that the deal goes off without a hitch. You know that I love you best in the world, but I have to do this myself."

Just like, when it came time to do his mandatory army service, he chose to be on a base far from home in the dusty desert, because she didn't sign for him to be in a combat unit. He would come home once every two weeks, dirty and sunburned, say practically nothing, hug his skinny mother, swing her in the air, devour everything she'd cooked for him. Sometimes his friends would come as well, and they also ate and laughed, went out afterward, and then slept until noon.

◆　◆　◆

"Mom," he would ask on the other end of the line when she was silent, "are you there?"

"Yes," she would say. She was always there. Always. That's exactly what she was. The one who was there. On the other end of the line, waiting, present, quiet. She was there when he said they had decided to extend their stay. She was there when the shiva was over and he hurried back to America. She was there when he said he had to work this summer so they wouldn't be coming this year, but that's okay, isn't it? Because he'd been with her only a short time ago, on Memorial Day. But that was without Dana, Carmela said, and he said he'd bring her sometime this year. She was there when he promised that next year, they'd come. She'd told herself so many times that maybe she should have yelled at him and said no, but she didn't yell. Maybe she shouldn't have answered the phone. But she did. And again she said it was okay. Again and again she kept silent and was there. Now she's confused and she doesn't know how many years of silence have passed, but she does know that last Memorial Day he didn't come.

And now he said again that just this once they weren't coming.

She takes a blank piece of notepaper out of her pocket and writes on it, "Dana came!" Then throws it into the garbage can.

2

✕

Irina stops in front of the police station, takes a very deep breath, summons her courage, and goes up those few steps she never believed she would climb. She holds on to the handrail for support. She has been imagining the scene all day, thinking about what she'd say, how to explain why she's worried. She'll tell them that ten days have passed since her daughter left, but her phone has been turned off for the last four days already and she knows she hasn't read the texts because they don't have those little blue lines. She checked every few minutes, and she checks now, too, a moment before she goes inside. Maybe coming here, to the police, is stupid. Soon it'll be the Seder night and maybe Nina will come back because who can she spend the Seder night with? His wife and children? She'll definitely come home.

Lying in her bag is the letter that was waiting for her in the box this morning. An official letter to her Nina with the army logo on it. A letter from the IDF. It must be a draft notice. "Just don't go far away from me," Irina had asked her before she went for her predraft interview, and Nina hugged her and said, "I want to be a real soldier. And wherever I am, I'm all yours. Always." Irina knew that girls in the army here carry weapons and are stationed at the border, and she was afraid for her Nina. Now she remembers those words, the bond they had, and thinks about how much has changed this year since she shot up and started watching what she eats and her cheeks aren't like two jelly doughnuts anymore, and the admiring way she always looked at Irina dropped away along with her baby fat.

This was a different Nina now.

It's been a long time since she curled up beside her in bed, and in fact, she hardly touches her. Her new girlfriends didn't say anything to Irina when they saw her and tried to avoid eye contact. And Nina began to ask her why she didn't get a more regular job. Maybe it's time. Your back is ruined, you can do much better than that, you have to think about the future.

"I didn't go to school," Irina told her, "but I raised you, and look, you don't have everything you need? Is there something you didn't get from me?" she asked with a smile, trying to keep things light, but Nina didn't laugh. She didn't think it was sweet or funny anymore, and she was sick and tired of the guilt that fell on her thin shoulders every time those words were spoken, laying the burden of responsibility on her. She hadn't asked to be born, hadn't planned for her mother's life to end because of her, and that sacrifice was suffocating her. How could she even begin to pay her back for that? There was no way.

She barely spoke Russian now. She, who had been Mommy's little girl and spoke only Russian, refusing to speak Hebrew no matter what they said, and the kindergarten teacher told Irina that it couldn't go on like that. Irina told her not to worry, Ninotchka understands everything. Because even when Nina pretended to be shy, Irina knew it was out of loyalty to her and to Babushka, who stayed with her during the long hours she was at work. When Babushka went into the hospital and everyone there spoke Russian, it was weird for Nina, and Irina told her she had to be careful when she spoke because here everyone understands Russian. She was happy to speak Russian with strangers, and the nurses pampered her and smiled at her, but the look in their eyes was hard. And Babushka never came home. Nina was already in the first grade and had not only begun to speak Hebrew, but also to translate for Irina when the fruit-and-vegetable man or an office clerk said things she didn't understand. When she got older, she used to help her mother write and fill out forms. Irina had such beautiful handwriting in Russian, but when she wrote in Hebrew, it looked as if someone had dragged a knife along a wall.

One day, Nina saw a want ad for a kindergarten teacher's helper pasted on a tree in the park near their house. She took the ad to Irina, who said it wasn't enough money, and Nina replied that there were only two of them now, they didn't have to worry about Babushka, so they didn't need so much. Irina smiled sadly because it hurt her that Nina had to worry about money at all. And she was sad that at her age, she already understood what money was, how important it was. She wanted so much to give her a life free of worry that she did everything she could to put some money aside. But every once in a while, Nina would find another ad for a course and say, "This way you can get ahead," because Nina was upset by the sight of how her proud mother, who had once been tall and straight, had become stooped. It pained her to see how her exhaustion and aching muscles were devastating her. Then at some point, it began to make her so angry that she stopped giving Irina the Friday-night massage she'd been giving her from the time she was a little girl, when Irina used to laugh and say, Look, she already has a profession, a masseuse, and Nina would get angry and say, I'm going to be a manager. Then Irina would reply without a smile, as seriously as possible, "Of course you will. Definitely. You'll be whatever you want to be."

But that idea, to work in a kindergarten, never left her mind. And about a year ago, after she had accumulated a small amount of savings to fall back on, she started working in the day-care center in the new neighborhood. It wasn't enough, so she also worked three afternoons a week, twice for Haviva and once for a different family in the neighborhood, and on those days, she would come home too tired to stand up. On the other days, when she came home early, they were together. That was worth everything. Gradually, she began to work overtime and afternoon shifts at the center, substituting for anyone who asked her. The salary grew a bit larger, and after Irina went to the bank to check, she even dared to believe that the day was coming when she would be able to buy a small place instead of throwing away money on monthly rent. But for the last few months, Nina had hardly been home. Sometimes she didn't even come home from school. Now the manager of the center suggested that Irina take a course given by the MOL. Level One Child Care Worker. Twice a week. Eight hundred hours. That seemed like so much, eight hundred hours, but at least she could sit, give her legs a rest, so it wasn't too bad. The only thing that scared her was the exams, because of the writing. Shoshi the manager told her not to be afraid, it would be fine, you don't have to write on those exams, just mark the correct answers. She said she would make sure they helped her with the language, and she would definitely succeed. Irina was so thrilled that Shoshi cared so much that she didn't ask her what a Level One Child Care Worker was and planned to ask Nina that evening, but Nina wasn't there again.

The next day, Shoshi told her about the man Nina was running around with. Shmueli. And when Irina came home, instead of telling Nina about the course, they fought about that man. The first fight, after which there would be many, many more fights. Fights that ended with her being worried now. So worried. And it was too bad she couldn't tell her, Nina would definitely have been thrilled to know that she had started a course. And all by herself, she read on the Internet that the MOL is an abbreviation for the Ministry of Labor.

◆ ◆ ◆

Her eyes filled with tears this morning when she saw the letter. "Your draft notice came," she texted Nina, then took a picture of it and sent it to her. "Should I open it?" But there was no sign that Nina had seen the message, just as there had been no sign that she had seen all the other messages she'd sent over the last few days. It worried her, but it also surprised her how emotional she felt about her daughter becoming a soldier in the Israel Defense Forces. And it would also take her away from that bastard, she thought. Suddenly, a base far from home seemed like a good idea. She wanted to open the letter but was afraid, Nina would be furious if she did. But Nina isn't here, she reminded herself. She has to find Nina. Maybe something happened to her. He's no good, that Shmueli. Maybe she should go to see him instead of the police, talk to him? She decides not to tell them his name.

Maybe she should go to the shopping center, she thinks, sometimes he sits there with his friends, and if he isn't there, then the guy who sells lottery tickets will definitely tell her where he is and when he's coming. Better than going to the police. He might get angry if she goes to the police, and besides, what will she tell them? That she has a daughter who doesn't care about her mother? Who's throwing away her whole future right before she graduates from high school? That she has the most beautiful handwriting of anyone in her class, and now it's been months since she opened a notebook? And she's worrying her mother to death. The tears roll down her cheeks; there was nothing she didn't give her. Nothing.

Irina turns around. She'll go to see him, she decides, and walks down one step. She'll put on nice clothes. And makeup. She'll wear the beautiful short dress that Nina made her buy when Racheli, the young helper at the center, got married. Yes, that's how she'll go to look for him in the shopping center. And she'll smile, but not too much, because she still hasn't had a new crown put on her tooth after the temporary one fell out. She was waiting to go to the dentist at the end of month when the money is deposited in her account. So she'll only smile a little. She fakes a smile with her mouth closed. She'll find him and ask where her Nina is. And she'll ask him to tell her that her draft notice came. From the IDF. The one she'd been so eager to get. But tonight's the Seder night, so he must be at home. She'll go to see him in the shopping center after the holiday. Then she realizes that that's at least three days away. And she knows she won't be able to get through the holiday without a sign from Nina.

Irina turns around and goes back up the steps to the police station.

In her pocket is the money Haviva paid her for the Passover work she did for her. They labored for hours, and now the Seder night is about to begin. Maybe she'll go home first to see if Nina came back, but that's stupid because she's already here, at the police station. And even though she doesn't want her neighbors to wag their tongues about her, she calls Michal and asks her to go see if Nina's home, because she's not answering, maybe she fell asleep. Michal says she has pots cooking on the stove and shouts to her youngest, Menachem, to go and check, and he comes back and says he rang the bell and knocked and no one's there.

"Why, what happened?" Michal asks. Irina had avoided her all week, she didn't want to tell her that Nina ran away. She kept thinking she would come back. That it wasn't so serious. Now she's been uneasy for a few days already.

"Nothing, I just wanted to know whether she bought matzos like I asked," Irina says, and Michal says, "I have loads, if you want."

◆ ◆ ◆

"Just tell me you're okay," Irina wrote in the first text she sent her, two days after the fight. She didn't try to make nice, didn't write "I'm sorry" or "Come home, Mamushka." She just added, "I'm worried." Nina saw those messages. The next day Irina left her a voice message. "I'm your mother," she said, "always." But there was no sign that Nina had seen the messages she sent over the last four days.

Now her heart tells her that something is wrong. That man was trouble from the beginning, what business did he have going around with a high school girl?

"You could be his daughter," she told her when it was just starting, and Nina replied, "He couldn't be my father. He didn't have kids when he was in high school, like you. He has really young daughters, and for him, I'm not a little girl. I'm a woman and he loves me."

"He already has a wife," Irina said.

"He loves me, do you understand? Do you know what love is?"

◆ ◆ ◆

Irina goes into the almost deserted police station.

"Yes?" the policewoman behind the counter asks, bored.

"My daughter disappeared," Irina says.

The policewoman picks up a form. Asks for Irina's details, ID number, address, phone number, and writes down what she says.

"How old?"

"Thirty-seven," Irina says, taking a deep breath to keep from losing her temper.

"The girl."

"Eighteen."

"How long?"

"More than a week."

"A week?" the policewoman says, suddenly alert. That's a lot. Usu-ally parents come after two or three days. That's about how long it takes them to cool off and realize that the kid knew they were angry, and start to worry.

"Longer. A little more than a week."

"You had a fight?"

"Yes."

"She went with her boyfriend?" the policewoman asks.

"Yes."

"That happens a lot," the policewoman says, bored again. Now it was clearer. "She'll calm down. She doesn't feel like talking to you. She's probably having a good time with him somewhere."

Irina feels the anger begin to blaze inside her.

The policewoman sees that the woman is upset. Maybe she went too far. She changes her tone. "Listen, you can fill out a missing per-sons form," she says kindly, sympathetically, the way she was taught in her course, "But you're sure it wasn't just an ordinary fight? Maybe she's just avoiding you."

"It never happened before that I didn't hear from her for days," Irina replies. "And for the last four days, she didn't read the texts I sent."

"You know what, let's call her," the policewoman says, extending her hand and introducing herself: "Ilanit."

"Irina."

"What's her number?" Ilanit the policewoman asks, and while Irina is telling her, she picks up the phone lying on her desk, puts it on speaker, and taps in the number. "Usually, when they see a blocked number, they answer right away," she explains.

The number you have dialed is not in service, the reply comes through the speaker.

"Maybe her battery is dead," Ilanit says. "Who's her boyfriend? Maybe we should call him? What's his number?"

"I don't know."

"How long have they been together?"

"Six months."

"And you don't know his phone number?"

Irina lowers her glance and shakes her head.

"Have you tried her girlfriends?"

Irina feels uncomfortable admitting that she didn't think of that, that she doesn't know the numbers of any of Nina's friends. What kind of mother is she if she doesn't know her daughter's friends? How can she explain that Nina built a wall between them and her mother, whose rough hands always stay dry no matter how much cream she puts on them.

"You think their mothers are better?" Irina once said to her. "Who, the mother of the one with the bangs who had a boob job and walks around all day with them hanging out so everyone can see? Or the fat girl's mother who's always home, just laundry and food, with four kids and a husband who talks to her like a doormat?"

"Like *she's* a doormat," Nina says.

"That's what I said."

"No. The way you said it, it means that *he's* a doormat."

"Don't get fresh with me!" Irina said. "I'm the one who's ashamed of you. Ashamed of the daughter who's ashamed of her mother!"

◆　◆　◆

"So should I file a missing person's report?" Ilanit asks, as if they shared a secret. As if they were in it together.

Suddenly Irina feels stupid for being there. After all, she knows that Nina ran off with Johnny Shmueli and they're probably living it up together and he's pampering her little girl and buying her stuff and she's enjoying it and doesn't understand how inappropriate it is, how fake it is, and how, in the end, her heart will be broken.

"I'm going home," Irina says to the policewoman, who now seems really nice to her. "She'll definitely come back for the Seder. Or maybe she's even there already, waiting for me."

"I'm sure she'll come back. And if not, I'm here. Stuck here for almost the whole holiday. I really got screwed with this shift," Ilanit says, making a face. The truth is that she didn't care about skipping all the preparations for the holiday, the hairdresser, the manicure, the clothes shopping, but now she suddenly misses everyone and feels like being with the girls and hearing them ask the four questions at the Seder. "But at least I don't have to help my mom with the dishes. Happy Passover, Irina. And tell your daughter not to turn off her phone like that and to answer when her mom calls." And she wonders what she would do if her daughter went off and didn't answer her phone.

◆ ◆ ◆

Carmela wakes up from her afternoon nap, goes to wash her face, and looks in the mirror, which once again reflects the image of an old woman that has nothing to do with her. She wants to shatter that image that insists on exposing the years, the truth, the wrinkles on her face. Her clearest moments are when she wakes up, and it sometimes seems to her that sleep has woven the net of details, has gathered together scraps of lucidity into a calming blanket of familiar knowledge. But it's not a blanket, because it's as thin as a silk scarf and as sharp as needles, and in another moment it will fade and vanish. And once again she will spend the rest of the day with the humiliating half-awake, half-asleep feeling that makes her tongue heavy and her thoughts stick on something she is unable to understand, unable to say what she should or wants to say and doesn't remember how.

Trying to hold on to the last moments of clarity, she takes a small piece of paper and a pen out of the pocket of her housedress and writes: "Tell Itamar about my condition." She wants to stick it on a corner of the mirror frame and discovers that there are three such notes there already, three notes that say: "Tell Itamar about my condition."

Suddenly she remembers. Dana is here. Dana is here. And she writes a note: "Dana is here." Tears of joy run down her cheeks. She's here, her granddaughter. And it's real. She feels that it's real. She won't be alone now because Itamar sent Dana here. Or maybe she ran away, maybe she fought with her parents and maybe they'll follow her here. If only they would already. She remembers leaving her mother's grave a moment before she and Itzik boarded the ship for the land of Israel and she knows she would never have left her mother there like that, alone, if she had been alive. We came to Israel, Carmela had once said to Itamar, your father and I. And we chose this place over all the others—and suddenly it hits her. With pain so strong that it makes her double over. The memory. Memorial Day. Uri's grave. Itzik's cries. And his silence afterward. And now all she wants is for that fog to come and wipe away the memory of it. The grave. The officer saluting and giving her the insignia of her Uri's rank. She doesn't want it, she only wants her Uri. And now an old image springs up out of the fragments of her memory, Uri and Itamar on the beach in the Sinai, Uri as dark as Itzik, who shouts, "Come see how enormous this fish is," and the children run to him. Uri dashes over to him, but the water is too cold for Itamar so he looks back at her, standing in the distance with a kerchief on her head, then turns around and walks back to her, and she hugs him. He always tried so hard to catch up to

Uri, to be the first to reach their father, to reach his heart. But Itzik was in love with Uri. Uri the big one was his and Itamar the little one was hers. Even after Uri was no longer there, even then, Itamar never managed to reach Itzik's heart. And the hole in his father's heart grew and grew, until in the end, his heart broke.

That painful moment arrives, as it does every morning, reminding her of what will become dimmer later in the day. Itzik isn't here, and Uri isn't here, and Itamar isn't here. And she doesn't know what hurts more, the one who isn't here because that was his fate or the one who is happier far away. And how far away he is. The other side of the world. Everyone there is a stranger. A place it takes days to reach, and enormous airports and going up and going down and transfer and connection and Itzik trying to help her, but like her, he doesn't really understand the questions of the bored clerk who checks their passports. The passports Itzik ran with back and forth to the embassy so they could get visas, coming home more tired each time.

"One more year and that's it," Itamar told them. "We'll stay there till the baby is born so he can get an American passport in case this country comes to an end," he said, and it was Naama's words she heard coming out of his mouth.

"How do you have the strength? I don't," she said to Itzik when they arrived exhausted somewhere on the other side of the world, a day before the new grandchild's brit. She was so worried about Itzik during the trip that she didn't sleep a wink, but he managed to muster all the strength he no longer had, the strength the doctors didn't believe he'd be able to muster for the trip. "I am going to be at my grandchild's brit," he had said firmly. And even though the trip was much longer and harder than they had thought, and they were completely adrift at the airport, like children who've lost their mother in the market, Itzik was still overjoyed at the ceremony. He even accepted the fact that it was a doctor who performed the circumcision and not a *mohel*, because Itamar explained that he had a lot of experience, and the rabbi was smiling all over the place, trying to say as many words as he could in Hebrew for them. Itzik sat on the large chair in that place that looked like a church and not a synagogue and held the baby on a pillow as if he really was the Prophet Elijah. For one evening, all the exhaustion and pain left him and a bit of his strength returned. She was so happy for him and thought that maybe this was what would sustain him, and Itamar was also so happy for him. All the other people there couldn't have cared less.

No one was excited because no one knew them, that threesome left behind after Uri was taken from them. They had remained quiet and connected, staying close together because otherwise, it hurt too much. And none of the others could understand what it meant to Itzik that he had a grandson. Ariel Ben Zion.

After the brit, Itamar told them that he had received an offer he couldn't refuse. "Try to understand, Mom," he asked, and she said no, she can't understand. "You said only until the baby is born," she shouted. "Don't do this to me!" And he asked her not to make a scene now.

"It's not a scene," Carmela said. "It's the truest thing I've ever said. Don't do this to me."

Itzik put a hand on her shoulder and stroked it, and then said slowly and clearly, "Itamar, don't do this to your mother. You've already stayed a year longer than you planned, it's enough."

Before they flew back, she took advantage of every minute to be with her Dana'le, to teach her a little more Hebrew, to laugh at her mistakes.

She doesn't know Hebrew at all, she told Itamar, and again asked them to speak Hebrew to her, and he said he does, but he's home so little, and Naama tries, she really tries.

"Come," Itamar has said to her so many times since then. "Please come."

"It's so far. I can't, I just can't."

"It's only one connection," he told her, and that word was enough to scare her off. She knew she wouldn't be able to change planes and manage alone in the airport. "You said it's only one more year," she told him, "and then you'll come home." But a few months later, he said it won't work out this year because Ariel is too little, and she suggested that he come only with Dana. A year after that, Itamar came. Alone. For Memorial Day. He promised he'd try to bring Dana in the summer, but he didn't. Or he didn't even try. Everything gets mixed up in her mind and she no longer remembers exactly what year he came and what year he didn't, all she knows is that Dana never came. Never. She doesn't even remember to be angry. She's just sad.

At the end of Itzik's shiva, he repeated what he'd been saying all week, and what her neighbors said when they came to see her, and the suppliers they worked with at the store, and everyone who knew them.

"You have no more excuses," Itamar said. "That's it, we're finished with the store now. It'll take another month or two, and then you'll come to live with us."

"And leave Uri?" she asked.

"There is no Uri," he replied.

There is Uri, she thought, but said nothing. The military cemetery, Kiryat Shaul, Block 8, Row 7.

Nor did she say that Uri never would have left.

◆　◆　◆

She doesn't know how much time has passed since then, but she saw on the computer how Ariel grew, the grandson she didn't know.

"Come here, Mom," he told her. "It makes more sense."

"You're not coming back soon?"

"I still don't know," he replied quietly. "Come here for a little while. Go back with me. I'll take you."

"When you're here, we'll talk," she said.

But he didn't come that year because there was a problem. He didn't come for Uri's day either, and for the first time, she was alone at the grave on Memorial Day. Uri's girlfriend brought her daughter. Carmela didn't know whether to be angry. Whether it was disgusting or nice. Hagit from the minimart came, and another few friends who hadn't forgotten came too. But for the first time, she stood there without anyone to lean on. Not Itzik and not Itamar. All by herself.

Luckily, the army arranged a chair for her. That was the first time she used a chair and sat down.

But now Dana is here. And she's so big. How many years they'd lost. But the main thing is that she's here now.

She'll make sure that Dana stays here. That's her job now, to see that she doesn't go back there, to America. That she helps her on Uri's day.

◆ ◆ ◆

A car horn startles Nina awake. It takes her a moment to remember where she is. Light filters through the slats of the shutters and the smell of mildew mixes with the sweetness of the clean sheets. Once again, the angry driver honks his horn outside, and doesn't let up. Someone else joins the ruckus that is heating up down there on the narrow street, and now another car starts honking and a woman yells from her window, "People live here! Have a little consideration," and Nina doesn't understand how people can live in all that noise. She has to decide what to do, but for that, she needs a little time. Just a little time. The problem is that, in the end, the confused old lady will want to know who she is, after all, she'll realize she isn't the Dana she's thinking of. And Nina also wants to know who this Dana is so she'll know what she can and cannot say, because if someone catches her out, she can get into trouble. That old lady might even report her, or her family might suspect Nina took something from her. Maybe she'd be better off just getting out of here. Take her stuff and go right now.

But she has no stuff. No phone and no wallet. Not even shoes. And the panties she's wearing are for a twelve-year-old girl. Maybe she'll ask the old lady for a little money. Not take, just ask. But then the old lady will have questions. Who she is and where she's from, and she doesn't feel like being interrogated right now, and she has nothing to say anyway.

She hears shouting coming from outside. "Who do you think you are? You're blocking the road, you stupid bitch," the man yells. "*Yalla*, drive already, cunt," and that word makes her feel nauseated.

She hears the old lady's steps in the apartment. The yelling and honking must have woken her up too. "Was that so hard? Bitch!" the angry driver yells right before he drives off and restores quiet to the street, but Nina knows she won't be able to get back to sleep.

She tries to think of what to do. She can't go back home now, Shmueli will be looking for her. He was angry at her for showing him up in front of his friends, and he'd definitely try to shut her up so she wouldn't go to his wife and his girls, who he takes—one from kindergarten and the other one from school—for pizza in the shopping center, all dressed up in pink clothes pulled tight over their chubby bodies, so like him in their mannerisms, the way they walked, potbelly forward, and she feels like taking a shower again. And again.

What an idiot she is. She should have kept quiet for another few days, showed him love, softened him up. Made him addicted to her again, because he was over that. He didn't really care about her anymore. He'd had her and now onward, next. She should have pretended to be crazy about him a little longer, and on that terrible night, she should never have asked to go out with him and those disgusting people he hangs out with. She should have stayed locked up in that apartment, but she already felt so suffocated and she'd lost all her confidence and was so scared, of him, of his buddies, of the fact that he didn't protect her anymore. She'd waited so long for him, had made the apartment kosher for Passover, and he'd promised to bring matzos. She'd planned everything, how she'd be so, so sweet and maybe he'd take her to a hotel or something, or even just come back alone. But time didn't move. She smoked what was left and thought about her mom, who'd have a Seder alone, but her pity was mixed with anger. She deserved it, the way she'd spoken to her. How could she have said that she had no place to come back to. But she also missed her a little, and started to be angry at Shmueli for leaving her like that. Waiting. As if she was nothing. If she had a phone, she would text him, and he would probably text her, the way he used to all the time behind his wife's back, to tell her how much he missed her. But she didn't have a phone. That punishment made her angry and she was bored without her phone. The hours passed and she drank some of the red wine, and maybe because she didn't eat, she felt a bit dizzy, and she asked herself what had happened to all the restaurants and parties he'd promised. She didn't even know exactly how many days she'd been in that apartment and they didn't go out at all, he would just bring his revolting friends over. And suddenly she realized that none of it made sense, because why in the world was he punishing her? What was she, a baby? She wanted to leave the apartment and look for a phone, but she was afraid he'd come, after all, he'd told her not to go out, only if there was a fire in the house. "Because you have everything here. What else do you need?"

Nina started to cry. Out of frustration. It seemed like her mom was right, she hadn't lived it up, she'd screwed it up, and she didn't know how to get out of it and how she could face her, because after all, her mom had tried to warn her and she didn't listen because what did she know. Nina knew she had to go back with something to show for herself so she could prove her wrong, prove to her that she'd bad-mouthed Shmueli for no reason. She had to get on top of this before she went home, she had to go back with all kinds of stuff or with something, anything, and she would never tell her mom how awful it had been, never tell her she'd missed her, and never tell her he'd let his friends touch her.

The smoking and the wine made her mind fuzzy, she had a head-ache, and it was already long after midnight. She fell asleep and woke up and didn't really know what time it was, only that she was alone in an apartment in the big city. A beautiful apartment, the kind you dream about, all white with a great view and a lobby. But she didn't care about that anymore. All she could think about was her mom alone in their apartment while every other home was filled with hol-iday songs and smells. This would be the first time they weren't to-gether, like they always had been, the two of them, since Babushka died, the two of them who were a world unto themselves, who didn't need anything else. Now they would be apart, each one alone, and it made her heart ache.

◆ ◆ ◆

Nina wraps herself in the pink blanket in the room of that Dana—who'll come back God knows when—and she knows that as bad as it was, she still could have put an end to it somehow, but when she insisted on going out with them that stupid night, that possibility went out the window. Because now it's a problem. They went to a club just to "take care of some work shit," like Shmueli said, and after what she saw there, there's no way out. Shmueli would kill her if she opened her mouth.

"Why are you afraid of me?" he'd asked her a few days earlier. "Am I not good to you? Didn't I get you out of your house? Didn't I buy you presents? Didn't I teach you what good wine is? Cheap vodka was all you knew how to drink. I made a lady out of you. Didn't I take you to the best photographer? Didn't I open doors for you?"

◆ ◆ ◆

She lay on the bed, tears spilling from her eyes, remembering how he'd taken her to a photographer a few days earlier and how she felt like she was floating on a cloud of joy, with a wonderful makeup artist who laughed with her as if they were friends, and a hairdresser who told her she was amazing, her beauty was one of a kind. And the pictures the photographer took, with the fan that blew her hair around. She had never been so beautiful. Never.

And the makeup artist told her she could make it. She had what it takes.

It had been a perfect day, and she'd wanted to hug the whole world. She'd been angry at him, her Johnny, for no reason. Just look, he's doing what he promised. Making her famous. Every once in a while he went out to make calls. And when he came back, she ran over and told him to come see what beautiful pictures the photographer had taken, and she asked him for her phone so she could snap a few herself. He took it out of his pocket, and after she snapped some pictures, he smiled and took the phone back again. She didn't feel comfortable about making a big deal about it in front of everyone, even though she really wanted to know what was happening back home. With her girlfriends. And what they were doing now during the Passover vacation.

The makeup artist said bye and left, and the hairdresser had gone a long time ago, leaving her with the two of them, Shmueli and the photographer. They drank a little. And the photographer let her look at the pictures on his computer. Then he said, "Let's take a few more shots. And show me a little shoulder." She was thrilled about that day, the day her dream was coming true. With the makeup and the heels and the lovely clothes, which the makeup artist had taken with her when she left, and she was again wearing the too-short dress he'd bought her.

The photographer said she had to show more, then more, and why are you embarrassed, and a little more, and then he put his mouth close to her ear and whispered, now we'll make a movie, because we have enough pictures. He started filming and asked her questions about the things she liked about her body and what she likes with guys, and she giggled, embarrassed, and called Johnny to come in, and he shouted from outside, "Just a minute," and the photographer asked her to pull down the straps of her dress and Shmueli, who had just come in, smiled at her and said, "Sure, babe, do what he tells you. He's the professional." And the photographer said, "Show a little more," and she wanted Shmueli to tell him no, she's his baby, his doll, and he's the only one who's allowed to see her. But her Johnny didn't say anything and went out because his phone rang again. The photographer gave her a blanket and said, Take off the dress, it doesn't photograph well, wrap yourself in this. She was on the couch, and Shmueli came back, looked, smiled, and said to the photographer, "Was I right or was I right?" and the photographer went over and started to take the blanket off her. She tried to pull it back to cover herself and he touched her a little, but Shmueli didn't say anything. She looked at him through tears, knowing that everything has a price. And she was paying it now. Everything had been perfect until now and she'd forgotten for a minute that there is no perfect.

"Smile, honey," the photographer said. "Why such a long face?"

"Smile," Shmueli said. "You wanted to be a model."

The photographer told her that this is how it is, if she wants to succeed, people have to see how she really looks, no one will work with a shy model. Shmueli told her, "They're only for us, the pictures, right?" and the photographer said of course. "No one else will see my beautiful doll," Shmueli added, and they both laughed.

Shmueli went over to her, she was already tired and hungry and thought, okay, now he'll cover her and hug her and finally take her out of there.

But Shmueli took her picture with his phone and smiled. "So I have something to show your mom."

◆ ◆ ◆

Irina comes home from the police station, takes off her shoes, and lies down on the living room couch. Coming from outside are the voices of families going out to friends or family for the Seder. "Come on already," mothers tottering on high heels shout at their unruly children. "*Yalla*, get moving," they urge the men, and she can already hear the cries of "welcome" along with shouts of joy and the sound of noisy kisses coming from other houses as guests arrive. If she had the strength, she would get up and close the window just to keep from hearing the holiday bustle that was choking her. The bustle she loved so much when the three of them celebrated. Babushka, Nina, and her. They missed Babushka on the holidays that came after she was gone, but there were always the two of them and they were content together. Once they were joined by an aunt from Ukraine who had come for a visit and was stuck here for the holiday, and Nina was excited that they had a guest and helped Irina clean and organize and decorate, and on the Seder night, she stood on a chair in her white dress and red patent-leather shoes and sang the four questions as if it were opening night of the opera season in Kyiv. And she also left a chair for the Prophet Elijah.

Now Nina's chair is empty.

It can't be that she won't call her. It's not possible. She hugs her phone. After all, she's alone too, her Nina. And then she begins to think how strange that actually is. She certainly isn't celebrating the holiday with him, he's with his family, with his wife, probably sitting at the table and not lifting a finger, the king. Leaving her Nina alone somewhere as if she were a piece of trash. But where is that somewhere? It has always been the two of them alone, but together. She never thought anything could separate them. Only rarely did she feel sad that they didn't have a bigger family, and that was mainly after Babushka died. "Friends are a little like family," Michal her neighbor once said to her, and Irina smiled because she didn't want to insult her. She had been her only friend for years, but Irina didn't really talk to her either. Now in the day-care center, she let people get closer, it took months for her to open up a little. To loosen up. And that's exactly when the whispering began. At first, she didn't understand what was happening. No one had ever talked about her behind her back, she had never been the subject of gossip. She had become an expert in being invisible in the homes and offices she cleaned. Unnoticed. She had learned how never to make eye contact and to always nod when people asked how she was or said hello. She just mumbled a heavily accented thank you, thank you, avoiding relationships. She had no need of them, and she understood that no one really wanted to know her. People felt uncomfortable with someone who saw their dirty laundry and knew more about their lives than they were willing to admit. Especially when that someone seemed happy with their lack of interest. And they preferred that someone to remain a stranger to them.

Until they began whispering about her in the day-care center.

Then there was the conversation with Shoshi, which seemed planned. Shoshi came in to make coffee at the exact moment Irina was in the small kitchen and began to ask her about her life, was she married once, and what about her daughter, and where did she go to school, as if she didn't know where she went to school, and Irina only said thank God, everything is okay, all the things she learned to say in order not to say anything. And then Shoshi closed the door of the little kitchen, took Irina's hand, and apologized for sticking her nose into it, but she thinks it really isn't healthy for Nina, maybe it's even dangerous, he's, well, not a good man, Shoshi said, shaking her head. "Not good. And also married."

Irina wanted to die, and a moment later, wanted to scream. How humiliating. If Nina had been standing next to her, she didn't know what she would have done to her.

"Yes, I know," she said, smiling at Shoshi. "I just didn't know he was like that. I thought he was a good person," she said, not revealing that she didn't know anything. That Nina was hiding it from her. That Nina was lying. And that's how she went home, in turmoil, her pulse pounding in her temples. And again, Nina wasn't home. This time she waited for her. Waited on the sofa she is now lying on.

And at two in the morning, Nina sneaked in. Barefoot, carrying her high heels in her hand.

"You don't have to sneak into your own house," Irina said in the dark, and Nina almost froze with fear.

"I didn't want to wake you."

"They say he's not a good man, Nina."

"Mom."

"Nina."

"Who says that? Maybe we'll talk in the morning?"

"I'm asking you to leave him."

"He's my boyfriend."

"He's married."

"I love him."

"What nonsense," Irina said.

"You can think that, I don't care what you think, good night."

And from that moment on, nothing was the same.

"How is this night different from all other nights," the neighbors across the way are singing the holiday song when Irina wakes up.

Everything is different, she thinks.

And she would give everything if only Nina would come in now. Because enough is enough. The whole crazy business has gotten out of control.

◆　◆　◆

Nina has to pee. And drink something. She has no choice, she can't stay in this sweet, pink Barbie room and never go out. "Here goes nothing," they had shouted on their annual school trip when they decided to show the boys they weren't afraid to jump off the high cliff into the small lake. In the end, she chickened out and didn't jump. And she didn't care when they laughed at her. Because it wasn't like it used to be. It used to be that when someone laughed at her, she almost died of mortification. Now she was the queen. It didn't happen all at once, but very slowly. Her baby fat dropped away, she started to stand up straight, dress well, wear her hair loose, like a gladiola, she began to stand out and the boys stopped talking when she walked past, and the girls ran to her, and it was like a drug, that thing that emanated from her. Then Shmueli came along. He started picking her up with his car and everyone whispered. "What do I care," she told her girlfriend, "I have a ride home," and Ortal asked her if she was afraid. "Of what?" Nina asked. "Of him," Ortal said, and with reddened cheeks added, "He doesn't want it?!" Nina laughed and said, "So what if he wants it, what's the difference, he's like all the boys in our class, they want it too, but he also knows how to buy presents." And she caressed her new phone, the very latest model, that made all her girlfriends crazy jealous.

◆ ◆ ◆

Here goes nothing, Nina says to herself and gets out of bed slowly, hesitantly, because everything hurts, opens the bedroom door carefully, and hurries into the bathroom. She sits down on the toilet seat and sees a large black-and-blue mark on her thigh, flushes, and looks in the mirror as she washes her hands. The area above her left eye is swollen and there's a red bruise on her cheek, but except for that, her face is okay. All she needs is a little makeup.

She opens the medicine cabinet, which is loaded with a jumble of toiletries and medications, and starts looking for a toothbrush. She opens another small cabinet, and also the drawer under the sink and finds everything there. Shampoo, toothpaste, even a shower cap. Like in that hotel Shmueli took her to, where he couldn't keep his hands off her, "ROOMS BY THE HOUR" the large sign said, but she didn't feel cheap, she wanted to be with him, to satisfy him, high on the feeling that he was addicted to her, to the smell of her. In the beginning, when they first met, it was enough for her to lie beside him, naked, he didn't need any more. Just for her to touch him a little, nothing else. He was faithful to Ofra, his wife, that's what he said, he couldn't do that to her. But he had to have her, his Ninush, to sit on the chair in front of her so he could see her, feel her a little, touch her a little. Smell her. He laughed at the things she said and explained things she didn't understand. But when she took a cigarette from him, he snatched it out of her hand and yelled at her. Don't ruin the way you smell, he told her. "Stay like this, my little girl. My love. I gotta have you."

He tried to wean himself off her, tried to distance himself, but after two days, he would relapse. Once it took a week. She was actually happy during that week, she'd had enough. The whole thing was getting too creepy. Too demanding. And a little gross. It wasn't fun anymore. And wherever he took her, people looked at them. She felt that those looks were dirty, hiding warped thoughts that made her and him and their relationship dirty. They didn't understand that he needed her. That she was his heart and it was almost spiritual the way they were meant for each other, except that it was the wrong time and place for them.

Even though she was a bit relieved when they didn't see each other for a few days, she admitted to herself that she was confused when her Johnny didn't call or text her at night, and she had a hard time with the feeling that she wasn't all he wanted and needed and had to have. And then Michael, from one of the other twelfth-grade classes, asked her to come to the smoking area with him. He offered her a cigarette and Nina refused it, saying, "I'll just take a drag of yours, I don't really want to smoke."

Michael didn't ask why she'd come with him. He knew. She'd been looking at him for two years already, and he'd pretended not to notice. He was with Noy, they were the royal couple. And Nina used to watch him, them, from a distance. A girl with that admiring glance he was used to getting from girls. They were always there, the ones who looked at him, and he—he only saw Noy. That was enough for him. And now Noy didn't want him. She's suffocating, she said, and he knew she wanted someone with a car. It made her crazy that they were stuck there and couldn't go out, even though Eliran was always happy to drive them and didn't care that they went with him only because he had a car. Noy said that Eliran was glue, and she didn't talk when he was there because she didn't trust him, and Michael told her that Eliran would "give his right arm" for him, but she was tired of having him around all the time, and *yalla*, Michael should get a license already. But Michael wasn't at all sure that he could drive his dad's car, because the insurance for a new driver cost thousands. He came to pick her up again with the electric bike he'd bought with money he'd made working all summer as a lifeguard's helper at a kiddie pool. He didn't know how to tell her that he was so stressed that he failed his second test, the one he didn't even tell her he was taking. Noy asked and asked, and in the end, she called his driving teacher, and was furious when she found out what happened.

Michael said he thought she loved him and why was a car so important to her? And then something inside him broke. His love for her seeped out of him the way the air seeps out of a inflatable floating mattress before you take it home from the beach.

◆　◆　◆

Nina walks slowly down the hallway and peers into the living room. Carmela is sitting there and Nina takes a deep breath to calm herself, says "Shalom" as if it's the most natural thing, and goes over to her. But something is beginning on TV right then and Carmela mumbles, "News. Wait a minute. News," with profound seriousness, as if something terrible will happen if she misses the broadcast. Nina doesn't recognize the young newscaster, and there are items about holiday preparations and traffic jams, and then she berates someone about prices, and Nina thinks about how much she wants to be like her, a TV journalist. She's interested in current events, and compared to her friends, she knows a lot. She even wrote on her military preference request that she wanted to take the test to be a military journalist, because she writes really well, but the exam was too difficult. In the part about general knowledge, there were a lot of old things she never learned about or heard about, like Moshe Sharett and *Waltz with Bashir*, and weird things like the National Security Council, but she did know what Meghan Markle and the prince had named their son, and she also knew a lot about the National Insurance Institute and the public health clinics and she also knew Russian, but they didn't ask about that. Now she wonders what would happen if she was like that news anchor, Yonit Levy, and all of a sudden someone showed up with the pictures that horrible photographer took of her. And she feels nauseated about herself and how stupid she's been.

Nina looks at the notes pasted everywhere, reminders about Itamar, about Dana, about Itzik, and wonders what exactly is wrong with this old lady who thinks she's her granddaughter. Maybe it's Alzheimer's. She saw a story about it on TV but doesn't remember how they treat it. When she has a phone, she'll check it on the Internet, even though right now, it's pretty convenient that the old lady is so mixed up. She reminds herself that she shouldn't get too comfortable. She has to get out of here in the next day or two before they figure out who she is and that'll be the end of her.

Suddenly, from the corner of her eye, she sees his face on the TV, on the news. It can't be. No.

Nina runs over to Carmela and takes the remote from her. Her hands are shaking and her pounding heart threatens to explode out of her chest. Luckily, the cable box is the latest model and she can go back to the beginning of the item. "Body," they say, "Central Bus Station," and on the screen is a picture of someone who looks exactly like the scared guy from that night. "Leonid," the reporter says, and when they show pictures of the street, there's no mistaking it, there's the door the woman came out of screaming, "Leonid!" The announcer switches to the weather forecast and Nina sits down, stunned, trying to understand what it means.

Carmela doesn't ask anything, she just keeps staring at the screen.

The phone rings. Nina jumps up, startled, and Carmela tries to get up quickly but almost loses her balance for a moment. Nina goes with her, telling herself that she has to buy a cell phone. If God forbid she falls, that'll be the end. She knows from her mom that that's what old women are most afraid of. Falling.

"Itamar," Carmela says, her face shining. "Itush. How are you? Yes, I'm fine. No, don't worry. Why worry? When are you coming? But Memorial Day is not far away. Yes. But you'll come, right? Try. Please try. I know you're busy, but try. Okay, sweetheart. Yes, right, I didn't ask, I'm a little tired."

She picks up the notebook that's lying next to the phone and reads what's written on it in large letters: "How is Naama?"

And waits for the answer.

With fingers that need their nails to be cut, she points to the next line and asks: "How is little Ariel?" and after he replies, she asks another question.

And after every one of his answers, she says: "Wonderful, wonderful."

He asks something and her finger reaches the line where "Dana" is written. Carmela looks at Nina and skips to the next line: "And how is work?"

And he tells her.

"That's so wonderful," she says. "Wonderful."

Then another question from him, and she says, "Yes, Dana is fine. I know. She's big already."

Silence on the other end. He begins to speak and Nina doesn't hear what he says, but Carmela doesn't say "Wonderful" again. She just says, "Try. Please. And if not, at least Dana will be with me. She'll stay here. Okay, bye, sweetheart."

◆ ◆ ◆

Nina's heart is hammering. She keeps going over in her mind what she saw on the news. It can't be. This is not happening to her. She knew something bad happened that night, but it never occurred to her that it would be on the news.

Johnny came back to the apartment late that night, again not alone. He was with those friends of his, the ones she already knew and two new ones. Nina was so angry that she almost cried. He asked, "What's with the sour face?" and she replied, "I waited for you," and he thought that was funny, and she said it again, angrily, "I waited for you," and the angrier she got, the more he laughed. His friends laughed too.

"Oh, the girl is pissed off because I'm late," he said, looking at them with a big smile, "You missed my crown jewels? You need 'em? You gotta have 'em?" He hugged her and pulled her hand down to touch him, and she whispered that she was just so alone and worried about him because he promised her they would go out. Shmueli put his hand under her dress and asked, "What do you have to worry about? It's not your job to worry. I take care of you. Come on." Nina tried to push his hand away, but he was hugging her tight, so tight that it hurt her, and he led her to the bedroom. His smile vanished when they went into the hallway. He wasn't really nice to her anymore. "Just stop it," he said, "I had a tough night, my wife broke my balls trying to make me stay home, and I do everything to come here to you, and now you put on that face. That's not what I keep you here for."

Nina tried to tell him that she was suffocating there, but he took her panties off quickly, too quickly, and when she tried to say, "Not now," he whispered in her ear, "I have pictures of you that you don't want anyone at home to see, right? So don't piss me off."

"I'm sorry," she said, "I'm sorry." She didn't apologize because of the pictures, but because he scared her.

She didn't know that that was his power. That's what allowed him to control people. He recognized their fear. He smelled fear from afar and knew how to play on it. That was his weapon. He was always surprised that people didn't understand how obvious their fear was. How much it stank. And he hated cowards. Now she, the little girl who wasn't afraid of anything when they first met because she didn't understand what it was to lose, now she was scared too. And he knew why she was scared, it was because she felt that she didn't have a hold over him anymore, that he was done with her.

"What are you scared of?" he asked. "I'm scary?"

His friend came in from the living room and handed him a phone, as if she wasn't lying there half naked, and said, "It's urgent. It's all fucked up there."

Shmueli bent over and whispered to her, "You're right to be scared of me," then he got up, zipped his pants, took the phone, and roared at the person on the other end, "Why are you busting my ass right before the holiday?" and when he heard the response, he threw her panties at her and said, "If you're so hot to go out, come on. Get dressed. We'll take you out for some fun."

And they went out for that damn fun, which she now understands has got her into more trouble than she realized. If only she hadn't gone out with them.

◆ ◆ ◆

Itamar goes into the bedroom. Ariel is sleeping there beside Naama, as he has been every night recently. He lies down quietly next to her.

"My mom doesn't sound right. She's really weird," he whispers. He thinks about the questions she asks, always the same questions, during every phone conversation. Once it amused him, but tonight he said to her, "Mom, change a few questions every once in a while, I won't answer any of the old questions anymore." She didn't reply.

"She's old," Naama mumbles. "We'll talk in the morning. I'm wiped out."

"She's alone too much."

"Your mom was never sociable. She doesn't really like people."

"Since my dad died," Itamar begins to say, and Naama puts the blanket over her head, then pulls it down and says angrily, "She can come here to visit. Like my parents do, and my sisters. Do you have to bring all that guilt here to our bed?"

"She's much older. And she isn't all that independent. She'll get lost."

"Can't this wait until morning? All I need is for him to wake up now."

Naama hasn't slept for almost a week. Ariel is entering the fear stage and he won't move from her side and can only fall asleep in their bed. Itamar comes home late at night, she barely manages to see him and he certainly doesn't help her. And today she fought with Dana, who is busy with her own nonsense and doesn't help at all. Acts like she's a baby, not like a girl who wanted a brother so much. "I wanted a sister," Dana corrected her with the annoying sullenness that has been part of her more or less since she was born. Sibling rivalry, they call it, a friend once said when she mentioned it to her, but

Naama no longer had the patience for psychology, and she was fed up with Dana never thinking she had to do something around the house.

It took Naama a while to get used to America. She always felt like the boss wherever she was, and here she was lost, the sheer size of everything, and the hard-to-understand rapid-fire English, but she gradually discovered how comfortable it was. Comfortable in the spacious house with the large garden Dana could play in. Comfortable in its tranquility. Comfortable in the absence of a need to explain what she was doing, or not doing, and why she hadn't conquered the world, after all, she was such a successful person. But it wasn't clear what she was successful at. And here in America everyone was so pleasant, with their have-a-nice-days and white, ear-to-ear smiles. And although she had found that obvious phoniness funny at first, now she loved it. It was nicer than the kibbutz, where everyone told her to her face what they thought of her and her family, and the way her father ran the factory and why the privatization benefited him and not the others. Everyone meddling in everyone else's life and bank account. She loved to paint, loved museums, and always pestered anyone who was driving to the city to drop her at a museum, where she could get lost for hours. Talking to strangers. Enjoying being someone else. Inventing herself. Not being the Naama everyone knew. Being slightly mysterious. Even as a child, she knew she wouldn't stay in the kibbutz. And here, as far as possible from the kibbutz, she finally feels at peace.

All she wants is Itamar and the kids. And a few girlfriends to chat with. She doesn't need anything else. She doesn't have the energy.

She remembers how, in school, everyone studied until the small hours, and then got up early to work on a project and she would fall asleep.

"I don't see any work here," the lecturer she admired in her first year said to her. "Art is something you give your life to." He talked about the absinthe that finished off Toulouse Lautrec. The earlobe that Van Gogh sliced off. She tried to tell him that there's also Jeff Koons, who married Cicciolina. It doesn't have to be "art or death." She wanted to tell him that it was just computerized graphic design, they weren't exactly at the Bezalel Academy of Art and Design, and it was also possible to use pretty colors and produce feel-good work. Not everything had to be edgy. But she kept quiet because she didn't want him to lower her grade, and he kept shouting, "If you just want to play on your computer, you can take a course at your neighborhood community center."

And that was what actually attracted Itamar. The fact that she never made an effort. He would say she was a princess who'd come here by mistake, and she would laugh and say, "There are no princesses in the kibbutz." Now, when they argued, he accused her of not caring, said her apathy—the same apathy that had once drawn him to her—drove him crazy. If he only knew how much she had been criticized for not having energy. She'd never had it. As if someone had taken it from her when she was still a child. And each birth seemed to have taken more life out of her. Another drop from the limited spring of her energy. That's why she's happy here. Because no one knows what and how much she hasn't done. Except for Itamar. Only he knows that she isn't capable of more. It's part of how they function as a couple. He's used to making an effort. He needs more and has to prove himself, even if it's about watching his weight, and it all comes with much teeth gnashing, while Naama never makes an effort. Whatever she has is fine. What she doesn't have— that's okay too.

◆　◆　◆

Gently, Itamar picks up Ariel and takes him to his bed, recalling that Naama told him, "This is an opportunity to have an American child."

He thought about all the benefits and about how some Israelis see it that way, like an admission ticket to some exclusive club. A work permit. The parents' license to stay. An American child. "We'll stay a little longer after the birth, maybe even six months, and then we'll go back with a shipping container," she said at some point when it seemed so far away. A lifetime ago. During his first crisis there.

So they stayed. And he took out a subscription for the Israeli television satellite, and checked out how Bnei Yehuda, his favorite soccer team, was doing. A long time has passed since then. They could have sent a shipping container a long time ago. And they don't argue about going back anymore, only about whether to buy the house at the end of the block that everyone says is going for a bargain price. And he had to decide in the next few days.

On his way back to the bedroom, he turns off the lights in the kitchen and the large living room, stops at the couch to arrange the throw pillows that match the cream-colored walls. The sound of his footsteps is swallowed up by the thick, wall-to-wall carpet, and for a moment, his feet long for the feel of cold floor tiles.

He goes back to bed, lies down beside Naama with open eyes, and listens to her breathing. His mother is getting old and maybe it's just the confusion of old age, but he knows for sure that something inside her has changed. And there was also something evasive about her, this time she was the one who ended the conversation.

Itamar embraces Naama and she lets him. They haven't touched that way in a long time.

"Talking to her kills me. Tears me apart," he says a moment before falling asleep.

"You're a good son," Naama says. Which doesn't help him at all.

Because he feels like the worst son in the world.

3

Carmela peels a cucumber very slowly, puts it on a cutting board, and slices it. Moves the slices to a plate, sprinkles a bit of salt on them, and opens the fridge to take out a yogurt. It's the last yogurt.

Nina is standing at the kitchen door, watching her. She's thirsty and wants to drink something. And she wants to call someone, to talk over what she should do, even just hearing a familiar, friendly voice would help her now. But she has no one to call. Who can she even tell what happened? And without her phone, the only number she remembers is her mom's. And she won't call her. Or anyone else. After yesterday, Johnny wants to find her for sure. And if he does, it's the end of her. She saw what happens when he's pissed at someone. Without a phone in her hand, she feels as if she's lost a limb. She went crazy when he took it away from her. Yes, she's addicted, who isn't.

At first, when he came to the apartment, he would immediately take her phone out of her hand and look through it, checking that she hadn't texted anyone. No boys' names were allowed. No pictures either. And Nina didn't text anyone. She didn't reply to any of her girlfriends who wanted to know where she was and what she was doing. They were all sure he'd taken her abroad, maybe to Paris, and she surfed the Internet about Paris so she would have something to tell them, but one day, Ortal wrote that she saw Johnny in the shopping center and she should tell her where she is and why she's making things up. When she realized that rumors about her were flying all over the place, she wrote to them that she was in Tel Aviv, having a fantastic time, and they'd never seen such an apartment and such a place in their lives. They asked her to send pictures, and she sent two, in one you can see the living room, and in the other the sea, and she framed them in such a way that made it look a million times more glamorous and amazing than it actually was, because it was really only a very white and empty apartment. Then suddenly she panicked and immediately deleted the pictures and the whole history and texted Ortal not to show them to anyone, and Ortal swore she wouldn't download the pictures, and Nina deleted those messages too.

"Why do I bother to check?" he laughed on the fourth day, when he came and saw again that no one had texted her. "Who would look for you but me? Who? No one. You have no one and you don't want anyone, right? You're mine. Right, babe? Only mine."

As soon as he left, she grabbed her phone and saw on Instagram that her girlfriends were on Passover vacation, meeting at the mall and posting selfies, as if anyone was interested. Only Ortal whined that she was working while everyone else was having fun. When they all went out on Friday, she saw Michael alone in the pictures, Noy wasn't there, and she was annoyed at herself for caring.

Then the girls started complaining about the days crammed with studying for a big biology exam they'd stuck them with in the middle of the vacation, and she thought about how the teachers would wonder why she didn't come and where she'd disappeared to. Maybe they'd even call her mom. And what would her mom tell them? What would she herself tell Galit, her homeroom teacher, who had believed in her so much and would be so disappointed in her?

"It's not like you," she'd told Nina when she was late to school again, fell asleep in class, and barely passed her big math test. "You're smart, all the doors are open to you, look at how all the boys look at you and how the girls admire you, what more do you need? Everything else can wait. Everything. Take the exams first—and then all the fun stuff."

And Nina said nothing. She knew that Galit was right, but she was already swept up in that whirlwind of things he bought her and gave her and did for her. She tried to tell him that she needed a little time, and he said that the Passover vacation was now, and what did she want—to be stuck here or to come to a beautiful apartment in Tel Aviv where there'd be parties and restaurants? "And after the vacation, I'll take you back," he said. "Come on, we live it up for a month and then you go home."

Not a month, she said, two weeks. And Johnny said, great.

But everything had changed those last few days. He'd changed too. And after they came back from the photographer, he took her phone, punishment for resisting. Behave yourself with me on the Seder night, he told her, and she—idiot that she was—instead of behaving herself, nagged him to take her out for a while.

"You brought her for us?" the skinny guy with the smile asked when they were going down in the elevator.

"Watch your mouth," Johnny said, and the skinny guy and the young guy who was the driver kept quiet. She tried to clear the air and be sweet, and she smiled and stroked him. She wanted her phone back so much and knew he'd give it to her only if she was happy and charming to him and his buddies. Just don't show him you're angry, she reminded herself, tomorrow you'll find a way to escape. She'd find a way somehow. Because it had gotten out of hand. And the Tel Aviv Johnny was absolutely not her Johnny. She could handle things if only he'd give back her phone.

So she played the game, but disgusted herself, giggling and covering him with kisses. And when they reached the car, he sat down next to the young driver and she squeezed into the back between the skinny guy and another guy who stank of cigarettes and smiled at her.

They drove and drove, and the brightly lit apartment towers with shiny lobbies were slowly replaced by peeling buildings, and there were a lot of foreign workers on the street. The driver explained to Shmueli that the bastards were two weeks late already and they couldn't just go back on the deal like that, it made him look bad. Everyone was angry and cursed and then the car stopped. Shmueli and one of the guys sitting next to her, the smoker, got out and went over to a building. Just then, someone came out, saw them, got scared and started to run, and they ran after him. The young driver joined them, and the smoker grabbed the guy who was trying to get away. Shmueli walked slowly over to him and the guy got down on his knees. A passing car lit up his face and Nina saw the fear. She'll never forget his face, the expression. The horror. The skinny guy and the smoker dragged him into an alleyway between the buildings, and Johnny Shmueli followed them.

She should have made her escape then, but she was paralyzed.

A woman wearing high heels came out to the street and screamed, "Leonid? Leonid!" One of the guys grabbed her and tried to drag her behind the building, but she got away and ran, screaming.

◆　◆　◆

Nina approaches the old lady and touches her shoulder, and she starts in surprise.

"Good morning," Nina says to the old lady, who seems to have a rushing river of question marks on her face, as if she's looking for a clue in Nina's eyes, while a smile is frozen on her lips, and it seems as if somewhere behind her eyes gears that have been blunted for a long time are screeching and the machine is malfunctioning.

Suddenly Carmela looks outside and says, "It's almost nighttime."

That scares Nina. These old ladies always think that someone is robbing them. She'll tell the police that the girl tried to rob her. And who will they believe? The old lady with the stupid smile. For sure. She would get the hell out of here, but she has no idea where to go, and she doesn't have any money. Now with this story on the news, it's even more dangerous.

"I just woke up, so I said good morning."

The old lady keeps looking at her with an uncomprehending smile.

Nina can no longer bear the suffering of that old lady trying to connect the features of her face with some fragment of a memory, and she's beginning to feel the pressure, the tension in the air. It's not healthy for the old lady, and she decides to whisper to her, "Dana."

It works like magic. The old lady is herself again, showing signs of life.

"Dana dear," the old lady says, holding Nina's face in her withered hands, wet with water and cucumber, and her eyes fill with tears. "My Dana, you came to me, you came."

Nina looks into her eyes, into the cloudy layer that, with the years, covers old people's eyes, and thinks about the fog blanketing her thoughts.

"Eat something," the old lady says, sitting down and placing the cucumber and yogurt on the table, where a closed box of matzos is standing.

Nina opens the fridge. It contains only half a bar of butter, some margarine, jam, eggs, and a lot of grime. She looks around. Unlike the dusty but tidy room she sleeps in, everything here is pretty filthy and messy.

"Who helps you clean?" she asks.

"Dana'le came," the old lady says, her face shining with joy.

Maybe she imagines she's the cleaner, Nina thinks, and that would be the best thing. The cleaner is great. I can be the cleaner or caregiver. She goes over to wash the plates in the sink, but hunger overtakes her. She opens a cabinet, then another, and in the third one she finds a bar of bittersweet chocolate. Milk chocolate would be better, but this will do. Until this place is clean she won't be able to eat anything that doesn't come in a package. She opens the box of matzos and takes a piece. Carmela is glad, and takes a piece for herself too.

A computer, she suddenly realizes. If not a phone, at least a computer. She thinks she saw one in the living room. She'll log in and check to see if anyone's talking about her or looking for her. But why should anyone be looking for her? She remembers Johnny laughing when he said, Who's going to look for you? No one.

She washes a glass, fills it with water, and goes to the living room, where a computer and an old monitor are sitting on a table. Turned off. She turns the computer on. Welcome, Windows tells her with fake friendliness.

She wants to shout at the old lady, "Is it okay, ma'am, if I use your computer?" but realizes that she can't call her "ma'am." Unless she's the cleaner. But she doesn't think Dana is the cleaner. If she's her granddaughter, then she has to call her "grandma." The name Ben Zion was on the door, but what's the old lady's first name?

Without noticing, she has finished off the bar of chocolate. The bittersweet kind was actually good.

She'll have to decide what to do. And what she clearly won't do anymore is take that big biology exam she was supposed to have taken the day before yesterday.

She needs a mouse. "Do you know where the mouse is?" she asks the old lady, who has come into the living room.

Frightened, the old lady moves closer to her: "A mouse?! Where?!"

Nina smiles. This is the first time she's smiled in a long while.

"No," she says. "A mouse for the computer."

"Oy," she says, "I don't like the computer. Itamar's angry, but I don't like it. He says that with the computer, you can speak and see. I promised him I would try."

"Can I open the drawer and look for the mouse?" Nina asks her.

"Mouse?!" The old lady lurches toward her again.

"I'll just set up the computer," Nina says.

"If it's Itamar, I want to talk on the phone," the old lady says. "I didn't fix my hair for television."

◆ ◆ ◆

The voices of people coming up the stairs make Nina's body tense. She's alarmed. She looks worriedly at the old lady, who doesn't react, and then she hears them ring the neighbor's bell. A second later, the door opens and she can hear cries of "Happy holiday" and the noise of children running on the stairs and sounds of great joy that are swallowed up by the closing door.

Suddenly the phone rings. Carmela hurries over to it, her eyes shining. She moves so quickly toward the phone that Nina is scared and follows her, watching to see that she doesn't fall.

"Hello," the old lays says hopefully, warmly. Someone responds on the other end of the line. And her face floods with disappointment, her smile vanishes. "No, thank you, Hagit. Thank you. That's so nice, but no. I'm fine. Yes. No, I'm not alone. Fine. Everything's fine. Happy holiday. Thank you for inviting me. Yes. Happy holiday to all of you. Thank you."

◆ ◆ ◆

Nina sees a few bottles of alcohol in the glass display cabinet in front of her. There's no vodka, only brandy and liqueurs. She opens a bottle and smells it. "Should we drink to a happy holiday?" she asks Carmela.

Carmela smiles at her. Nina pours them something sweet.

"Happy Passover, Grandma," she says. And suddenly that word sticks in her throat. She said it so that sweet, pathetic old lady would feel good for a little while, would enjoy the holiday for a little while. But Nina knows the truth. She just lied to her. She can no longer say it was a misunderstanding. A mistake. That the old lady didn't understand. She's lying to her.

"Happy holiday, Dana dear," Carmela says with a smile, her eyes bright. "I'm so happy you came."

◆ ◆ ◆

The sound of Passover songs enters through all the windows, and Irina recalls once again that terrible evening she'd tried to suppress. The evening when the shouts of Shmueli and the neighbor coming from outside blended with the car horns and the noise of suitcase wheels crossing the small apartment and the slamming door.

She would regret many times not running over to Nina right then and hugging her. That she didn't tell her she had someplace to come back to, that this would always be her home, always. She didn't know this would happen. If only she had known. She would have told her she's her daughter forever. That she should come back if she's unhappy. Now she just sits there, sad, recalling how everything went downhill, crying quietly, the tears rolling down her cheeks trying to wash away the hurt.

Her daughter, her whole world, Nina. Said that to her. In those words. "Who needs you."

"You'll come back to me in the end and say you're sorry," Irina said. "He doesn't love you," she shouted at her in that combination of Russian and Hebrew. "You're stupid. Stupid."

"He loves me and he'll take me away from here, I won't be like you," Nina yelled back in Hebrew, proud of her non-accent. Proud not to be like her. She's not a foreigner—she's from here, this place is hers. She understands the laws her mother will never understand, the mother who is so afraid of everything that's rough, prickly, everything that's Israeli. Of the heat and the sun. "Take a hat," she used to beg Nina, running after her with it. "Not to get burned."

And at night, when the cold descended on the desert, Irina would stand at the window, open it wide and push the plastic shutters deep into the wall openings, stand there and breathe deeply, and every breath caressed her on the inside.

Little Nina would lie in bed and watch her mother's back, the steam rising from her breaths, and sometimes the moon would peek at the image framed in the window, and she imagined all the memories from Ukraine returning to her mother with the cold air.

Unlike her, Nina loved the hot, dry wind of the desert, she loved watermelon and flip-flops. Too-short clothes. She couldn't imagine life in darkness and cold, being wrapped up in layer over layer, choking.

"You look like a whore. My daughter doesn't go out like that," Irina said and went to stand at the door, blocking her way, while he honked the horn of his blue Jeep impatiently downstairs. He hated waiting. Hated people being late. Nina knew he'd be angry at her, and she didn't have the strength to deal with that. She'd apologize and he'd explain that she has no manners, and then he'd hurt her a little, "Because you love it," he'd say. "Bad girls love it." She didn't love it, but she did think she was a bad girl and she did love him. And the power and the respect. The knowledge that he'd look out for her and take her away from here.

"You're not going out like that," Irina said quietly, and Nina laughed too loudly. "As if you're the one who decides what I do."

"If you go out with him now," she told her, "you're not my daughter anymore. You have nowhere to come back to."

"Who needs it!" Nina yelled, and he honked again, and Amsellem, the neighbor who's always nice, shouted at him, "Quiet! Our heads are exploding from the racket you're making."

Her cell phone vibrated and flashed. She answered as she walked to her bedroom and said, "Be right down, my mom is driving me crazy," and he laughed. "Come down already, you're killin' me here." And she threw more and more clothes into the small suitcase, the panties she bought in the Central Bus Station, three for twenty shekels, and also her toiletry bag. Her mother stood in the doorway, her eyes wide.

"Nina," she said, "you have to study for your exams, you're finishing high school, it's not a joke, it's your matriculation certificate. Don't ruin it now."

"And what'll I do with that certificate? What difference does it make in this shithole whether I have one or not?! You need something that will open doors in this life, and high school grades won't do it. You need to know how to take advantage of opportunities," she said, knowing she was talking to the wall. A wall like the one where her mom had hung the certificate they gave her when she completed the Welfare Ministry computer course a few years ago and she was so proud of herself for knowing how to write an email, as if it was like flying a spaceship.

What does her mom understand. She doesn't know anything about the latest celebs, she's not on Instagram, doesn't watch TV shows about rich people with their swimming pools and bikinis, with their champagne and fancy stores, she has no idea what Victoria's

Secret is. She doesn't understand her small dream to be part of that, of all that beauty and wealth. Nina knows that her beauty will help her, she just needs to have the door opened a little, that's all. And her Johnny promised her, he has lots of friends in the industry and he'll help her. He showed her a picture of him with another celeb in the gossip pages, one with that singer and another few girls on a balcony overlooking the sea, and another one in an elegant restaurant. Who the hell cares about exams? This is life, now.

"You don't understand," Irina said in almost a whisper. "You're giving up on your future."

Nina closed her bag and walked past her on her way out.

"He'll throw you away," she yelled. "He'll use you and throw you away. You're his whore."

Nina froze. Neither one spoke. Nina turned around and moved closer to Irina, very, very close to her makeup-free face, with her red capillaries and her patchy eyebrows. "Just because Dad threw you out," she says, looking her in the eye, "doesn't mean I'll be thrown out."

At least that's how she planned to end her sentence, but it didn't happen.

The sudden slap stopped her.

Her mother's expression was cold; neither of them moved. Nina just put her hand on her red cheek that showed the imprint of a hand, and held back the tears.

That was the first time her mother had raised a hand to her.

Humiliation and pain blended together.

Her mother was the first to turn around and walk away.

Nina knew that was it. There was nothing here for her anymore. It was over. This place, the two of them who had always been everything to each other. Everything. A mother and daughter who were both sisters and friends, who slept together in the same bed. And had slowly drifted apart.

And now it was over. She would leave now and never come back. Ever. And her mother would regret what she said to her.

The horn honked again downstairs and the phone kept vibrating.

And Amsellem the neighbor yelled, "Quiet! People live here! I'll call the police."

"Ooh, I'm so scared," Shmueli yelled back at him. "Tell the cops at the station that Shmueli sends his regards."

She answered the phone and said, "On my way."

◆　◆　◆

Naama lowers the back of her chair. Ariel has already fallen asleep and Dana's on the phone. It was stupid to drink so much wine, but it was the Seder night and she's allowed to get drunk one time, and it was also terrific wine, everyone said so, and she realizes that she's beginning to differentiate between just any wine and fine wine. It still feels weird to celebrate the Seder night here, but she has to admit that Zipi did a really nice job and followed all the rules. It was an experience, and she even got emotional. It was certainly better than the small and slightly pathetic Seder they'd had for a few years with the elderly Jewish couple that invited them, and this year, had moved to a retirement home. Itamar never wanted to make a big deal about the Seder, and cared even less about it now that he was in the middle of the never-ending merger she was sick and tired of hearing about, but they talked about Passover in Ariel's music class at the Jewish Community Center, and they also needed a bit of Judaism for Dana, and Zipi—her name was really Tzippi, but Zipi was how they pronounced it here—was so insistent that they come to her Seder that they didn't feel comfortable refusing her.

Between Zipi's crystal glasses, the grayish gefilte fish they bought at the deli, and the Haggadah in Hebrew and English, Naama found that she missed the kibbutz, even Israel a little, and she was glad she had been insistent with Itamar and they'd gone to the Seder. She saw that he too was a bit emotional.

◆ ◆ ◆

It's already noon, but everything in the apartment is dingy. The heavy rugs are loaded with dust and Nina decides she has to air them out. She goes over to the large balcony shutters and opens them. The exposed apartment is flooded with glaring light. The old lady covers her eyes.

"It hurts," she says. "It hurts my eyes."

Nina goes over and strokes her hand. "Your eyes will adjust in a minute," she says. "You need a little light. We have to clean up here. It's a holiday."

Suddenly the doorbell rings.

Carmela keeps eating her cucumber, her yogurt, and the bits of matzo, as if the doorbell has nothing to do with her. A slice of cucumber, a spoonful of yogurt, then a small piece of matzo. A slice of cucumber, a spoonful of yogurt. Nina looks at her when the bell rings again and again.

"Carmela," someone shouts on the other side of the door.

All at once, the old lady comes back to her senses, as if from a dream. "Someone's here," she says. And remains seated.

Just let it not be the police, Nina thinks.

"Carmela, don't be afraid," someone shouts. "It's Hagit's son from the minimart. I brought you some things." He knocks on the door. "Come on, Carmela, in the end they'll call the police. I can't shout like this every time."

"Maybe tell him he should leave the stuff at the door?" Nina says. "I'll bring it in later."

The old lady smiles at her and doesn't move.

The man knocks on the door.

"Come with me," Nina tells her. "Just say thank you and please leave it at the door." She holds out a hand to the old lady to help her up and walks with her to the door, but even before she realizes what's happening, Carmela turns the key in the lock and opens the door a crack.

"Carmela," a young voice says. "You scared me. My mom was angry you didn't come to the Seder last night. Are you okay? She's worried. Says no one should be alone on the Seder night. I brought you some groceries, and she also sent you some food from yesterday."

Nina is standing beside her, tensed. Hoping he won't come in.

But suddenly Carmela opens the door all the way. He's surprised to see Nina.

She remembers the blow to her face and lowers her head so that her hair will conceal the bruised cheek and most of her face.

She peers at him, avoiding eye contact. Not tall, broad shoulders. Built a little bit like a tough guy, but with a baby face. And curls. He comes in with a box that holds some vegetables, dairy products, a box of matzos, and plastic containers of homemade food.

"Nice to meet you," the guy says. "Eitan from the minimart downstairs." Thinking about what name to give him, she holds out her hand, but both of his are holding the box and he smiles in apology while her hand remains hanging in the air, and she's embarrassed.

"I see you have a guest," Eitan says to Carmela. "A guest that doesn't speak."

"I speak," Nina says as he places the box on the kitchen table, but she tries to stay far away from him so he won't see the bruise.

"Carmela, should I help you put everything away, like always?" he asks.

"I'll do it," Nina says, wanting him to get out of there. A minimart delivery guy, why the hell is he sticking his nose into our business. And it's a holiday, so it's really weird that he came.

"Great," he says, and now his hands are empty and he holds one out and says, "Eitan."

"Nice to meet you," Nina says.

"This is my Dana," the old lady says. "Came from America. Came to her grandmother."

"You're Dana?!" he says in surprise. "Wow, you've grown up. I remember you being younger."

Nina smiles. And she's scared, still trying not to look him in the eye.

"Carmela, I'll tell Mom you weren't alone yesterday," he says to the old lady. "She'll be so happy. She drove us crazy, said that no one should be alone on the Seder night. No one. And definitely not someone who gave so much to the country. She'll be so happy Dana's here."

Nina tries to slip away to her room.

"Is everything okay here, Carmela?" he asks her too loudly. People very often speak like that to the elderly, too loudly. "Everything okay with the TV? The computer? You need something?"

"Thank you," Carmela says, nodding in a strangely mechanical way.

"Do you happen to know where the mouse is?" Nina returns to the kitchen and asks him.

"She had a wireless one, must have wandered around the apartment with it," he says, trying to catch her eye. He knew Carmela had a granddaughter, but he didn't know she was so grown up. About a year ago, she showed him pictures of Dana, but Carmela, she's a little confused. For some reason, he remembers meeting her when he was a kid, and she was a lot younger than him. But never mind, maybe he doesn't remember, the most important thing is that someone came to be with Carmela. He'll tell his mom, who always worries about her. Says it isn't nice that her son went away like that, and how can you leave a mother alone without anyone.

"Always make sure everything's okay with her," she tells him every time he brings her a delivery. "And if it's not okay, tell me."

◆ ◆ ◆

Eitan still remembers Carmela and Itzik's hardware store. It had everything. Brooms and thread, light bulbs and irons, pails and can openers. Whatever you needed. Everyone bought from that lovely couple. When they walked together, she leaned on him and he leaned on his cane. And the store was always open. "Except when they went to America," his mother said with a smile not too long ago when they were talking about it and he said she had to take a vacation. Even now, at Passover, Hagit won't take time off. She just covered the shelves that held *chametz* with his old childhood sheet imprinted with nursery rhymes. She didn't care that people reached behind the sheet and took pasta or something else that wasn't kosher for Passover. "The law only says *chametz* can't be shown in public," she told him.

"Only my old sheet is shown in public," he said, laughing. Two weeks ago, he offered to take her place. For three years he'd busted his ass in the artillery corps, then he rested for a few months, and the academic year would be over soon, so now was the time to help her.

"I'll kill you if you take my place in the store. I've suffered enough with this inheritance your grandfather left me. This is an inheritance? This is slavery. I feel like closing it for good."

"Enough, Mom," he said, laughing. "Close it? What are you talking about. You're making piles of money."

"Don't get carried away, honey," she said, "I have your tuition and the mortgage on the roof renovation. Don't make me mad." He no longer said that maybe Dad would help. He'd understood years ago that Dad wouldn't help them. Maybe he'd help his new daughter. Until the last few years he hadn't realized how strong his mom was, never whining or complaining about his dad in front of him, never saying a bad word about him. He's your father, she would say, we talk about him nicely. And yet he sometimes caught her yelling at him on the phone, but not more often than she yelled at him or her workers. That's how she was. Blew up quickly. But also loved a lot.

She still felt uncomfortable about Carmela, about the fact that less than a month after Itzik died, she already broke the wall and added the space of Itzik and Carmela's store to her grandfather's store, and since then, it has been "Hagit's Minimart." She could have waited another month.

And she has been angry at Itamar since then. The way, in the middle of the shiva, he came to close the deal with her because he had to fly back on the weekend. Hagit couldn't believe his wife didn't come to the funeral, and if not to the funeral, at least to the shiva.

"Just for the time being, Mom," Eitan said with a laugh. "Until I make an exit and we move to a penthouse," and she hugged her good boy and said, "Then I'll go back to painting."

And he decided that's it, he would sign her up for a painting class. That's her dream and she has to fulfill it. In her heart, she's still an art teacher, a graduate of Beit Berl College, as she liked to point out. And he still remembers how once, when he was little, she took part in an exhibition and he was so proud. Her father, who was still alive then, managed the grocery store, and when Hagit was busy, they left him there and he had the greatest time. His grandfather let him sit on the counter, and Itzik from the hardware store gave him marbles to play with and Carmela would shout, "Are you crazy, he'll put them in his mouth and choke."

Grandpa and Itzik used to laugh at Carmela for being so uptight. And Mom used to say that Carmela was allowed. She was allowed to be uptight and worried about kids. And her eyes would grow sad.

Eitan told her several times that she should go back to teaching. "You can hire someone to manage the grocery." That's what they called the minimart before they broke the wall, and she said she'd promised Grandpa she would manage it. An outsider would only steal and nothing would be left. He should also remember that people came here because of the personal attention. And with the supermarkets choking them, it was hard enough to keep the business going. "Sales. Everybody buys what's on sale. They don't care about anything else. I give them attention."

They both knew that almost everyone in this big city was living here temporarily. Young people who rent for a year or two with roommates and IKEA shelves. And you may think that personal attention doesn't matter to them, but that's not true. His mom might be addicted to work—she even admitted that sometimes—but those young people really do want to shop where they can feel a little bit of home. Where they are seen in this huge city.

After Eitan's grandfather died of a heart attack, Itzik got tired too, but he would still open the store every morning and slowly take two chairs outside, one for himself and one for Eitan's grandfather, who would no longer be coming. At noon, he would nap on his chair and Carmela would sit inside at the cash register. At four o'clock, she would wake him to take her place and she would go home to rest and come back at six with some sliced fruit. Then they would drink tea. Every day. Every day.

The store was closed only on Memorial Day. And always, when

the siren sounded, he would think of that couple and the sweet boy in the black-and-white photo that hung behind the counter, the boy who was their son.

Now the frozen-food section in the minimart stands where Itzik and Carmela's hardware store used to be, and Eitan laughs at her for feeling guilty that she's glad their store became available, because otherwise, they would have had to move to the expensive new building across the street. There's a bit of truth in that, but sometimes Hagit feels guilty because she once kissed that soldier in the black-and-white photo, and loved him, and was angry at him for leaving her.

◆ ◆ ◆

"If you don't find the mouse in the fridge or wherever she put it— call me and I'll bring you the one I have at home," Eitan says. "And if you need help with anything, we're here in the minimart across the street," he adds and hands her a magnet. "Here's our phone number, if you need it." Carmela goes over to a drawer, takes out a hundred-shekel bill, and gives it to him. He knows what the girl is thinking. One hundred shekels is much more than what the old lady should give him. Eitan hands the money back to Carmela and says, "This is too much, Mom will kill me." And Carmela smiles. "Nonsense," she says, "you are her heart and soul. Take it. Invite a pretty girl out for ice cream."

"Do you know if there's a password or code?" Nina asks.

"For the supermarket?" he asks with a smile.

"For the computer. The Wi-Fi." They smile at each other, and she lowers her gaze.

Carmela one-two-three-four. Carmela in English, with a capital C.

"Thanks," she says as he turns to leave, and that moment stays in her mind, that fraction of a second when he looked deeply into her eyes. And she into his.

Mistake. She has to keep avoiding his gaze.

Because no one should notice her.

Carmela goes to her bedroom and as Nina begins looking for the mouse, she sees how dusty and dirty everything is in the apartment. She finds a floor rag, a pail, and a few half-empty bottles of detergent and starts to get the place ready for cleaning while she continues to look for the mouse. She moves furniture and collects all the doilies and tablecloths to be washed. But she still doesn't find the mouse anywhere.

In the kitchen, she opens one of the boxes the guy brought. Stuffed peppers. She really loves stuffed vegetables. Michal their neighbor makes fantastic ones. "Look at your little Russian girl," Michal would say to Irina. "Ready to kill for a little bit of delicious Moroccan food. Poor thing. With those *pirozhkis* and all that tasteless food of yours." Irina would tell her that stuffed vegetables are Hungarian, and they would both laugh.

Nina's stomach rumbles. She opens the microwave to warm up a pepper, and the microwave is dirty too. She cleans a spoon with her shirt and eats the pepper cold out of the box. It's good. The kitchen will be her first job. And then that whole filthy apartment. But now she's wiped out and goes to bed. Everything hurts her.

◆ ◆ ◆

Carmela wakes up, but doesn't open her eyes. She tries to hold on to another minute of peace until she starts to remember. Uri, Itamar, the store, Itzik. And then there's no Uri, there's Dana, then no Itamar, no Dana, no Itzik, and no store. The list of what-was-and-what-isn't that lashes at her dozens of times a day, day after day. And then she remembers that there is Dana. Dana's here. A hacking cough shakes her. She almost chokes, and it scares her. She coughs again and sits up in bed, and Dana comes in and hurries over to her. "Are you okay?" she asks.

Carmela nods, trying to see her face, but it's blurred. She sees the skinny legs and thin hands, and she's so white. The way she herself used to be. My Snow Princess, Itzik called her. I can't believe you're mine, he told her so many times. He, rough and sunburned from the construction work, who had come to Sofia when he was sixteen. Alone. Far from the remains of his extended family, which had fled to the village with a few other families during the war. There it's better, they were told. Here it's dangerous. So they left, taking what they managed to carry, and arrived somewhere. And stayed there even after the war ended. Because there was nowhere to go back to.

"Farming? What do I know about farming?" those city men with their ties and white shirts said. But slowly, they learned. Because they had no choice. And soon enough, the white shirts were no longer white, and the delicate hands became callused.

Itzik and his mother lived with an uncle. His mother was ill and tired. The years of her life had clenched into a fist and beat her. Until the war had ended. Up to then, she had watched over him. Had taken such good care of him. A widow with one pampered son. "You spoil him," the uncle said, and she replied, "He's all I have in this world."

But he had already been bitten by the travel bug. "You're too young," the uncle said. "But after what happened to our families," he said, "I have to look out for myself. No one will look after us, Mama, no one, do you understand?" People had begun talking about America and Palestine, but his mother would never survive the trip, and he wouldn't leave her to go to a far-off country. So he thought only about going to the big city. To Sofia.

And he left her. He left her there in the village. "I'll send you money," he promised. And she said, "Son, all I want is grandchildren. Only grandchildren. Go and come back with a grandson. So I can die in peace."

"First a wife," he told her.

And she said, "Who wouldn't want my Itzik?"

He hugged her, eager to be on his way to the big city, to the world, suffocating in the vicious circle of hardship, poverty, and people beaten down by the memories and scars of that war and the people it had taken from them. More and more widows in black.

"*Un loco quita cien*," his mother would say laughing, one crazy person makes one hundred people crazy, and then she would cough. That coughing finished her off slowly.

And Itzho, his cousin, decided to go with him. Itzik and Itzho. The two Itzhaks. Cousins. Wild men. And then, there they were, in Sofia, the big city, doing construction work, Itzho, big and strong, and Itzik, small and strong. There's a synagogue open to you, a rabbi told them. Come. The High Holidays. And Itzik sat in the synagogue and remembered how his mother had prepared for the holidays when she still had the strength. With great solemnity, as if she were doing holy work and not stuffing vegetables.

◆ ◆ ◆

"Are you okay?" Nina asks, trying to bring Carmela back from wherever she'd been pulled into.

"Dana'le, bring me some water," she asks.

Nina goes, and Carmela is suddenly drained of her strength. She realizes all at once how frightened she is of this aloneness. The aloneness and the confusion. And how much she hasn't allowed herself to let go. And where was the cleaner who used to come. She hasn't been here in a long time. Or at least that's what she thinks. And how good it is that Dana is here.

"Mom," Itamar told her after Itzik died, "let me bring you a caregiver."

"I'm fine," she told him, "I'm managing."

But slowly, she lost her confidence and began to be scared, started walking carefully, very carefully. Just not to fall. Just not to break anything. Who would come if she fell? No one would come. No one would knock on her door. She would die and no one would know.

And when another year passed, Itamar said, "Mom, it's dangerous to be alone like that."

They had the same conversation over and over again. And at some point, she wanted to tell him that, yes, she needs help. That it's hard for her alone. That the fear is hard for her. The fear of being alone if something happened to her.

"Come here and we'll talk," she said that time. She already felt the fog of forgetfulness creeping into her, enveloping her, and began writing the notes. It'll pass, she reassured herself after the doctor asked her a few questions and told her to keep a record and come back for a follow-up because he couldn't give a diagnosis without data. She didn't go back. She'd go with Itamar when he came. There was even a note for Itamar that had the doctor's name and said: "Give to Itamar!" But Itamar didn't come to visit. And the cleaner stopped coming, and she explained why, but Carmela doesn't remember. Maybe she took a vacation, but that was a long time ago, she doesn't know how long.

And now her Dana'le is bringing her water. She's so thrilled that she's here. That she's not alone anymore. It feels good. Maybe Itamar was right about a caregiver. But Dana is better.

"Don't go barefoot," Carmela tells Dana, "you'll get a cold." She points to the shoe cupboard and says, "Take something," and Nina smiles at her and says, "Okay, Grandma, okay." She takes out a pair of soft, embroidered, blue velvet slip-ons and steps into them. Even though they're a bit too small, they feel good.

Nina is upset and worried about what she saw on the news, and she's dying to turn on a computer and see what the Internet says about it. She knows he'll come looking for her, Shmueli, and she thinks it's a good thing she's here, where no one knows who she is. She'll hide here for another two or three days and then decide what to do next. If only they don't find out where she is. She has to be careful.

◆ ◆ ◆

Irina tries to think about how she can find Nina's girlfriends. To ask them about her, the way the policewoman suggested. She goes out to the shopping center in the afternoon, maybe one of Nina's friends is there, or maybe she'll see him. She's already seen him there at the kiosk where they sell lottery tickets. But the center is deserted. It's the second day of Passover and everyone is still home with their families. The holiday stretches out like a piece of chewing gum. Everything is closed. The pizzeria is closed because it's Passover. She remembers that Hezi's kiosk is closed too. "I don't have the strength to clean the shelves," Amalia whispered to her in Russian a few days ago, "just to hear my upstairs neighbor tell me later that it isn't kosher enough. Last year they brought me the rabbi because of the whiskey I put on the bottom shelf and I had such a fight with Hezi. He said I didn't understand what it means to be a Jewish woman and I opened such a big mouth on him, in the end we almost went to that rabbi to get a divorce. Who knew that whiskey is bread? I told Hezi that this year, I'm going away. Listen up, all you rabbis, I'm on vacation. To tell you the truth, Irina." She gestured for her to come closer and Irina looked at her overdone nails. Even though they made it hard to tap the cash register buttons, Amalia wouldn't give up those fancy artificial nails because she loved the tap-tap-tap of plastic on plastic. "And anyway, no one's here. Nothing's in the cash register. No woman lets her husband sit at the lottery kiosk on Passover. So *yalla*. We're allowed once in our life. Hezi and me, we're going to Burgas. It's cheap like you wouldn't believe."

"But it's cold there on Passover," Irina said.

"Who cares, the main thing is not to be here. Hezi's dying to be in a casino. Everyone tells him it's something else there, and he's dying with jealousy. Dying to hold some of those chips in his hands and that's why he doesn't care if I go shopping. They say the malls there are out of this world."

"And you're not afraid he'll lose?" Irina had heard enough stories about men who lost everything playing cards.

Amalia laughed. "That cheapskate plays with a hundred euros and thinks he's an Arab sheikh."

She has to find one of Nina's girlfriends. And she remembers that the one whose mother got new boobs works in Castro in the mall. But the mall won't open until tomorrow and she can't wait. She's so anxious. Something is wrong. She hasn't had a word from her Nina for almost two weeks, and for more than a week, there had been no sign that she'd seen her messages.

It's starting to get dark and she decides to go back to the police station and report Nina is missing.

Inside, she calms down when she sees the same policewoman from last time, who recognizes her.

"She still hasn't come back?" Ilanit the policewoman asks in surprise, embarrassed that she doesn't remember the name of the woman or her daughter. The woman's sadness moves her. She thinks about her loneliness on the holiday; she must have waited the whole time for her daughter. She herself has wanted a little loneliness her entire life. A rest from her two sisters, who fight about everything, and her two brothers, who hit each other. She has never had a corner of her own.

◆　◆　◆

It seems to be just another case of a stupid young girl who fought with her mom and ran away from home, but something smells fishy to Ilanit.

"Come on, I'll check whether anyone's heard anything about her," Ilanit says. "If there was a report."

"What does that mean?"

"We'll check to see if something's happened. Wait a minute. Let's start over," Ilanit says, opens a document on her computer, and begins to type in the details Irina has given her.

"I'll check on the computer."

"What?"

"Whether a policeman reported something."

"Like what?" Irina asks, not understanding what she means, and then she panics. "Hospital?!"

"That too," Ilanit says, and when she sees that Irina is freaking out, she asks, "Is her boyfriend from here?"

"Yes," Irina says.

"You know his name?"

"Yes," Irina says.

"He's from her class?"

"He's older."

"How much older?" Ilanit asks.

"A father. With kids. A man."

"Fu . . ." Ilanits starts to say, then remembers her uniform.

"Did you talk to him?"

"I don't have his number."

"Name?"

"What for?"

"I'll call him. You want me to call him?"

"She'll be mad. He'll be mad. No." Irina is afraid of both him and Nina, who'll kill her. But she's already stopped breathing. She's crazy with worry.

"You want to find her or not?" Ilanit says, starting to lose patience.

"Just check for me, okay?" Irina asks, looking at her with sad, tired eyes. "I don't know. The hospital, something. That's what scares me."

Ilanit looks up from the monitor. Something is weird here, something this woman is not telling her.

Irina says nothing and looks around at the policeman who is smoking outside. At the other policeman who's playing on his computer.

Seeing this, Ilanit suddenly understands. "You're afraid."

Irina nods. "He's a scary man. There are always other people with him."

"Whisper it in my ear," Ilanit says, leaning over the counter.

"Shmueli," Irina whispers, and Ilanit takes a deep breath. This is something she definitely wasn't expecting.

"Johnny Shmueli?" Ilanit asks just to be sure.

Irina nods.

"Okay," Ilanit says. "Let me think a minute. Let me think." She knows she has to ask Ashkenazi for permission. The situation between the police and Shmueli had finally calmed down a little and they'd reached an understanding, an unspoken agreement that the police would ignore their small-time stuff, and in exchange, Johnny Shmueli and his gang would keep things quiet in the streets. Ashkenazi won't want some policewoman fucking it up for him now. She has to be smart about this.

"So we shouldn't call him?" Irina asks.

"I have to talk to the chief about it," Ilanit says, looking at Irina's haggard face. Her heart goes out to this woman who came here in such a pitifully helpless state. And she begins to get angry. That Johnny is disgusting, is this all he has to do? Destroy young girls whose mothers have a hard time as it is? Whose lives have never been a walk in the park?

"You'll tell the chief his name?" Irina asked.

"Look, this is someone we all know."

"I don't want you to. I don't. Can't you just ask him, with no names?"

"Let me think about it. Let me just sniff around a little."

"What does that mean?"

"Check it out. Try to find out quietly whether he's home and what the story is."

"But without saying it's me?"

"If that's what you want." Ilanit understands her. Her fear.

"I want. No, never mind. I just want you to check the hospital and that kind of thing."

"Let's see what the computer knows about her." Ilanit types, and it seems to Irina like an eternity until she says, "The hospital, no." And after a lot more typing, "And other police stations, no. No complaints and no reports. Not on unidentified young girls her age. There's nothing." Ilanit looks pleased.

"That's good, yes?"

"Yes. That's good. It means the chances are your daughter is lounging around somewhere, in some hotel or something. And maybe her phone fell in the pool. I'll sniff around about him a little. Quietly. I promise. And when my chief comes in tomorrow morning, I'll talk to him. And if she doesn't come back by tomorrow, we'll call him. Okay?"

"I don't know."

"I'll call you before I call him. Okay?"

"Thank you very much," Irina says, slightly reassured to know that Nina isn't in jail or in some hospital.

Ilanit looks at Irina, who leaves the station and holds the railing as she goes down the steps. On her way to another night of loneliness. She comes out from behind the counter and goes after her. "I'll ask the chief to ping her phone. Okay?"

"What's that?"

"It lets us see where her phone is located. At least where it was before it fell into the pool," she says, trying to make a joke, but Irina doesn't smile, she only says, "That's good. Thank you. Try tomorrow. You have my phone number too, yes?"

On the way home, her worry increases with every step. And so do the number of questions. Irina is beginning to understand that even the police are afraid to touch Shmueli. Now she's not only worried, she's angry. She feels the anger rising in her. She'll wait one more night, and that's it. Enough. She'll go back to the police tomorrow and ask them to look for Nina's phone and to call him. Let them question him. What does she have to be afraid of? She hasn't done anything wrong. She's just looking for her daughter, who he took. Let him give her back.

4

His phone conversations with Carmela were long at first, like journeys outside of time. "Don't call if you're in a hurry," she told him once. "I don't deserve to feel like a nudnik, Itamarinka. It's hard enough for me that you're not here. That none of you are here." And he swore he wouldn't rush. She could go on and on explaining which air conditioner had stopped working and Itamar would reply patiently, knowing that their conversation was the high point of her week. He got used to pouring a glass of whiskey on the rocks for himself, laughing at how American that was of him, as if he were preparing for a ritual in which he mentally cut himself off from the rat race, from the fact that he had to be stingy with his time and managed to find a moment of quiet, a window of opportunity among all his commitments.

At first Naama was a bit jealous of the long conversations, especially because he came home late as it was, and more than once, she asked him why he didn't call his mother from the car, from the road, and he tried to explain that talking from the car was different, but after Ariel was born, Naama was actually happy for the chance to go to sleep early and forgo another evening of their regular, amusing dance of "should we watch some TV or talk or go to bed, and if it's bed, then will it be yes or no." It was mainly no, because it was late already, but sometimes it was yes, and then they both remembered the good thing between them, which had been eroded by the daily routine of work and chauffeuring the kids and running errands.

There had always been something fragile about his mother. People thought it was because of the tragedy that had befallen them, and it was true that she had become worse after that, but she'd actually been that way before. Like one of the delicate porcelain cups with the blue and gold stripes that were carefully taken out of the china cabinet only on holidays. "Are you being careful, Itamari?" she would remind him.

His father was different. From the moment he touched the warm earth of the Holy Land, he understood Israeliness and got along. He had the right temperament for it, and something about that Israeli roughness suited him. The way clothes, both cheap and expensive, suited him. He insisted on going to work in a suit every day, then he took off the jacket in the store, hung it on a hanger, and remained in the button-down shirt he wore over his undershirt. At the end of the day, he put on his jacket and walked the half block home with Carmela.

For the last few years, Carmela hadn't had the strength to iron a shirt for him every day, so she bought him those shirts with two buttons, polo shirts, and gave the button-down shirts to Igal from the dry cleaner's, though she thought that was immoral self-indulgence and apologized for it countless times. "You work hard enough," Itzik would tell her, and she would smile in gratitude.

She grew more tired as the years passed and spent less and less time in the store. Also, there wasn't enough work to justify the presence of two people for the entire day. She would come around noon so Itzik could rest. She told him he wasn't getting younger and he replied that if they took him out of the store, he would die. She knew that was true. His relationships with their regular customers and the conversations with the occasional buyers were his oxygen. He would explain every little thing patiently to each customer, and for the regular ones, he would make coffee and sit with them at the small table outside, arguing about politics or asking how their wife and children were, enjoying their stories, and when someone updated him that his son had gone abroad, he would say, "My son is in America too," and immediately add, "But he'll be back in a year or two." And the people would always say, "Good for him," or, "I wish him success," thinking to themselves that they all say they're only going for two years.

◆　◆　◆

Carmela was a listener. She loved to hear Itzik's arguments and also loved the moments he sat outside and women she knew came into the store and, while she was making them a new key to replace a lost one, or finding them the right light bulb, they would chatter away, reporting on everything that was happening in the neighborhood, and so she was always up to date.

Once she had a sewing machine in the store, for small alterations. Until threading the needle became impossible for her.

She maintained the customs of the old country, wearing dresses sewn to the exact measurements of her body, not loose and not too tight, always in soft colors, and she spoke in a hushed voice that still held vestiges of the accent that decades hadn't eradicated, different from all his friends' moms, with their jeans or minis and their hair dyed every shade of red or streaked with blond. And she was also older than all of them. And he, the child born when his brother was already in the second grade and she was approaching forty, he was hers. Intertwined with her. From the beginning. As if he had been born so someone would be with her. And they suited each other. She and Itamar. The way Itzik and Uri suited each other. They loved to arm wrestle and go fishing on Friday afternoons, while Itamar loved to be in the kitchen with his mom, to draw while she cooked and set the table, a large dish, a small dish, and a soup bowl on top of them.

She used to serve soup on Friday nights even if it was ninety degrees outside because that's how it had been at her parents' house. And Itamar felt enveloped and serene inside that elegance of hers, as if there were in her a small alcove meant only for him. Like a kangaroo's pouch. They shared a special intimacy. He understood her without a need for words. Both before and after. He knew when she was waiting for Dad to finally stop talking, when the tears would burst forth, and when he could wheedle a small, embarrassed smile out of her, after which she would grow serious.

"You're allowed to laugh," he once told her when her smile vanished and he knew she was thinking about Uri.

"But I don't want to," she told him.

"But Uri would want you to laugh," he said. She hugged him and her body shook and her tears wet his head. He was only fifteen then, just two years after his big brother, the hero, was killed in the line of duty, and he already knew that even if he was the funniest person in the world, his mom would only laugh for a moment. A fragment of a moment. It was the most she could manage.

The first year, Itzik tried to take him fishing. But they just sat facing the water in silence. A few weeks later, as he was preparing his rod, Itzik told him, "I think your mother needs you to help her with dinner today," and Itamar stayed with her, the way he used to, except that he set the table for three, not four. Not with the fancy dishes, but the everyday ones.

And ever since, Itzik had gone fishing alone. And had begun to be silent.

◆ ◆ ◆

"I understand that it's important if you want to get ahead at work, but . . ." Carmela said when he told her they were going to America.

And his father shouted at her, "Why make it hard for him? It's hard enough for him as it is."

He asked Eitan, Hagit's son, to help his parents with Skype. At first, they managed to have some Skype conversations, but then Eitan went into the army, then they tried FaceTime, and later, Itzik died, and since then, Carmela hadn't wanted any of that. "I'm fine with the phone that has no television," she said.

Itamar closes his eyes and finds it hard to breathe. Is something really wrong with Mom, or is it him, with his feelings of guilt for what he did? He, the deserter. The traitor. The coward. The sellout. How many times had he heard his parents say those words about their friends' children who left the country. Words used by Israelis of their generation who built the country and saw their children leaving it, trickling out. His generation gives it a different label. Relocation, they call it. Fulfilling themselves, realizing their potential somewhere in Silicon Valley, in the London Stock Exchange, maximizing their abilities, the global generation, the international generation with the world at their feet, as accessible as a meal at McDonald's. But at the end of all that globalness, he thinks, is an old woman who's been left alone on the other side of the ocean.

Because her son is in America.

With time, their long conversations grew shorter. He already knew most of the questions by heart, and the replies also repeated themselves.

How's Dana doing at school—she's a great student. What's Naama doing now—she just finished planning/organizing/starting the renovation. And the question about Uncle Ronald, who's called Ron, will they be at his place for the holiday, a question she asks even when there is no holiday—and no, he tells her, Ron lives really far away, but they have friends here who live relatively close. Yes, the kids like to go there. He dresses up the truth for her when it's about the sweet, elderly couple the kids aren't interested in and they flop onto the couches pretty quickly and become engrossed in their tablets. And yes, sometimes they take trips, during vacations, he tells her, remembering their trips during his childhood, when the store was closed. Itzik would take a map and had something to tell them about every intersection, explaining how, when he first arrived in the country, they sent him to the army to work in transport, and look, this is where they spent two months, and here almost a week, and that's where he was wounded, it's not clear how, but he's had a limp since then, and he would tell them about his buddies and the things they did together when they were young and stupid. And how he always worried about Carmela because he was older than his buddies and the only one married, except for that religious guy. Who was killed later. In each city they passed, there was always someone with whom he did reserve duty, the reserve duty that always meant leaving Carmela alone in the store, and that was a lot of pressure for her, but Itzik wouldn't give it up, so Uri would step up and help her, and little Itamar knew he had to behave really well because Daddy was in the army. And whenever those buddies of Itzik's were in Tel Aviv, they would come to the hardware store and he would introduce them to all the store owners and take them to the restaurant on the corner across the street that served homestyle meals.

"Look." He would say someone's name and point at a few red-roofed houses located at the foot of a hill. "You see, he lives right there." Itamar remembered how Uri would scrunch his face into an

I'm-so-bored look to make him laugh. Mom would say, "Itzik, take pity on the children, enough with the stories." And even though Itamar actually liked the stories, he never said anything. And here, driving with Dana and Ariel, he doesn't have a single story to tell them. And he doesn't have a single friend in any city they pass.

◆　◆　◆

He tries to remember how she was before Uri died of his injuries. The images blur in his mind and he doesn't know whether he romanticized it or everything had really been so pleasant and peaceful. Two brothers who almost never fought, the elder his father's child, the younger his mother's. Eating lunch with her almost every day, telling her about school. And then boom.

That moment when everything that had been was shattered. Crushed.

He had awakened in a panic, not understanding what that noise was. It took him a while to realize that Itzik was crying. He had never heard his father cry before. It was a low sound, the sound of someone whose life seemed to have been wrenched out of him, like a lion trapped in thick vegetation, roaring with the knowledge that he was helpless, that he couldn't do anything, a sound that came from within the hell of despair. And the pain. That's what pain sounded like. And then howls burst from the living room. "No," he heard him scream. "No." And his mother mumbled. He covered himself with his blanket and tried to understand.

After that, there were no more lunches. "I'll stay in the store," Itzik said, making the excuse that he had to adjust to the new era in which the malls set the rules and stores didn't close at noontime anymore. And there was no more laughing and hardly any happiness. There were hugs. His mom would hug him tight, sometimes even hurting him a bit, as if she were trying to paste him onto her. Make him seep into her. So that his skin was her skin. So he would never leave her. Never distance himself from her. Sometimes, after one of those long hugs, he would feel drained, exhausted. As if the strength had been sucked out of him.

◆ ◆ ◆

"It's okay," she says in a weak voice, and even she doesn't believe herself. "If you can't, I understand."

She hangs up and he's left with his phone in his hand and no one on the other end. His energy gone. His body hurts where the hug used to be, as if he himself has become the mother kangaroo discovering that her baby pouch is empty.

She's angry that he isn't coming to stay with her this year either, and rightly so. But on the other hand, it's so complicated to go to Israel now just to be silent with her on the day she doesn't speak. And it's always hot and crowded during the Memorial Day ceremony, and those traffic jams, and there's never any parking at the cemetery. They're lucky to have Menashe, who has been driving them there for years, from the time Itzik was alive, and always waits for them. He takes the job very seriously, polishing his taxi the day before, feeling that he's doing something for the country's bereaved families. Over the years, he learned that Menashe drove there the day before to arrange the plants around the grave. So they wouldn't look neglected during the ceremony. And Itamar has no idea who asked him to do that. He has to remember to find out if Carmela pays him.

◆ ◆ ◆

Memorial Day is in less than a month, but there's the presentation everyone's been waiting for, hoping that this time, that's it. The merger is finally happening. He trudges into the bedroom and finds Naama and Ariel sleeping, as usual, and takes little Ariel to his own bed and turns off the lights.

He thinks about the fact that Carmela hasn't told him anything for a long time, she barely responds, just asks her regular questions, as if she were only waiting to ask the next one, and it was he who prolonged the conversation. "Did you see Dana's end-of-year picture? They called her onto the stage to receive her certificate of excellence," he tells her, but she has already moved on to the next question. The burden of guilt he feels is much heavier than he admits, and recently, it has attacked him in all sorts of unexpected places. When he's looking for a parking place in the endless mall lot. When he throws his coffee cup with the green Starbucks logo on it into the trash bin at the entrance to the offices.

◆　◆　◆

It's a good thing Grandma isn't very focused, Nina thinks, smiling to herself as the hot water washes over her. It's her second shower today. She showers at least three times a day in the new shower stall that someone renovated in this dilapidated apartment. No one turns off the water heater here. No one tells her not to waste water, and only joy radiates from Carmela's face every time she sees her coming out of the shower, and she immediately says, "Dana'le, Dana'le, it's so wonderful that you came here. Do you need anything?"

Nina closes her eyes under the flow and the images that have been haunting her return, a mishmash of sounds and colors, of laughter and vulgar words, of everyone jumping out of the car and chasing the guy who was running away, and the woman screaming, "Leonid!" As soon as the gang was back in the car and Shmueli started the engine, the woman ran to the back of the building, and Nina can still hear her screams.

Things are beginning to connect and become clear. Something happened in that apartment that was much worse than a few joints and alcohol and exhaustion. Entire days were lost to her and she had no idea what happened in them. People spoke to her as if they knew her, and she didn't remember them. She sees flashes of men looking at her, she's lying down and they're standing around her, images race through her mind and the nausea rises in her throat again. That's why she showers so much and scrubs her body until her skin is red, to cleanse herself of all those hands that touched her, of all the words they said to her, the sound of them laughing to her face and behind her back. She tries to remember when she started to lose control, when hours began to be erased from her memory, and she remembers that photographer. That's where it began. That's when she entered the cloud that swallowed her up. Until those screams. "Leonid! Leonid!" shook her out of the strange blurriness that had shrouded her.

She remembers how stressed out of their minds Johnny and the others were when they got into the car, shouting, speeding away from there, and the guy next to her, the one who had shoved her head violently down to his open pants earlier, trying to say something that came out garbled and Shmueli screaming at him, "Shut your face, you bastard." Nina had never seen him so furious before. Then he yelled at the guy who had torn her panties, saying he couldn't trust them, he had to do everything himself. "How did this happen?! How could you drag me into this fuckup? You piece of shit, you fucked me, you know that? Me!"

She looked around while they were yelling at each other, and tried to move closer to the car door, tried to minimize her presence as much as she could. When they had gotten out of the car and she remained inside, she was already planning to escape, decided to count to ten and looked around, but then they suddenly came back and the yelling started. All at once, she realized she was in danger. Something really bad just happened, she told herself, unable to understand what, and now, once again she hears the screams of the woman who had run, looking for Leonid, and she thinks maybe that was what shook her awake, what made her finally escape. Her body, which until then had been limp, suddenly filled with strength, maybe because she had been alone in the apartment for two days, had slept and had not taken anything, maybe because she realized she had crossed a line, that she was in danger, but whatever the reason, she knew for sure that that's what she had to do. Run. The first chance she had. But they sped away. She squeezed against the door so they wouldn't remember she was in the car, and then the moment came. They stopped for a light and the sidewalk was full of young people and there was even a bar, and she knew that was the moment and she opened the door and started to run. Just like that. She ran like a madwoman, like the wind. Without her purse, without anything, even without her high heels, which fell off her feet. She sneaked a glance back and saw Shmueli looking at her from the car. The two guys in the back seat jumped out and began to run after her, and Shmueli's driver honked and tried to drive faster after her. Everyone watched suspiciously and two guys even tried to stop them, saying, "Hey, what's the story? Leave her alone," and while they fought, she ran into a side street, then into another street and then into the front yard of a building, and from there to another front yard. Only then did she stop for a moment and hide among the trash bins, waiting, surrounded by the stench. Then she came out and ran to another front yard. And tried to open the door to the building, but it was locked, so she ran to another building. She tried not to go out onto the street, but kept running from yard to yard. She stepped on things and couldn't decide what was worse, the pain or the repulsion. But she didn't care. And then she came to the one door that was open.

◆ ◆ ◆

Nina turns off the faucet and wraps herself in a towel, and it's so nice inside the soft, clean cloth. And it's also nice that the old lady's house is beginning to smell better. She still has a lot more work because everything was so filthy and musty, but she's made a start and she's proud of herself. She has to go to the grocery store. There's no choice. She needs detergent, and the stuffed peppers are finished, along with the other things the neighbor sent. She made pasta for them, and only afterward did she realize it was *chametz*, but Carmela didn't seem to care.

She also had to figure out how to use the washing machine.

"Dana'le, Dana'le, where are you?" she heard Carmela. Sometimes she asks once. Sometimes twenty times. Sometimes she stops because Dana answers that she's here and will be there in a minute, and sometimes, after Dana answers, she immediately calls her again and asks where she is, and Dana answers again. And Carmela asks again.

Every time Nina goes to her and says, "Grandma, I'm here," Carmela fills with joy and tenderness, reaches out and draws her closer, clasps Nina's head to her chest and strokes her cheek.

"I'm here," Dana shouts and goes to her, still wrapped in the towel, looks at the rolled-up newspaper lying on her lap.

At dawn this morning, Carmela once again began her journey down to the mailbox. It was a long, slow journey, during which she walked out of the apartment, left the door open, went downstairs, exited the building, opened the mailbox and then slowly returned, climbed the two flights of stairs to the second floor, stopping to rest on the chair on the first floor. That's how she found Nina. On her first morning in this apartment, when Nina heard her go out, she leaped out of bed and followed her. There was no newspaper that morning because of the holiday, so Nina didn't understand the reason for her journey. Today, when she heard Carmela get up and leave, she followed her downstairs again to make sure she didn't go out for a stroll by mistake. Because she was so confused that who knew if she'd find her way back. After her strenuous journey, Carmela returned to her armchair.

Nina turns on the TV. "Thank you, sweetheart, thank you," Carmela says and strokes her arm, and a moment before Nina goes to get dressed, the man on TV says, "New details on the murder in the Central Bus Station," and the picture of Leonid appears behind him again. The neighbors standing in front of the area the police cordoned off yell at the policemen, "It's impossible here with the illegals and the prostitutes, where are the police!" A hoarse woman explains to the TV reporter that they're fed up with being ignored, and they're already preparing for an impromptu demonstration against the Supreme Court and the police and the government. The reporter nods, turns to the camera, and says that the police are asking for the public's assistance, and anyone with information should call the police, and one of the demonstrators shouts, "Why don't they put enough cameras in this area? Don't we deserve to be defended?"

Nina knows she's supposed to report it to the police. That they're looking for information. Maybe there were street cameras there, a thought that frightens her very much. No, she won't do it. She won't report it. She takes the newspaper from Carmela and right on the first page she sees Leonid's face. She reads the headline, then turns to the page with the story. It's lucky she ran away. It's lucky she isn't with

Johnny now, he must be freaking out, and it's a good thing he doesn't know where she is. She just hopes they don't come to ask her questions because what will she say? And she's scared he might find her. This is the first time she's glad she doesn't have a phone because he could locate her through the phone, he has connections. He even has friends who are cops. Nina saw him meet with them, the backslapping and guffawing. "Cut the crap, bro. You can't bullshit me," he said to the older-looking cop in uniform who came to ask him for something, she didn't hear what. Shmueli was being nice, they sat in the café and talked, and suddenly, the cop got up and said quietly, but loud enough for everyone to hear, "Don't try me." All his pals in the café looked away because they didn't want to meet Shmueli's eyes or the eyes of that cop, who looked like he was very high up and clearly wasn't afraid of anything.

While thinking those terrifying thoughts about Shmueli and his connections, Nina tries again to figure out how to turn on that annoying washing machine. She got it working only once, after pressing all the buttons for almost an hour. She reminds herself to add laundry powder to her shopping list. It's already a long list, maybe she will call that guy from the supermarket. She remembers how her mom used to laugh at women who always managed to ruin their prettiest, whitest blouse because they washed it with colored things. "What's so hard about separating? What?! A lawyer she knows how to be, but separating white and colored clothes she can't manage?" she would say to Nina. Irina would laugh if she saw Nina struggling with the stubborn machine now, cursing and banging on it.

Carmela comes over, presses two buttons, and the machine starts working. Show me again, Nina asks, and Carmela shows her. Nina smiles. "Now I'll remember."

"Should I make you lunch, Dana'le?" Carmela asks.

And Nina says, "I have to go shopping. There's no laundry powder and we need some other things."

Carmela tells her there's a place downstairs owned by a really nice woman. "She was my Uri's girlfriend. Once. A long time ago. Tell her you're Carmela's. She'll write down what you owe. Or you can call and that sweet boy of hers will bring what we need."

"I'll go there," Nina says, feeling that she has to get some air.

She goes to get dressed, tries to find something that won't look like a baby's pajamas. There are no pants in Dana's room that will fit her, so she takes a beige pleated skirt from Carmela's closet and doesn't care that she looks a little like a religious girl. And with those velvet slip-ons yet. She tells Carmela she'll be back soon, and Carmela takes her wallet out of the handbag that's hanging on the back of the chair, gives Nina her credit card, and says, "In case you need something else. And buy yourself a present from Grandma." Nina hugs her. Not because of the money, but because something inside her has softened. Because Carmela is taking care of her. This confused old lady who doesn't remember who her granddaughter is, but knows how the washing machine works and who her son's girlfriend was who knows how many years ago. Nina sees how Carmela constantly tries to hide her confusion, but all those notes give her away. And Nina decides to ignore it.

Carmela gives herself over completely to Nina's hug, and even holds her a little bit longer. It feels good. The scent of clean hair. The touch of young skin. Touching. She doesn't remember how long it's been since someone touched her. Even held her hand. But her body seems to remember.

"You've grown up," Carmela says suddenly.

"Hagit was Uri's girlfriend?" Nina asks, because written in large letters on the note at the front door near the phone is "Hagit—Minimart. Son—Eitan."

"Yes, yes." Carmela's eyes awaken for a moment. "She was so sweet, but a child, and he wanted someone prettier. She loved him with a passion from the time they were little, but he was a better catch than her and wanted more in a girlfriend."

The truth is cruel, Nina thinks, when it isn't wrapped in the civility of what isn't nice to say. It's scary.

◆ ◆ ◆

Eitan wakes up embarrassed that he dreamed about her, and in the dream, he tried to move her hair out of her eyes and look into them again. He remembers how almost transparent her lashes looked when her eyes were downcast. It's stupid that he's thinking such things about her, that he can't get her out of his head, after all, he only saw her for a few minutes, and now he's trying to find a convincing excuse to see her again. Even for just a moment. To understand what happened there. He'll ring the doorbell to ask her about the mouse she's looking for, and if she hasn't found it, he'll give her his. He doesn't use a mouse at all. He lies on his bed with his laptop and telephone, it's much more comfortable. Sometimes he raises his head and finds that he's been surfing sites with idiotic jokes and stupid videos for hours. After asking about the mouse, he can ask her out, but that might be a little forward, might seem like he's trying too hard. Because they don't really know each other and it's really stupid to plan things with her, she's probably going back to America next week. But why the hell can't he get her out of his mind? He'll think of something they need or he forgot to bring from the minimart, or make something up. And he won't charge her for it.

"Don't ring it up, it's Eitan's friend," Hagit would tell the girl at the cash register when he came from school with a friend. He lost so many of them when he found out that they came with him after school just to go to his mom's minimart and take things. Hagit didn't care about the ones who were considerate enough to take only one thing. Or two. But there were some who thought it was an open buffet. It was a test of character for grade school kids. And his mom was right. The ones who showed respect, who didn't snatch everything they could and were happy to get an ice cream pop or a candy bar, continued to be nice to him. And he got along with them. He hated that Hagit was almost always right and it embarrassed him that everyone knew her, that she was a neighborhood fixture. "Oh, you're Hagit's son," the neighbors would say, thinking they knew him.

"Don't you want to go backpacking now that you've finished the army?" Hagit asked him, but he really didn't want to take a long trip. Throughout his time in the army, he missed going home and being in his room. For almost three years he was with people constantly, and that was absolutely enough for him. He saw that his mom was worried, wanted him to have a more active social life, but he had never been like that, and the few friends he did have were spread around, two on a long, post-army trek, another one in the university in Beersheba. He enjoyed the quiet, and he also enjoyed his classes at the university, which surprised him by being so different than he expected. Different from high school. Here he could disappear in the crowds of students that take the huge first-year introductory courses. He was comfortable watching everything from the sidelines. He had already begun recognizing faces, mainly in the classes given by the teaching assistants, where they were divided into smaller groups. In no time at all, he had given each one a label. The joker who insisted on making people laugh. The one who always had questions. The arguer. And he, who had always been the nerd, understood that now he could decide who he wanted to be, the tough guy or the nice guy. And he was letting his hair grow longer, and longer, and longer. His mom kept pushing him to cut it, but he didn't care. He'd hated the army haircut, felt too exposed, and now his soft curls caressed him and tickled the back of his neck.

And he thinks about the touch of her hair, trying to imagine himself stroking it, stroking her, lifting her chin and looking into her eyes.

He glances at the clock. Too early to call Carmela. If he knew Dana's number, he would text her to say he's bringing the mouse. But he hadn't had the courage to ask her for it.

He laughs at himself. What a big deal he's making. After all, she's a kid, too young for him. He won't hit on a kid. Maybe she's fifteen. He thinks she looks seventeen or eighteen, but these days, you can't tell. Girls mature so much earlier than boys. And the ones his age are sometimes so childish.

He can't decide whether to tell his mom. For years, they've been dancing a careful tango. He knows everything about her and she knows everything about him, except for a few small secrets they keep to themselves. They weren't ever dramatic things. But now he's holding a bomb. Because he knows that Hagit would be happy to hear him talk about a girl. Very happy. She's always trying to fix him up, and maybe that's why he doesn't want to tell her. Every time he thinks about hiding something from her, he remembers Aida and her green eyes, and knows that his mom was very glad when she stopped working in the minimart. She also used to clean Carmela's house, and every time she finished there, she would say, "How could they all leave her like that? Carmela, such a good soul, and they left her all alone. She doesn't deserve that."

Since Aida left, Carmela's apartment has become very dirty and smells kind of moldy, and he's glad Carmela isn't alone now.

"You know that Aida gave birth to a girl a few months ago?" Hagit asked him not too long ago.

And he remembers how, on her last day at the minimart, he went to shake her hand and could feel the tears welling in his eyes, which embarrassed him, and she came over and whispered in his ear, "I'm an Arab, don't cry over an Arab," and that time, instead of laughing at the joke, he found himself hugging her, and their tears blended with their laughter. He thinks about all the years she was with them, and now she's married and has a child, and he still doesn't know what he wants out of life.

He should have asked his mom who was cleaning Carmela's place, but he didn't. Because who even thought about it. Now Sisi, an Eritrean, works for them, and he doesn't seem to like Eitan. Maybe the army uniform Eitan wore when he came home the last few years threatened him. Maybe he suffered a trauma back in Eritrea, maybe he was persecuted. And his mom was on the phone all day with the organization that looks out for immigrant workers' rights, and she was always giving that Sisi money to help him, and sorry, I hate to admit it, but the more she helped him, the angrier he seemed to be and the longer his list of complaints grew. And his angry expression reminded Eitan of the way the young Palestinians looked at them when he and his buddies in the unit went into their villages. It was the same look of exploding testosterone boys that age have. The age right after adolescence that doesn't really have a name. The age when, once, people used to get married. Aida and Hussein got married at that age and are busy trying to make a living, adding another floor to her parents' house, without a building permit. That's also why, on the street leading to the main road, a row of gaping rectangles has sprung up which will have windows someday, and now they give the illusion of being unfinished, but inside, the structure is totally finished. Hagit and Eitan were welcomed warmly at the wedding, and it was strange for him to see Aida like that, wearing a traditional dress and head-covering, and she didn't look him in the eye.

He misses her a bit now, and also that long summer before he went into the army, when he spent his days in the minimart and his nights with PlayStation, and he and Aida organized the shelves and the orders and he began doing deliveries. "If we don't do free deliveries," his mom explained to him, but really to herself, "that'll be the end. They'll eat us alive." When she said "they" she meant the big supermarket on the corner. "The Deal," she said bitterly. She hated them. "We have no choice," she added at some point. "We need to have sales."

When Hagit told her mother about it, she said, "Next you'll want us to have our own members' card."

"That's right," Hagit said.

"But they're a chain, we're just a grocery. Since when does a grocery have its own members' card?"

"We're not a grocery!" Hagit shouted. "Come and see how big it is, we're a minimart!" And she shouted the word *minimart* as loudly as she could. Since she took over the store that used to be Itzik's and the one that used to be the shoemaker's—she no longer remembers who the last person in that place was—and broke through the walls and renovated, she insisted that people say "minimart" and wanted to change the sign. She and Grandma argued so much. "It's not Levy's Grocery anymore," she told her, and her mother said, "You can't erase Papa, it's not nice," but Hagit was already sold on the name suggested by a customer who worked in an ad agency, Hagit's Minimart. And one day she just changed the sign. Then she told her mother, who surprised her by saying, "Whatever is best for the business."

Because in the end, that's how it is in the homes of the self-employed. The business comes first.

◆ ◆ ◆

He gets up to go to the bathroom. The sun is beginning to shine and Hagit is already having her coffee and a cigarette on the balcony.

"What are you doing up?!" she asks him.

"I'm sleeping. You're imagining things," he says and goes back to his room.

"Eitan," he suddenly hears her shout. "How is Carmela?"

"She's fine. Her granddaughter's with her."

Hagit shouts, "Really?! Dana's here? And Itamar?"

"I don't know," Eitan replies.

"Oh, come on." Hagit is suddenly at his door, a second before he puts on his headphones and goes back to sleep, and asks in surprise mixed with profound shock. "You didn't ask?"

"No," he says calmly.

"Boys," she says, shaking her head in despair.

"Sorry, Mom," he says.

"I can't believe you didn't ask," she says. "You didn't take money on the holiday, did you?"

She looks at him and knows right away. "I don't believe it!" she says. "You did!"

"She insisted!" he defends himself. "Besides, I told her I'd bring them a mouse for the computer."

"Great, so when you go there tomorrow, you'll ask about Itamar."

"Why, was he hot?"

"Stop it, Eitan," she protests, and then laughs. "That's no way to talk to your mother."

"So he was hot," Eitan says with a smile.

◆ ◆ ◆

A knock on the door wakes Irina and she sits up. Then freezes. Waiting to hear if the knocking continues, if it's on her door or someone else's. Or maybe she dreamed it. She had a restless night, sleeping and waking up, waking up and falling asleep, and now it's almost seven. She needs to hurry. She has to be at Talia's mother's house at seven thirty. How did this happen to her? She jumps out of bed. She never gets up this late. This weeklong *yob tvoyu mat* holiday has messed up everything, I just want it to be over already. And being alone without Nina is hard. Luckily, Talia's mother asked for help with her daughter for a few days. That'll make it easier to get through at least part of the week. Yesterday she went to the mall to look for Nina's girlfriend, to try and get her to talk, maybe she knew where Nina was. She went to the store manager, who knew immediately who she was talking about. He was boiling mad and explained that he'd fired her, what a nerve she has, insisting on going to Eilat for the holiday week. "When I need her here the most. Look at how many people there are in the store, and I'm alone. She won't get a job in this city, you'll see. I'll tell everyone how Meital left me high and dry on the holiday to go away with her girlfriends. Here's her number." He wrote it on piece of paper and said, "And tell her to stay in Eilat, there's nothing for her here."

"She's a high school kid," Irina tries to defend Meital, even though she can't stand her. "You know how they are at that age. They just want to have a good time."

"I'm not a nightclub," he said, and Irina thought that maybe Meital was actually right, she still had a lot of years to be a hard worker, to worry about her salary, now she should go to Eilat with her friends and roast in the sun on the beach. Irina couldn't believe she was thinking that, and smiled to herself at how much she'd changed. Once she thought going to Eilat was the biggest waste of time there was. Now it seemed like life itself. The life she missed out on.

Meital answered the phone and said, "I don't know where she is. I really don't. No, she wasn't in touch with me. Don't worry about her, she must be living it up somewhere. I'm in Eilat. With some girlfriends. We sent her a WhatsApp, but she didn't answer. Maybe she lost her phone."

She finishes brushing her teeth and then hears the knock on the door again. It wasn't a mistake. She's not imagining things. But who would come here before seven in the morning? Maybe it's Nina? Why would Nina knock if she has a key? Another knock on the door. Hard, too hard. "Just a minute," she shouts. "Who is it?" She zips up her pants as she goes to the door and asks, "Who is it? Nina?" And she shouts, "Ninotchka?" And as she turns the key, she sees him in the peephole, but too late. She has already opened the door.

And he's in her living room.

"Where is she?" she asks the large man who has entered her home as if he had permission.

"Let's not play games," he says, pleased with the time he chose to come. People are most surprised when it's early in the morning. Most confused. It would have been better to wake her up, but he couldn't get up this morning. Too many thoughts had kept him awake at night.

"Where's Nina?" he asks.

"What?" Irina says in alarm as she gathers leftovers of her meal from the living room, embarrassed by the mess. She never imagined anyone would show up out of the blue.

He understands that he has to start differently. "Shalom, Mrs. Absiovsky," he says, extending a hand. "Nice to meet you. I'm David, but everyone calls me Johnny. Is this how you always welcome visitors? No coffee? No cookies?" Irina is paralyzed. She stands there, holding the plates she picked up, unable to find words. He walks around the living room, touching things. She snaps out of her paralysis and goes into the kitchen to boil water. There hasn't been a stranger, definitely not a male stranger, in her home for years. Nina's friends have been here, but never a man alone with her. The tension makes her perspire, soon there'll be underarm sweat stains on her blouse. She takes a deep breath, tries to calm her pounding heart. Tries to control her voice, to not shout, and asks, "How do you like your coffee?"

"Turkish. Strong."

"I don't have that. Instant or tea?"

"Diet Coke?"

"I have regular."

"So regular."

She brings out a bottle and a glass. He scares her, a man that size in her living room. With such a piercing glance.

"Should I wait for her here?" Shmueli asks. "You know when she's coming back?"

"What do you mean? She's not with you?"

"No," he says, looking surprised by the question. "I haven't seen her for, I don't know, something like ten days, maybe two weeks . . . Why, where is she?"

"She hasn't been here since she . . . since the two of you . . ." She tries to understand what he's saying. Nina went with him. To be with him. She's with him. That's what she'd been thinking all those days. Why has he come here looking for her? She, Irina, is the one who should be going to him to look for Nina. That's what she planned to do. It confuses her that this is upside down.

"So I'll wait here for her," Shmueli says. "When do you think she'll be back?"

"Where is she?"

"Don't play games with me," he says softly, smiling as he sits down on an armchair and puts his feet on the coffee table.

"I'm worried about her," Irina says in almost a whisper. "Very worried. Where is she?"

"How should I know?"

117

"She went with you."

"With me?!" He chuckles. "What are you talking about?!"

"I saw you take her lots of times. All her friends . . ." She stops talking. She mustn't talk so much. Listen and don't talk, she tells herself. Try to understand what this bastard's story is. Then you'll find out where she is.

"Yeah, we went out a few times." He smiles. "She was crazy about me, probably a complex because she has no father. Followed me around everywhere. How many times can a man say no to a girl who offers herself like that? I told her I'm too old for her, but she was in love. Wouldn't take no for an answer. Maybe she liked being taken out like I took her out. Nobody ever pampered her like I did. Did anyone ever take her to a suite in a hotel?! To a restaurant in Tel Aviv where she can order whatever she wants and everyone asks her does she like it and is she enjoying herself? You ever go to the mall with her and tell her, whatever you want, take it?" he says and looks her over from head to toe, wondering if in twenty years, Nina will look like her. Like someone life tossed aside. "Did anyone ever pamper you? You deserve it too."

"Where's Nina?" she asks again, and in a state of shock, she asks it over and over again in her mind, her body swaying forward and back, as if she were praying. What did he say, that man, she's trying to understand where that evil in him comes from. There's no wound or pain in her life that he isn't prodding and poking and bruising. There's no father. No money. But she reminds herself that now is not the time to take offense. Later, she'll plan revenge, she'll bring his world down around him. But for now, listen, she tells herself. Understand what he's doing. He's not looking for Nina. He's trying to rewrite his story with Nina for you. Trying to make you believe that she chased after him. Try to figure out why. He's scared. He's worried about something. Otherwise, he wouldn't have come here.

"The last time she left here, it was with you," Irina says.

"When?" he asks, pretending to try to remember. "The day she argued with you? When she said she would never ever come back here? When was that, even before Passover, more than two weeks, right? I told her that was between you and her, I won't mix in. And I don't know you, Mrs. Absiovsky, I didn't have anything to do with it. She was really mad at you. I mean really mad. She said she would never forgive you. That was a tough day for her, I told her the same day that I wanted to stop seeing her, I couldn't do it anymore. She came down with a suitcase, so I saw she had some fantasy in her head. I have a wife and kids and I have to be with them. My wife already started hearing things she shouldn't, and Nina comes down to the street with a suitcase in the middle of the day, like what the hell? She wants to put the suitcase in my car so everyone sees it and talks about it? No way. And she cried her eyes out, that daughter of yours, she begged me, kissed me, threw her arms around me, she would have done anything, she even tried to hit me," he said and laughed too hard showing teeth that were too white and too new.

"But she . . . it wasn't like that." Irina tries to sort out those two weeks in her mind. Suddenly, it all looks different.

"She told you she would never come back here, right?" Shmueli asks, looking at her as if he sympathizes. "That's what she said she told you, and she thought she was coming to sleep at my place, but sweetie, I told her, you can't sleep at my place, I have a wife and kids, so I put her in a taxi and gave her money for a hotel in Tel Aviv. And that was it. I haven't seen her since."

Irina is breathing heavily, trying to absorb his words, and Shmueli keeps talking. "All of a sudden I was worried, I thought she must have used up all the money, so I tried to call her, but she didn't answer. And I tried her again before the holiday, and nothing. So I came to see if everything's okay. It's all right I came, right? I'm worried about her. She was so upset. After all, a girl without a dad to take care of her."

Irina can't believe what she's hearing. Is her little girl alone in the big city just because of what she said to her, just because of one argument? It can't be. She would have come back. For sure. And maybe not. She's so stubborn, Nina. Strong. Never shows when she's having a hard time. But what is she doing all by herself in Tel Aviv? Where did she sleep when the money was gone? A sea of questions threatened to drown her.

"So how was the Seder night with her?"

"She wasn't here," Irina says, her heart pounding. She has to talk to the police. Her Nina, help! She'll tell them everything. If only he'd get out of here already. "Where's Nina?" she mumbles.

"That's just what I'm asking," he says, and the truth is that now he's worried. Shit. He was sure she'd be here.

"What did you do to her?" Irina whispers, looking him in the eye. "What did you do to her?"

"Calm down, Mrs. Absiovsky," he whispers. "Your daughter doesn't talk to you for two weeks and you don't ask where she is? Don't take an interest? You really surprise me. My mom would have turned the world upside down to find me. Now I come and you pretend like you're worried?"

Irina isn't listening to him. "What hotel did you send her to?"

"I told her to pick one herself," Shmueli says with a shrug. "I don't know what she decided."

◆ ◆ ◆

He begins to believe she's not here. He smells the fear coming off this woman. She's not lying. She really doesn't know where the girl is. He checks out Irina, sees the vestiges of her beauty, the high cheekbones, the light-colored eyes and skin which, with a little more makeup and a little less neglect, could still attract a man. That's what Nina wanted to run away from. From that neglect. He's momentarily sad for that girl. She really drove him crazy. Too bad he gets over it so fast. As soon as the girl is his, he loses interest in her. That's his disease. And the time between getting turned on and turning off gets shorter with every girl. But he didn't come here because of that crap. He has to find her, to make sure she doesn't talk. What a stupid, unnecessary fuckup.

"She called?" he asks.

"No. Just tell me she's okay," she pleads, covered in sweat.

"I don't know. Looks to me like you didn't educate her right," he says with a smile. "That's why a daughter runs away from her mother." Then he moves closer to Irina, runs a hand along her cheek, down to her neck and then to her cleavage. "When she comes home, tell her not to open her mouth. I know you didn't manage to educate her so far, but maybe this time you will. You're not that stupid. Not stupid like your daughter. So tell her."

He takes a step back, checking to see how his words are affecting Irina. As if they were a new dress she was wearing. And then he sees her phone lying on the table.

He reaches out and picks it up.

"What's the code?" he asks Irina.

She looks at him uncomprehendingly.

"To unlock the phone, lady. What's the code?"

She tells him.

"Happy holiday," Shmueli says. He opens the door, turns around at the threshold, and adds, "And don't go to the cops. Don't. That would be a very bad mistake for both of you."

And he leaves.

Irina sits there like a sock forgotten in the washing machine. Unable to comprehend how all that happened. How could he send her to Tel Aviv all by herself? And how will she find her now?

She promised to go and watch Talia, and she's late. No one in the center can know, even though there are other employees who babysit privately on vacations. Shoshi doesn't like it. But Talia is big already and Irina is worried she might tell. She'll tell the mother that's it, this is her last time. It was stupid to say yes. She mustn't jeopardize her job at the center.

Irina reaches inside her bag for her phone. It's not on the table. She realizes that he took it. Shmueli has her phone. And then she understands why. If Nina calls her, he'll answer. That's how he'll find her Nina. Before she does. He'll reach Nina before her. What does he want from her? And why?

Irina collapses in tears, drops to the floor and pounds it with her hands, muttering, Nina, my Nina. My Nina.

◆ ◆ ◆

Every few minutes Nina recalls Leonid's face from that night, and from the TV, and she remembers that the police asked the public for help, anyone who knows something should call, and every time she remembers this, her throat closes up and she perspires with fear. She takes the remaining detergents out of the cabinet to see what they need, and their pungent odor reminds her of the cloud of smells that enveloped Irina whenever she came home from work, and she remembers how Babushka would try to clean the apartment to make it easier for Mama, and how when she was little, she would help in order to surprise Mama, who would come in and just collapse on the couch. And later, when there was no Babushka, everything was so sad. Nina was too young to stay alone on holidays, which were Irina's busiest times because none of the women she worked for were willing to do without her for even a minute, so she would take her to work with her. They all agreed to let the child come along, just so long as Irina came to clean. Some of them were nice to her and some ignored her. And some weren't even home, and then the two of them really had fun. They would ride the bus together and Irina let her ring the bell to get off, and then they would stroll to the new neighborhood and go into the large apartments that Mom had the keys for. Nina imagined that her mother could open every house with her huge bunch of keys.

"Did you work in any of those places?" she would sometimes ask when the bus drove past some beautiful houses, and Mama would say no, until one day, when she asked again, her mother bent down to her and said, "I did work in one of those houses. But a bad man lives there. So I didn't go back."

Nina didn't ask what a bad man was, but after that, she always worried about her mama and waited to hear her come back from work.

"I don't want you to work for bad people," she told her.

"She won't get in the way," Irina would always say when they went inside, emphasizing her accent a bit, and she, Nina, would open a pair of innocent eyes so they wouldn't see how much she loved it. Loved wandering around other homes, looking at all the things in them and learning about the people who lived there. She learned about the children of the house from what Mama took out from under the bed. Sometimes, when they got to the kids' rooms full of stuff, she thought that if she took something, they wouldn't even notice, but she didn't dare. "You don't touch anything, understand?" Irina would warn her. "It's about our reputation. This is my job."

Nina tried to help her, but Irina always said, "It's my job," and told her to draw. When Nina was older, she used to tell her to do her homework. Nina didn't want to do her homework, she wanted to help her mama. Make it easier for her. So she wouldn't come home afterward and put the hot water bottle on that hollow at her lower back. On the spot where it hurt. "When you're big, you can help me. Now you'll just get in the way," Irina said, but when Nina was a bit older and could help, Mama stopped taking her to work. "That's it," Irina told her, "you're old enough to stay alone." Nina asked to go with her anyway; staying alone scared her. "You have to finish the work your teachers gave you to do on the vacation," Irina replied, but Nina knew that was just an excuse. Only much later did she understand that Irina didn't want her to see her cleaning and hear the way the ladies spoke to her. Not always with respect. The first time Nina stayed alone, she was scared. She wasn't used to being home alone in the morning for so many hours. She checked the door every minute to make sure it was locked. But gradually, she got used to it. And she even liked being alone. After a few times, during the vacation between the sixth and seventh grades, Irina asked her, "Maybe you should ask a girlfriend to come over?" Nina was surprised. She hadn't thought of that. When she was younger and all the girls invited their friends over, she didn't want to invite them to her house. She thought they were noisy and different, and her mom was tired.

"Don't open the door for anyone you don't know," Irina warned her, and once a man argued with her for a long time. Said her mom had asked him to come. Nina didn't open the door for him. And afterward, her mom said that he was the neighbor Michal's son-in-law who'd come to check something in the bathroom and she did the right thing by not letting him in. "It's always better to be too careful."

That summer, Nina decided that was it, she's starting middle school differently. She'll be different and she'll have girlfriends, she's grown up and she has to stop being with her mom all the time, enough is enough. But she didn't know that it would be much more complicated than she thought. She had to learn how they spoke and dressed and what they did. She had to observe them for a while before she figured it out. She learned that boys were the key. Boys were easy for her, she got along with them, they weren't complicated like the girls. And then the girls started talking about her behind her back because she got along with the boys, and at the same time, they tried to get close to her, and for the last two years, she really understood how to do it, how to become popular. She became queen of the school. And the boys began to distance themselves. She was no longer in their league. And definitely not when Shmueli's car waited to pick her up at the gate at the end of the school day.

❖   ❖   ❖

Her mother was stingy with words. She wasn't a big hugger either. Nina didn't understand that until she got older and began to go to her girlfriends' homes. To their noisy homes with the TV always on and their moms shouting and their sisters and brothers fighting. One of them took the other's something and the other one was hurt and angry. And they hit one another. She would freeze every time. Because it all came as a surprise to her, how quickly those arguments started and escalated into fights that included yelling and kicking and hair-pulling, and the mother would shout from another room, "Quiet!" and "Let her take it!" or "Let him take it!" or just "Stop the noise already," and never came to separate them unless it had become a situation with potentially irreversible injuries, or if one of the sides was really older than the other.

She wanted so much to have someone who would fight with her.

Yell at her. Just so she wouldn't be surrounded by all that quiet anymore. So she began talking, telling her mom everything. Everything. At first, about school and her teachers, and then about all the kids in her class, about the girls and the boys, and when she began to go to her girlfriends' homes, she would talk about what she saw there. She asked her mother about her day, and Irina would reply that she had nothing to say about it.

For the last two years, Nina had been pestering Irina to stop cleaning houses, because she was capable of so much more, and she should stop killing herself. The first time, Irina was shocked and couldn't decide whether to be happy that Nina thought of her that way, or angry that Nina didn't appreciate how much she was sacrificing for her. It became an obsession with Nina. She would bring up the subject all the time. And they began arguing. "Don't try to run my life," she told Nina, and Nina replied, "You run mine, so I'm allowed too," and Irina told her not to be fresh. Until the time Nina said, "I think you want to be a cleaner because you're afraid to try something else." Irina couldn't believe Nina said that, thought that. She was so hurt that she didn't even raise her voice. She just turned around and walked out. Nina ran after her, but Irina closed the door to her tiny bedroom. To the small balcony that their neighbor Haim's worker had closed off for them practically for free after Irina realized why Nina didn't invite girlfriends over. "Girls come to their friend's house to be in her room," Nina explained to her, but she didn't mention how everyone in the class whispered about her after Romi and Moran had been to her house and told them that Nina didn't even have her own room and slept with her mom.

Not everyone has their own room, Irina told her, and Nina explained that it was okay to share a room with your brother or your sister, but not to sleep with your parents.

And that was it, Irina decided it was time for separate bedrooms. For Nina's sake.

They moved the washing machine to the bathroom and closed off the small balcony where it had been so that Irina could sleep there.

Irina never admitted how good she felt there. Alone. In the silence. Not hearing every one of Nina's breaths. Not waking up every time she moved. And she was surprised when she began to feel her body. As if it had come back to life. Once she even woke up after a pleasant dream and saw that she was caressing herself. That made her laugh. And she thought that maybe it had something to do with the new neighbor. The one who opened a café in the mall. He interviewed waitresses all day. And he had a table outside where he sat with his friends and they smoked. They say he got divorced not too long ago. Maybe because of the waitresses.

5

Irina sits there, totally drained, perspiring and exhausted, even though she has to run. She's been late for a while already. Talia's mother will call her and won't understand who it is that answers. But she doesn't care. She just wants to know what happened to Nina, because what Shmueli told her doesn't make sense. It can't be that Nina isn't with him. And it can't be that she would just throw her studies in the garbage, along with everything they had together, and for what? She thinks about everything she gave her Nina, how she has worked her fingers to the bone all these years for her daughter, her only daughter, who was more important to her than she herself was, so she would have food and shelter and could devote herself to her studies.

That man is lying, she knows he's lying. He made her Nina crazy, came along with his power and money and dazzled her. She'd never seen such things, and he knew that. He's smart. Smart, but there was so much evil in him. He saw exactly where all her Nina's open wounds were and tore into them ruthlessly. He saw that she had no father and no one to pamper her, that she didn't have what other girls have, and he gave her all that in spades. So she would want more and more. He made her addicted to it.

Irina knew that game, knew how youth and beauty connect with money and power. Two sides that need each other, feed on each other. What are power and money worth if they don't make you feel young, and what is youth worth if it doesn't free you from worry, if you can't devour life. She came here, to this new land, to escape all that. There she couldn't break through the ceiling, couldn't support herself and her little girl. Especially because she wasn't willing to play the game, to settle for a man who would be there, who would help and support and then toss her away. So she decided to come here because they told her that here, it was easier to make a start. Here they give new immigrants financial aid and they would help with housing and kindergarten for her little girl, and she'd be able to manage. She thought that here, no one would pay attention to the kind of shoes she wore and the kind of house she lived in. But here too they look at you and check you out. And that piece of garbage, Irina thinks, who Nina believed in, in his love for her. She believed she was stunning and special and he was entranced by her. That's what Irina tried to tell her. That she was too much in love with herself, with the power she had over men. She needed a little humility. Maybe it's her fault, because she complimented Nina all the time, always told her how beautiful and smart she was. Always tried to compensate her for what she didn't have. A father, an extended family, siblings, money, an educated mother.

You have a roof over your head, food and love, she used to tell her, and that's a lot. Not everyone has it.

But Nina recognized the apologetic tone in her voice and wanted more. And she was sure she had the ability, the beauty, and the intelligence to get more. But there was one thing she didn't understand—that there are people who will exploit you. People who smell your hunger from a distance. Who take advantage of the weakness of people like her.

◆ ◆ ◆

Irina goes down the steps and out onto the street and sees the neighbor from across the way getting into his taxi.

"Excuse me," she calls him. "Excuse me, can you take me?"

"Sure," he says. "Where to?"

"The new neighborhood, 3 Hatzivoni Street."

"That's five minutes from here."

"Not on foot," she says with a laugh.

"I'm on my way there anyway," he says and doesn't turn on the meter, but now she doesn't care if he robs her blind.

"Are you okay?" he asks.

"Yes, it's the holiday," she replies. "You know. It's not always easy in this country without a family."

The neighbor doesn't know what that's like. He grew up here and lives here, surrounded by family, always together, always invited out or having guests, and there's his mother and his mother-in-law, and except for the times his wife insisted on flying to some cheap all-inclusive hotel deal abroad, he would have settled for Eilat. Just driving to Eilat would have been enough for him, and even there, after two days he wants to go home.

"Here it is," he says when they arrive.

"How much?" she asks.

"Forget it," he says. "It's on the house."

"I don't feel comfortable not paying."

"This holiday is the time for giving," he says, smiling at her.

"Thank you," she says, thinking, look, this is how it starts. Someone sees you, is nice to you, how pleasant it is. How easy it is to make a woman happy.

That's what the bastard did to her daughter, a million times worse. He should burn in hell.

The worry is choking her and she can't breathe anymore. It's a good thing Talia is too young to understand that she doesn't have anything in her eye, that she's crying.

◆ ◆ ◆

Itamar gets up, puts coffee in the percolator, and fills the house with the aroma of morning. Soon the whole house will wake up. He wants to tell Naama about his need to go to Israel for Memorial Day, but that's not a conversation to have over breakfast, which is the most important meal of the day, like the Americans always say. Maybe that's why he, like so many Americans, needs to diet, he thinks. Naama hasn't gotten back to herself after the birth either. And it's been a few years already. He looks at his small potbelly. Tomorrow he'll go to the gym, he promises himself every day. But rarely follows through.

The kids went to sleep late, Passover vacation at home. He doesn't know whether the school gave Dana the seven-day vacation because she's Jewish or Naama decided on it herself. They've been at home for a few days because of Easter too, but he had a lot of work to do on the presentation, and in the end, they didn't do much together, and Naama was giving him angry looks again. And maybe rightly so this time. He should have arranged things better and spent time with the family instead of going to the office now. And he still hasn't decided about buying a house. She tried to show him the numbers again, saying how stupid it was to throw money away on rent. His throat constricts with all the guilt he feels. About the wasted vacation, about being so far from his mother, who sounds so weird and needy, and about being unable to make the decision to buy the house. He pours coffee into a large cup he'll take to the car, and admits to himself that it has been a while since they had any plans to go back. They only talk about visiting. And that seems strange to him. Because Israel is home, he loves that it's his, that there he can be angry and complain. It's true that reading the news about Israel makes him angry, but it's his. And it's true that everything there is too sticky and people are nosy and there's something so comfortable here in America. Here no one looks at you through a magnifying glass. You're just another person. Just another suit, as they say. Until now, that's been fine with him, but suddenly he does want to have a say, to be someone whose opinions are taken into account and who has the right to speak up, instead of being just another person who comes here in pursuit of the dollar. And that seems strange to him, because he always preferred being a bit distant, the quiet one on the sidelines. Uri was at the center. The one who stood out. The tough kid with the big mouth, the king. Itzik's son. Since that role was taken, he was left with a different one. He was his mother's son. Curled up in that softness of hers that enveloped him like down. She heard his every whisper so that he never had to shout. But he's not a child anymore, he's here, far from her. And she isn't so warm and embracing anymore either. After Uri was killed, she held on to him like a person drowning in a swirling current and he was the one with the lifesaver. Sometimes she would clutch the outstretched hand, sometimes she would lose strength and be dragged away. And since Itzik died, she's been withdrawing deeper and deeper into herself. During the shiva, she was in shock. Total shock. Maybe he should have stayed a bit longer afterward, to be with her, but Naama really pressured him to come back. It was hard for her with the baby and Dana, who was starting to become jealous, Dana the good girl was beginning to act spoiled, and Naama was right when she said it was crazy to fly a little girl and a baby less than a year old halfway around the world to sit shiva.

"We'd be exposing the kids to such negative energy," Naama said. "And there's nothing for Dana to do there, and she's in the middle of the school year. We'd be putting her through all that just to see her dad and her grandma cry."

He went to the airport alone, tears for his dad choking him, and when everyone at the shiva asked where Naama was, he explained, "The baby," an explanation that sounded reasonable to them there in America, but here at the shiva, seemed so unfeeling. Just try to explain in Israel how the Americans see motherhood. Everything is different there. There is no day care for babies that age, so the mother stays with them, and they don't have grandmothers they can summon for help when something sudden like this happens.

Naama called during the shiva to ask how he was, and after two minutes, when she began to complain about the new nanny, he got angry and wanted to say, Deal with it, I lost my father and all you can think about is the new nanny who only speaks Spanish even though she said she knows English. But he didn't say it. Nevertheless, she understood he was angry at her, and said it wasn't fair because she's the one who's alone with the two kids, so he promised he'd come home right after the shiva. He never imagined how powerful his feelings of guilt would be when he left his mother two hours after they visited his father's grave on the seventh and final day of the shiva.

Throughout the flight, he thought about the difference between his mom and Naama. And it wasn't that Naama wasn't a good person or didn't love the kids, and him—although she loved him less, because it made sense that mothers love the kids more—but she always put herself in the equation. She wouldn't let anybody step on her. For too many years, she wasn't taken into account because that's how it is on a kibbutz, she had explained to him so many times, and there was no one to take your side with the other kids, it was just you and how strong you were. And for her mom, there was no such thing as being weak. Actually, that was true of that whole generation. For them, *spoiled* was apparently the worst word in the kibbutz dictionary. Naama and her friends were a different generation, they talked about themselves, about personal fulfillment, about feelings, words that were antithetical to kibbutz principles, and an intergenerational war against communal sleeping raged. Gradually, those battles became irrelevant because there were more important things, and when agriculture was no longer the leading source of income, it was industry that replaced it. And Naama loves America. Very much. And she wanted the house they'd seen. She thinks it's stupid to go back to Israel, Itamar should be here, should sit in the company offices and make sure they don't make mistakes. Because they were about to issue stock and become the hottest new thing. He really should be here to make sure they don't miss their chance. It was supposed to happen very soon. But it's been just one more month for years now. And one more board meeting. And one more discussion with the investors. Yes, there's good buzz, but it has dragged on endlessly. They've already been on the list of most promising startups twice. They're still promising, and Itamar wants that promise to be kept.

But there's another promise he hasn't kept.

He promised his mom he would go back. And not only did he not go back, he didn't go to see her last summer either.

He thinks about the weird Seder night at Zipi's place. Zipi is the mother of Charlotte, Dana's school friend, who doesn't speak Hebrew because her dad is American. He thinks about how Naama told everyone that she's looking for a nanny, and that she advertised everywhere, even at the Jewish Community Center, that she was looking for someone to help her with the kids because she wants to start doing something with herself. "I'm tired of always being packed and ready to go," she said, as if she wasn't the one who wanted to stay because soon there'd be a baby, and it'll be good if he's American, and we'll go back after I give birth. Then it was the middle of the school year for Dana and it would be a shame to leave, because Dana's school is fantastic, and isn't it great that her English will be so good. And another year passed. And Naama organized, painted, and designed the baby's room. Three years had already passed since Ariel was born. And she'd been a full-time mom ever since they'd arrived. Something that hardly exists in Israel. And there are lots of couples here where the father works around the clock and the mother devotes all her time to the kids, and every time she said that, she made sure to give him the feeling that what he did was less important.

And now his Naama was also becoming the one always rebuking him.

For years, she'd tried to be like the American women and fit in here, but in the end, she sits with Zipi while Dana and Charlotte play pretending they're in a spa, putting on makeup and polishing each other's nails, making TikTok videos, chattering away in American English, which Naama doesn't totally understand.

Sometimes Naama says about Israelis, "Look at how Israeli they are," when they speak loudly in a restaurant or argue with the guy in Starbucks when he doesn't understand what they want. And he thinks, yes, they're Israelis, just as they themselves are. Just as he is. A week ago, two CEOs arrived from Israel for the board meeting, and Itamar took them to lunch with two others from the office. They chattered away about Israeli soccer and cursed the coach and laughed loudly, and instead of being ashamed of them, which he would have been if Naama had been with them, he really enjoyed himself, and for the first time, he didn't care what the Americans thought of them. He also totally agreed with the bald CEO that Berkovic was the best player. Better than Benayoun.

And he realizes that that's what he misses. Being with those noisy people, people he understands. With them, he can relax.

◆ ◆ ◆

Carmela stares at the TV. She's crocheting a small lace doily, and occasionally, she looks away from the TV to the doily, and occasionally, from the doily to the TV. Nina, who is totally dedicated to the cleaning project, is running around the apartment. She airs out the rooms and wipes away layers of dust from the sideboard and the bookshelves. She finds it funny that she knows how to do this, and especially that she's doing it like a pro. Looking around, she begins to be satisfied. She's finished the kitchen and the living room is already in pretty good shape. After she vacuumed the heavy carpet, she rolled it to the side and swept. She needs to wash the floor, but doesn't have the strength for that now. Her body is still recovering and she's weak. She arranges the things on the coffee table and sees a photo album under a book and a newspaper.

Nina looks at Carmela, who is engrossed in the TV and doesn't react at all to the storm of cleaning raging around her, so she sits down, opens the album, and looks at the photos that, with time, have faded so much that they look almost monochromatic, sepia colored.

Suddenly, Carmela sees her with the album and shouts, "Give it to me!" and Nina is alarmed by the shout and the look in her eyes, so she gives it to her and whispers, "I'm sorry. I'm sorry." Carmela clutches the album to her chest, and Nina begins to move away, saying quietly, "It's me, Grandma. It's just me. Everything's fine."

Carmela hears the words and her expression softens, as if she only just woke up, and it seems impossible that the shout that rang out only a moment ago came from the same fragile, gentle woman, who now murmurs, "My Dana, Dana'le." She extends an emaciated hand laced with blue veins that her thin, pale skin cannot hide, and her expression is sad now. She looks so tired. So old.

"Come," Carmela says, gesturing for Nina to sit beside her, and she opens the album. "This is Uri's birthday. His twentieth. Look at him. The way he's looking at his Niva. So beautiful. They fit together like a hand in a glove. They were together a year, and she had no idea how happy she made him. He came home from the army and only wanted to be with her. Not with his father, not with me. Nothing interested him. Not even your father, my sweet Itamar, who so wanted time with him. But Uri didn't have time. None at all. We celebrated his birthday early and I don't like to celebrate birthdays early.

"Niva asked me, 'Why not?' and I didn't have an answer, maybe it was the conversations with Uri when he talked about what was happening in the north, and I said, But the war is over, and Uri hugged me and said, 'Mom, you should know that it's really serious there, really. And such a mess. For you here, it's like nothing is going on, but there it's real. And I don't know if I can come home next weekend. They let me go this weekend because they haven't allowed soldiers to be away from home without leave for so long.' And they had that business with the house that got blown up, and after that, his eyes were sad because he saw all kinds of things a boy shouldn't see, and right then and there, I decided we should celebrate his birthday. Niva was glad I agreed and spoke to his buddies, and the ones who didn't have to stay on their base for the weekend came right away, and we had a small party. The three friends who had desk jobs close to home felt uncomfortable, and looked at him with so much admiration, and your grandfather—he spoke so beautifully. About how proud he was. They all had tears in their eyes. Afterward I asked him why he didn't write it down, at least then we would still have it. For years, I remembered every word he said. And I wrote them down on a piece of paper, before I started to forget a little, because I forget a little now. And look," she says, pointing to a picture, "That's your father. That's your father."

"Sweet," Nina says. "And that's you?" she asks, pointing to the picture.

Carmela nods.

"How beautiful you were." Nina looks at her in her light-colored dress, holding a cake with loads of candles, and in another picture, she's sitting on the side, and the one she calls "your father" is sitting next to her, his head on her shoulder, as they watch the others celebrating and laughing, seeming to be in a bubble of their own, separate from the crowd of people partying in the small living room. Some pieces of furniture that appear in the pictures are still here, as if frozen in time. And there's the same large window, only the tree outside it is smaller.

Carmela hands her the album, and Nina browses a bit more, and suddenly, the pictures are no longer faded and the colors are sharp, and there's a lovely family, mom and dad and a sweet little girl surrounded by boxes in a house that looks like it's not from here. "You were so adorable," Carmela says. "And how I cried when they took you there. How I cried."

Nina looks at the picture, tries to understand if there is any resemblance between her and the girl in the picture. And there is some. The straight hair. The kind of roundish face that, really, all babies have, and she can't see the eye color, so she browses some more and finds a close-up of the girl. That's not you, she reminds herself, that's Dana.

And she looks carefully at the pictures of Dana's parents, trying to understand what role she should play.

On the last page are pictures of Carmela's husband, who looks terribly old, sitting on a luxurious chair and holding a baby. He's the *Sandek*. She remembers what that means from the time they went to Amalia's grandson's bris and Amalia wouldn't let anyone call her Grandma, only Amalia. And her husband Hezi's father sat on the same kind of chair.

"Are Mom and Dad on the way?" Carmela suddenly asks, giving Nina an unreadable glance.

Nina freezes. Startled. "Aah . . ." She searches for words. "Maybe. We should ask them." And her heart skips a beat, more than one. "Are they supposed to be coming? When?" And she thinks, What will happen if they come and catch her here? They'll report her to the police. She has to get away. "Okay," she says to Carmela, "I think I have to go. I'll go now."

Nina gets up. And remains standing. She's confused. Where did it come from, the idea that those parents were coming? What should she do now? What is she supposed to do? She thought she had come to a safe haven. That here she would have some peace and quiet. Shmueli knows she saw what they did to that guy in the alley. This is the best hiding place for her. But if Dana's parents are on the way, she can't stay.

"No," she hears Carmela whisper. "No. Don't go. Come here," and she gestures for her to come closer, then hugs her. "Don't go, Dana. I've waited so long for you. So very long. Stay. No one's coming here. No one. Only you. I waited so long for you. Come to me," she says, gets up, and pulls her by the hand, "come," and she takes her to the pink bedroom. Raises the blanket. "Get into bed, Dana'le. Get in." Nina crawls into bed. Confused. Frightened. And Carmela tucks her in. Tightly.

"I'll take care of you," she whispers to Nina. "I won't let anyone take you from me, no one."

"If Mom and Dad come, I'll have to go with them," Nina whispers. And the word *Dad* feels strange on her tongue. Unfamiliar. The word that was never spoken in their house. That she never said.

And now Carmela has that look in her eye again, the one she had when she grabbed the album and shouted, a hard look, her eyes blazing like hot coals. "No one is coming," she says. "They're in America. That's far away. It's difficult to come. Difficult."

Nina breathes a sigh of relief, and then reminds herself not to depend on that. Nothing is certain in this house. Maybe they're in

America and maybe they'll walk in the door in another minute. Suddenly, the tiredness loosens its grip on her and the embrace of the blanket tucked around her keeps her from falling, watches over her. And Carmela's eyes are once again soft and kind.

◆ ◆ ◆

Nina takes the magnet and goes over to the phone. It has been years since she spoke on a phone attached to the wall like this one.

The phone rings and a woman with a Russian accent answers, "Hagit's Minimart, shalom."

"Ah . . ." Nina stammers. "Ah . . ."

"Miss, what is it?"

"Can I speak to Eitan, please."

"Eitan," the woman yells. "There's someone here who wants to talk to you. Make it fast, the store's packed today."

"Hello?!" Eitan says, surprised. No one ever calls him there. He has a cell.

"It's me, from Carmela's house."

"Yes! What's up?"

"Okay, so tell me, about the mouse . . . do you have one?"

"I'll bring it to you after work, no problem."

"Eitan," the woman with the Russian accent shouts, "there's no time, *yalla*, love affairs later."

"I have to go, we're really busy here," Eitan says. "I'll bring it to you."

"Never mind, I'll come to you. I need to buy a bunch of stuff."

◆ ◆ ◆

Nina leaves the house and Carmela goes to the large living room window to watch her the way she used to watch Uri and Itamar when they went out, or when she waited for them to come home. The trees were smaller then and you could see the street. Now you have to strain to see a small strip of it. Someone honks and she stands there, in front of the window that is almost always closed but is open now, looking through the slats of the shutters, and a moment later, she doesn't remember what she's doing there, who she's supposed to be watching. Her sense of time and place is fading again. A spring-scented breeze comes through the shutters, caressing her. Suddenly, she's upset. It's starting, the hammering heart and shortness of breath. She has no idea why she's standing at the window, but there's no mistaking that smell, which arouses her body, like an animal sensing the rain before it starts. It can't be that she missed it. It just can't be. No! That's her worst fear. Breathe, Carmela tells herself. Calm down and go to the phone, everything's written next to it, neat and organized. What you don't remember will be there. She goes to the phone and sees a large piece of paper with a phone number and "Menashe Taxi to the cemetery" written on it.

She dials. No answer. She dials again. She's about to give up when he answers, "Carmela, shalom."

"Shalom, you remember?"

"Yes, of course I remember. But we still have about two weeks. Don't worry."

"I know," she says with a smile. "I'm just checking that everything is all right. That you remember. That you're okay."

"Yes, I'm fine. The day after tomorrow, I'll go to the plant nursery and then I'll drive there. I'll call you. Don't worry. I don't forget."

"If I don't answer, don't give up."

"I never give up. And I never forget. This year we'll bring some beautiful plants. And I'll help you prepare the grave for Memorial Day. Don't worry."

"Thank you, Menashe."

"Please don't thank me. This is between me and Itzik, may he rest in peace. I promised him that as long as I'm still standing, I'll take you there. You don't know how much I owe Itzik. How much he helped my son. Tell me, do you need help with anything else? The fridge or the washing machine? My boy just opened an electrical appliance store and he has the best prices. If you have something that broke, just say the word and I'll bring you a new one."

"Thank you so much. I don't need anything. Everything's fine. But maybe Dana does. She went out for a little while, but when she comes back, I'll ask."

"Dana's here?"

"Yes," Carmela says, and it feels so good to say it. Her heart fills with joy again. She didn't forget Memorial Day and she also remembers that Dana's here. She's okay. It's a curse, this disease, a curse, but no one must know. She has to hide it. So they don't take her away, so they don't hospitalize her. She's ready for anything, even death, just not the hospital. Just so she doesn't have to go through what Itzik went through, fading away in front of her eyes, it ended so fast there. He wasn't a large man before, and in only a few weeks, there was nothing left of him. Just the tubes that took away his life.

"There are some fantastic places these days," Itamar told her during one of their phone conversations, and not for the first time.

"You want to put me away?!" she shouted.

"No, Mom, it's a retirement home, protected living. Like a suite in a hotel. You wouldn't believe how beautiful those places are. There you won't be alone. You'll have friends. You'll have a small apartment of your own."

"Come and we'll talk," she said. "This is not for the phone. How is Dana? How's school? Is she learning Hebrew?"

"She's fine. We speak Hebrew to her, but she answers in English."

"How is Naama?"

"Fine. Mom, listen, those places have a doctor on call twenty-four hours a day, seven days a week."

"Okay, come and we'll go to see a place," she said, knowing that she'll leave this house only after she dies. But she can't die yet because who will go to Uri's grave? Who will clean it and bring flowers now that Itamar's there in America? She has to stay here until they come back from America. Uri won't be one of those who never has visitors and no one stands beside them on Memorial Day. But Dana's here. Dana can help her.

"If you come back, I won't be alone," she told him.

Itamar couldn't believe she said that, she usually didn't play the victim card. Absolutely not. And she wasn't sarcastic either. And he couldn't believe how much it hurt him to hear those words, which dredged up from the darkness of his thoughts the price tag that turned the entire adventure in America into something oppressive and suffocating. It destroyed the whole idea of distance, of proving himself. To them. But who are they? The kids that used to meet on the bridge on Yom Kippur? His schoolmates? Who was his success for?

Assaf is doing a postdoc in Cleveland. Haim opened three restaurants and pictures of him with models he's dating appear in the gossip pages. Gali married a millionaire and seemed sad when they met once in the airport business lounge during one of his work trips.

To prove to someone you went to school with that you're more successful. To please his parents, who expected him to be a great success. The greatest. Because he had to succeed for Uri as well, to fill the void. To make Itzik happy, to make him proud. So that if someone in the store asks him, "So what's Itamar doing?" Itzik can answer proudly, "Startup, he even sold a part of it to America." But he had been wrong. The money they received for the first merger didn't interest Itzik, all he cared about was Carmela. For the first time since Uri, she blossomed again when she became a grandmother. That move to America sank them all. And instead of one year, he had already completed his sixth year there and was already deep into his seventh. After Itzik died, all the air went out of his ambition. Who would he prove himself to? Who cared? He could go back and spin tales about himself, who would even know? His mom couldn't care less. As far as she was concerned, he could sell nuts in a kiosk, just as long as he was back with her. Just as long as she'd be near the grandchildren. And Dana Dana Dana.

◆ ◆ ◆

Itamar already knows that he has no one to blame. He didn't do it to make his parents happy, he did it for himself. And no matter how far away he goes, it will pursue him. Even here, they check you out at every social gathering, at every business meeting, they casually check out your watch, your car, trying to figure out whether you've hit the jackpot or you're one of those who remain here to try to make it big, because it's right around the corner, maybe the next business. The next project.

And when his mom says, "Come home," he can't lie to himself anymore about the cost. It's true that Naama feels as if she's having the adventure of her life and the kids will have perfect English, and Ariel will be a citizen with a passport. An American kid. And if everything works out, they really will put a down payment on the house this week. "If something happens and we go back, then the rent we get for it will pay the mortgage," Naama said, using the English word. It makes him laugh, the way English words suddenly pop into their heads when they talk about money and business.

He drives slowly in the heavy traffic and thinks that it's been a long time since he asked himself what *he* wants. Where *he's* happy to be. Phone conversations with his mom depress him. And this whole America thing is such a drag with all the meetings, and the sale, and a suit first thing in the morning, and always selling himself. The company has succeeded. He's working on the final part of the merger and that's it, they'll be part of a large corporation, and he hasn't celebrated at all or unwound or been reckless with money. Everything is so organized and measured. He took on the responsibility to see the merger through to completion while his partners took off on a two-month vacation to spend some of the money and think about what they would do next. There's no end to developing a product because there will always be new markets. Another company to do business with. Enough, he's done his part. He has to move on now. He'll call Hanoch, his partner, and tell him to come and release him.

◆ ◆ ◆

His dream was that if he had enough money he would buy a small place near the seashore, somewhere north of Tel Aviv. A kind of summer home. And now he has the money, but he doesn't even dare to fly business class to Israel and go to his brother's grave on Memorial Day because it's expensive. While Ariel's day care for next year will cost as much as ten round-trip tickets. So he calls the company's travel agent and says he wants a flight to Israel. She types something into the computer and says that he has lots of miles, almost enough to upgrade him to business class, and it would cost practically nothing. Itamar books the ticket and feels totally corrupt. He tells himself that he won't say anything to Naama, she always wants to save the miles for bonus tickets, but they don't use them because they don't go to Israel, and in the end, she gives them to her mom. A moment later, he realizes that he's earned it and he's allowed. True, they don't have the means to live as if they were in a Hollywood TV series, but he has enough. And what am I saving for? he asks himself. Dana's college fund? Really, he laughs at himself. I've become a joke. You can't pay college tuition with airline miles.

◆ ◆ ◆

Far from there, in Tel Aviv, Carmela goes back to sitting in front of the turned-off TV until she can breathe again.

She didn't miss it. There's still time before Memorial Day.

◆ ◆ ◆

Ilanit the policewoman knocks on the open door to Chief Ashkenazi's office.

"So," he asks, "how was it working on the holiday?"

"It was quiet," she says, not giving him the pleasure of labeling her someone who complains about her shifts.

"Good. So?" He wants her to leave his office already.

"Listen, a woman came here looking for her daughter."

"So?"

"Her daughter is seeing Johnny Shmueli."

Ashkenazi looks up. He's not bored anymore. "So?"

"The mother hasn't heard from her for two weeks, and her phone has been disconnected for a few days. I told her to call him. She didn't want to. Was scared. I said I'd ask you what to do. Maybe ping the phone? I thought you should decide."

"I'll call him."

"I told the mother I'd check with her before we call him, to see that it's okay, that the girl hasn't come back."

"So report back to me."

Ilanit goes out and dials the number the mother gave her.

"Irina?" she asks, surprised when a man answers.

"No."

"Is this Irina's phone?"

"Not anymore. Who's this?"

"Excuse me, but who are you?"

"Miss, you called me." Shmueli wants to ask about Nina, but is wary.

"Where's Irina?"

"Changed her number," he says, and disconnects.

Ilanit wants to call back and say she's from the police, but can't decide. She doesn't want to screw up here. She goes back to Ashkenazi and tells him that the woman didn't answer the number she called. Someone else did.

"I'll take care of it," Ashkenazi says. "I'll talk to him."

"Should I go to her house?" she tries because she feels uneasy.

"I'll take care of it!" Ashkenazi says firmly, putting an end to the discussion.

◆　◆　◆

Irina gets off the bus. For the entire time she babysat Talia, she kept replaying in her mind the conversation she had with that horrible man in the morning. Yes, he warned her, actually threatened her, not to go to the police, but who is he to decide. She'd thought he was the only one who could know where Nina is, but now she realizes that he isn't. He doesn't know where she is. And she can't bear the thought that Nina is alone somewhere in Tel Aviv. Her delicate Nina. Her too-beautiful Nina. She called her from Talia's mom's house again and again—but her cell was disconnected. She has to buy a new phone to replace the one Shmueli took.

And then she sees him. He stands out like a candle in the dark. Young, wearing a black button-down shirt tucked into skinny jeans, leaning on the fence. She keeps walking, and he follows her. It's obvious that he's following her. If he planned to do it secretly, he was doing a lousy job. For kilometers, he stood out in this neighborhood with his stylish clothes. Then she understood, he wasn't supposed to do it secretly. He was sent so she would know she was being followed.

And now she knows.

And she also knows that the police won't help her find Nina. After all, they'd rather not deal with Johnny either.

◆　◆　◆

For the first time in days, Nina's outside the house. She thinks about Leonid and about Shmueli, who knows she's an eyewitness. She's a threat. She begins to understand that she's part of a story that's bigger than she thought. And suddenly, she realizes that it isn't only her. That he'll go to see her mom. Oh. No. No. She has to warn her. How did she not think of that sooner?

She sits down on a bench on the center strip of the boulevard and tries to organize her thoughts. She mustn't make a mistake. She and Irina might be in real danger. She remembers the technique Galit, her homeroom teacher, taught her once when Nina told her she was so stressed during exams that she couldn't concentrate. Galit asked her if she feels her heart pounding, and Nina whispered yes, she did, and Galit said, "It's a small panic attack. Close your eyes and take a few deep breaths," she said and taught her how to breathe deeply a few times to get her pulse and her brain activity back to normal. The day after the exam, Galit caught up to her before the break and Nina thanked her. Galit explained that she does yoga and it's a technique she learned, and it's important to inhale through your nose and exhale through your mouth. Since then, Nina has done it sometimes when she's really stressed. Like right before she ran out of the car. Thinking about Galit reminds her that everyone is already going crazy with finals and matriculation exams and soon it'll be days of intensive study because Galit gives her heart and soul to help them do well, and for sure, she doesn't know where she is. And she must be so disappointed in her. She always supported Nina so much, in the most crucial classes, and this is their last year of high school. They fought for Galit to stay with them for another year, almost organized a demonstration—and in the end, the administration agreed that it would be better to leave her with them than to bring in a new teacher for the last year.

◆ ◆ ◆

Nina takes another deep breath, closes her eyes, and lets the dry breeze caress her, and she's able to hear the rustle of leaves before a motorcycle blasting away at full speed deafens her. She inhales deeply and slowly and exhales, like Galit taught her, and realizes that she is screwing up her life now in a way she never thought she would.

Maybe she should just get on a bus and go home. Back to Mom. She'll promise Shmueli that she won't talk. She'll swear to keep silent. Come on, she says to herself, who are you kidding. Like he'll really let her walk around and put him in danger by possibly opening her mouth at any moment?

A guy riding a bike down the street looks at her, and Nina remembers that her clothes are really weird, a pink Minnie Mouse shirt, tight and much too short, because that's what she found in the closet, and a beige pleated skirt.

She should ask Carmela if she can buy clothes in her size. But gently, she can't press too hard. Old people can go crazy when it comes

149

to money, especially old ladies. That's what Irina told her when she came home crying one day because the old lady from town claimed she'd paid Irina and Irina said she hadn't, and the old lady shouted at her that she was a liar. "I know they're crazy when it comes to money," Irina said, in tears. "That's because they're afraid they won't have enough to support themselves until the end. That they'll become a burden. I understand. And I know it's not because of me, but it's so humiliating. You can work for years, always come on time, never say anything, never argue, nothing, be economical with the detergent so they don't have to buy more, and in the end, they'll think you're a thief."

She knows Irina is crazy with worry and she knows she has to let her know she's okay. She's not angry at her anymore. The anger was crushed under the wheels of her panic. And she misses her. And is worried about her. She gets up and walks to the minimart. That's it, after she does the shopping, she'll go upstairs and call Irina.

◆ ◆ ◆

Nina goes into the minimart and the woman standing at the entrance seems to be studying her. She must be that Hagit, she says to herself. Beside her is a rack of newspapers, and Leonid's face is spread across all of them. Shit, she mutters as she takes a cart and frantically tosses things into it. She's hungry, but her stomach is cramping from nausea. In another minute, she'll vomit here in this minimart with all the weird items she'd never seen in their grocery. The images haunt her. His face in Carmela's newspaper, the TV report with the pictures from the scene of the crime. She feels like smoking something. Swallowing something. Forgetting. Somehow stopping the nausea and repulsion that are choking her. She puts a bottle of vodka in the cart, but remembering that she needs to show ID to buy it, she returns it to the shelf. It's a bad idea to get wasted now. She needs a clear mind to figure out what to do. She must not attract attention, maybe it was stupid to leave the house. She'll buy only what she needs and go straight to the apartment. She puts back the stuff she doesn't need, leaving only detergent and the items she thinks she can use to cook for Carmela and herself. Now she's sorry she didn't learn how to cook from her mother.

At the checkout counter, she realizes that she bought too much and won't be able to carry it all herself. "Can I take the cart home and return it later?" she asks.

The cashier looks at her with eyes wide in surprise and says in Russian, no, definitely not.

"What?" Nina asks in Hebrew, as if she hasn't understood, even though the cashier's body language was clear even without a translation.

"Oh, I'm sorry, I thought you speak Russian," the cashier says with a forced smile.

Nina doesn't smile back.

"Hagit," the cashier shouts, and the woman who was standing at the entrance smoking a cigarette says, "What?"

"This girl here wants to take the cart."

Hagit frowns at Nina. "Where do you live, sweetie, because I don't recognize you."

"I'm staying with Carmela. She said to say hello."

"Oh! Carmela." A huge smile lights up the face of the woman who was suspicious earlier. "How is she? I worried about her on the Seder night, but Eitan said she isn't alone. That Dana is with her, so I stopped worrying. You're Dana?!" she asks, surprised. "I thought you were younger. A lot younger." Goodness, what do they eat in America, Hagit asks herself.

"I look older than my age," Nina says, averting her eyes, upset that Hagit is clearly studying her. "Grandma and I had trouble with the washing machine," she says, trying to explain why she's wearing half a pajama set.

That's it, she said the word. Now she's a liar. She's already picturing the cop who'll question Hagit, "She said she was her granddaughter, or did you just assume she was the granddaughter?" and reminds herself that she has to be more careful. A lot more careful.

"You're Eitan's mom?" she asks.

"Yes," Hagit says proudly. That's her favorite title.

"Is he here?"

"He'll be here later," she says. "But why should you shlep the cart, he'll be here soon and bring everything to you."

Hagit looks at her. She doesn't resemble Itamar at all. Maybe Uri a little. It's strange that she's here in the middle of the year.

"Did your dad come with you?"

"No."

"Will he be here for Memorial Day?"

Oops. Nina wasn't prepared for that.

"He still hasn't decided," she says, and Hagit's dissatisfied expression makes her add, "But I think he'll come."

"He didn't come last year and it was hard seeing your grandma like that," Hagit says. She wanted to say to this granddaughter that it was really heartbreaking, and what Itamar is doing is terrible, and they didn't come in the summer either. But she doesn't think it's fair to dump everything on the head of this girl, who seems to be in total shock.

Nina tries to solve this family puzzle of Carmela and Itamar and what will happen on Memorial Day and when she should get the hell out of here. She has to be more careful, she reminds herself.

But first of all, she needs a phone. To warn Irina. She can buy one now with the credit card Carmela gave her, and then she won't need a mouse or anything.

"Is there a cell phone store around here?" she asks her.

"It's bit late," Hagit says, looking at her watch, "and it's also Passover vacation now. But try. You see that sushi restaurant across the street? It's right next door."

"Thank you."

The news is on the TV above the checkout counter and Leonid's picture appears again. She has to talk to her mom. Shmueli will go to her house to look for her, and who knows what he's liable to do to her. He can hold her hostage. A marathon of gangster movies starts running through her mind, and she realizes that a low-budget crime movie took place in her neighborhood and she had a role in it. All the guys around Johnny with their identical swagger, hairdos, and tight clothes, along with all the people who kiss his ass, and all the scared people who bring him things and envelopes, sweating with fear, and how at first Shmueli would come to pick her up but sometimes he would send one of his guys to take her home.

"Why doesn't he ever come upstairs?" Irina asked when he honked outside. "Our building isn't fancy enough for him?"

Nina didn't say anything.

❖   ❖   ❖

"Look," the cashier said, pointing at the TV. "Do you know what's happening here under our noses, they turned south Tel Aviv into the Wild West. Murders. And nobody cares. Don't we deserve a little peace and quiet?!"

Maybe she should go to the police, Nina thinks. It's all too much for her. Calling her mom from Carmela's apartment seems too dangerous now. He might find out where she's calling from. And he'll come to Carmela's house. She wouldn't put it past him. If she calls from there, she'll expose the three of them to danger. We're talking about murder here, and Shmueli will do anything to shut her up. She's already seen what he's capable of.

Better to call from a different phone. Maybe she'll find a pay phone somewhere around here. Or maybe she'll ask someone on the street to let her call Irina from their phone. She'll say hers was stolen, and if it's possible, please, just one call.

◆ ◆ ◆

Dana was born when Naama was in the middle of establishing her business, which had sprung from the wonderful idea of opening a place that would be both a boutique and a café that offered lectures on styling and mindfulness. She opened the place with Esti, a friend who invested money, but Itamar was not enthusiastic. Not about the partner, Esti, and not about the idea. He wanted to support her, but he thought that that kind of business did not suit Naama. She explained that they shouldn't be afraid and had to take the risk, because only the risk-takers succeed, and he looked at her, at his Naama who grew up on a kibbutz, speaking the new, trendy language of empowerment she had learned at a coaching course that gave her a lot of confidence, maybe a bit too much. In any case, it alarmed him. Because that wasn't the Naama he knew, the Naama who only wanted to be at home, to paint, to design websites, to bask in their love, which was all she needed. Dana was born into the whirlwind of the business and the commitments, and Naama wasn't really there. Not with her whole heart. Itamar got up at night because she was always tired. He didn't care that she had stopped nursing, that was her right, of course, but it was hard for him that she wasn't really with him and Dana then, when they were building their family, learning to be together. And he was angry at himself for not being generous enough with her.

And he saw how his mom looked at him when only he and Dana went to see her.

"So Naama didn't come?" Carmela would ask, and he would explain, and Carmela would say, "Business is hard. The owner has to be there." Actually, they enjoyed being together, just the three of them. His mom, seeing the black circles under his eyes, would send him to sleep and stay with Dana. And how much that baby loved her. How she would run to her when she had just learned to walk.

The two of them would go out and walk to the store, to Itzik. And the minute the door closed behind them, Itamar would sink into the most restful sleep in his parents' bed, calm in the knowledge that Dana was with her grandparents. Those two hours of sleep would sustain him for a few more days of juggling the startup that took up his entire life, and Naama's business, which barely broke even, but took her away from him and Dana. Because Naama spent every minute in front of the monitor, on Facebook or the Internet, advertising and promoting and calling all her friends because there was another sale and another lecture, and end of season and pop-ups, because there were goals. Esti's husband had built a business program, and now his Naama, who dreamed of art, was pushing it and they didn't even have time to argue. And she hadn't painted in ages.

Then Esti decided to leave the business because she wasn't having fun anymore. Naama was angry and disappointed, knowing that she couldn't do it alone, and began to look for partners, and that was exactly when their merger with a large company in America took off. The champagne flowed that evening, and they were happy, and when the bubbles ebbed, it turned out that someone had to go there. And it made the most sense for him to be the one.

Itamar didn't know how to tell Naama that he was going to America and leaving her and Dana, who was a baby at the time. He was sure she would strangle him or throw him out of the house, but she surprised him. And immediately came up with the idea of taking Dana and joining him. True, she often fantasized about living somewhere else for a few years, but this also gave her a legitimate excuse to dissolve her company, because no matter how much she gave and did and worked, she wasn't succeeding. You might even say she was failing. Again.

So here they are now. In America. And the business she established and dreamed about is now being run in a bedroom community somewhere in the Sharon area by a yoga teacher whose husband bought it for her as a hobby. And that doesn't even bother her. Because she's so happy to be a mom here, in suburban America. A 100 percent mom. Feeding her family organic food. Processed food is the enemy. Sometimes Itamar sees Ariel getting all of Naama's attention and is sad that Dana never had that. Maybe that's why they're always a bit edgy with each other, why they never really get along.

"Daddy's girl," Naama would joke, but she wasn't really joking.

"That's how mothers and daughters are," he told her. "Complicated."

"How would you know?" she said, immediately regretting her words.

And a few months ago, she told him, "I found a kindergarten for Ariel."

"I didn't know you were looking."

"I wasn't," she said over the cold broccoli. "Someone told me about a fantastic place. And I went there. It's very special. It's based on home education."

"Doesn't home education mean being home?" Itamar asked even though he knew that would annoy her.

"A few moms who don't want to send their kids to kindergarten got together, and every day, two mothers are with the kids, and that way, they have three days a week off."

"That's great." He said what she wanted to hear, and in fact, was expressing what he really felt. Because he was a little tired of their conversations about diapers and development and growth curves. He even had moments of missing her store and Esti. At least their conversations were more interesting then. "I'm happy for you."

"I thought you were glad I was staying home with the kids."

"Sweetie, I don't want to fight. I'm just happy for you. You seem enthusiastic about it."

"I am."

"So I'm happy for you. I just want you to enjoy your life."

Before they go to sleep, Itamar peeks into Dana's room, where Ariel is also sleeping. Sometimes he was willing to sleep with Dana and give them half a night alone in bed. Dana didn't care if he was there with her. For the time being. But it won't be long before she gets tired of it.

He closes the window in Dana's room and thinks about how Naama reinvents herself every few years. And how he just wants her to be happy. Because he doesn't really know what to do with her when she's upset. When she can't find peace. And it threatens him. Like when she began working on her company. Like when they first came here and she tried to be more American than the Americans, and in the end, like most Israelis, she found it more comfortable to be with other Israelis. He hasn't seen her this excited in a while, finally that I-don't-know-what-to-do-with-myself expression is gone from her face. And he was happy that she was excited about the home education kindergarten. And sad that she didn't understand that he really was happy for her.

He covers Dana, and can't believe how big she is already. And next to her, Ariel looks so much like a baby.

◆ ◆ ◆

Eitan steps out of the shower, shaves, and dresses, hoping he hasn't slathered on too much aftershave, and takes the mouse he promised Carmela's granddaughter. He's been walking around with it since yesterday, trying to find the courage to talk to the girl who filled his thoughts. And nights. There's something delicate about her, vulnerable, that makes you want to rescue her. He tries to picture her eyes, their color, but can't. She didn't look him in the eye, unlike the beautiful girls in school, the noisy, self-confident, aggressive ones who made him feel like the biggest loser. Nothing he tried worked with them, the book would fall and the pen wouldn't write and his cheeks reddened.

"Are you trying to find out if I'm gay?" he asked, surprising his mom when he realized what was behind all her questions about his social life back in high school, and laughed. "I'm not, not that I didn't worry about it myself," he said.

She said that was natural and it's fine.

And he said, "Maybe you'll let me talk? I'm not. I know I'm not. I'm just shy."

"How did I give birth to a shy kid?" Hagit said, hugging him lovingly. "How?" Adding, "And if you are gay, that's okay."

"Mom, I'm not."

"Great," she said. "So bring me home a girlfriend."

Several years have passed since then. He graduated from high school and even went out a few times with Noga, who was in his physics class. They had a nice time and talked about the science fiction movie they saw, and he really wanted to hug her, and they walked hand in hand. On their next date too. They both talked too much, because they were nervous, and it was only on their third date that he suddenly kissed her when she was in the middle of a sentence. Afterward, she said, "That was nice."

He thought she talked an awful lot, but he liked it. Because the thing he hated most in the world was silence.

His mom never shut up, she was always saying something. His father stayed quiet. And he hated that.

◆　◆　◆

Carmela's granddaughter seemed different to him. Maybe because she came from America. Maybe girls are more mysterious there. And quiet. He thought about Sharon, that sweet girl from Haifa he met in the army. Somehow, he wasn't as shy with her, probably because they both knew it wouldn't last long. She was about to be discharged and take off on her long post-army trip.

She told all the girls at headquarters that they'd gone out on a date but she wouldn't tell them what happened because they'd both sworn not to. She told him she knew what kind of reputation she had in the army, but she wasn't like that. She'd been the shiest girl in high school, and she felt like being different in the army. When they sent her to this hole in the wall, with all the combat soldiers who rarely went home on leave, she suddenly felt that they noticed her, were attracted to her. For the first time, she got a whiff of that smell of sexuality in the air. In the way they looked at her butt. At her breasts threatening to burst the buttons on her army shirt. That smell woke her up. And she stopped being shy. And enjoyed it.

And when Eitan, that sweet guy from the base, came to Haifa to see her one Friday night, they told her parents that they were going to a movie, but they went to a hotel. And laughed all the way there.

159

She acted like he was her millionth, even though he was only her second.

He was gentle and considerate. And she almost fell in love with him. But she already had a plane ticket to South America. Maybe we'll see each other when I come back, she told him after the unit toasted her on her last day. He hugged and kissed her, saying he would miss her.

And she said, "Hey, we promised not to be emotional." And he replied, "There's no such thing as not being emotional. I'm an emotional guy."

She laughed. But she was glad they'd done it, because her first time had been so disappointing.

And she didn't know that she was Eitan's first. Because he was too shy to say.

◆ ◆ ◆

"Dana," she hears someone shout. "Dana." It takes her a moment to realize that someone is calling her. She turns around and sees Eitan standing at the traffic light across the street with a supermarket cart. She waves in his direction, thinking he'll help her. That guy with the innocence in his eyes. She'll twist him around her little finger the way she did with guys better and older than him. Yes, she has no choice. That's the only way she can survive. It was a miracle that she saved herself. A miracle. And now she has to find a way to save Irina. And fuck that nerdy idiot.

A delivery boy, she laughs at herself as they both wait for the light to change. How mortifying. To get turned on by a supermarket delivery boy. But maybe that's what she needs. A naïve guy who won't play games with her. All those big dreams of hers screwed her up. The thoughts of shortcuts, of someone strong and rich who would appear suddenly and take her into the world of glamour. That's what her girlfriends think. They look at someone and think, What kind of life will he give me? As if they are the ones who give us, the women, life. As if it doesn't depend on us, just on them. Looking back now, she understands that that's what her mom tried to tell her. This is you, and it's up to you. And your studies are the most important thing, they are what will decide who you will be.

But now she's going to miss the matriculation exam in biology. An exam she didn't even need to study for. She's really good in that subject, which didn't especially interest her mom. "The most important things are English and math," said her mom, who didn't know English. Nina taught her. Irina constantly bit her tongue trying to make the *th* sound and gradually accumulated word after word, but the tenses and verb conjugations were too hard for her.

"A woman has to stand on her own two feet. So no man tells her, I bought you this, I gave you that," Irina said more than once. "If it's a small gift, okay, but not something you can't manage without. Don't make the same stupid mistake my generation made in Russia. Babushka's generation too. Here it's different. Here a woman has power. In Kyiv it was different too. But we were far away, in a place where you live according to who your man is. And no one will take you if you have a baby. That's why I came here. To stand on my own two feet."

And stand on her own two feet she did. She stood on them until her ankles swelled up. She would come home, put her feet up, and cover her ankles with hot water bottles. Nina would bring her tea and food to the living room, and they would both sit around her ankles, which were on the table, and argue about whether to watch channel 9 or channel 2. Irina was everything for her in those days. But Nina saw her and knew she didn't want to live like that. There had to be another way. She would succeed.

She was jealous of other girls in high school, all the ones who lived in cliques and everything was easy for them. They lived in their own small, limited world where things were ridiculously simple, and why shouldn't they? She was the one who wanted to break out because the small town wasn't enough for her. And now she's missing the matriculation exam she was so eager to take. Screwing up the beginning of her life. Maybe the army too. They're sticking out their tongues on Instagram and she's hiding from a killer.

I thought they were stupid, she says to herself, but this time the joke's on me. I'm the moron.

◆ ◆ ◆

"Here's the mouse you wanted," Eitan says, taking it out of his pocket.

"Wow, thanks," Nina says, trying to sound upbeat. "Do you always walk around with mice in your pocket?" And then she says, "I'm just going to see whether the phone store is still open, and then you can bring me the stuff from the grocery."

"Minimart," he corrects her. "If my mom heard you call it a grocery, it would be the end of you."

Nina doesn't understand why he laughs, but she smiles because his smile is so pleasant.

"I'll walk you there," he says.

He's nice, but she reminds herself to be careful, to make sure he can't tell she's not Dana. She needs to keep hiding at Carmela's place for a few more days and he mustn't know. If he does suspect, she'll try to manipulate him so he won't say anything. She has to make him think she's helpless. Weak and pitiful. That's how boys are. They love being the prince from fairy tales.

Shitty fairy tales, she thinks.

The phone store is already closed, and Nina curses herself for not going there before the minimart. Eitan peers through the window and sees a man inside who signals to them. "Sorry, closed." Nina asks for one minute. Just one minute. The man lowers the security gate halfway, Nina gives him a pleading look and presses her palms together in an emoji of prayer, but the man inside gestures that he's sorry, he has no choice.

"I need a phone," she says to Eitan. "Mine broke."

He knocks on the window. "Danny, open up for a minute."

The man comes over to the door and opens it a crack. "Eitan, don't do this to me, Ayelet will kill me."

"If you don't do what this young woman wants, I'll kill you."

"Psshh," Danny says, his expression brightening as he looks at her although he doesn't even look at a newspaper without Ayelet's permission.

"What do you need?" he asks

"A phone."

"No!" he shouts in alarm. "I thought you wanted a charger or something like that. Not now. No. I have to get going."

"Danny!" Eitan shouts. "It's an emergency." And they can really hear the wheels in his mind turning as he weighs the pros and cons.

"Listen, I'll give you a replacement phone," he says, staring at Nina. "You can use it until the end of the holiday and then come back and I'll fix you up. You have a SIM card?"

"No," she says, and Danny waves his arms in desperation.

Eitan asks him to let them in and he says, "No! No one is coming in! Wait here and I'll bring it to you. Bro, I'm on the way to a B-and-B up north and the traffic's already backed up and I'm screwed, Ayelet's with the kids and she's really pissed at me. Enough. Passover vacation. Let it go. I'll give your pretty little friend here a phone and a SIM card and we'll talk after the holiday. Okay?"

He hands her a phone and a SIM card, comes out, lowers the security gate, and locks it.

"What about the money?" Nina shouts as he hurries away.

"Come after the holiday. If not, then your boyfriend will pay."

"He's not . . ." she starts to object.

"Is that a nice thing to say, that I'm not your boyfriend?" Eitan smiles at her and notices again that she doesn't really look him in the eye. He hasn't met a shy girl in a long time.

"You're the best!" she says, raising her head, and for a moment their glances meet and he finally sees her eye, light brown, with a touch of green. It strikes Nina as funny that, in the middle of Tel Aviv, the big scary city, people act the same way they do in her small neighborhood. People help each other. And give you a phone on credit.

"So you'll invite me over for a cup of coffee?" he asks.

"Oh, I didn't buy coffee! So add a jar of the kind you like and when you bring the delivery, you'll get a cup."

"Come on, I'll buy you a cup at the café on the corner."

"I have to go back to make a call. And you have deliveries to make."

"Forget my deliveries. Besides, it'll probably take you a while to set up the phone. You want to call from mine?"

Nina hesitates for a moment. It might not be such a brilliant idea, but she's worried about Irina. "Thanks, that's great," she says, and Eitan hands her his phone as he taps his code. His wallpaper is a picture of his legs with the sea in the background. "Is it a local call?" he asks, and immediately regrets his words; let her call the moon, you idiot. What do you care?

"Family. An aunt I promised to call but my phone died."

"And you know her number by heart?"

"Yes," she says. "My dad really wanted me to stay in touch with her. She even came to visit us there."

Her behavior seems really weird to him. She absolutely doesn't seem American, but maybe that's how Israeli kids are there. Or maybe, like his mom says, he just doesn't understand girls because they're a lot more sophisticated than boys. Boys are stupid, she'd say and laugh.

Nina's heart pounds as she taps in the number. It feels like years since she's spoken to Mom, and she recites the words in her mind, *Mamushka, Mushka, Mama.* No, she mustn't say *Mama* or *Nina* and she mustn't speak Russian. She won't say anything, that's the best thing. It rings once, twice, and in another minute, she'll hear Irina and she still doesn't know what she wants to say. She only wants to hear her voice. She misses her so much.

"Hello," a man's voice answers.

Nina freezes. Eitan looks at her.

"Hello, hello," the voice on the other end says.

She can't believe it. It's him. Johnny. She takes the phone away from her ear and looks at the display, wondering. Maybe she called him by mistake. But no. It's Irina's number. And Shmueli says, "Hello there. Looking for Mom?"

She disconnects, panicked, but forces herself to stay calm, hands Eitan his phone, and says, "You were right. I called the wrong number. Memorization is not my thing."

The phone begins to vibrate as Irina's number appears on the screen. She sits down on a bench and Eitan answers.

"Who is this?" a man's voice asks on the other end.

"Sorry," Eitan says. "Wrong number."

"Nina?"

"Do I sound like a Nina to you?" Eitan says with a laugh.

"Where's Nina?"

"I don't know, I dialed wrong. Sorry."

He's lying for her. This is a good beginning, she thinks. And gives him an unconvincing smile.

◆ ◆ ◆

She recalls in her mind the number she's known by heart since she was a little girl. From the long days she stayed alone at home when Mama was at work. Before she left, Irina made her recite the number to be sure that Nina would know how to call her if there was a problem. I'll come home in a taxi if I have to, she told her, and Nina felt like the most important person in the world. They only took taxis to important weddings. To the most important meetings. Only rarely did Nina call her.

And now Shmueli answered instead of Irina. He took her phone, Nina thought in alarm. What else did he do to her? Where is she? She had to talk to her.

Eitan laughs when he sees how shaken she is. "Who remembers phone numbers these days."

"Sorry," she says. "I apologize."

"Everything's fine, it's nothing."

The phone rings again and Eitan answers. "I apologize, sir. Yes, I shouldn't have hung up on you. Sorry."

He sees how upset she is. He doesn't really understand why. And he thinks happily that she isn't fifteen. Definitely not. At least seventeen. He smiles, proud of himself for not showing how excited he is, for being so cool. He has never before invited himself for coffee with a girl and rarely joked around with one. It's a good thing they met here. This is his kingdom. This spot on the street where he grew up and everyone knows him. Here he's the king and she's the confused new girl.

"I'll go back to Carmela," Nina says. "Thank you." And she hurries off in the direction of the building. She can't breathe. Fear is choking her.

"Wait a minute, the delivery," he shouts after her when she's almost at the entrance to the building. She looks back in alarm, and he hurries over to her with the cart. "I'll help you," he tells her, and she says, "You don't have to, just leave it here."

Eitan understands that this isn't the time to argue, so he takes out the bags and leaves.

Nina carries the bags into the building with her.

A man who is parking his electric bike in the stairwell asks her suspiciously as he removes the battery, "Can I help you?"

"I'm going up to Carmela's."

"Carmela? How nice. Finally someone has come to visit her. How do you know her?"

"I'm her granddaughter," she whispers.

"Great. Ah, from America!" The man smiles, reaches out to take two of the bags, and starts climbing the stairs.

How come everyone knows about Carmela's granddaughter? she thinks. It won't be very pleasant when Eitan finds out who she is, or who she isn't. It'll be a lot more than just unpleasant. She feels a pang of regret, because she likes that Eitan. She only hopes he won't call that number back. He seems curious and he might ask Shmueli questions. She's surprised she's even thinking about him, good boys never interested her. And he's from Tel Aviv. Curls. Shy. They have nothing in common. Water and oil. What could they talk about? She'd eat him alive. And yet she actually likes his gentleness, that distracted look he has. But how could she, who has lived through things a pampered kid like him could never understand, explain to him what happened? And how long would it take for him to realize that she isn't who she says she is? That she isn't Dana. He'll go straight to the cops. After all, she's assuming someone else's identity. They might even arrest her. But maybe you can use him, an inner voice says. Turn him into a boyfriend, someone who will protect you. What crap, a different voice shouts, you need to disappear before it all blows up. Get yourself away from that old lady and her apartment. You just need to get your hands on a little money and take off. But the only way she can get money is to steal from the old lady. And then, where would she go? she asks herself.

She has to find a way to warn Irina and let her know that she is fine. But how?

◆ ◆ ◆

Carmela stands up from her armchair in front of the TV and, with Nina's help, goes to bed. Then Nina sits down in the dining room and inserts the SIM card. Finally she has a phone. She connects to Wi-Fi with the password *Carmela*, with a capital *C*. But she doesn't have a number. Her old number is with her old phone, so she can't get into WhatsApp. And maybe it's better that she doesn't have her old number because then he would find her. Damn. She wanted the phone so much, and now, nothing. It's no help at all. No contacts, no Instagram, no Facebook. She tries to download some apps, but she needs a credit card. She can use Carmela's, but she doesn't want to without asking her. She'll ask her tomorrow. Maybe she should take a picture of her agreeing to give it to her, in case anyone asks. She tries to synchronize, but nothing works and she feels like smashing the phone. She puts it down to charge it and then connects the mouse to the computer and searches for "Murder in Tel Aviv." There are reports and articles on riots that broke out because of the murder. A lot of hatred of foreigners, and the fury of the Tel Aviv residents who have to cope with the many illegals and asylum seekers, as if it isn't hard enough in that neighborhood as it is. She types "Johnny Shmueli" and all kinds of old stuff comes up. Gossip in the local papers. Nothing comes up when she types in her mom's name. There are a lot of other Irinas. At least there's nothing there about her mom. She tries to get into her girlfriends' Instagram pages, but most of them are blocked to anyone who isn't a friend and their profile pictures show them with blurry faces and protruding lips. Nina realizes that she's angry at them, they're not really her friends, they didn't try to rescue her, to stop her. True, she was dazzled by all that pampering and didn't realize the price she would have to pay for it, but why didn't they say anything? Would she have stopped a girlfriend who was going out with Shmueli? Her mom tried to say something, but she wouldn't listen. The truth is that they did try to tell her and she didn't listen. Maybe they're even searching for her and she doesn't know. She looks at a few of their Facebook pictures, and they're all normal. As if nothing has happened. On Michal the neighbor's Facebook page, she sees pictures from the Seder night, everyone wearing white clothes. And it's all so normal that it seems strange to her. How come the whole neighborhood is not out combing the streets for her? She was sure everyone would be talking about the murder, about her mom, about Johnny. And nothing. There's something reassuring about that, but only a little. Johnny still got to her mom. And took her phone.

She has to find a way to warn her and tell her that she is okay. Her eyes are closing, it'll wait until tomorrow, but she mustn't get too confident. She can't let herself enjoy this weird game too much. She has to get out of here. And a new voice rises from inside her and asks quietly, What about Carmela? How can you leave that poor old lady who's sinking deeper and deeper into oblivion and darkness? That's not your problem, the survivor's voice inside her says. Run.

6

The next day, after hours of Internet surfing and efforts to get a new phone number, Nina goes out for some air. She walks into the drugstore downstairs and puts a pair of underpants her size into her cart. Shampoo. Eyeliner. She even finds some beach flip-flops on sale. She waits patiently in line to ask the nice pharmacist a few questions about Carmela's confusion, and he says he's sorry, but he's not a doctor. You need a doctor. As if she didn't know. She still has no idea how to get hold of Irina. And she's really worried. Tonight she'll do something. It doesn't matter what.

◆　◆　◆

Carmela moves away from the window. She doesn't know how long she's been standing there, but she does know that she wants to go outside for a bit. The idea of the stairs tires her, and she remembers how Itzik objected to an elevator. "It's important to get some exercise," he said. Afterward, she was sorry she gave in to him because the time came when he no longer had the strength to go up and down the stairs. And now she's the one who doesn't have the strength. And the morning journey to get the newspaper that she forces herself to make is becoming more difficult every day. But now she wants some air. So she goes out the door and walks carefully down the steps, then from the stairwell to the street.

A pleasant afternoon breeze caresses her face. She doesn't know whether she's cold or warm, nor does she remember when she was outside the last time. She walks slowly down the street, watching her feet as her slippers clatter on the pavement. A moment later, she raises her head and takes a deep breath of the sea smell carried on the breeze. And she walks along the street toward the breeze. She misses the sea.

When they were young, they used to walk to the beach every Saturday morning. Uri would build sandcastles and then go into the water with Itzik. She was always afraid that Itzik wouldn't be careful enough. He loved being Uri's god so much. It was his favorite role. Then Itamar was born, and Itamar didn't like the sand and was afraid of the waves. Itzik laughed, saying that this son had turned out to be a daughter. And she asked him not to say things like that. "Never say that again," she made him swear.

"If he's like that," Itzik said, "then he's like that and nothing will change him."

He's not, she told him. He's just used to being with me. Spend a little more time with him, she told Itzik, but Uri wouldn't let him. He kept Itzik all to himself, ran to him the minute he came into the house. He went to the store to bring him lunch when she put baby Itamar to sleep and nodded off with him.

Uri was six when Itamar was born, and he was terribly jealous, ignoring him so much that Carmela started to worry.

◆　◆　◆

At the crossing she looks right and left, overdoing it, as if she were a school crossing guard. A voice inside her tells her to stop. Stop. Maybe you won't know how to get back. She looks around and knows that she doesn't know, that she has no idea why she went out and where she's going. And that knowledge breaks her heart.

And then everything loses clarity again.

She sits down on a bench, waiting for the wave of blankness to flow through her and pass.

Carmela knows that clarity will come. It'll take a minute or an hour, she has no way of knowing how long. But she's fighting it. Struggling against that fog. And just as with fog—there's no point in waving your arms, no point in running away, all you can do is wait for it to lift. The first time it happened, she screamed. Alone at home, she screamed. When consciousness returned, she felt as if she had been swept back to the shore after a storm. She tried again and again to fight it, until she realized there is no point. It comes and goes. She doesn't know where she is anymore. Present or absent. In time, she learned to let it go. Not to fight. To let the fog embrace her and wait. And only deep inside her, when she feels it coming, she mumbles, Uri. Uri. Uri. She has to remember him. Who will remember him if she doesn't? Itzik isn't here, Itamar isn't here either. He has his own life. And he's so far away. Look, she remembers. And soon it'll be Memorial Day. She has to remind Menashe the driver not to forget. To keep trying even if she doesn't answer. She'll call him today. What is she doing outside? Maybe Menashe is coming to pick her up? Maybe it's today? She looks down at her clothes. Sitting on a bench wearing slippers and a nightgown. A crazy old lady, she mutters to herself and smiles. Go home, crazy old lady. But the spring breeze comes, bringing with it the smell of the sea. And a memory of walking down the street pushing a baby carriage. With Itamar inside. Her dear baby. Who came along when they had already given up. For months, she ignored her stomach, ignored what was growing inside her. She didn't want to be disappointed. To lose another fetus. "Was it a girl?" she asked the doctor after one of the miscarriages, and he was silent for a moment before saying, it wasn't a baby, it wasn't anything yet. She wanted to tell him that it was something, absolutely something, it was hope and expectation, something that she and Itzik wanted so much, even Uri wanted it and knew. After the next few times, she didn't tell him anymore, and one time Itzik didn't know until it was over and she cried as she told him. She doesn't even remember how many times it happened. We have Uri, Itzik told her. We have Uri. It's a miracle. Let's be happy for him, he said, trying to cheer her up. And she said it wasn't enough. They needed another one. At least one more. When she looked at them, at Itzik and Uri, she knew that for Itzik, it really was enough. Only later did she understand that he had no room for another one.

He loved Itamar, but his heart was Uri's. And hers was Itamar's. She was in the NICU with him for a whole month. Never left his side. She slept there, right beside him. She didn't care about anything else. And when she came home with the baby, Itzik and Uri were already an inseparable pair. With their own private jokes and experiences. It was difficult to get Uri back into a regular routine. Once he even yelled at her, "It was more fun when you went to the hospital and stayed there with him."

"He's your brother," she told him.

"It's more fun with Daddy," he said.

And she replied, of course. It's always more fun with Daddy. And she knew he was absolutely right. Everyone loved being with Itzik. How much she missed him.

She stood up to go back home but sat down again. She'll stay a little longer. A tiny bit longer. Until her mind is clearer. Uri, she mumbles in the fog. My Uri, Uri'le.

Itzik will finish work soon and maybe they'll get ice cream and go to the seashore. She'll wait here. She feels like eating ice cream. And dancing. She hasn't danced for so many years. How she loved to go dancing with him in those small cafés there used to be in the old days of Tel Aviv.

She looks at her wrinkled hands and her slippers and closes her eyes.

She's waiting for Itzik. He'll take her dancing.

And for a moment, some of the fog disappears and she remembers that Dana is here. And her heart warms.

❖ ❖ ❖

Itamar is getting ready to leave for work. He has to decide whether to sign a contract for the house, he thinks. It's clear what Naama wants and what Dana wants.

"Dana." He knocks on her door and says in English, "It's time to go."

"Coming," she replies in a whiny voice, as if she were already a teenager, and he packs her lunch while Ariel, dragging his blankie, goes from her room to their bedroom and gets into bed, a bundle of sweetness.

"Dana, you're late! Bye!" he shouts and leaves the house and Dana runs after him.

He hugs her and she says, "Stop, Daddy," and pushes his hands away.

"*Nudnikit*," he says.

Dana asks what that means. Go explain. So he says, "Pretty girl," and puts his Omer Adam playlist on in the car. The price she has to pay for driving with him. That was the deal. After Poliker and Artzi were banned.

"I look at you, everything you are," he sings along. "You won it all. And then it hits me, everything I am is you."

He has to go to see his mom. Tonight he'll tell Naama he's booked a flight. Nothing else matters. This Memorial Day he'll be with her. The guilt he'll feel if he doesn't go will be the highest price he could pay. And yes, Naama will say it conflicts with Dana's party, but Dana's here in the car with him, and she couldn't care less. She doesn't care about him. And he doesn't really know her. They drive to school together every day, and they never say anything to each other. Not a thing.

Omer Adam keeps singing, "After all the years with you, now I understand / You've made me a better man."

Two weeks ago, Naama thought she was pregnant, but it was a false alarm. He was glad. It would be too much for him, three children. He still hasn't gotten used to two. But they need three. He doesn't want Dana to have to bear the same burden he carries. And he thought about his mom, all alone there.

"She insists on not coming to live here, and for no good reason," Naama said the last time they argued about it.

"She won't leave Israel for good," he told her.

"We haven't left Israel for good either," she said angrily. "Aren't we allowed to travel? You're a citizen of the world, we're citizens of the world. Stop being so provincial."

"As if you're not 'the Israeli' here," he said.

"So what?" Naama snapped. "Isn't someone else 'the Japanese guy' or 'the Lebanese girl'? Your mother can stay with us for a year. What does she have there? Nothing."

Her words bring to the surface everything he's been repressing. It's true, she has nothing there. His mom, who gave them everything, who never asked for anything and wanted so little, has nothing. And even the little she did want, he took from her. He put it on a plane and took it to America.

He says goodbye to Dana at her school and wonders if one day she'll feel the same about him. If she'll feel that she owes it to him and Naama to be with them. And if they go back to Israel, will she stay with them when she grows up or will she go back to America?

◆ ◆ ◆

Suddenly Carmela sees him and jumps up from the bench.

"Uri," she shouts at his back. "Uri. Come here."

But no one stops.

"Uri," she keeps shouting. "Don't go. Uri."

People look at her. The young man she is shouting at gives her a quick glance and keeps walking, his arm around his girlfriend.

Carmela looks around for someone to help her, and yells, "Itzik, tell him. Itzik. Itzik."

The young man stops and turns to look at the old lady and realizes she's talking to him, but Shira, his girlfriend, pulls his hand impatiently. "Come on, let's go."

Half of Dizengoff Street is looking at them, at the shouting old lady and at them. And suddenly, it's clear to him that he hates Shira now. Her arrogance. Her selfishness. He saw those traits of hers, the ones he's been pushing out of his mind for months, silencing the inner voice warning him that she isn't what he needs. Yes, she's too beautiful for him. And he knows she thinks he's not good enough for her.

He begins walking toward the old lady, who greets him joyously, "Uri. My Uri."

"Yaniv," beautiful Shira shouts, "what are you doing? She's crazy. Be careful," as if that fragile old lady could hurt him.

But he doesn't turn around. He gets really close to the old lady, takes her hands, and says, "I'm Yaniv."

Carmela touches his face, turning it so the setting sun illuminates it, and she sees.

"You're not Uri," she says, and all the sadness in the world is in her expression.

"Excuse me," she says. "I'm sorry."

"Don't worry, everything's fine. Where do you live?" he asks.

"Yaniv," the beauty shouts, "I'm going. Are you coming?"

"It's okay, Itzik will come to get me. I'm here," Carmela says, turning back to the bench.

"You're sure?" Yaniv asks, and she says she is. "Go," she tells him. "Go. Live. Enjoy."

She sits down on the bench to catch her breath. And now the fog is beginning to envelop her again, and she's a bit cold, but not terribly, she'll wait for it to pass and then go home.

◆ ◆ ◆

A mother walks past with her little boy, urging him, "Come on, already. I don't have the patience. It's time for supper. Come on." Her voice wakes Carmela. She finds herself on a bench and remembers how she was torn between Uri, who ran forward, and Itamar, who walked slowly and stopped to look at every leaf. The fog is lifting now. And everything is so sharp and painful. Uri, she mumbles. My Uri. Uri'le. The agony of missing him rips through her. What is she doing here on this street, where there's a sea breeze and so many benches? She wants to go home. But which way to go? If only the fog would come back, she thinks, to fold her in its arms. So it won't hurt anymore.

And then she remembers that Dana's here. That calms her down a little, she just has to wait.

Dana will come to get her. Dana will come. She can relax.

◆ ◆ ◆

"I'll go for Memorial Day in any case," Itamar tells her on their way to dinner with the partners.

To his surprise, instead of getting angry at him, Naama is almost thrilled. "So this summer, we'll go to Florida," she says.

He always associates that place with old people dozing, decked out in checked polyester pants, pastel-colored shirts, and sneakers.

"And not take the kids to see my mom again? She hasn't seen Dana in three years."

"It's stupid for all of us to go, to make the kids crazy with those long flights and a week of jet lag in each direction, not to mention that it'll cost a fortune. For what? I give Dana an hour, tops, until she's tired of it and locks herself in her room with her cell and complains to her friends that her awful parents took her to an uncivilized country."

"I want to take them to the desert and then spend a night in the north. She and Ariel need to get to know Israel. They even answer in English when we speak Hebrew to them. Dana barely understands what we're saying."

"Oh, right. I can just see Dana climbing Masada." Naama smirks, and when he sees the small wrinkle on her forehead, he's glad she stopped the Botox. After her first treatment, they almost fought. Itamar said she was beautiful even without it, and she laughed and hugged him and said it was sweet that he was blind when it came to her, and he said he wasn't blind at all and admitted to himself that he was afraid that in another few years, Naama would look like the women here with their skinny bodies and faces swollen with plastic.

"You want desert?" Naama asks. "So let's go to the Grand Canyon. When you're in Israel, convince your mom to come."

On Her Own

"She can't handle the connection. No way."

"Did you speak to Dana about it?"

"She didn't take out her earbuds."

"It's the age," Naama said, rubbing his shoulder.

"Were we like that too? With our heads up our asses?"

"I was."

"I wasn't," Itamar says, knowing that he never actually had the opportunity.

"They'll have a lot more years of Grandma when we go back," Naama says. "If you want to go this summer too, go right ahead. I'm not flying to Israel in August."

◆　◆　◆

Naama doesn't know how long they'll stay in America and wants to take advantage of every minute she's here. Her entire family is happy she's here. On every visit, her mom steps off the airplane into a whirlwind of shopping, as if Israel were besieged and it's the fifties now with the austerity measures and she has come to the land of plenty. Her mom was just here for a month and they had a great time together. She postponed her flight back three times, to Itamar's displeasure, even though it was actually good for both of them. He stayed late at work without feeling guilty, and Naama was glad he wasn't walking around the house with a sour face in the presence of her mom, who was starting not to like him. And everyone liked Itamar.

"I told you he wasn't easy," Naama told her.

The big surprise was Dana, who enjoyed her grandmother's visit and for the first time wasn't embarrassed about introducing her to her friends, despite her terrible accent, her dyed red hair, and her loud voice.

◆　◆　◆

It took Naama a long time to understand that she had to arrange play-dates for Dana at least a week in advance, otherwise her girlfriends wouldn't come. A year ago, she started a playdate planner for Ariel.

"It's funny that kids need their parents to decide who they'll play with in the afternoon," Itamar said. "We used to go downstairs and play with whoever was there."

Then he remembered those six months, in the third grade, when Igal threatened him and he was afraid to go down to the street. Until one day, Uri asked him what had happened, and Itamar told him. Uri left the house, came back fifteen minutes later, and told him, "Don't be afraid anymore. Do whatever you feel like."

On the way home from school the next day, Igal kept his distance. And stopped harassing him.

Within a week of arriving in the States, they became a branch of the kibbutz in a foreign land. Anyone coming to the area stayed with them for a few days, and it wasn't that mobs of people invaded the way they would have if they lived in New York, but there were more than Itamar expected. Naama was on cloud nine. She became the tour guide for shopping, especially at outlets, and also, the tax here was much lower than in New York and anyone who came from Israel swooned when they saw the prices and flew back with an additional suitcase.

At first, Itamar liked the enthusiastic guests who came, but later on, he became sick and tired of them. "I want to come home and be with you and the kids," he told Naama, "not be a host."

"We're not hosts," she said. "They're our friends."

He said that maybe that's the difference between someone born on a kibbutz and someone who wasn't. She was used to being with people. Used to strangers in her home. For him it was an effort. He was used to quiet. To intimacy. To the gentle way Carmela and Itzik touched each other, the way he put his hand carefully on hers, as if she were a fragile statue. Even when he was a child, their home was pretty quiet. Even before the Great Silence. Only Uri was a bundle of noise barreling through the house like a storm, always with a story or something he had to tell them, almost always with a ball, and Carmela would get angry and say, "No balls in the house," and Uri would kiss her and say, "Mom, you worry too much, I'll be careful," and if Itzik was home, he would smile at her and she would smile back.

Carmela didn't stay angry for long. Certainly not at the kids. Not at the customers either. But every once in a while, in a long while, someone would get on her nerves and that was it. Forever. They tried everything to make peace between her and Rachel from the nail salon. But nothing they tried or said or pleaded—after all, they had neighboring stores—managed to restore their relationship. Rachel didn't say what had happened because everything had begun when she said something Carmela didn't want people to know. And she would rather die than make Carmela angry again.

After Naama's mom flew back to Israel, Itamar said, that's it, no one is staying with them anymore until they finish remodeling a guest suite. Naama was delighted to start the remodeling. She already had plans, the house filled with interior decorating magazines, and then Zipi told her that their neighbors were selling their house. And then it was full speed ahead for Naama's campaign of persuasion.

"Isn't paying rent like throwing away money?" she asked Itamar. "The down payment here is so small, we can get a mortgage with the money we waste on rent."

He was stressed about the plan. Naama, who knew Itamar, knew it was better to give him time to let the idea stew.

But now they had to decide because there was another couple that had already made an offer on the house.

Itamar and Naama reach the boss's house and park in the large driveway next to all the glittering cars. She smiles at him, and before they get out of the car, he takes a deep breath and says, "I'll try to persuade her when I'm in Israel."

◆ ◆ ◆

Nina inserts the key in the apartment door, gives it a half turn, and goes inside.

The TV is on at full volume, so she puts the bags on the table and goes to lower it, finding it strange that Carmela isn't sitting on her armchair in front of it. She checks the bedroom, goes into the kitchen, then heads to the bathroom. If only she hasn't fallen in the bathtub, God forbid, she thinks in alarm, it would be really terrible if she slipped and broke her leg or something. But Carmela isn't there. She dashes through the bedrooms, the kitchen, the living room, and no, the apartment is empty.

In an instant, she realizes what happened. Shit, Carmela left the house. That's not good. It's really not good that she's wandering around the streets alone, she won't know where to go and how to get back. She flies down the stairs and out onto the boulevard, looking right and left, but there's no trace of Carmela. When did she go? In which direction? Why did she even leave the house? Someone honks like a madman and Nina's heart jumps. Carmela could have stepped into traffic and been run over. She isn't aware of the dangers around her.

She walks and looks around, hurry up, she urges herself, and she's already out of breath, where the hell did that old lady go, it couldn't be too far. And maybe she went in the opposite direction? Nina runs back the other way, onto the sidewalk, looking in all the stores, then back again to the center strip. No Carmela. She thinks about calling her name, but it seems stupid to start shouting "Carmela" now in the middle of the street. If she's in a fog she won't answer anyway. And if her mind is clear, she'll come back on her own. Nina tries to calculate how much time she's been out of the house. No time at all. Maybe half an hour or a little more. How did it happen, damn it, and where could she have gone? As she tries to breathe deeply the way her teacher taught her, Nina continues to walk down the boulevard, and then thinks that maybe Carmela has returned while she's been out looking for her. She runs back home, but Carmela isn't there. Then she goes back to the boulevard. And that's it. She's all out of air.

◆   ◆   ◆

I need to call for help, she thinks. But who should she call, the police? And what would she say to them? That she's Nina or Dana? It'll end badly, especially if something happens to Carmela. They'll blame her. For pretending to be Dana. That maybe she wormed her way into the confused old lady's house to rob her, to get control of her money. Because it's the easiest thing in the world to blame someone like Nina. Someone who's not from here, who has no one to defend her. And Itamar will certainly come for the trial. Itamar, the one who tossed away his mom and doesn't give a damn about her, lets her live in a pigsty, confused and filthy, he'll come and blame her. Now Nina's sorry she cleaned the apartment. The cops won't believe the kind of repulsive conditions that gentle old lady lived in. But the truth is that, even if they saw it, it wouldn't make a difference. After all, they'll have the girl who tried to rob her. All those thoughts race around in her mind, but her heart pounds wildly with apprehension and she realizes that she doesn't care about anything else now. All she's worried about is her, the sad, fragile queen who took her into her home.

And at that moment, she knows that Carmela knows she's not Dana. Not always, not when she's lost in the fog and her brain plays tricks on her. But in her lucid moments, when tears run down her cheeks, she knows.

◆ ◆ ◆

She'll ask Eitan for help. She has no choice.

If only he doesn't ask too many questions.

She has to look calm. So he doesn't think there's any drama here.

She goes into the minimart and asks the cashier, "Is Eitan here?"

"Yes. In the storeroom," she says and moves her head in the direction of the back of the store.

"Eitan," she calls quietly from the door of the storeroom, forcing herself not to scream.

He comes out, a dirty towel on his shoulder that he wipes his hands on. "Listen," he says. "That guy from the wrong number called today too."

"You didn't answer, right?" she asks, and to keep him from thinking she cares, she adds immediately, "Weird, why is he making such a big deal about a wrong number? He must be bored."

"I told him it was a mistake and he should stop," Eitan says.

"And he stopped?"

"He called again, but I didn't answer."

"Listen, there's something more important now—I need you calm and collected now," she says, and he likes that she needs him. A good start.

"What happened?" he asks calmly, ordering himself to be cool. He has to impress her.

"She's not in the apartment," she says, looking deep into his eyes, and he wants to sink into her eyes, but tries to listen and resist his desire to throw his arms around her and run off with her for the rest of his life and forever, it doesn't matter where. He has to have her in his arms. Has to feel her.

"Do you understand what I said?" she asks.

"Yes. And you don't have a key?" he asks. "Maybe my mom does. I think your dad left it with us once."

The words *your dad* give her the chills. No one ever said "your dad" to her. Only when they asked, "What happened to your dad?" They usually asked her how come she has no dad. And she never had a good answer.

"I have a key. That's not it."

"So what is it?"

"Carmela. She's gone."

"What do you mean, gone? Not home? Went out and didn't tell you where?"

"I don't know where she is. She doesn't usually go out."

He sees that she's really upset, and her eyes are even bigger, looking at him with even more hope, and he doesn't really understand how someone so beautiful could be so desperate. "She'll probably be right back. Maybe she went to buy something?" he suggests.

"No, she doesn't really know what's going on. She's not really"—Nina searches for a way to say it—"with it."

"Oh no," he says, then remembers that his shock and concern might stress her, and corrects himself. "I get it. Shit."

"Right. Now come help me find her."

I'd follow you to the moon, he wants to tell her, but instead, offers her a bottle of Diet Coke from the fridge, and they set off.

"I'll go that way and you go the other way," he says, taking control of the search operation. "You still don't have a phone, right?"

"I couldn't get it to work. There's a problem with the number."

"So we'll meet here. Come back here every few minutes. Whoever finds her brings her to this bench."

They split up, each one going in a different direction. She walks quickly, scanning the area. Eitan walks slowly, climbs onto a bench to see farther. A grumbling old man tells him it's not nice, with his shoes on, people will sit here later. Eitan says that he's right, and he's sorry, but he's looking for his grandma who disappeared.

A car honks and he tenses. He runs to see what happened. Just an argument between two drivers. It's not Carmela. But now he knows what they have to do. And quickly.

He goes back to their meeting place.

"We have to call the police," he tells her. "It's dangerous."

"She'll come back," Nina says, alarmed, looking all around.

"Look at me," he asks. Her eyes are darting back and forth, searching, and he takes her face in his hands. "Look at me, Dana. You know that she won't come back on her own."

Nina averts her gaze. It's hard for her to look him in the eye, it makes her lie worse. Tears fill her eyes.

And when Eitan hugs her, it's so good. She needs that, to be held by someone who is taking care of her. Irina used to hold her that way when she was proud of her. When she brought home a good report card. When she came off the stage after receiving her certificate of excellence at grade school graduation. It happened a long time ago, before everything began. That hug she was willing to work hard for. And this is the first time she has felt this way with someone who isn't Irina. She hugs him tight as uncontrollable tears spring from her eyes.

"Please don't. Give me half an hour," she says.

"Why? They'll help."

"I'm asking, please don't."

"Dana, no one will blame you."

"I'll blame myself," she says. She's worried about Carmela, but she's also afraid that the police will expose her.

"Just a minute," he says. "I'll text some friends."

◆ ◆ ◆

He remembers a small group of friends from high school that, a few months ago, texted that they needed another person to come play basketball with them, and he went, but afterward, didn't feel like it anymore. A while later, someone texted that they were meeting to celebrate the birthday of a member of the group, and whoever came should bring something to drink. In high school, he avoided birthdays, and when Hagit found out, they fought, and she took him to a therapist. She worked with him on social relationships, but Eitan preferred to be alone. Being with others at school was enough for him. He didn't like large groups. He used to drown in the talking, lose the thread, and suddenly, everyone was laughing at something he didn't really understand, or hadn't really heard, and he never knew if they were laughing at him or someone else and why, and he would remain serious while everyone else was roaring with laughter. Or they would argue loudly and he didn't understand why. As if they were all going full speed ahead and he was in low gear. As if they were rolling down-hill and he was pedaling on an endless upward climb.

And Hagit wanted so much for him to be a leader, to be popu-lar, to be less attached to her, that she sometimes felt as if she were pushing him away. She would explain to him, teach him how to stand out, how to lead, but he was content with his PlayStation and her minimart. Everything was clearer there. When the employees in the minimart laughed at something, he asked what was funny. And they explained it to him. That's how he learned about life. And since it was sometimes in a different language, they would translate, and that's how he learned Arabic and a bit of Russian, and also how to tell the difference between a Ukrainian and a Moldovan, and how each felt superior to the other, and how to drink vodka, and what Ramadan was. One night, in the army, when they went into that village and the boy was really scared of them, he sat down next to him and spoke Arabic and reassured him. His commanding officer asked, "Bro, are you a plant? What's all this Arabic?" And go explain to him that when you were a kid, you were in love with Aida with the green eyes and chocolate skin and ringing laugh, who worked for your mom.

It's not love, Hagit told him back then, it's hormones. Start looking at the girls in your class before I fire her. That was one of their biggest fights. Her family arranged a match for Aida when she was nineteen, even though she didn't want to get married. "That's how it is with us," she told him. "It's even a bit late." But what about love?" he asked. "Love, it's dangerous," she replied. The next day she came to work with a hijab and her smile was no longer the same, and she left even before the wedding. Seeing her at the wedding, he realized how stupid he'd been.

Since then only Jewish girls worked at the minimart checkout counter. Most spoke Russian, and they were all older than him and stern. They were there to work. They were nice to him, but they weren't his friends.

It was a good thing Aida left before she saw him in uniform, he thought as he lay in bed at night, staring into the darkness, an exhausted combat soldier in a dusty uniform who had awakened from a pleasant dream about a green-eyed cashier, and if he met her on patrol tomorrow, she would spit on the ground. And his body was aroused.

◆　◆　◆

Eitan keeps his arms around Nina, feels her body shake from her weeping. "I'll look out for you. Don't worry."

"You don't understand," she whispers.

"I do understand," he says. "We'll talk later, let's go and find Carmela."

She breaks away from his embrace, looks at him with eyes swollen with tears.

"I only want to know what your real name is," he says.

She's not so surprised. Tries to decide how and what to tell him. Then she hugs him. Rests her head between his shoulder and his neck.

"Nina," she says.

"Nina," he rolls the name around in his mouth. "Nina. Let's go and find Carmela. Before things get even more complicated."

Eitan calls Hagit. "Mom, listen. Carmela left the house and got a little lost, and before we call the police, if you see her, call me."

"We?" Hagit asks curiously.

"Now's not the time, Mom."

"It's always the time, honey," Hagit says, smiling from ear to ear.

And Eitan can't help smiling too.

"Oh no, Dana?! She's just a kid!!" Hagit's upset and feels like shouting "Eitan" but he has already hung up.

"Hey, friends," he writes to the group. "Remember Carmela from the hardware store? She left the house two hours ago and she's a little confused, so if anyone's in the neighborhood and sees her, let me know."

And those tough guys actually reply. "Oh boy, hope she's okay," someone texted. "Haven't seen them in years."

"I'm in India," someone else texted. "Let me know when you find her. I liked her Itzik. He was a great guy. *Namaste*."

"Sending to my mom," someone texted. "She walks in the neighborhood this time of day."

"What's she wearing?" Eitan asks Nina. Now they're walking together. Looking around.

"A brown nightgown, a kind of *galabiya*. And I think a sweater.

Also brown. Or beige," she says. All Carmela's colors are like that. Like sand or soil. Not the warm, damp soil things grow in, but dry and hard. Soil that contains no life.

"If we don't find her in another fifteen minutes," Eitan begins, but Nina stops him and says, "Okay. Another fifteen minutes."

They reach the pedestrian crossing where the boulevard ends and the main road and the bustling city begin. Buses and taxis and traffic and honking. And everyone is moving. People don't even stand still at the traffic light. A guy in running clothes keeps running in place. Another guy is talking on his phone and pacing. She doesn't know how long she and Eitan have been holding hands, but now they let go. As if here, it's inappropriate. In a minute, they'll be at the sea. And she wants to go back. There's the promenade, too far for Carmela, she thinks, looking north while Eitan looks south, and suddenly, as if this were a movie where everyone is moving, she sees one woman who isn't. She's sitting on a bench facing the sea, her back to them. But Nina recognizes her. She touches Eitan's hand and points at Carmela.

On a bench, wearing earth-colored clothes. Red slippers. White hair. And the final rays of the sun are sinking into the sea.

Eitan remembers something his grandma told him once: "If you close your eyes and make a wish when the last rays of the sun are sinking into the sea—it will come true."

He makes a wish. That he can spend the rest of his life with her. Nina. He says it silently, getting used to the name.

◆　◆　◆

A driver honks at Nina when she jumps into the road. "Watch out," Eitan says, pulling her toward him. "Take care of yourself for me."

"Some nerve," she says, laughing. "Who do you think you are?"

"I save your life and this is the thanks I get?"

Nina hugs him. With all her heart. She wants to cry, to shout, to flood the street with tears, to spit out all the stress and the scenarios that have been running through her mind, including life in prison.

Eitan hugs her tight and they cross the road.

"Carmela." Nina touches her shoulder and Carmela looks up at her. Her face is covered in tears.

"We're here," Nina says and hugs her. "We're here."

And Carmela's expression is blank. Blank.

Nina takes her face in her hands. "I'm here," she says, watching Carmela slowly return from that somewhere, and it's heartbreaking. Nina's touch, like electricity in her veins, brings her back to the here and now. "I'm here with you. Everything's okay."

"My little girl," Carmela says. "I've been looking for Uri. He went away. Itamar too. I can't find them. Can't find them. Where are they?"

Nina helps her up. "Come home now."

"Is Itamar home?" Carmela asks. This is the first time that Carmela has asked about him when she's in the fog. About Itamar. Not Uri.

Eitan texts Hagit and his group of friends that Carmela is back.

◆　◆　◆

"Want something to drink?" Nina asks Eitan after she puts Carmela to bed.

"You want to go out tomorrow to get a little air?"

"I'm afraid to leave her alone."

"So we'll take her with us," he says with a smile.

Nina laughs. "Carmela doing shots at the bar—that would really be something."

She hasn't laughed in a long time. She always puts a hand on her mouth when she laughs because of her slightly crooked tooth. A dentist explained to her that she needs braces, gave her a ridiculous price, and said she should bring her mother and "I'm sure we'll come to an agreement." She knew there was no way. His receptionist called a few times to make an appointment, but Nina didn't answer. She just decided to be careful when she smiled. To cover her mouth.

And now she doesn't put her hand on her mouth, but just laughs, normally, without hiding anything.

"There's a place with a view of the sea," he says, "that you have to see. You know what? We'll take Carmela too. My first date with a grandma."

"Date?" she says. "Cool it. I still haven't said I'd go out with you."

"Should I stay here with you?" he asks. They both know there's a conversation they should have, but Nina still isn't sure whether she can tell the truth or she has to keep lying. If she lies, she'll have to make up a story. And her entire body hurts from the tension and the worry and the running around.

She has already told him that her name is Nina, but all he really knows is the Dana story, and suddenly, she doesn't have the strength. For anything.

Seeing the tears running down her cheeks, he puts his arms around her. He moves her head gently to the hollow between his neck and his shoulder, and Nina closes her eyes, breathes in the smell of his body mixed with the remains of his deodorant, and she no longer wants to disappear. All she wants is to stay in his arms.

Eitan strokes her head. "Sshh, everything's okay now," he whispers. "Everything is fine."

She wants to tell him that nothing is fine, nothing. He doesn't have a clue. Shmueli will find her and finish her off, his Tel Aviv toy. She moves away from Eitan and withdraws into herself, thanking him silently for not questioning her now.

"I'm curious," he says, as if reading her mind. "But it can wait. Go to sleep now."

They walk to the door. He wants to tell her something but doesn't know how.

"I'll talk to you tomorrow," he finally says.

"I'm here," she says, smiling sadly.

It's weird, how she's stuck here now. With this old lady she barely knows who has found a way into her heart and this guy she misses even before he leaves. And she knows that she'll stay because of him, even though it's stupid.

7

After the main course, Itamar took his glass of wine and went outside to look at the huge pool. The maid came out to tell him that dessert was being served. He looked at the manicured garden, the mowed lawn, the roses, the white garden furniture, and knew that his life was heading there. He should have been jumping with joy now. The dinner was being held in his honor, to celebrate his new position. "This is what we need," the boss said. "The way you think out of the box, the originality and daring you brought with you. I know you will lead the department forward and we are already excited about your taking on this new role." And he looked at his suit, his shoes, which he bought for an exorbitant price because that's what was expected of him, and thought about that out-of-the-box he will have to supply. But he feels so in the box. Submitting to all their rules. To all their "how do you dos."

At the table, they are all sitting as couples. Playing their roles. Most of the women are simply accompanying their husbands. There are almost only men at the top of the corporate ladder, except for the required token woman. And she usually comes from human resources. The wives chatter among themselves about education and children and colleges, and the men tell jokes, straining to be pleasant and actually saying nothing.

He looks at Naama as she speaks avidly with the company president's wife, trying to impress her, and it pains him to see how hard she's trying. He thinks about Carmela, about her stillness and gentleness, how she never fought to be accepted. How she maintained the customs of the old country. How different they are. Naama is trying to absorb the new place, establish relationships, fit in. His mother never tried to deny her foreignness. She even hung heavy curtains to shade the house from the blazing sun. In the summer, she wore a wide-brimmed hat and an off-white suit when she was out in the steamy, sticky street, holding his sweaty hand as they walked to school, and he was proud, feeling as if he were being escorted by the queen. And they would both look at Uri, with his short pants and long hair, as he ran far in front of them.

That's your future, he thinks, a pool and roses and a polite maid who works for the out-of-the-box guy who is totally in the box.

◆　◆　◆

"I need to think about it," he says, interrupting Naama's enthusiasm on the drive home.

"Itamar," she says, in that annoying, empathetic tone she learned in the coaching course. "You're fulfilling your dream. This is the important promotion you've been waiting so long for. This was your dream! What happened?"

"Sometimes I feel like such an outsider here."

Naama strokes his hand. "You're stressed, and that's natural, but you'll be great at it. And I'll get a nanny, I won't nag you about the time you come home. I won't make it difficult for you. I'm with you. We'll do it together."

Itamar thinks about his father, who didn't get to see how successful he is. Even if he were still alive, he might not really understand. And his mother, the more successful he is here, the more miserable she is there. His daughter is turning into a spoiled American kid who thinks her dad is embarrassingly provincial. He remembers how his father used to go fishing with Uri. What a shame he doesn't have that kind of relationship with Ariel. But go explain to an American kid what the difference is between Hapoel Tel Aviv and Maccabi Tel Aviv. Here, everyone's into baseball, and he hasn't even managed to learn the rules.

"Do you understand that you did it?!" Naama says, turning her entire body to him and rubbing his shoulder. "It's amazing. Did you see how much he likes you? They're even crazy about your accent." She smiles, referring to his boss's imitation of his Israeli accent.

She can't decide whether to talk to him about buying the house.

"You're right," he says, "I should be happy. I don't know what got into me."

"So let's celebrate."

"I want to go home," Itamar mumbles.

"Do you want me to drive?"

"This is not my home."

"Could you maybe stop that? Who's waiting for you there? All your friends would be happy to come visit you here. Spend an evening cracking sunflower seeds together. Here. In America. Just invite them and you'll see, they'll come, and they'll be so proud of you. And yes—maybe a little jealous too. This is the best home you could have, Itamar! You built it with your own two hands. With your talent and skill."

"When will we say it's enough?"

"Why do we have to say it's enough? Why can't we keep living this good life here?"

"So we're never going back?" Itamar asks. "We've left Israel for good?"

"Why look at it that way? Think of it as relocation."

"We came for a year. Six have passed," he says, realizing that he has never dropped anchor here. Everything is rented: the house, the leased car, even some of the furniture and electrical appliances. Everything's "in the meantime." Temporary. Until we go back.

Naama has nodded off. Red wine always knocks her out. He's happy for the quiet. Everything is in such turmoil inside him now, a mishmash of contradictory voices. The promotion, the new house, and Memorial Day is getting close, all forcing him to make decisions. But before he does, he has to figure out what he really wants. For himself.

Even at this hour, on the freeways around the city, so many cars are hurrying over the bridges and along the interchanges, the red taillights and white headlights look like blood cells flowing through the veins of this place, an endless blood transfusion of the land of opportunity. How easy it is to get lost here, Itamar thinks, to be part of the crowd, to disappear.

When he was little, people said that if you were dying in the middle of the street in America, no one would stop. In certain neighborhoods that might be true. In most cases, however, someone would definitely call the police. But as long as you didn't die, they didn't interfere in your life. It embarrassed him to admit to himself that sometimes, he did want them to see him. He wanted to say, hey, look at me. I'm the nobody from somewhere in the Middle East. With a terrible accent and a passable vocabulary, I did it. I made it. I'm set for life. But the truth is that no one here cares. No, he doesn't want to be another tiny blood cell in the veins of this alien body. He's sick and tired of English, of the game. All this foreignness is hard for him, and he feels like a foreigner with his American children, with all those people, as if this were a game or a grand performance, and he wants to go home and take off his shoes. Walk around in sandals. In flip-flops. Walk down the boulevard to the sea, sit on the beach with his feet in the sand and breathe in the salty breeze, look at the Israeli women who have a freedom they don't even understand. Not everything with them is perfect, and he thinks they're still sexier than any woman coming out of a spa looking as if she's just stepped out of a magazine.

It's clear to him that already now, Dana will object to leaving America and hate Israel, and with every passing year, her objection will grow stronger. Naama will say he's out of his mind and she won't stop counting the money they lost until the day she dies. She'll list the experiences they missed. It'll be a heavier cross to bear than his mother is. For a moment, he's angry at Carmela, at her unwillingness to let him go. To really let him go. But a moment later, he remembers how she looked during his last visit, withered, a shadow of herself. Her sadness seeps into him from the distance and Itamar wants to run to her, to embrace her. To ask forgiveness for leaving her so terribly alone.

He doesn't want to be like those people who were at his boss's villa who only want more and more, to achieve and trample and acquire, and the race will never end because there will always be someone who has more. Much more. This knowledge envelops him like a soft blanket. You never conquer a mountain here. You climb and climb. But you never conquer.

He wants to go home.

◆ ◆ ◆

Looking out from the mirror at Irina is a tired, older woman, her hair as messy as if she had been caught in a storm. She changes her blouse three times. This one's too tight, that one's too low-cut, and the other one is too black. She feels comfortable in the fourth one. The end-of-holiday stillness is in the air. In only a few more hours, the first three stars will come out and it's okay to start eating *chametz*. She's planning to go upstairs to help Michal get ready for Mimouna, the Moroccan celebration marking the end of Passover. She was at her place yesterday, but didn't tell her much, just that her phone is broken, and she used Michal's phone to call and text Nina, who didn't answer.

She went to the mall twice during the Passover vacation to buy a phone, and that shadow followed her both times. She ignored him and went into the store, and he walked right in with her. She's going out of her mind. Home, without a phone, she's going crazy with worry. Tomorrow she'll buy herself a new one even if he follows her. And if he tries anything, she'll scream.

Irina texted Nina in Russian that if she has a problem, she should call Michal, she always has her phone with her. Then she deleted the text from Michal's phone and told her that Nina was fine. She's in Eilat.

"She'll probably come back burned to a crisp," Michal laughed, even though she was worried about Irina. There was obviously something she wasn't telling her. And where was Nina?

◆ ◆ ◆

Irina is waiting for evening. Michal is having a lot of guests and she'll try to find out what they know, to get a sense of what people in the city are saying. It's not easy for her to be with people, and it's even harder for her to need them. In another minute, the building will be crowded with Michal's guests and those coming to the other neighbors, they'll all go from house to house, and the whole neighborhood will turn into one big party. Happy music, everyone in colorful clothing.

It's always the most lit up night in the neighborhood. It's only her brain that is racing around like a sleigh in the snow, where is Nina, what's happening with Nina, why doesn't she call, and what does Shmueli want? What's really bothering him about Nina? He's hiding something serious, and Irina doesn't have a clue. If only she could tell Michal, but she mustn't. Absolutely not. She'll just be with her, help her with all the trays of food, and that's all. Michal knows Shmueli. She knows that Nina is with him. At first, Irina tried to hide it, but there was no point, half the neighborhood was talking only about them, and the other half was talking about them a little less.

"There's nothing you can do about it," Michal told her during that conversation. "You know *Romeo and Juliet*? So that's it. That's how it is when you're in love, your brain goes on pause. There is no brain. Not for the man and not for the woman. You just have to wait, and it'll pass. Just don't fight with the girl."

How could she not fight with her? How?

"Stop with that tough Kyiv thing," she told Irina. "Your daughter is total sabra. Total. Except for her complexion, oh, and also that slimness you have from Russia, damn you all. Until you came, they thought we Moroccan girls were hot."

"He has a family!" Irina said, gaping at her. "He's married!"

"So," Michal said, holding out her arms in despair, "you never heard of such a thing? There are a few women here in the neighborhood who want to send you all back to Russia just so their husbands will come home."

"I never took anyone's husband."

"Too bad," Michal laughed.

And Irina told her it wasn't funny. "I'll kill her. I'll tell her that I won't allow it."

"And you think she'll listen to you?" Michal asked.

◆ ◆ ◆

Nina had no intention of splitting from Shmueli just because her mom objected to him. After their first argument about him, Irina went crying to Michal, who told her, "The best thing to do is laugh about it. She's smart, your Nina, she'll snap out of this craziness. It'll take another month. Another two months. The main thing is that she shouldn't get pregnant. Did you take care of that? Did you get her something?"

"Don't say that, even as a joke," Irina said.

"Did you talk to her?"

"She's a good girl."

"What do you think he wants from her? To do homework together? Wake up, sweetie."

Irina choked. She couldn't even imagine them together. She couldn't imagine him touching her little girl. Her delicate little girl. But she understood that she had to speak to Nina. She had to. But she had no idea how. "What should I tell her?"

"Be nice," Michal said, "and smile and say, 'I'm with you, my little girl,' and take her to a doctor who'll give her pills. That's more important than sitting here in my kitchen and washing my floor with your tears."

Irina tried at first, she really tried not to preach to Nina, but it weighed on her, and sometimes she criticized her. Gently. "This is not for a girl your age, there are such nice boys your age."

And Nina would yell at her. Her delicate, educated Nina, who now had a mouth like a toilet, and Irina's heart would break. She tried not to say anything, until that terrible fight, the last one, on the day Nina took her suitcase and left. And now, who knows where she is, what happened to her.

Irina looks out the window and sees him standing there. The one they sent to follow her. She doesn't know if it's the same one or if all the soldiers in that piece of garbage's army have the same clothes.

She goes out to the stairwell, but she's so afraid that she can't breathe and she realizes that she can't be with people now. She'll fall apart, she can't, and she goes back to her apartment.

◆ ◆ ◆

"Did you call him?" Ilanit asks Ashkenazi when she sees him at the station, even though she's afraid he'll yell at her for butting in.

"Who?"

"Shmueli."

"Yes. He didn't answer. I'll try him again." It's clear to both of them that he tried and then completely forgot about it.

"Should I drop by and check with the mother?"

"Yes. Tomorrow. Good idea. I'll probably see him the park tomorrow."

◆ ◆ ◆

"Bummer," Eitan texts Nina, after she explains that from now on, the farthest she can go to is to the bench on the boulevard, from there she can see the entrance to the building and make sure Carmela doesn't come out.

"Tonight's Mimouna," he says. "I have a friend, we all go to his place every year." He really wants to celebrate Mimouna with her. He pictures the two of them dancing, surrounded by all the colors and the scarves, but she's right, they can't leave Carmela alone.

"Everyone goes there, no matter what. There'll be tons of pastries and candies and jams. His mother's a wiz in the kitchen."

The description instantly transports her home, to Michal's Mimouna, to the noise and the glittering, gold-embellished costumes.

"Thanks," she texts him. "I adore the sweet stuff they serve on Mimouna."

"You know Mimouna?" Eitan is surprised, and then remembers that she isn't really from America. "So now you're going to stay with her all the time?" he texts.

"I don't know. I have to think about what to do. Maybe after the holiday I'll start looking for help. A professional caregiver. Go to your friend. Have a great time," Nina replies.

He could ask his mom to stay with Carmela for a little while, but then he'd have to talk to her. And she'll ask too many questions. And she'll suspect too many things, mainly that the girl isn't Dana. That she couldn't be her. Dana is much younger than Nina. He rolls the name around on his tongue.

◆　◆　◆

The sounds of traditional Mizrahi music of the holiday come from the neighboring roof. She misses home, misses the kids in the building who grew up together outside, the pastries and candies and jams Michal made for Mimouna. For a full week she worked and complained after she removed her glittering rings and put them on the small shelf, and then mixed and kneaded, her manicured fingers rolling dough with surprising speed.

"So don't do it," Irina would tell her. "Be someone else's guest for once."

"Are you kidding?" Michal shouted at her.

Nina loved sitting in her kitchen with her, rolling the sticky dough, painting it with food colors, dipping it in sesame seeds and coconut, licking her honey-covered fingers. She loved the brightly colored ethnic dresses with the tinkling coins, and Michal would sing and then cry, why does she only have boys, and who will do all this when I'm gone, and Irina would say, "Your daughters-in-law." And just the idea that other women would take away her princes angered Michal, who said, "They'd better watch out for me," and Irina would laugh.

Every year the guests were flattering the beautiful spread Michal had put out with all those special jams. Michal's sons would help her mother-in-law up the stairs. "Such wonderful grandchildren," the grandmother would say, "like their father, such big hearts. He was that kind of kid too, good like them."

Nina thinks about all the people at Michal's place now, and she suddenly realizes that that's the solution. She can call Michal. Irina must be there too.

◆　◆　◆

Naama is scrolling through the pictures on her phone, waiting for Ariel outside the Gymboree. She looks at a picture of Itamar. The straight, beautiful nose. The slightly fleshy chin. The potbelly. He's gained some weight. The food that's always accessible on every corner here, the huge portions, America. And she thinks she doesn't tell him enough that she loves him. And that she's happy. That she doesn't need anything else. Maybe just a little more strength. Maybe she should go to a dietician, she thinks, she has no energy.

For the last few months, she's been going to Pilates with some Israeli girlfriends. With the American women, she feels like it's all almost. Almost close. Almost nice. Forced. With the Israelis, she feels at home. They can laugh and gossip and no one thinks anything of it.

She waits here once for Dana and once for Ariel, the chauffeur-Mom. That's the price you have to pay. A big house, everything easy and comfortable, accept all this abundance, the American promise and the dream, and in exchange, forget about fulfilling yourself. It's addictive. And the strangest thing is that it makes her so happy.

Sometimes her friends in Israel ask, "So what are you doing?" and she explains that here it's okay, that a lot of women with academic degrees who graduated from the best universities, whose parents used up all their savings to pay for the degree, are full-time mothers, sitting in front of the Gymboree, feeling fulfilled and happy. There are also women who work, but it's really fine if you don't. "You should have some kind of role in the community," Zipi said, explaining that it's part of the admission ticket, and Naama thought she'd take on responsibility for the Hebrew library. She's already scheduled a meeting with the head of the Jewish Community Center. Maybe later on she'll set up a Hebrew writing workshop or book club. She used to read more, but since the kids—who has time? She began preparing a list, how many women here read in Hebrew, she should find out if she needs to get Israeli books in Hebrew or ones translated into Hebrew. Which is always different. She still doesn't really enjoy a book in English. Reading in Hebrew speaks to her heart, her soul. Hebrew passes through her senses and her memories. The smell of pine trees when she reads about woods. The humidity of Tel Aviv. The kibbutz. English has none of that. The question is will there be enough copies of every book for the reading group? Maybe she should first speak to the woman who opened an Israeli bookstore here, she'll know how many Hebrew-speakers want to be in a book club.

◆ ◆ ◆

Nina finds Michal's home number on the Internet. She hasn't called a number with the 08 area code for years. Who still has a landline? she wonders, waiting for someone to pick up. The phone rings and rings. No answer, and she keeps trying until finally someone picks up. Nina hears music and noise, and she shouts, "Hello, hello," but the call is disconnected.

She calls again and again, and finally someone picks up. She hears the sound of someone drumming on a *darbuka*, and remembers that Michal's Ronen always sat among the guests on the roof with his *darbuka* and didn't stop drumming until all the Ashkenazim yelled at him from their windows.

A little boy's voice answers, "Hello."

"Who's that?" she asks.

"Rami," the boy replies.

"Rami, go get Michal. And don't hang up. Okay?"

"I don't know her."

"Call a grown-up to the phone."

"Coral," he yells, "Coral, come here, someone's on the phone."

Coral takes the receiver and she's a little kid too, but she goes and comes back and says that Michal is busy and nervous and wants to know who it is, and Nina tells them to call Omer to the phone and they go to look for him, and after an hour on the line and Ronen's *darbuka* in the background, she wants to scream. Omer comes on the line and says, "Hello, who's this?"

How nice it is to hear his voice.

"Omer, this is Nina. Listen. It's a secret, so don't say anything to anyone. Is that clear?"

"What's up?" he asks, and without waiting for her answer, adds, "Your mom isn't here."

"Why not?" she asks, alarmed.

"She's tired. Didn't feel like it."

"You saw her?!" Nina asks.

"Where are you? Come on over, Mom made really yummy *mufletot*."

"Did you talk to my mom?"

"Mom sent us down to invite her but she didn't want to come, and then she sent us back to bring her some sweets and we made her at least open the door. Honestly, she looked happy about the food. Your mom said we were good kids and everything's fine, she's just tired and we should let her be."

"Was she okay?"

"Yes, you know your mom. Not exactly happy."

Nina smiled in relief. Her mom is home, they saw her.

"Omer. I swear, if you tell anyone you talked to me, I'll cut your head off."

"Go against you? Never, you're crazy."

"I'm crazy about you."

"So will you marry me?"

"Yech. You're a baby. Never."

"Just wait and see."

"*Yalla*, noise, I can't hear a thing. Bye."

Nina rests her head on the pillow. The sounds of a *darbuka* from the neighboring roof fit right into her thoughts about home, and everything suddenly seems a little less menacing. Omer can help her. And she knows Irina is okay. But the more she thinks about it, the less sure she is. What's the real reason Irina didn't go to Michal's place? Maybe she's hiding black-and-blue marks? Who knows what Shmueli did to her. And so more and more questions and worries pile up in her mind, but she tries not to worry. Omer would have said if something was wrong. But what does he understand? Shmueli could be in her mom's house right now. Holding her hostage to keep her quiet.

◆ ◆ ◆

Irina takes out a large bunch of keys and opens the door of the daycare center. She's glad the vacation is over. Since Nina ran away, everything has been so crazy, but this last week of vacation was the worst ever. Every morning she would wake up with the hope that it was all a bad dream, a terrible dream. But no. And that shadow who never leaves her watches her every move from his car. The first couple of days, she was afraid he would attack her or try to do something to her, but he just followed the bus she was on. Three stops to Talia's house, and back. Now, surrounded by all the dolls, toys, and books that calm her down, she peers out the window and sees that he's there.

After two weeks of endless attempts to call Nina, and after so many days have passed, it's obvious that she isn't getting her texts. And even though her own phone is with Shmueli and he's just waiting for Nina to call her on it, and even though she knows there's no chance Nina will answer—the first thing Irina does when she goes into the day-care center is call Nina again. No answer. Disconnected. And she's disappointed to hear again the "The number you have dialed is no longer in service" recording. Because she hoped so much. She tells herself that it doesn't make sense for Nina to answer because if she did, Shmueli, that piece of garbage, would find her. In fact, that's what cheers her up every morning when she sees the shadow. It proves that Shmueli still hasn't found her Nina. It means that her Nina is hiding from him. But where is she? Where? And what's happening with her? Irina is falling apart. She knows she won't be able to play the game. The tears threaten to spring from her eyes, her heart is thumping in panic, she hasn't been able to sleep more than half an hour at a time before waking up trembling and anxious.

She opens the windows, airing out the rooms of the center that have been closed up more than a week, arranges in a circle the small chairs on which the young, innocent children will soon be sitting, making their sweet noise. She loves the mornings here before the commotion begins. Soon Menachem the guard will arrive, followed by the parents who bring their little ones here, happy to be rid of them after the vacation. She has noticed that the parents are more grateful and smile more at the staff after every holiday. The long days they spent with their young children have exhausted them and they're just waiting to drop them off for a few hours and return to being the career people they are.

◆   ◆   ◆

Usually the fathers come in the morning. That's their job. So they can check off "taking care of the kids" and stay at work until evening. They've done their part. They took the kid to day care. But she's not angry at them, they're so nice, so young, and so bleary-eyed from lack of sleep. And the kids are so attached to them. She admits that she's jealous, how much she wanted to have someone at her side to help with Nina, to lend a hand, to help support them and share the worries. She didn't even dare to think about love. Just look, her Nina fell in love and was tossed aside so quickly, like toilet paper blowing in a field. Getting stuck on a thorn and fighting the wind. Her tears flow for her Nina. How did this happen to her, how could she have run away from her like that? And where is she? Her stomach hurts from the sweets Michal sent her. She devoured them at night when she couldn't fall asleep yet again.

The phone in Shoshi's office rings. She doesn't have to answer. She lets it ring. And then she thinks that maybe it's a parent who wants to check whether the center is open today. Irina already knows that Mimouna is an elective holiday and there are parents who get confused. She runs into the office, but the ringing stops. A few minutes later, it rings again. Irina runs back into Shoshi's office.

"Hello?"

"Mom?"

"Nina! Nina!" She doesn't believe it. Her legs are shaking. She sits down on Shoshi's chair. "Nina."

"Are you okay?"

"Yes. Are *you* okay???"

"Yes."

"I've been so worried."

"Me too."

"Your boyfriend has my phone."

"I know. He's not my boyfriend."

"Where are you? Do you have food? A place to sleep?"

"Yes, Mom. Don't worry."

Silence.

"Nina? Ninotchka?" Irina whispers. "My little Ninotchka. Are you all right? Are you okay? Oh, how I worried."

"I was so worried about you." Nina begins to cry.

"I love you. So much. My little girl. Come home. Please come home."

"I can't."

"Why, Nina, what did he do to you? Are you healthy? Give me a phone number so I can reach you."

"I don't want you to have my number. I don't want anyone to know where I am."

"Why not?"

"It's too complicated to explain."

"Nothing is complicated. It's only complicated when you're not with me. I have no life like this. I don't want to live without you next to me. I don't want to! *Yob tvoyu mat.*"

"Let me think about what to do," Nina says.

"Give me a number. So if something happens, I can find you."

Nina looks at the fridge. On the minimart magnet is a phone number for deliveries. She dictates the number to Irina. "Ask for Eitan. And say you want Carmela's Dana."

"Go slower, I'm writing."

"Mom," Nina says, "I love you. Very much."

"And I love you. And I'm sorry, my little girl."

"No, Mom, I'm sorry. So sorry."

"I'll come to you. Where are you? Tell me where and I'll come."

"Is he watching you?"

Irina hesitates for a moment. She wants to lie so she can go to Nina, but she knows she doesn't really know what's going on. "Yes. Someone's following me," she says.

"Let me think. I'm really okay now. Really," Nina says and hangs up before she starts to cry.

◆ ◆ ◆

"What happened?" Menachem the guard asks when he comes in to put his things down and sees her crying.

"Nothing," Irina says and wants to tell him that she's crying with joy. Her Nina is okay. Her Nina is okay.

"A beautiful lady like you, crying like that about nothing?"

She looks up at him. No one has told her she's beautiful for years. Many years. She hasn't felt beautiful for such a long time.

"Be careful, Menachem. I'll tell your wife."

"She knows. I didn't go blind. I just got married."

Parents begin to arrive with their kids, along with the rest of the staff. Irina goes into the kitchen to prepare breakfast and write a list of things for the kids' lunch. She listens to the voices of the parents, who are chatting with the teachers about the vacation, and the kids who are starting to cry, and the parents who promise them presents if they don't cry, and I'll come at lunchtime and we'll buy you ice cream. She feels as if two tons have been lifted from her heart. She goes out to greet the kids with a smile and asks Menachem the guard if he wants coffee.

"So what's with the smile?" he asks.

"Crying wasn't good. Smiling isn't good. So what's good?"

"Smiling is good," he says. Irina tells him that she's happy to be back, and he says she's crazy because she loves to work.

"We went, the whole family, to the Sea of Galilee," Menachem says. "Slept in a tent. I could go for another month like that."

Being outside with a lot of people, sleeping in a tent, with mosquitoes, doesn't sound to Irina like much of a vacation, and she doesn't want to hear about it and doesn't feel like being jealous of people who go away on vacation. A few years ago, she went to Eilat with Nina, and the child was so happy that Irina thought it was a shame they hadn't gone sooner. She met so many Russians there. Including that man who tried to start something with her. And that really scared her. Now she's sorry she refused and she misses that feeling of being wanted. What is she saving herself for? What is she, a saint? Why doesn't she let herself enjoy and be happy? Someone who wants her. Yes, she wants someone to want her. Now that she knows Nina is okay, she wants to start living. She thought her life was over because without Nina she was better off dead. And now Nina has called her, is worried about her. And isn't running away from her.

Irina smiles to herself and looks outside, and sees him sitting in his car. Watching her. The shadow. And she smiles. So let him follow her. That's his problem. Her Nina is okay. For all she cares, he can follow her for the rest of her life, the main thing is that he isn't following Nina.

◆　◆　◆

"Shalom." Two people walk into the station, and although they're in civilian clothes, they seem extremely confident.

"Is Ashkenazi here?"

"Who are you?" Ilanit asks.

"Detectives from Tel Aviv," they reply, and one of them shows his badge. She thinks they're so full of themselves. Wearing civvies and acting so important.

"I'll see if he's here," she says, picking up her two-way radio. "Ashkenazi. Chief. Two guys waiting for you here."

"Half an hour, I'm there."

"Okay, Chief."

"Tell him to hurry up," the older guy says, the one who didn't show his badge.

"I won't say that to my chief," Ilanit says, raising her chin in an attempt to show that they're not her bosses.

The younger one wants to say something, but the older one puts a restraining hand on his shoulder and smiles at her.

"Can I get you some coffee?" she asks.

"Good idea," he says.

◆ ◆ ◆

Her head hurts from the day before. She shouldn't have had anything to drink.

"I have the morning shift tomorrow," she said to her husband, when he brought her another drink.

"This is how it's always going to be with you now?" he asked.

"No." She laughs. "It'll be worse when I'm a detective. You won't see me at all."

"How did I end up with you?" he said, hugging her, and they laughed and drank. A lot. He's crazy about her and proud of her. And even though he's pretty fed up with those holiday shifts of hers, and the angry faces his mother made when he arrived at the Seder with the girls and without Ilanit again, unable to accept that a woman could leave her husband alone on a holiday.

Ilanit is extremely happy to be on the force. It was her dream. She insisted on going to the course and taking the exams. She doesn't care that everyone thinks she's just a police clerk, including her mom, who never believed in her. Ilanit knows she'll be promoted to detective. She doesn't have the slightest doubt. And she was also happy to go to work this morning. The girls had been on vacation for two and a half weeks. And it was a lucky thing her mom agreed to take the older one today too. She took the little one to day care, thank God it opened today even though it was Mimouna, and then hurried to the station. But her head still hurt.

She has just made herself a cup of coffee and sat down behind the counter to browse through the newspapers when they walk in. Plastered across the front pages are colored photographs of politicians wearing *tarbooshes*, eating *mufleta*, singing, smiling endlessly. She remembers all the sweets she devoured and curses herself. She has to slim down, she can barely get into a size 42. Her problem was always her backside. That's why she insists on wearing heels. This is the only place where she's at her natural height. Because that's how it is in the police.

◆ ◆ ◆

"When did you leave to get here now?"

"A quarter to six."

"If you called, we would have gotten ready for you. What would you like? Turkish? Espresso?"

"No kidding, espresso?" the young guy says.

"Yes, there is espresso outside of Tel Aviv," she says, smiling at him. "Ashkenazi brought a machine. His, from home. You know him? Should I give him your names?"

"No. Not on the radio."

"I'll make my own coffee," the older guy says and walks to the coffee machine with her. "So tell me, you know Shmueli?"

"Johnny Shmueli? Everyone knows him," she replies, thinking it's weird that he's the person they're interested in.

"What's he like?"

"I don't want to get in trouble with Ashkenazi. Why do you ask?"

"Talking about Shmueli will get you in trouble with Ashkenazi?"

That older detective is nice, she thinks, but he's too pleased with himself.

Her phone rings. Ashkenazi asks who's waiting for him and she hands the phone to the detective.

"It's about what went down in Tel Aviv," the detective tells him after introducing himself. She makes a mental note of his name. Ron Danieli. "Come in. Let's talk quietly."

She smiles. Ashkenazi doesn't believe in quiet. And she sees the patrol cars approaching the station and everyone is trying to find out who these guys are and why they're there.

And thank God, Ashkenazi comes out really quickly and the three of them go into his office.

Everyone in the station comes to ask Ilanit what's happening. There hasn't been any action here in a long time. They're all keyed up, knowing that nothing has happened there to justify the sudden arrival of detectives from Tel Aviv. And what concerns them most is that there's no shouting coming from Ashkenazi's office.

"So what did they say?" one of the veteran cops asks.

"They were waiting for Ashkenazi."

"What did they want?"

"Coffee."

"You're a tough cookie."

"I'm scared of Ashkenazi," she says. And that's it. Now they realize that she's hiding something. That's what cops are like, they have a sixth sense for lies and evasions. Now they know that she knows why those detectives came from Tel Aviv, she just doesn't want to tell them.

"Just wait until you need something," says Liron, the computer expert who's already on the net, typing furiously and trying to figure out what this is all about.

The older detective says, "We'll know about it soon anyway. Why are you playing hard to get?"

"Listen, I'm new here. If I say something, Ashkenazi will put me on his black list," she says, "and I'll be stuck here behind the counter until I retire and I'll turn into the crabby old cop who gives her neighbors tickets for not tying their garbage bags, and that's not what I want."

Ilanit knows that if she shows even a drop of fear, that'll be the end of her in the station, but their arrogance annoys her and she gets up resolutely, goes over to the chief's door, and knocks.

"Who is it?" Ashkenazi asks impatiently as she walks in.

"Coffee, Chief?" she asks, and his angry expression turns into one of pride. This is how it should be. So they can see how respected he is here.

"Yes," he tells her. "The usual. Anyone else?"

"I already had coffee. Thanks," the older guy says, looking her in the eye. She's embarrassed, it's been a while since a man she doesn't know has looked at her like that. Admiringly.

"So we shouldn't arrest him?" she hears Ashkenazi ask when she comes back with the coffee and some cookies.

Their indifference annoys Ashkenazi. He doesn't understand the logic in keeping it quiet. Go and take him and threaten him, his businesses, tell him you'll tell his wife everything, and if that doesn't work, then beat the hell out of him and he'll spill it all, he'll sing like a canary.

"We need a witness," Danieli says. "We have a theory full of more holes than Swiss cheese. We have no proof. Just a body. Everyone's afraid to talk. We have a prostitute, excuse the word, but that's her work." He smiles apologetically to Ilanit, and Ashkenazi signals with his eyes for her to leave as Danieli continues, "And she won't open her mouth. She just cries all day, 'Leonid, Leonid.' There are neighbors who saw him there a few times. And a few snitches who said he actually runs the place. Apart from that, nothing. But it helps make sense of a few things."

Ilanit leaves the office and whispers to Zvia from accounting, "Tell me, how does Ashkenazi like his coffee?" She has never made him coffee before.

"Turkish, weak, with milk," Yakov the guard says, and Ilanit laughs. That description in itself would be enough to make Ashkenazi angry.

She starts connecting things. It's a murder case. And it's somehow connected to Shmueli, that toy gangster, who goes around with lowlives. Drugs and sex, not the kind associated with the rockers and rollers, but the kind that ropes in easy targets like the minorities here in the desert, the needy people who exist outside of the big party of life going on somewhere in the center of the country, and are drawn into the whirlpool of robbery and debt and crime that destroys their families and makes their lives a misery.

After almost a year on the force, she already knows that those are the Shmuelis of the world. They're the ones who bring the poison. The money game that puts the wrong ideas into guys' heads, that takes them away from their families, makes them break into houses at night to steal money to buy more things they don't need because all they have in their minds are dreams about girls and fun and sex.

Everything looks so shiny and seductive in the red light of yet another apartment where you're drunk or high, until the police bust in because the neighbors are sick and tired of all those men coming and going. Ilanit sees the girls rescued from those places after they didn't think they could be rescued anymore, because their innocence had been slapped around too much and was in terrible pain, hiding in the place where their dreams were buried, and who knew if they could ever break out of the vicious circle of money and drugs. At first, she thought it was so easy to break out of it, but it definitely was not. And she sees the devastated parents who come to tell them that once she was beautiful, or a good student, or something else of which there is no longer any trace under their flashy clothes. But sometimes no one comes, maybe the parents have given up altogether, and she watches the newly rescued young girls leave the station with their little evening bags, which are all they have in the world, with nowhere to go except back to the same place they've just come from. And the saddest thing of all is seeing the glitzy cars that come to take them back until the next round.

◆ ◆ ◆

Ilanit thinks about that woman who was here before the Seder night. Who was looking for her daughter. The one who went with Shmueli. And after she connects the dots, she realizes that she might be onto something. It fills her with pride. This is her chance to prove to Ashkenazi what she's capable of. But only if she's clever about it. She wonders where that girl is and hurries to the computer to find the woman's name. She'll ask about her. But if she just mentions Shmueli's name, they'll know immediately that it's connected to the investigation. Then she reminds herself that this is a girl in distress, and who knows. Maybe she's in some kind of danger.

The VIPs come out of Ashkenazi's office. He walks them to the door of the station. "Where can we get some good food around here?" one of them asks. And Ashkenazi says, "Try Menachem's, the shish kebab place. Ilanit, direct them." Ilanit goes out with them, and the older guy asks her, "What's your number?"

That pisses her off. "Hey, who do you think you are?"

He smiles and says, "In case Ashkenazi doesn't pick up."

And she knows she just made a fool of herself. They both smile. But he smiles more.

"Type 'Menachem's Shish Kebab' into your GPS. When you get there ask for Rachele and give her my regards, she's my aunt."

"Are you a good cook too?"

"No. I get takeout from her place."

He starts to walk away, then turns and smiles. He remembers the good days he had as a young policeman in a small station full of volume and passion. It's been a while since he missed his ex so much that it hurt. Yes, he's about to return to an empty apartment, but in the end, he's happy this way, without her complaints. Without her questions. Without all that pressure he was so eager to get away from. And now he sleeps on a mattress on the floor, starting all over again. He needs someone like this Ilanit, who won't know how to cook, who won't know anything, just how to look at him that way. And he feels like leaving everything and moving to a station like this in the boondocks.

"So? What do you say?" the young detective asks him.

"I think he's the guy. Let's go eat and find out more about him there. But, kid, be careful. They'll immediately run to tell him."

"And you better be careful with this Ilanit." The young detective laughs.

"Get outta here, you jerk."

"Man. You have no idea what's going on these days."

◆ ◆ ◆

Ashkenazi leaves his office and puts on his sunglasses, and Ilanit goes over to him.

"Chief, I wanted to tell you something."

"Not now," he tells her, and shouts to his deputy to come.

"It has to do with this."

"With what?"

"With this," she says, and then she sees it starting in him, the nervous smile, and in another second, he'll roar at her here in front of the whole station, so she moves closer to him and says, "With Shmueli and with what they said."

"Come with me," he tells her, and she follows him out to his car.

As his deputy turns on the engine, he stays outside the car and says, "What?"

"Remember I told you that a woman was here on the holiday looking for her daughter who went out with Shmueli? And she didn't answer my call?"

Yes, he remembers. "I called him. Sniffed around. He didn't understand what I wanted."

"I thought maybe I'd drop by to see what's happening with her. I'll go to her place. Ask her a few questions."

"Okay."

"Okay," she mumbles, surprised he didn't tell her not to stick her nose in it.

And now she's a bit angry at herself for not checking with Ashkenazi even sooner to find out how the business with the mom and her daughter turned out. Maybe it's connected. She could already have been part of that story that brought the detectives from Tel Aviv.

220

◆   ◆   ◆

After she heard that Irina was okay, Nina calmed down. She finally managed to breathe, as if a rope around her neck had been removed. In the end, she entered Carmela's credit card number in her phone, and since then, she's been lying on the living room couch, filling in gaps. First she tried to access her girlfriends' profiles without her username and read some of their stories and public statuses. But most of them were private. Then she thought that Shmueli and his collection of fuckups probably didn't have a clue about social media. She remembered her password, logged on to her Instagram page, and saw everything. Her friends meeting at the Aroma café in the mall, the nights in the abandoned shopping center, a party at Moran's house with the Jacuzzi her dad installed in the backyard, where her previous party had made her instantly popular. Nina saw how all of them fell all over her for a selfie and noticed that Michael, from the senior class, was sitting with some girl. That could have been her, in the Jacuzzi with Moran, fantasizing about Tel Aviv and settling for Michael and his clean kisses. And she feels dirty again.

◆   ◆   ◆

Suddenly there's a private post to her from Noa. "What's happening? I see you're online. Are you coming for the matric exam day after tomorrow?" Nina's so alarmed that she doesn't reply, deletes her password, and logs out. And tries to remember which exam they were having now, and what a bummer, she's really screwed herself, she thinks, and a wave of anger rises in her, a terrible wave of anger that makes her muscles contract instantly, and she leaps off the couch and runs to wash her face. Maybe it's because she finally knows that Irina is okay, that he hasn't done anything to her, and she is momentarily free of fear and worry, that she's allowing herself to be angry. Really angry. At that man who destroyed her whole life with his games. She knows now that it was a game for him. Falling in love. That's his hobby. To wallow in it until it's over. To immerse himself in it. To experience it like in the movies. And then move on. Everyone around him knows that. She was the only one who didn't understand that it was his pattern. The hero of an action movie with a girl clinging to him on the poster. She thought she was using him, but he took everything from her. Her relationship with her mom. Her matriculation exams and all the years she had worked so hard at her studies for which she got such good grades. Her friends. Because she could never go back to them. Ever. Even if this whole story ends, she can't go back. They would always think of her as Shmueli's whore. That's what they'd say about her. And rightfully so. Because one of his pals who was in the apartment and saw how he treated her would show up one day and tell them. And even if she kept away from those friends and just stayed home with her mom, and even if she went into the army or brought home a boyfriend, someone would tell him. There will always be someone who recognizes her. Someone who might tell. And that would be that. Her head was exploding with the things Irina tried to tell her. And after a few days of feeling okay, she was nauseated again as all those images flooded her mind, and she wanted to vomit. There was another matriculation exam the day after tomorrow and that's where she should be, studying for it. The girl she had been before she met him. Before he took her, took away her dream of going to college. Because how could she be a student without matriculation exams? But you don't get off easy either, she tells herself, you played the game too. Your mom tried to warn you, but no, you're smarter than that cleaning lady, that immigrant with an accent, yes, you're an Israeli and you know how to twist everyone around your little finger. You're stupid, she says to herself. So stupid. And she runs back into the bathroom and vomits.

When she washes her face, she looks in the mirror and understands something she hasn't thought about until now. That she escaped. She ran away before it got even worse. Before she lost herself completely. Before Shmueli gave her to them too. To use her. That's what would have happened if she hadn't escaped. Look, already on that horrible night, he didn't intervene when that guy with his smelly aftershave tried to push her head down to his crotch. Johnny couldn't have cared less. And for a brief moment, a very brief moment, with the sour, disgusting taste of vomit still in her mouth even after she brushes her teeth, she's proud of herself. For running. For saving herself.

She wants to get out of this stifling apartment for a little while. To buy something sweet. Ice cream or something that will wash away the vileness in her throat and in her soul. Carmela is sitting in her armchair staring at the blank TV screen, and it worries her to see her like that. Carmela is deteriorating too quickly. She needs to get her moving. She'll give her the laundry to fold. Encourage her to help with the cooking. And go out. Yes, they have to go out. A little ice cream won't hurt Carmela either.

She goes over to her and asks, "You want to go out for ice cream?"

"Yes, Dana'le. Yes, I really love ice cream. Itamar does too. Chocolate is his favorite. What's yours?"

"Vanilla. Let's go out for some air, Grandma."

Carmela goes to her room to get ready. Fifteen minutes later, she comes out, her hair gathered into a tiny ponytail, wearing a neatly ironed off-white dress and holding a small matching handbag, and she takes a wide-brimmed hat out of the closet near the front door.

There's no connection between the determined woman standing

at the door, ready to go out, and the muddled old lady with the un-
kempt hair who, only two days earlier, walked down the boulevard
looking for her little boys, or the lost old lady with the empty eyes
who sat and stared at the blank TV screen only a few minutes ago.
Those gaps between the shrinking islands of awareness and the sea
of confusion that is rising among them so quickly are so large that,
in another minute, all consciousness and understanding will be swallowed up. They both know it's only a matter of time. I have to find
her a doctor, Nina thinks, to consult with, and she offers Carmela her
arm to lean on.

For a moment, their glances meet and now it's clear: Carmela
knows she isn't Dana. She knows everything. She thinks that, in another minute, Carmela will scream at her, throw her out, hit her with
her elegant handbag and scream, "Thief! Get out of here! Who are you
anyway?" but then something softens in Carmela's face and she hands
Nina the key. "Lock the door." And she starts to walk down the steps.
Then stops.

"Dana, look," she says, pointing at her feet and the red slippers.
"Look. What a stupid, confused old lady I am. What a grandma you
have. A disgrace." And she starts back up. "Let's go back."

"No," Nina says. "You don't need shoes, your slippers are more
comfortable. Who cares. We're in Tel Aviv! We're not going back. Ice
cream in slippers. It's a new trend!"

"What's a trend?" Carmela asks with a smile and keeps walking
down the steps, unable to believe that she's about to go out like that.

"It's what you used to call fashion."

They go out to the street. Every time she leaves the apartment,
Nina is struck by the huge, impersonal commotion of Tel Aviv, but
also by the way the people act as if it were a small neighborhood. A

woman spreads a blanket on the boulevard and puts her baby on it as if all the buses weren't spitting black smoke at him. One guy is sprawled on a bench as if he were in the middle of a park.

"Is there an ice cream place you like especially?"

"American waffle in Café Oslo."

"Where's that?"

Carmela smiles at her. "In Café Oslo."

"You know which way to go?" Nina asks Carmela.

Carmela smiles at her but doesn't say anything. That's the way she reacts when she's not here—that's how Nina thinks of those absences of hers.

She takes out her phone and calls Eitan. "Feel like ice cream?"

"I remind you that my mom owns a minimart. You're invited to the ice cream freezer."

"Carmela and I are taking a little walk. Come with us."

"On my way."

"We're on the boulevard. She wants to go to Café Oslo. Where is that?"

He shouts the question to his mom. And then says to Nina, "Closed a long time ago."

"Where can I get an American waffle?"

"Don't know. Wait for me. I'm coming."

◆ ◆ ◆

"On Fridays," Carmela tells her, "after Itzik and I closed the store, we would go to the Oslo and that was my special treat. After Uri was born, we went there with him too. But when your father was a boy, he was addicted. Addicted to sweets. And dreamed about the whipped cream they put on the waffle and would try to convince me to go in

225

the middle of the week too. Where will it end? I used to ask him, and he said there was no such thing as too good. No such thing. And I didn't understand that. I didn't understand."

"Now we're good," Nina tells her. "Not too good, but good."

Carmela strokes her face. "I feel good that you're with me. I was afraid of being alone. It's good you came."

Eitan arrives, panting. He has to learn to look a little less eager, Nina says to herself. If she were his sister, she would teach him that you shouldn't show girls you want to be with them.

"Shalom, Carmela," he says, kissing her cheek.

"When did boys start kissing like that?" Carmela says with a laugh.

"Since we taught them," Nina says. "So where can we get waffles?" she asks, and Eitan tells them to follow him. They stroll down the boulevard, an elegant lady carrying an evening bag and wearing slippers, a young girl wearing flip-flops and a pink shirt over a cream-colored slip, and a cute boy wearing a heavy-metal-band T-shirt.

"I think you need more clothes," he says.

"Are you saying I don't look good in pajamas and an old lady's skirt?" she asks, laughing.

Carmela takes a credit card out of her wallet, points to a store across the street, and tells her to go buy herself whatever she wants.

"I don't feel comfortable doing that."

"Feel comfortable. I'll wait here on the bench if you take me for an American waffle afterward."

"I promise," Nina says, and hugs her. She wants to say, "I promise, Grandma," but tries not to lie around Eitan. They still need to have that conversation. But not yet. A little later. When they get better. When they get to know each other. Besides, she won't initiate it. Let him ask.

"I'll stay here with her," Eitan says.

"And who will tell me what looks good?"

"Call me and I'll tell you."

She goes into the store across from the bench and comes out immediately, with a grimace on her face that tells him it's absolutely not for her, so he signals for her to go into the adjacent store.

That store has a few items of clothing, some accessories, and some household furnishings, everything in shades of gray and black and white, and a pleasant smell of cleanliness and money in the air. Nina feels like a fish out of water. She's not used to this kind of boutique. She looks at the stuff that's on sale, and sees a few things. She goes into the fitting room to try on black pants and a gray shirt, then walks to the entrance of the store and shouts, "So?"

Eitan and Carmela look at her and he immediately gives her a thumbs-up. Carmela looks at him, smiles, and imitates the gesture.

She tries on another shirt, white this time, and jeans. Eitan approves, Carmela a bit less, and as she turns to go back into the store, her eyes fill with tears. For a moment, she feels as if the three of them are almost a family. And for a moment, she believes that everything will work out. Because she feels happy and calm after being afraid for so long. Almost the way she once felt with Irina before she learned what money was and that they didn't have any, and what it means when everyone thinks your mom isn't worth much just because she's not like everyone else and doesn't cook and wait at home for you and because you have no dad and your house isn't renovated and your kitchen cabinets are crooked.

The nice saleswoman suggests that she try on some things from their new collection, she'll look great in them. Nina says they're expensive. The saleswoman brings her something from the storeroom in back. "And this?"

Nina tries it on. It's a black dress made of soft material that caresses her skin and makes her pale complexion even paler against the black. The saleswoman pins her hair up and hands her a pair of pumps, and she goes to the entrance of the store again.

Eitan and Carmela stare at her.

She looks incredible. Absolutely incredible.

Eitan looks at Carmela and smiles. Carmela whispers, "Don't lose her. Don't be stupid."

He blushes.

The saleswoman gives Nina a discount after Nina tells her that she has never in her life bought anything so expensive, and the saleswoman says with a smile that neither has she, and they both laugh, and Carmela's card slides through the credit card reader like butter. Nina leaves feeling like the heroine in a Hollywood movie.

And they go for ice cream.

Eitan can't decide when to tell her about the people who came to the minimart the previous day.

Carmela leans on Nina's arm, and he watches her match her steps to Carmela's. How gentle she is. He doesn't understand what the connection could possibly be between her and those two people who came to the store looking for her yesterday.

"Just a girl who lives on the street," he told them, repeating what he said to the people who have been calling him. They showed him her picture and he said he didn't know her. He wasn't sure they couldn't tell he was lying. One of them went over to the cashier, showed her Nina's picture, and asked if she'd seen her.

"No," she replied, even though she had. She didn't like that guy, acting like people owed him, who was he to ask her questions.

"Excuse me," interrupted Hagit, who had just come out of the washroom. "Who are you and what do you want from my employees?"

"I'm looking for my sister," he said and showed her Nina's picture. It caught her unprepared. He saw that.

"Your sister? What happened to her?"

"A fight with Mom. You know what it's like."

"I wish. I'm dying to fight with my mother a little."

"Someone saw her in the area."

"You want to leave your number? In case we see her?"

He couldn't decide. He went outside and shouted to his friend who was standing with Eitan, and they looked like a pair of roosters competing to see which one could puff out its chest more. Hagit didn't like that. She wanted them away from her son. They made her nervous. They gave her a phone number and left.

"This is not good," she says to Eitan as she lights her second cigarette in a row.

"Mom, if you keep smoking like that, it'll end badly."

"Don't tell me how to live."

"Let me find out what the story is, okay?"

"They scare me."

"Right now, she and Carmela are staying home. Let me check it out."

"Don't play Captain America."

"Tell the crew here not to talk."

"If I tell them that, they'll talk," she says, and almost lights another cigarette, but seeing his expression, she puts it back in the pack.

"If you paid for each and every cigarette, you'd see that you're smoking away my inheritance."

"Yes, but this way you'll get it faster."

"Mom."

Hagit thinks for a minute, then says, "I think I have to talk to Itamar. So she doesn't steal everything Carmela has, including her savings."

"Who's Itamar?"

"Carmela's son."

He's speechless.

"I'm not as stupid as I look."

"Give me a few days," Eitan says.

"I don't like this," Hagit says, realizing that he knows too.

"I do."

"You're just horny."

"Mom! Yechs."

"Be careful."

❖   ❖   ❖

Deputy Superintendent Ashkenazi walks among the families in the park and wishes them all a happy holiday. He comes here every year on Mimouna, so it doesn't seem odd to anyone. Someone puts out a joint when he sees him, but the smell remains. It's clear even to Ashkenazi that the years' long war against adults who get a little high at the end of the day is over. Kids are another story, it's not really good for them, but the people who want a brief escape from their hard lives, their debts, and their worries at the end of a day's work, more power to them. The alcohol concerns him more. Also the hard drugs. Over the years, he's seen enough people who've screwed up their lives with them. The ones whose old mothers would come to him when it was already too late. What can I do, he would say to that mother who looks at her forty-year-old son who's all skin and bones and almost toothless and still sees in him her little boy. The young man he once was. He knew some of them because they grew up with him. But there was nothing to be done. For some people, that's their destiny.

Relatively speaking, there isn't a lot of crime in his city. "Your city."

His wife laughs at him sometimes. "At most, a town, and not exactly yours." But a great little town, he tells her, shrugging off the scorn. He's had so many conversations with fathers and sons right before the kid got swept away to a bad place, and so many times the conversation changed the kid's path. Not arresting the kid but threatening that next time he wouldn't be so easy on him. He knew that some of the fathers would beat the hell out of their sons when they left his office, but it would get them back on the straight and narrow. It was so easy to get lost here, in the boredom. But over the last few years, their town had grown, more and more people had come and more and more tall buildings had begun to surround the little houses in the old center. And since they opened the pub in the mall—that was it, people felt like they were in Vegas. That Shmueli, with all his swaggering, is the only thorn in his side. But he'd succeed with him too. He does most of his filthy business outside the town. With the bedouins in the area, with the yuppies from Tel Aviv, who don't understand that kind of shit, and Shmueli makes fools of them and then tells his pals, who roll on the floor with laughter and say, You're the man, Johnny. Only the way Shmueli uses young girls repulses him.

"They're not young girls," Shmueli once said, smiling like a sated cat, and Ashkenazi told him that soon his daughters would be that age, and we'll see how he feels then. He tried to tell him that there are enough women here who just want a little pampering. The ones who still haven't found a husband and you can see the desperation on them, the ones whose husband left them and all they want is someone to help with their tough day-to-day lives, the ones who carry the whole burden on their shoulders, who occasionally want to leave their kids and go to the city, to feel that their lives aren't over. Why young girls? "It's legal," Shmueli said with a smile. And Ashkenazi thought, yes, it's legal. But disgusting.

231

Now he walks among the families, speaks to all of them, but his eyes are searching for Shmueli. The smell of barbecuing meat and the smoke are too strong for him this early in the day, not even noon, and all the women push food at him, but he rubs his potbelly, which he can't get rid of and is still full of last night's Mimouna sweets, and when the men invite him for a beer, he says thank you and reminds them that he's on duty. Some of them say, "*Yalla*, get rid of the uniform and come sit with us, you deserve it," but really, they admire him for it. He watches over them. They admire him for serving them. For keeping an eye on this place. For a while now, he's been toying with the idea of running for mayor. And this shitty business has dropped in his lap now, of all times. He doesn't know what's going to happen and how they'll react here if he fucks Shmueli. They all know him here, and they all owe him something. This one got a loan from him. With outrageous interest, but who else would have given it to him. And that one got a car for a week, or bags and bags of food for his mother's shiva, and Shmueli said it was "to honor that righteous woman."

And he will fuck him, that man everyone tiptoes around but also loves. He'll turn him over to those Tel Aviv guys because of what he did there, who even cares. His poor wife will stay in the town with the girls, and Shmueli will be in prison, and there might even be a war here. In the end they'll probably blame that little Russian girl, even after all he did to defuse the tension between the older residents and the new ones, and the Russians aren't even that new anymore. And they all get along. Looking at all the families on the lawns, he feels that he plays a large role in the community that has been created here. Because first of all, it's quiet here, thanks in large part to him, to the cameras he convinced the previous mayor to install. And although it's true that not everyone knows everyone else, the place is still small enough for him to persuade the majority.

His wife is the only one he doesn't know how to persuade.

Are you crazy? she screamed at him, aren't we happy enough the way things are now? Why do you need that headache? And she reminded him about his cousin, who burned up all her savings running for councilwoman, and after she lost, was left with debts. Besides, you think they'll all vote for you? she asked him and laughed. She apologized afterward, but he was hurt. She didn't know he could be hurt that way. And things haven't been right with them for two months since then. And nothing she does helps.

When Ashkenazi sees Shmueli's wife and daughters and her mother and sister, he walks over to them, and how are you, and what's happening. He asks where Shmueli is, casual like, for no real reason, and his wife replies, "In Tel Aviv, work, said not to wait for him with the meat and he hopes he'll be here for dessert."

Suddenly Ashkenazi doesn't really know what he's supposed to do with Shmueli when he sees him. Maybe the best thing is to call and tell him to come to the station when he's in town. To talk to him. Better in the station. Maybe record him.

"Happy holiday," he says and walks away, and Shmueli's wife looks at him, worried. He speaks to other families, but she's gotten the message. She takes out her phone, calls her husband, and says, "Don't come for dessert."

"Baby," he says, "it's work, don't start."

"Don't come. Forget it." She can't decide whether to tell him. And she doesn't feel like telling him anything ever. Let him start paying the price. But she can't. He's the father of her daughters. And if he goes to prison, she's the one who'll be left alone, like a dog.

"Ashkenazi was looking for you."

And she hangs up. She doesn't have the strength. For the last two years, she's seen it coming closer to him. The circle closing around him. And the end, when she's left all alone. Really alone. And today she realized that it might take a little longer, but that's it, the end. He's done for.

For the last few days, she's been hearing the whispers around her. Something's happened. Something big and bad. And all of a sudden, he's home. For almost the whole week of Passover vacation. Just phone calls. And tension. He doesn't go out, and he jumps every time the doorbell rings. The girls get on his nerves too quickly and they understand and go to their room and barely come out. And he didn't go to her sister-in-law's Mimouna last night. And after this whole week, today, of all days, when they have their family picnic, he went to Tel Aviv.

Ashkenazi turns to look at her and she sees something in his eyes. He's coming for Shmueli. It's clear to her.

And Shmueli knew why he left this morning.

◆ ◆ ◆

"Drop me here," Shmueli tells the driver.

"Cigarettes?" the driver asks him.

Shmueli gets out of the car and says, "Drive, give my wife the car. I'll come later."

"Boss, how will you get back?"

"Did I ask for your help? Go."

And he went. Shmueli feels the roll of bills in his pocket. It'll be enough for a few days. He needs to think about what's next. He walks along one of the streets that leads to the sea, feels the salty breeze, and sees the entrance to a sleazy hotel, three stars. He hasn't stayed in a place like that for a long time. He pays for three days up front. In cash.

"I need a credit card."

"I don't have one." Shmueli hands him two more two-hundred-shekel bills.

The guy gives him a key and says, "Room 304."

Shmueli takes the key and goes outside. He walks toward the sea, and like him, a few young couples and families are hurrying to the beach, all wearing light-colored, summery clothes, enjoying the recently arrived spring weather, their skin still white from the winter. He reaches the promenade, takes off his shoes, rolls up his pants. He sees himself through other people's eyes. A large, heavyset man, wearing dress pants and shirt. He reaches the shoreline, opens his phone and removes the SIM card, breaks the phone in half, and tosses it into the sea. And then Nina's mom's phone. It reminds him of the time before Rosh Hashanah when he went with his father to the traditional *tashlich*, a symbolic tossing of your sins into the sea, and his father told him that was the first time he actually went to the sea to perform that mitzvah. They were silent all the way home. And then his father said, "You don't need a lot, son. You don't need a lot. You always had big eyes. You don't need a lot."

But he didn't listen. Tears start falling now, behind the Armani glasses he bought in the mall not long ago for a price that only morons pay for plastic, just to see her gush over him, that snobby uptown teenage salesgirl with the white skin and overdone makeup who was trying to hide her age. Moron, he cursed himself, and kept muttering like a madman: You don't need a lot. You don't need a lot.

◆　◆　◆

Ilanit reaches Irina's apartment and knocks on the door. No answer. She walks around the building. Looks up at the window. Asks a few neighbors. "Yes, she lives here. Goes to work every day," one of the women says. "Cleaning houses or in the day-care center. Maybe both," she says. Ilanit asks when she saw her last. "Yesterday," the neighbor says. Ilanit takes out a card. "Tell her to call when she comes. Okay?"

"Don't get me mixed up in this," the neighbor says.

"I won't. Just give her the card."

◆　◆　◆

Irina gets home in the afternoon, lies down on the couch, and for the first time in a long while, falls asleep with a smile on her face.

In the evening, the neighbor knocks on her door and tells her that a policewoman was there. But Irina knows that Nina is all right. She asks the neighbor if she can use her phone, calls Ilanit, and says that everything's fine. Her daughter called. She didn't want to say where she was and didn't leave a number. Sorry for not letting you know. No, she doesn't know what happened with Shmueli. She hasn't seen him in a while, her daughter. And no, she's not planning to come back right now. If she calls again, she'll tell her to call Ilanit. Thank you. Thank you.

8

It takes Nina a minute to understand what's going on. A siren. Holocaust Remembrance Day. She turns off the faucet and stands in the kitchen, her hands wet, holding a scouring pad and a bottle of dish detergent. She tries to think about the wretched, starving children being led to their deaths, but she keeps seeing the image of all her friends standing at the school ceremony in their white shirts, and Moran singing like a nightingale. Nina had saved up her babysitting money for a year, filled out all the forms for financial assistance, and Irina ran herself into the ground working overtime to get the rest of the six thousand shekels for the trip to Poland, and in the end, she didn't go to Poland because that asshole said, "I'll take you to London, what do you need all that heavy stuff for?" And now she regrets it. When she saw all the pictures her friends posted on Instagram that showed them crying, bundled up in coats and placing flowers on the graves and monuments, and she read all the emotional texts, she knew she'd made a mistake. She and a few other kids who hadn't gone on the trip met in class because, like the principal said, "If you didn't go, that doesn't mean you're on vacation." Some of them were glad they hadn't gone, but Nina and a few others couldn't hide how upset they were that half the class wasn't there. She was so cut off that she didn't even ask the others why they didn't go, was it because they didn't have the money or because it meant nothing to them. That trip is something else that will never come back, another memory that has surfaced from all the ones that were swallowed up during those dark, crazy months he took from her. All the things that excited her then, the restaurants and presents and evenings with his pals and the smoking and the sex, it all seems so dirty now, and she doesn't understand what turned her on so much. Stop thinking about those things, there's a siren now, she tells herself, now you have to remember the six million.

◆ ◆ ◆

Last night, they sat on the boulevard, she and Eitan. Everything was closed. The city that never stops took a break in honor of Holocaust Day. For a few days, they'd been getting to know each other. Slowly, discovering a little something, then another little something. She still can't tell him everything, but at least she isn't lying anymore. She doesn't tell him the things that are hard for her to talk about. And he doesn't pressure her, lets her take her time. And she sees how he's putting together the puzzle of who she is from the little she tells him about her babushka, and her mom, and going to work with her mom. He's putting together the bits of information in his mind, but he still doesn't understand how she got here, and why Carmela, and why the break with her mom. And she tries to learn about him, but he laughs that there's nothing to learn. He's perfectly ordinary. And she laughs, because he isn't. He's so different in her eyes, talking about movies she never saw and singers she doesn't know, and he wants to show her so many things that are happening in the city, but they can go out only after Carmela has fallen asleep, and only sit on a bench on the boulevard in front of the house. She misses her mom so much. She calls her at the center early every morning. And thinks about how she can return to her.

If only she could turn back the clock. She's angry at herself as she begins to understand how she's ruined her life. All her friends are home knee-deep in matric exams, one exam after the other, coming down the home stretch, the last round of high school. That's where she should be now, in a white shirt at the ceremony, getting ready to complete her admission ticket to life with terrific grades. She keeps going over the past in her mind, re-creating the chain-reaction accident that had crushed her future and erased her past.

They touch each other gently, and that's exactly how she wants it. Slow. Holding hands. When he pushes her hair away from her face and she senses how scared he is to cross the line, he feels something he doesn't understand and she does, the fact that her body is still traumatized. And her soul. It's still hard for her. But she doesn't want to tell him. Doesn't want to dirty this relationship they are creating on the bench on the boulevard, amid the soot from the buses, with a tenderness that makes her realize even more how wrong and obscene everything was, and how her innocence was stolen from her.

◆ ◆ ◆

Suddenly, rising above the blaring siren, comes the sound of Carmela screaming and screaming and screaming, and Nina begins to run to her just as Carmela rushes out of her bedroom and attacks the front door, trying to open it, screaming, "Where's the key? Uri is waiting for me! He's waiting for me! Open it! Uri! I'm late. I forgot to go! My sweet boy. Wait for me! Mama is coming!"

Nina tries to hold her, but Carmela pushes her away, she's strong, frantic, desperate. Nina tries to calm her down. "You're not late for anything. Everything's fine. Everything's okay," and Carmela screams and Nina is helpless, and the phone suddenly rings, and Carmela bangs on the door and Nina pretends she's going to get the key, but she isn't, because this way, Carmela can't go out. In the other room, Nina puts her hands over her ears and Carmela keeps banging her fists on the door until her strength is gone, and the phone rings again, and all that noise is unbearable, and Nina starts to cry, realizing that she needs Irina. She needs her mother to come and help. This is too much for her. She can't. And Carmela crumples, exhausted, onto the floor near the door.

Nina goes to her and holds her. "What happened?"

"Memorial Day. Memorial Day. Everyone is there, I'm the only one who isn't there for my Uri. He's the only one who's alone. The only one. All alone."

"Today isn't Memorial Day," Nina tells her. "Grandma, it's Holocaust Remembrance Day. Holocaust Day."

"Really, dear? Really? You're not just saying that?"

"No, Grandma. It's Holocaust Day. Memorial Day is in another week. I'll remind you. You want me to come with you?"

"Of course you'll come with me. I want you to meet your uncle."

"I'll come."

"And you'll remind me?"

"I promise. We'll be there on time. I promise."

"I'm so afraid I'll miss it. He's waiting for me. I'm so afraid I'll forget. I don't remember anything anymore. What a pumpkin head. Empty." She hits her head hard, and Nina grabs her hands to stop her from hurting herself, and rubs her palms. Slowly, their tears begin to fall.

"I won't let you forget. And I'll come with you. Always."

"And when I'm gone?"

"Even then, I'll go to be with Uncle Uri. Always." That was the first time she'd said his name.

"You promise?" Carmela looks at her with glistening eyes.

"I promise," Nina says, and swears to herself that she will. That's what she'll do. Every year, she'll go. It doesn't matter how this crazy adventure ends. From now on, he will be her fallen soldier. Forever.

◆ ◆ ◆

"You'll win the employee-of-the-year award," says Oren, the driver of the first bus in the morning. Today too, she's the only passenger. It's just the two of them. Everyone else is just waking up. She always gets to the center before the others, but for the last few days, she has been in more of a hurry because Nina calls the center early every morning and they talk. Irina checks, and for the last two days, she's been sure that her shadow isn't following her anymore. It's as if none of it ever happened. No one asks her about Nina. No one waits for her at the end of the day. No one asks her how come she has no phone or why she doesn't answer their calls. Only Michal sent her son to tell her that it can't go on like this, and since then, she's been checking on her every day. Insisting that she come for tea when she gets home from work. To chat a little. At first only Michal chatted. And Irina was silent. Michal was worried about Nina, and Irina finally told her not to worry, Nina's fine. Michal practically jumped out of her chair and had a million questions, but Irina told her she mustn't talk about it. Michal hugged her tight, and since then, they don't talk about it.

Only one thing disturbed that silence, when that policewoman came to the center to ask her if she'd heard anything. The kids were really excited to see a policewoman there and told their parents about it, who all asked Shoshi why a policewoman had come to the center. Shoshi said she asked her to come because she had some questions about the distress alarm. The parents began to talk about cameras, look at all those stories on the news about kindergarten kids being abused by their teachers, and the committee called for a parents' meeting to discuss the subject.

Shoshi hadn't been that angry in a long time. Not at poor Irina, who carried all the sorrow of the world on her shoulders along with her concern for her daughter, but at the policewoman. On the way home, she stopped at the police station, went into Ashkenazi's office, and shouted, "You don't come to the center just like that. It upsets the children and the parents. If you have a problem, you can call and discuss it with me." Ashkenazi told her to calm down, they're trying to find out where Irina's daughter is. And Shoshi said angrily, "She's been gone almost a month and all of a sudden you woke up? It's about time, but can you please not bring it to the center? Now the whole city is trying to figure out what happened, and Irina feels uncomfortable about it too."

Ashkenazi apologized, but it was too late.

One of the children said that the policewoman was looking for Irina, and gradually, people began to connect Shmueli's disappearance and Nina's, her girlfriends talked about the relationship and the story became the talk of the town.

Irina couldn't bear all the whispering going on behind her back, as if she were deaf, and asked Shoshi if she could have a few days off. Shoshi agreed happily. She liked Irina, but the gossip about criminals and police was hurting the center's good name.

It wasn't until the end of the day that Shoshi asked her, "Is she okay?"

Irina smiled and said, "Yes, thank God. I was starting to think I was dying."

"She'll come back? Soon?"

"I don't know. She . . . it's complicated," Irina said.

If Nina came back now, everyone would gossip about her constantly, Shoshi thought, he has destroyed her reputation. Totally. But Irina can't live without her. It would be good for her to take a few days off. Maybe she'll go to see her.

"It's just that she's missing her exams—it's such a shame," Irina said sorrowfully.

◆ ◆ ◆

"You have to come back, Ninotchka," she tells her. "Isn't it a shame about your exams?" And Nina says, "Mom, it's complicated. Let it go. It's complicated." In the end, Irina asks her if she's pregnant, because that is absolutely out of the question, and that's why she's going to see her. Because she won't let that happen. She won't let Nina screw up her life completely. She touches the letter in her pocket. The draft notice. She has read it, she couldn't control herself one night and opened the envelope. She didn't care that Nina would yell at her. She'd tell her it happened when she didn't know where she was. They were sending her to train as a teacher. She knew that's what Nina wanted. That it was something good. And important. And every time Irina is sad about the matriculation exams, she tells herself that it's the lesser of two evils. The main thing is that this whole mess and that man are out of their lives. That Nina is talking to her again.

◆ ◆ ◆

Two days ago, they came in the evening, Ashkenazi and the policewoman, and asked her a lot of questions. Irina kept answering that she didn't know, she didn't know. And every time she didn't want to answer, Ashkenazi said, "You want to come to the station?" and she got tired. The truth was she really didn't have anything more to tell them. Because she didn't know where Nina was. They asked to see her phone, and she told them that he had it.

"Who has it?"

"He does. His friends. I don't know."

The next day they showed pictures of Shmueli on the news and in the papers. The police request the assistance of the public. And that did it. That's what everyone was talking about here. And she is so eager to know why they were looking for him. What did he do? And maybe he's just missing?

She didn't ask anyone anything, knowing that whatever she asked, they would say that she asked. She always knew how to make herself inconspicuous, but during those days, she managed to make herself invisible. The parents in the center would talk about her, never noticing she was right there.

Gradually, she began to realize that it had to do with something more serious. That they had some kind of break in the investigation in Tel Aviv, something to do with DNA they found at the scene. And they started talking. It was connected to a murder that took place at the Tel Aviv Central Bus Station a while ago, and they found a witness who agreed to talk to them. They didn't talk about it a lot on the news, the murder of some filthy pimp at the bus station is not a big story, but here in town, it was the only thing they talked about. The mothers in the center said that Shmueli's chubby little daughters haven't left the house and his wife cries constantly. Why is this happening to her, why, she cries in her one-hundred-square-meter living room with the Natuzzi furniture and the huge chandelier. All that luxury didn't bother her, she didn't throw out what he bought her, of course not. But now she's crying that they didn't need all that. How much blood was spilled, how many women's lives were ruined for that dirty money. And no matter how much the house is cleaned, it will always be filthy.

❖   ❖   ❖

"Where are they?" Ashkenazi asked her.

"I don't know. I told you, I don't know."

"Where is she? I have to talk to her. You can be mad at us, but we're trying to help you and your daughter."

Irina told him she had nothing to hide. And he shouldn't act like that to a woman whose daughter was kidnapped, and the police didn't protect her, and no one listened to her.

"I listened," Ilanit said.

"But you didn't help me. So I don't want to help you. I don't trust you."

"What's her phone number? And where's your phone?"

"I don't have one," Irina said, knowing it sounds so stupid that she doesn't have a phone. It's true that, for a few days already, that shadow hasn't been following her, but she's sure that everyone in the town would snitch on her if she bought a phone and they would know the number. She has to go to Beersheba, to the central bus station, where no one knows her. Or she'll buy one in Tel Aviv. The kind of phone no one can use to find her.

"He took my phone and I was afraid to buy a new one," Irina told them. "I'll buy one."

"And you'll give the number to Ilanit, okay?"

"Okay."

"You understand that he can take her hostage? He can hurt her, if he's desperate enough."

Irina understood how dangerous it all was, and what a mess Nina had gotten herself into. *Kibinimat*, damn her, she'll give her one hell of a slap. It's a good thing she ran away from him.

Ashkenazi stared at her without saying anything. Ilanit was afraid that in another minute, he would explode at this woman.

But instead, he leaned forward and looked her right in the eye. For a long time.

"She's not with him," he suddenly said to Ilanit.

Irina shook her head in shock at how he read her mind. "It's true. She's not with him. She ran away from him."

Ilanit knew she would remember that moment all her life. The moment she saw the difference between just another cop and a genuine detective.

"She's not stupid, your little girl," Ashkenazi said. "I understand from a lot of people that she's not stupid."

"She went with that piece of garbage. She's as stupid as can be. And I told her. It happened because she went with that piece of garbage."

"Tell me what we can do to help you."

"Nothing."

"When did she run away from him?"

"The day before the Seder night."

"Thank you. That's what I needed to know. Let me see your passport and hers." Irina brought them to him. They had expired a few years ago. Ukrainian passports. He handed them to Ilanit to photograph.

"You're not to leave the country. Is that clear?"

"Yes."

"Listen, I believe you. You don't know where he is. And you don't know where she is. I know you're angry at us, but for no reason. Ilanit did the right thing. She'll give you her cell number. If there's a problem, tell her."

Irina knows this is the last day, tomorrow she'll go to Nina. That's it. She has decided. And she'll tell her that today.

◆ ◆ ◆

Itamar opens the Israeli news app. When he first got here, he was addicted to it, opened it many times a day to check what was happening in Israel. He hasn't done that in a long time. He opens it only rarely to read the financial papers, to see what's happening in the Israeli market, whether there's any potential competition for them in the big data area, but he doesn't read the news. From here, it all seems so crazy. Not allowing *chametz* in hospitals during Passover, rockets from Gaza and Israeli retaliation bombings, the rising cost of living, political incitement. The struggle over fake news. Here in Trump's America, violence and aggression are also escalating from day to day. But here, it isn't his. And the more difficult things become here, the more removed he is. He opens the app now to see what's happening, because he'll be traveling to Israel soon. And it hits him right away. The funeral of a soldier killed in a terrorist attack. The pictures of the funeral summon up images from Uri's funeral. Carmela silent. Like the stone that would later cover Uri. She only cried silently. Soundlessly. But Itzik wailed for both of them. For the three of them. Because he couldn't wail either. He didn't understand. He hadn't taken it in yet. And he was angry at himself for that. And wept quietly. All he knew was that everything would be different from now on, but he didn't understand how much. How could he understand that what had been would never be again. Ever. Itamar looks at the pictures of the grieving family standing around the grave, and he knows that they still don't know. They don't know that there will never be joy without pain, that there will never be a really happy holiday. Or a Sabbath without heartache. And that the overwhelming sadness will be forever and ever. A few months ago, they brought some guru to hold a workshop for the employees here, and he talked to them about serenity and mindfulness, told them how to breathe and focus, to fall asleep more easily, and how they should be happy, enjoy what is good in their lives. He wanted to tell that guru that it was only here, far from home, that he dared to be happy, because it hurt too much to be happy there. But he understands now that, with time, it has become just the opposite. Being here is always like picking at the wound. Always paying the price. You went away. Abandoned them. Left them alone. Left her alone. She would never abandon you.

◆ ◆ ◆

Now the headlines appear on the app. Holocaust Remembrance Day. A memorial candle. Remember and never forget. The week he hates is starting, the week in which the days crawl by with quiet, painful slowness from Holocaust Day to Memorial Day. Days on which flags begin to appear on streets and bridges and all the office buildings. Suddenly everyone is patriotic. After an entire year of cursing, hating, and sowing dissension, suddenly Israelis are united, there are official speeches, children sell flags at intersections, and everyone is so proud of their strong, heroic country. But wandering around in his home were two shadows of people who had paid the price for that festival of flags, the price of power, two people on whom a blanket of darkness had descended, and the windows in the house were closed, and the color had drained from their faces. If they spoke, it was in whispers. The silence during those days suffocated him. And those flags. Counting down yet another night of Carmela weeping until Memorial Day.

He has to find someone to be with Carmela so at least she won't be so alone. Waiting from one Memorial Day to the next. As if Uri's gravestone cares whether someone comes to run their hands over it. Stone. And she doesn't really care about what's happening to him

at work, she can't even manage to fake an interest or try to understand what he does, not to mention the kids. Every once in a while,
he makes them talk to her on Sunday morning, the only normal time
to call her, and they're not in school. But that already seems pointless
as well. He emails her pictures of them, but he doesn't think she even
opens them. He has to teach her how to master the smartphone. If
she had a caregiver, she would also help her with that way of com-
municating. She loved Dana so much when she was little. How much
light she brought into both their lives, she even stole Itzik's heart.
After Uri, the only time they were happy was after Dana was born.

It's good that he's going to see her. Even Naama understands. He's
really cutting it close with the connection, the travel agent told him
that too, but he'll have his boarding pass, so he should definitely have
enough time. If only nothing unexpected happens at the airport.

He doesn't even have anyone he can tell that today is Holocaust
Day and his dreaded week is starting. His family's dreaded week.
There's an abyss between his old family, Carmela and Itzik and Uri,
and his new one. Family before everything, but what is this family, which
is nothing like the one he grew up in, where it was one for all and all
for one. This doesn't feel like a family. More like the fragments of
something. A communal settlement. Communal sleeping. And Itamar
needs to figure out how to deal with it. He wants a family like the
ones in Israel. Where everyone fights for everyone else.

It's good that he's flying there in another few days.

◆ ◆ ◆

Ever since the TV news reported last night that the police were looking
for Johnny Shmueli, the entire town has been up in arms. Ashkenazi is
glad he isn't the person who has to make the arrest. Shmueli left town
before national headquarters issued the warrant.

"You're sure he's not hiding out there?" asked Danieli, the detective who had been at the station.

"As sure as you are about who's on the line in your office and recording me," Ashkenazi said, knowing that the detective was thinking to himself that you don't see professionals like him on the force these days.

"Absolutely recording. Roni, say hello to Ashkenazi."

"Hello."

Now let them look for Shmueli, Ashkenazi thinks to himself with a smile. He's been eating his heart out since the detectives' visit. If he hadn't missed Shmueli by a couple of hours, he could have made the arrest of his life. But in the evening, sitting with his wife for their regular end-of-day ritual of tea and the cookies that keep his potbelly from disappearing, she said something smart that calmed him down. It's better this way, she said. After the five minutes of fame and glory, it could have developed into a big mess. He would have gotten into hot water with half the town. After hours of suffering because his name and picture would not appear on the TV news or the front page of the newspapers, he realized that it wouldn't have made the headlines anyway; after all, this was only about a dispute between scumbags in a backwater town. He'd been through enough in life to know that it really wouldn't have affected his career in the police. He used to dream about the big arrest and the TV cameras filming him, imagined being called to fill a position in Tel Aviv, but today he knows that at his age, that doesn't happen. At most, another letter of commendation to hang on the wall. So the loss wasn't great. The only thing he cares about now is becoming mayor. Elections are in three and a half years, and this time, he'll go for it. If he had arrested Shmueli, he could never be elected. They would hate him here. All the families around Shmueli who depended on him. The ones who worked for him, his own family, all the people he gave loans and help to, the ones he pulled strings for when they asked him to. It's a good thing he didn't make the arrest. He wasn't about to become chief of police anyway. It strikes him funny that, until not long ago, he believed he could climb from the bottom all the way to the top. But he sees how they bring people from outside to run the police. As if there isn't a single good cop who could be chief. They bring them from the army. From the security services. They even bring in civilians. As long as it's not someone in uniform. But why? It breaks their spirit. Apart from that, it's the glass ceiling for a local cop from the boondocks. That's how it is if you're not a hotshot detective from national headquarters. That's why he decided to go into local politics. And ever since, it's all he cares about. That's why not arresting Shmueli isn't a problem. Just the opposite. The two of them have been playing this game for years. Each one protecting his turf. And his opponent's reputation. That's the most important part of the delicate balance that keeps the town running. It's also the reason he and Shmueli reached an agreement after that business with Sasson's poor son, who approached Shmueli the wrong way and lost an eye. The entire town was on the verge of exploding. And right before there was an honor killing here—even though there's nothing honorable about killing—and right before two families ended up in prison—there's definitely nothing honorable about that—and most important, before the young people here were dragged into crime—they came to an agreement. An agreement that was signed with lots of backslapping, handshaking, and arm punching, without words, because everybody records these days and you can't trust anyone. They agreed that not here. That he wouldn't touch people whose families lived in town. And they both promised to make sure things were quiet here. And if people came into town from the surrounding villages, he would be informed immediately. Gradually, people began to feel that they were in the safest place in the southern district because they would come down hard on anyone who violated the agreement. When one of Shmueli's soldiers beat his wife and nothing helped, Ashkenazi didn't turn a blind eye. The guy was on parole after having been in prison for committing violent acts and he pleaded with Ashkenazi to look the other way so he wouldn't have to go back inside for five years, but Ashkenazi refused. And no matter how hard Shmueli tried, he knew there was no chance.

When he was a child, Ashkenazi saw his father hit his mother. That's what made him decide, at a young age, to be a policeman, to protect his mother, because she was his whole world. And then the day came, when he was in middle school, and stood between them when his father raised his hand to her again. His father tried to hit him, and Ashkenazi said, "Hit me. Come on. Let's see what a big man you are. Come on, do it."

And that was it, his father never showed his face in town again. Because everyone was talking about it. About the boy who disrespected his father, but he deserved it. Because you don't hit the mother of your children. That's not what a real man does. No. Only someone who's not a real man beats his wife. Be unfaithful, disappear, ignore her, curse her, but don't raise a hand to her.

Since then, no one crossed Ashkenazi anymore. Right after the army, he joined the force, and moved up the ladder pretty quickly.

◆ ◆ ◆

Ashkenazi is uneasy. He's worried about the girl. He was slightly reassured when her mom said she wasn't with Shmueli, but he's still trying to figure out where she is and what happened to her. The mother seemed frightened when he told her that detectives from Tel Aviv insist on calling Nina to give testimony.

252

"Never," Irina said.

"What?"

"She'll never talk to you if, because of her, he goes to prison. She won't have a life after that. Leave her alone. Enough. She's been punished already."

Ashkenazi can't blame her. That's what he would tell his daughter to do. And that makes him sad. He, a police chief responsible for upholding the law, knows very well that they can't always protect someone who testifies against a criminal like Shmueli. The truth is that he doesn't understand him. Johnny Shmueli hasn't needed that kind of nickel-and-dime stuff for a long time. Not since he succeeded in getting the mall at the entrance to the town built on his property and not in the shopping center, even though they had to build a bypass. The previous mayor thought a bypass was a waste of public funds, and that's why he isn't the mayor anymore. His opponent had no problem with the bypass, and he's now in his second term. And the mall is thriving, no one remembers what it was like here before and how they ever managed to live without it, except for the business owners in the older shopping center. Jacobi's son from the clothing store once dared to yell at Shmueli because of the damage done to his parents. Everyone was sure Shmueli would do a number on him, but Shmueli said to him, with surprising patience, "Bro, your parents worked hard enough, and we all bought in their store all these years. So tell me, how many times did they let someone get away with paying even a shekel less than the price?"

Jacobi's son apologized immediately, but it didn't help. Two days later, he was found in Eilat, beaten half to death, and no one knew who did it. Every year, his parents took a bus to spend Passover with their son. And they never told anyone exactly where he lived. It wasn't until old Jacobi died that the son came back to town for the first time.

Everyone was tense at the funeral, but Shmueli came and hugged Jacobi's son, who cried harder with joy about Shmueli forgiving him than with grief about his father. After that, he used to come to visit his mother. And a few years later, he came to live with her.

◆ ◆ ◆

Eitan hugs her. She puts her head on his shoulder and feels her body thaw, and her muscles, stiff and tight after weeks of tension, soften like bread crust in hot, homemade soup. In the arms of a guy who knows nothing about her, not who she is, where she comes from, or even her surname, but she feels as if he knows everything. Everything that's important. Everything that's true. Who looks into her eyes, and sees her heart, and she trusts him. His kindness and gentleness. She knows he will never hurt her. That he loves her for who she is, for who she really is. And doesn't want to take what so many wanted to take from her, and she doesn't want to take anything from him, she wants only this, the two of them here on the bench on the boulevard that is their whole world, a world made up of just the two of them and the little treats he brings from the minimart. Today he brought a new pink floor-washing bucket filled with ice and a bottle of white wine, and he didn't even forget an opener or bags of Bamba and potato chips. He has made a party for them. And yesterday, he brought Coke and chewy mint candies, and they checked out what really happens when you mix them together. The combination made the Coke fizz up like champagne, and they laughed. It was on that bench, so exposed to everyone, that they created the greatest intimacy, as if the entire world couldn't see.

"Am I the cheapest date you ever had?" she asked with a laugh.

"You're the first date I've ever taken a floor-washing bucket to, that's for sure."

And they talk about everything and nothing.

Now Nina is melting in his arms, and he runs a finger gently along the back of her neck after he moves her hair away, and the tenderness of his touch seems to heal her wounds slowly, restore her trust and serenity, blunting the thorns that surrounded her, that she sprouted to defend and protect herself.

How far away from the you-scratch-my-back-and-I'll-scratch-yours world she grew up in, from the hideous distortion of what she thought was love and turned out to be a dark game of power, money, and sex. That's what her mom tried to tell her, that it's not real, it's not what love is, but she didn't believe that that asshole was playing her, using her. That she was far from running the game, far from understanding the rules. Now she doesn't want to go back there, doesn't want to remember it, she wants to be only here and now. She doesn't want Eitan to stop, to move away. She breathes in the heat of his body that strengthens her, restores her. Makes her feel safe after weeks of fleeing, of being terrified.

And the smell of his shirt is so pleasant.

"What kind of softener?" she asks.

He laughs and says, "The expensive kind."

"Wow," she says. "You went for the best."

"You're the best."

"You don't know anything."

"I know what I need to know."

"Maybe the day after tomorrow or in another few days we can really go out," she says.

"What, really? Not just to the bench?!" He practically jumps with excitement and kisses her throat and her forehead. Then she cups his face in her hands and kisses him on the lips. A small kiss. And it's so gentle and lovely. She pushes away the memory of Shmueli's rough bristles and the taste of cigarettes he always had, and rests her head on Eitan's chest again.

"I want to take you to the beach so much," he says.

The beach that lay at the end of the boulevard, the backdrop of his youth. The place his classmates went to, some of them carrying surfboards, their hair burned from the sun, and he didn't surf with them, but mostly went alone. When he was happy or sad. When it was cold or hot. A child of the beach. He hasn't gone there often enough since the army. Only when he has to think. He can't imagine her sunburned, or in a bathing suit, he can only imagine the two of them at night, darkness on the sea, the city lights behind them. And they're barefoot in the sand. In another two or three days.

"People might even think we're homeless," she says after someone passes by and makes a "don't-you-have-a-home" face.

"I have no problem living with you here on a bench."

"Don't say such nice things," she says. "I don't know what to do with them."

"You can say you feel the same way."

"Someone has to look after Carmela," she says.

"I will."

"That won't be simple."

"It won't be so complicated either."

And she thinks about how good is so simple, so clear. How bad is so complicated and convoluted, how it suffocates you in the web in spins. And how good makes things easy and opens your heart.

He takes the wine out of the pink bucket and fills her plastic cup.

They make a toast, *"L'chaim."* To life. A guy walking his dog looks at them and smiles. And Nina blushes.

Eitan asks him if he wants some wine and hands him a cup. The guy takes it, raises it in the air, and says, *"L'chaim* to both of you."

◆ ◆ ◆

Irina stands and looks around the small apartment, trying to think whether she's forgotten anything. Over the last few days, she managed to sneak some empty boxes from the garbage room into the apartment. She filled them with Nina's things and things of her own that she wanted to keep.

It was surprising to see how little they had, only what they really needed. There are so few things she wanted to keep. She'd given two boxes with the important things to Michal yesterday, and thank God, she was smart enough not to ask any questions. She put three more boxes, with things no one needed but her, books in Russian, glasses, Nina's clothes, in the storeroom on their floor. Even if she never came back and someone took them, it wouldn't be a great loss.

Sixteen years packed into two boxes she left with her neighbor, she thinks to herself. Albums of pictures of Nina when she was little. Certificates of excellence. They weren't just things, they were evidence. Evidence that there once was a grandmother and a mother and a daughter who survived, who loved. Tomorrow morning she'll go to work like she does every day, and even if that shadow follows her—although he hasn't been around for a few days—even if he looks at her, he won't suspect.

He won't suspect that she's leaving this place and hopes she'll never return. There's only one thing she keeps making sure she has, the letter from the army, the draft notice.

It's not clear to her what will happen with Nina's matriculation exams, and worrying about it keeps her awake at night now that she's missed them. How much time they both invested in them, how they struggled with English pronunciation, how Irina got angry at her when she gave up and took an easier math course that would give her fewer credits. She won't let Nina mess herself up in the army too.

She pays her last month's rent. She never misses paying on the first. After transferring the money, she empties her bank account. They'll start all over again somewhere else. With different names.

The police, Ilanit and Ashkenazi, tried to question her again, they even brought her to the station and photographed her, probably so they would have proof that she wouldn't talk, because they had already stopped pressuring her. And she just looked at them and the camera and finally said, "That girl is the only thing I have in the world. I won't say anything."

❖ ❖ ❖

She gets on the bus. She deliberately doesn't take the first one, choosing to get on a bus with a driver who isn't Oren, a driver who doesn't know her. Who won't ask her why she isn't getting off at the center. Why she's continuing on to the bus station. As the bus passes the center, she remembers how, a few days ago, when the Holocaust Day siren sounded, the whole staff in the center stood at attention, and the little ones didn't understand what was happening. They came to her for a hug, and when little Bat-El burst into tears, she picked her up, and with the child in her arms, didn't move from where she was standing. The touch of those tiny hands was so lovely. Maybe she should have had another girl. But she hadn't had the strength. Images of the first time she came to this place, which seemed like the end of the world, return to her mind. She and her baby girl. And how she brought Babushka here. At the bus station, she asked again and again for them to check the note they'd given her at the absorption center so she would be sure to get on the right bus. And when she saw this town, which looked abandoned at first, she asked the driver if it was really the right place. And now she's leaving it like a thief in the night. Without anything. Without knowing if she would ever return.

Her eyes fill with tears. It's finally happening, she's going to her Nina. Nina, who is her place in the world, and her home and her family.

"There's a minimart," Nina told her when she gave her the address, "on the corner of Nordau Boulevard in Tel Aviv. Look across the street from the minimart and you'll see a really ugly old building with a large, beautiful tree at the entrance. It's there, on the second floor. Don't go up. Wait on the bench and I'll come."

She clutches her handbag, pressing it hard against her stomach. Against the money belt she keeps checking. She has never carried so much money. All the money she has in the world, and Nina's letter from the army. She doesn't need anything else. Only to finally see her. To hold her. She still has to give her the hardest slap of her life. But she knows she'll only hug her. Her heart aches from missing her. And so does the rest of her body.

◆　◆　◆

The voices wake Shmueli. The moans coming through the thin wall that separates his room from the adjacent one in the seedy hotel he's been holed up in for a few days now. He doesn't know how much longer it will go on. He thought, that's it, no one's interested in him anymore, but two days ago, he turned on the TV and saw his face spread across the screen. "The police are asking for the assistance of the public." It's a good thing he hasn't shaved for the past few days, and now he almost has a beard. It itches. He checks the Internet all the time, sees a few small items, reads about what they're saying on a police Facebook page.

The girl in the next room is making so much noise. "*Yalla*, come already," he mutters to himself. Let a person sleep.

259

For the last year, he's known he was walking a thin line. Too thin for such an overweight guy who has trouble breathing from all the cigarettes. All the warning lights started flashing a long time ago. His organization grew quickly. Yes, he was a big fish, but for the last two years, he's been swimming in a shark tank. And that was a mistake. He should have stopped a long time ago, settled for his earnings from the mall, which finally started making a profit. But he had to show everyone that he's conquered the big city. Had to prove himself to all his fans. But it was more than he could handle. He knew that. He wasn't the right age anymore, and he didn't have the courage, and he had too much to lose. And when you're afraid, you can't really succeed. And like everyone who's nearing the end, he went too far. With the girls, with the drugs, with the lies at home, with the people he allowed to get close to him.

Everyone thinks it won't happen to them. Every criminal says he'll retire before it happens. It's like thinking that someone will leave the casino table when he has a pile of money and his luck is running high. You never see when you're going to lose it, that slippery thing that can't be explained. There are people who have it, that thing you can't explain, that makes others listen to you. You have charisma, someone once told him, and he fell in love with the word. And he did have it. His whole life. For good and for bad. Teachers got angry at him even when he was behaving himself, and wanted him out of their class even when he sat quietly, because there was always a buzz around him. He was the center of things everywhere, and something in him made people do his bidding. He used to ask himself what it was that made them listen to him, follow him, but in the end, he realized he would never know. Even his father looked at him admiringly. His quiet father. His timid father. Who worked in a factory and didn't want too much. And as soon as he made some money, he bought things for them, gave them some cash, and they would tell him he didn't have to, just take care of yourself, you have to start a family, and they would give it to his sister, thinking he didn't know, but he didn't care that she was getting a little, she deserved it, the poor thing. He didn't believe anyone would want her, because she was the type no one ever saw, no one ever noticed. Whenever she told people she was his sister, they were surprised, not only that he had a sister, but also that it was her. But in the end, she found Kobi and they have a good life together, along with their two sons.

◆ ◆ ◆

Shmueli looks at his watch and feels like he has to go out for some air. For an hour. He's going crazy. Before the sun rises and the city starts to wake up. That woman's moaning is driving him up the wall. Once it used to turn him on, but now he doesn't even try to touch himself. The tension is killing him. At least he's keeping the diet he decided to start. He's even doing push-ups and sit-ups in the space he made by shoving the bed aside. Like in a prison cell. He laughs at himself without thinking it's funny, realizing that he's not far away from that. He hasn't exercised in years, and with every push-up, he understands how weak he has become. Only his money was strong. Now he's here, without all the swaggering and the hangers-on, just a man with a potbelly trying to sleep while some woman in the next room is moaning, and he can't even yell for her to shut up. And suddenly, she shuts up. Finally. But he can't fall asleep anymore. He gets up, brushes his teeth, puts on a hat, and goes out, wearing the flip-flops he bought at a street stand.

Out on the street, the end-of-night air feels good. The sun is starting to rise. He turns toward the boulevard. A homeless guy is sleeping on the street, and two women are out on their morning run. He doesn't have much time, he'll have to go back soon. He'll buy himself a few things. He sees a minimart and goes in. He feels like grabbing bags and bags of potato chips and cookies, but all he takes is a container of low-fat cheese and some pita bread. And some vegetables and apples. Health. He laughs to himself and adds a bottle of vodka. He goes to the cash register and is careful not to make eye contact.

"I can't sell you vodka now," the cashier says. "Not until six in the morning."

"And beer?"

"No."

"Okay," he says, thinking that once, he would have argued.

"Come back in fifteen minutes, if you want to."

"Thanks," he says, taking a Diet Coke.

He sits down on a bench on the boulevard. Watches the big city begin to wake up. He needs to go back to his hideout.

You asshole, he mutters to himself, thinking about his wife and daughters, knowing he's fucked up their lives. And his own. Maybe tomorrow he'll take a bus to Eilat. He has to disappear. From there he'll find a way to get to Jordan. Maybe the Sinai. Otherwise, he's finished. Finished. He definitely fucked up. He shouldn't be walking around outside. But he hasn't been out of his room for three days, he's suffocating, he needs air. Light. He lights a cigarette. The groceries he bought in the minimart are sitting on the bench beside him, the hat covers most of his face, the rest is hidden by his sunglasses and beard. He thinks the cashier stared at him and saw something in his eyes when he took off the sunglasses. But he doesn't care. She has no idea where he lives and she has no way of calling the police on him. She wouldn't call them anyway. That's how it is, the Russians don't call the police on someone. He knows he has to lock himself in the room again. Someone might recognize him and that will be the end of him.

262

◆ ◆ ◆

He looks at his watch, tries to decide whether to wait a few minutes or stop at a kiosk on the way. That cashier creeped him out. Russian women do that to him. Make him feel that he isn't good enough. That they're better than him. That's why he's crazy about them.

He thinks about Nina. Remembers how wild he was about that girl in the beginning, addicted to her scent and her touch. And look at what he did to her. He remembered that night, the way she looked at him like a hungry cat someone had spilled water on. And now it's all turned around, his fate is in her hands. And suddenly it seems so sick, so senseless to him. The way no one stopped him. The way they all kept quiet out of fear. And the way he destroyed her. Who is this man he's become, when did he lose his soul? And why didn't he think about his family? Maybe he deserves what's happened to him. He feels like screaming.

He remembers how he was beaten that night he was in jail, when they suspected he'd stolen a car. He'd just gotten out of the army, Ashkenazi was the one who suspected him and put him in a jail cell at the station, that's when they met. He actually seemed pretty okay. But then they came from the Beersheba station and took him to be interrogated, and there was this asshole in the jail there. When his mother saw what he looked like when he got out, she cried for a week. And he swore that never again. Never. He'd been careful ever since. And when things got a little sticky, he immediately called Yafit, the criminal lawyer who once worked in the prosecutor's office, before she became a blond. She taught him a lot about life. No one believes how smart she is. And the cops always make the mistake of underestimating her because of the high heels and fake nails. And he's crazy about her. She's so smart that she didn't even let him start to flirt with her.

The best thing would be to go to Eilat alone, quietly, to think. But he has no way of getting a car. And that bus takes too many hours and has too many people on it. Maybe a taxi. He'll take a taxi to Eilat. A driver who won't talk. He has to get the hell out of here. He has to. He won't survive prison. And if they catch him, he's going inside for a lot of years. A whole lot of years.

❖ ❖ ❖

He really fucked it all up. And for what? For some whore Leonid fell for so hard that he decided to take her away from the shit they'd dumped her in. He didn't really care, but the young guys who have such bloated egos that they call themselves his soldiers, who spend all their time keeping track of how much people respect them and him and the shithole they all came from, as if it were the center of the world—they told him, "He's making a fool of you," after Leonid took her in and turned her into someone who would take good care of him. As if anyone cared, as if he cared, as if the fact that Leonid's whore was now a saint who lit candles on Friday night would make a difference. That whole market had changed over the last few years. There was no money in it. All the big shots left the whore business and went into drugs, weapons, smuggling, bringing in construction workers from Romania. They left that garbage to bottom feeders like him. And he, like a moron, as if he didn't have enough money, went into the business so he would have something in the big city. So those kids could show off, could strut around Tel Aviv as if they worked for Al Capone, at the least. And now she's singing to the cops, they must have promised her a ticket to wherever she wanted to go, as if in that place, whatever it was called, she wouldn't spread her legs again and dream for years about Leonid, who was hers more than she even realized.

◆ ◆ ◆

And he remembers that fucked-up day before the Seder night, when they got to the apartment and Nina was sitting at that pathetic table she'd decorated with two pieces of matzo, how she smiled that hungry-for-love smile at him when he walked in, and then the others came in and started horsing around, and her expression turned into the saddest one there is. Suddenly, he felt a little sorry for her and he went over to her and she started with that anger because some people get their sadness and anger mixed up. He took her into the bedroom to calm her down, and because she was still angry, he got pissed off at her, so he tried to undress her, but she was wasted, maybe she'd been drinking or smoking. She was like a corpse when he pulled up her mini and tore her panties and stuck it in her, and that's when those kids barged in and the skinny one told him they had to go, there's a fuckup, and they all saw her lying under him. He pulled out of her and left her crying quietly and trying to cover herself with that tiny mini. He'd humiliated lots of girls, but never like that. Never like that, in front of people who grew up with her, who knew her from the neighborhood, from school. Who knew her mom. They were always women who played the game with him. Nina was different. A good girl he really felt something for. Until he turned her into a piece of crap you could fuck even while everyone was watching. Because he felt bad about it, he told her to come out for a ride with them. He thought he would make it up to her. And the skinny kid pushed her into the car because he didn't want any delays. If only they had delayed all of it. If only he'd stayed in the apartment with her, with the matzos and the wine. Wiped away her tears. He deserves it, everything that happened to him afterward. He deserves it. How did he become such a scumbag?

He looks at his watch and thinks about how much money he spent on it. Idiot. According to the time, he's been sitting here much too long. The city is starting to wake up. People are leaving for work, buses are pulling into stops. He gets up from the bench and starts walking toward his hotel.

◆　◆　◆

Nina wakes up when she hears Carmela go out on her daily trek to get the newspaper and even when she hears her come back, she can't fall asleep, she's too excited. She gets up and looks out the large window at the boulevard and the bench across from the minimart, hoping she described it well enough to Irina. She kept making calculations all night, how long will it take the bus to reach Beersheba, and from there to Tel Aviv, and until Irina finds the right bus from the Central Bus Station to here, to her. It'll take her another few hours. She probably didn't leave too long ago.

Of course Irina isn't there yet. Someone is sitting on the bench with his back to her. She goes into the kitchen for a Diet Coke. And then it suddenly hits her, like a flash of lightning—but it can't be. She runs back to the window to look at the man who was sitting there with his back to her. He's already gotten up from the bench and Nina sees him walking away toward the sea. Despite his weird clothes and the hat, something about the way he walks reminds her. She laughs, it doesn't make any sense. It can't be. He's thinner than Shmueli, but something about the way he carries his body is so familiar. She panics. It's him. He's here. That shit is here. She wants to run downstairs and look him in the face, grab him and scream, and she runs to the door, then goes back to the window, runs to the door again, but stops because she knows it's dumb. For him to know where she is. And it's definitely not him. Maybe she should call the police. But then they'll ask questions, and she doesn't want to be involved, she wants to leave all that behind her. Because if he thinks she's the snitch, even if he's behind bars, he'll send people to take his revenge. She can't be part of it. But what about saving other girls? she asks herself. She moves away from the window. Takes a deep breath. If she sees that he's getting away scot-free, she'll go to the police. But not now.

She looks at the figure walking away, disappearing in the crowd. It's not him, she tells herself, that guy is stooped, he walks like an old man. What's happening to her. It must be the stress.

◆   ◆   ◆

Shmueli realizes that he's stayed outside much too long. He walks with his head down to avoid making eye contact with anyone, reaches the hotel, and goes straight into the elevator without speaking to the reception clerk. He doesn't even nod hello. He feels like hitting something, smashing his fist through a wall. He goes into his room and starts doing push-ups, then sit-ups, and screams emerge from his mouth, from his heart, from his soul. In the next room, someone bangs on the wall and yells, "Quiet!" He wants to yell back, that fucking whore of yours should shut up, she kept him awake the whole night, but all he can do is laugh hysterically.

9

T here." The taxi driver points to the minimart. "It's over
there."

Irina got off the bus at the Tel Aviv Central Bus Station
and was shocked by the dirt, by the mobs of people rushing around
madly, so many foreigners she's not used to seeing, and apart from
a group of Filipino women, they all looked like they had collided
with the dregs of life in a hit-and-run accident that had flung them
here, casualties of fate, walking around this ugly place she had to escape from. She didn't have the strength or the ability or the desire to
start looking for a bus to the minimart. Everything looked scary and
threatening, and she decided to go down and take a taxi, however
much it cost.

She tried to go out to the street, to breathe, but the levels confused her, so it took a while for her to get outside, squeezed between
a remarkably tall and beautiful African woman and a thick-ankled
religious woman. She didn't want to think about how much she re-
sembled that thick-ankled woman. When was it that she put her feet
up at the end of a workday and realized that she no longer had the
beautiful legs she used to have?

She hails a taxi and says to the driver, "Nordau Boulevard."

"What number?"

"The minimart."

"What minimart? What number, lady?" he says aggressively.

"I don't know," she replies, ignoring his dissatisfaction. She doesn't care, she's in Tel Aviv, she's going to her Nina, no shadow is following her, no one knows she's here.

"Drive down the whole boulevard until we find it," she says calmly.

"Ah, Nordau, yes, I know where there's a minimart on Nordau."

And she didn't say, You see, you can be nice. And when they arrived, she even gave him a tip.

◆ ◆ ◆

Irina is sitting on the bench, looking around. Tel Aviv has only just begun its day. She thinks it's funny that it took her such a short time to get here. It always seemed to her like such a grandiose trip, the kind you only take once every few years. She's surprised she finds the city so pleasant, everyone hurrying to someplace and no one knows her or cares about her. She's no more interesting than a tree or a bench. She looks at the building across the street, a big tree in front of it, second floor. She also looks at the people walking on the sidewalk and the boulevard. Young yuppies with scooters and headphones. Tired young women pushing baby carriages, young fathers hurrying little kids along and finally picking them up and carrying them. And she thinks that, as long as there are young parents here, she'll have a job. It seems strange to her that once, she was afraid to think about living in a big city, and now, it suddenly feels easier and safer. She touches her money belt, which holds everything she took out of the bank, a little bit every day, and also what she'd hidden away for an emergency. She always put a little something aside. Because who knows what might happen to the banks. She looks in her bag for her phone, then remembers she doesn't have one. This handbag and money belt are all she has in the world. There's still a little money left in her savings account that she won't touch for the time being. And a few boxes. And she has Nina.

◆ ◆ ◆

When he went into the hotel without making eye contact, Yaara, who worked there, thought he was suspicious. Now she realized it was the man from the news. She says nothing about what she's thinking of doing. "You don't see anything and you don't hear anything," Yinon the manager told her on her first day at work. "You don't know anyone and you don't ask about his wife or kids, even if he's your neighbor."

She looks around. It isn't what she dreamed of when she started her hotel management course. But this is what she found. At least it was close to the apartment she shared with roommates and the hours were good for her. And there was something cool about the grunge of this hotel; three stars in Tel Aviv is like four in New Delhi and two in Thailand. Families of foreign workers, too-fat tourists, too-menacing Russians, and a cool bar that draws both tourists and kids from the neighborhood. She kind of likes Yinon so she's learning to be a little less of a nerd. To dress a little more Tel Aviv–style. How did she, a girl who wanted elegant hotel management, end up in this wild, boho-chic place? Couples come in every few hours, the guy asks about the hourly rate and the girl averts her eyes. Yinon allows that only after nine at night. He explained to her that every night the hotel isn't full is a loss, and she thought that they make the most money from her convincing people who drank too much to take a room for the night so they don't have to drive under the influence. Yinon laughed because he never thought of that, only a nerd like her would. And she realized again that she wanted him to wrap her in those strong, tattooed arms of his and kiss her and take her away from this world, where no one gives a damn about you.

She knows she has to do it. The guest in room 304 is the man whose picture has appeared on the news. She takes a deep breath.

She goes out of the hotel and dials 100. The policewoman at the other end of the line wants her name. "I don't want to give it," Yaara says. "There's a guy you're looking for in connection with what happened at the Central Bus Station. So I saw him. I'm not involved and don't know him." They both know that the policewoman has her number, but she refuses to identify herself. "He's in a hotel." She gives her the name and his room number and hangs up. Now she'll lose her job here and also Yinon, who she isn't really losing because he was never hers. And for the first time in her life, she feels really alone, maybe because of this disgusting hotel, which is full of pathetic, lonely people who have been crushed by life. And now she's doing something good but she feels like a nasty snitch who's destroying someone's life. And that's probably true. Someone and his family. Maybe he has kids whose father is going to be arrested now. And then she sees a car pull up at the hotel and two people jump out. The way they leave the car on the street like that without a second thought means they must be detectives. She didn't think it would happen so fast.

Suddenly it scares her that someone might think she's the snitch. She should get out of here. She has a chill and she starts hurrying away from there. Tears rise in her throat and she walks away and calls her mom, and the tears flow freely now.

"What happened?" her mom asks. "What happened? Are you okay? Yaara, are you okay?"

"Yes, Mom, I'm okay. I just want to come home."

❖   ❖   ❖

Nina looks out the window, and there's Irina. She came early, and even though Nina has been waiting for her, she's surprised. She longs for her so much that her pounding heart almost explodes, and she wants to run to her, but doesn't want to stop looking at her, she's here, she came. She sees Irina look toward the sea, then get up and take two steps, and she wants to shout to her not to move, yes, that's the bench, and she waves through the window, but Irina isn't looking in her direction. Don't go, she wants to shout, and then Irina goes back to the bench. She sits down and looks around, as if trying to figure out which direction Nina will come from. Then she glances at the building, almost at the window where Nina is standing, but she apparently doesn't see her.

Nina takes her key and runs downstairs, taking a few steps at a time, stumbles, and warns herself, remembering the time she lay in the stairwell here, injured in body and soul. So alone. And now that Nina is so alien and distant, as if she had been bewitched, as if a fog that had blinded her has been lifted. Nice words, she thinks, I was just a stupid idiot. Not blind. She runs, wanting to reach Irina and throw her arms around her. But she needs to be careful now. She can't screw it up. She knows that her plan is far from complete. Until she decides what story they're going to tell, she's afraid to be seen with Irina. She still doesn't know how and what she'll tell Eitan. And what he'll say to his mom. And she—to Carmela's son. He might still go to the police.

She's managed to get herself into a mess again, and again, her heart is leading her, not her mind. She should never have started that relationship: Eitan sees things through her, understands her, reads her thoughts. She has to tell him, but not everything. No, not everything. There are things she will never tell anyone in the world. What happened in that apartment. That, never. And he also has to promise her not to tell his mom, that's the only thing she'll ask of him.

Because except for him, who even knows her and her mom, who

in this big city gives a fuck about them, a mother and daughter who don't have a role in this big game of life.

Nina opens the door to the building, goes out to the street, and then stops. Calm down, she tells herself, no scenes on the street. She waits for Irina to look in her direction. It'll take another minute. She sees Irina looking around. And now their eyes meet. And the rest of the world vanishes, falls silent.

Nina smiles at her. Tears run down Irina's cheeks. She starts to walk toward her, not understanding why Nina isn't running to her, and instead, gestures for her to come. Irina reaches out to hug her and Nina pulls her into the darkness of the stairwell, which is fragmented by bars of light coming through the glass door. Only after it closes does Nina hug Irina. As tightly as she can. And Irina does the same. They sit down on the steps and Irina holds Nina's face, stares at it, trying to read everything she has been through, but doesn't see it. Once, she could see everything on her.

"My little girl," she mumbles, and pulls Nina to her again. "My little girl."

"Mama," Nina says. "Mama."

"Are you okay?" Irina asks anxiously.

"Yes. I'm really fine. Don't worry. It's just a painful lesson I learned. A very painful lesson."

"My baby," Irina mumbles, in Hebrew and in Russian.

"Come on." Nina helps Irina up. "We'll go to Carmela's apartment now. She thinks I'm her granddaughter, Dana. So call me Dana. Okay?"

"What? No. What did you do now?"

"I'll explain it to you slowly, and you decide what to do. Okay?"

"I don't want to lie. Lying is wrong. Ninotchka, what kind of trouble are you in now?" This is not good, she thinks. Not good at all.

"Not now, Mom, and please call me Dana. Okay?"

"No."

"Then don't call me by any name, okay?"

Irina cups Nina's face in her hands again. "Look me in the eyes. And the whole truth," she says, staring intently at her as if she were reading coffee grounds. Looking for pain. Anger. Details of what happened. She sees how much Nina has grown up in these last three weeks. Nina looks away.

"What is this here? Whose house is this? Why are you here?"

"Mom, calm down. Everything's fine," Nina tries to explain. "She's an old lady named Carmela. She's glad I'm with her. She thinks I'm her granddaughter, Dana."

"What granddaughter?" Irina is shocked. "*Yob tvoyu mat.* How did you get into such a mess?"

"She's not exactly sharp."

"And you?"

"What?

"You told her you're not Dana?"

"No. You don't know what it was like when I got here. Everything was filthy. Disgusting. She was living in her own garbage. She didn't see anything. I don't know how anyone can leave an old woman like her alone. I couldn't leave her. I can't leave her. No. I have to help her, Mom, but it's too much for me. Really."

"She thinks you're Dana?! What did you tell her?"

"I think she knows I'm not."

"What do you mean, you think?"

"Mom, calm down, okay? I don't want to fight now! I wanted so much for you to come. And I was worried. I don't know what's right."

Irina hugs her and Nina realizes that they're already the same height. It's been so long since they hugged like this. A real hug. A tight hug. She thinks that the last time was so long ago, and she feels like this hug is different, this is not how she remembers it, she remembers the hug of a large, strong woman who wrapped her arms around her, a little girl whose head rested on Irina's chest and not on her shoulder. But that must be wrong, because Nina's been a big girl for a while. It's just that she hasn't been held and protected in a long time. And it feels so good. But it's different from what she remembers. And Irina seems so different suddenly, not fragile but definitely no longer the rock she had clung to all her life, that had always welcomed her and strengthened her, until she smashed against it, smashed everything they had created together, that they had spun into the delicate threads that connected them, held them together.

"What did you tell her?"

"She doesn't want to know the truth. She wants me to be Dana. And I don't want to hurt her. She's very confused."

"Nina, we'll get into trouble."

"I know. That's why I need you. Let's figure out what to do. We have to straighten this out."

"Forget it. Let's leave this place. You don't want the police to catch you. You know they're looking for him," Irina says.

"I can't leave her. And I need help to help her. You'll see. She's really so miserable."

"And her family?"

"She has a son. His name is Itamar. He lives in America. He has a daughter named Dana. She had another son who died in some war. Uri. Every night she screams for him to come back. It breaks your heart. Sometimes he comes to her in her dreams, and then she's so happy, but then she wakes up and cries. So the dream isn't worth having."

"She saw a doctor?"

275

"I don't think so. Come on. Come in and meet her. I'll tell her you're the caregiver Itamar sent her. Okay?"

"And what's my name?"

"Stop, don't make me mad, Mom."

"I'm your mom?"

"I haven't decided yet," Nina says with a laugh. "Give me some time to think about it."

"You're such a strange girl. If I was a good mother, I would slap you hard now for what you did to me."

"Believe me, I've already received my slap."

"My love. My Ninotchka." Irina hugs her again. "I didn't mean it."

"Neither did I," Nina says.

"I'll never let you go away again. Never. I'll scream and I'll lock you in. And I won't let you go again. I cried so much. So much."

"Me too. Me too."

◆ ◆ ◆

They go into Carmela's apartment. She's sitting in the kitchen, the morning light coming through the window caresses her and illuminates the newspaper lying in front of her. Nina approaches her. She sees that the newspaper is upside down and turns it right side up.

"Carmela," she says, "meet Irina."

Carmela stares at her.

Irina comes closer and extends her hand. "Nice to meet you."

Carmela looks at her, and her expression doesn't change. Then she looks at Nina.

Nina says, "This is Irina."

"Why?" Carmela asks. "Why is she in my house?"

Nina recognizes when it begins, it has already deteriorated three times before, that short circuit between what Carmela understands and what she doesn't understand, and it's scary when it happens. The last time, she broke things and was really violent, she even attacked her. That was the moment Nina understood that she couldn't handle it alone. That it was too much for her.

"Shalom," Irina says again, and extends her hand again.

Carmela looks at her with empty eyes, and then pulls herself together and tries to find clues in the face of this woman standing in front of her, and leaves her hand hanging in the air.

Irina takes Carmela's hand and shakes it. "Nice to meet you. I'm Irina. I came to help you."

"Help me?"

"Take care of you. Clean. Cook. Go shopping. Help."

"I don't know." Carmela looks at her helplessly, as if everything Irina said to her places an overwhelming responsibility on her. "Dana takes care of me. Tell her."

"Okay, I'll explain to her what has to be done," Nina says. "Itamar sent her."

"Itamar? Wonderful," Carmela says, her face glowing with happiness, as if she has been thrown a lifeline. The name Itamar makes her eyes light up and her terrified, haunted expression vanishes. "Itamar is a good boy. Very, very good. This is his Dana. My Dana. Welcome."

"Itamar sent Irina to help us. She'll take care of you and help with the cleaning."

Irina looks at Nina, who is handling the situation, and now she's the one who's scared and confused.

Nina repeats the story she's made up for the time being. "Itamar sent Irina to be with us and help us."

"Nice to meet you." Carmela extends an emaciated, fragile hand. "I'm Carmela. Itamar's mother," she says, adding, "And Uri's. But he isn't here. He's not coming. Itamar's coming. Of course he's coming.

You know him? He's Dana's father. Our Dana. Our little girl." And she looks at Nina and strokes her hand.

Irina tries to smile, but it's not easy. She gives Carmela a fake smile but gives Nina a harsh Soviet look.

"I'll take Irina to her room," Nina says.

"No, Dana'le. No. You're with me, you're not going. No. I don't want Irina. I want you. You. You're not going! Tell Itamar that you're staying with me. That you're here. Don't go away. Don't leave me alone."

"I won't," Nina says, hugging her. "Leave you? Never. I'm here."

"I don't need Irina."

"Yes, you do, you do. I can't do it alone, Grandma. I can't. We need someone to help us. I told Dad. We need Irina. We do."

Nina caresses Carmela. Slowly, she calms down. And goes back to the newspaper.

◆　◆　◆

Irina gives Nina a worried look. They go into the kitchen after they take Carmela to sit down in her armchair and stare at the TV, even though the volume is too low to hear, and she occasionally looks at the scarf she has been knitting. It has gotten so long that it's piled up at her feet, made up of all the colors and thicknesses of wool Nina found in the apartment and gave her. The slow clicking of the needles has become the soundtrack of the apartment.

In the kitchen, Irina is pleased to see how clean and tidy everything is, knowing that it's her Nina.

"We have to see a doctor," Irina says.

"Okay, wait. Get to know her. Then we'll go."

"Which clinic does she belong to? Who's her doctor?"

"I don't know. She must have a card in her wallet."

"You look through her wallet?" Irina is not happy to hear that.

"You think she manages without me?"

"How did she manage before?"

"She didn't. There was a cleaner who disappeared. But she's really deteriorating. From one day to the next. It was terrible here before."

◆ ◆ ◆

Two policemen burst into the hotel and, like in the movies, show Yinon their badges and signal for him to be quiet. Another patrol car pulls up outside. "We're looking for him." One of them shows him the picture of the man on the third floor. The one who hardly ever goes out. Now it's clear why.

"What's his name?"

Yinon realizes it's pointless to try to help someone who doesn't know you, who you'll never see again. They didn't come here to arrest him for no reason. And another patrol car pulls up and two more cops get out and stand outside.

◆ ◆ ◆

In his room, Shmueli wakes up. Just a little nap. Suddenly he senses blue-red flashes. Dim. Just a hint on the ceiling. He has no way of seeing where the police car is, but he knows that it isn't moving. They're the flashing lights of a patrol car. He leaps up. It must be in his blood, he thinks, to wake up at the smallest hint of the police. In seconds, he puts on his shoes and pants, grabs his wallet, thinks for a moment about what he mustn't leave behind. He remembers the cash. He presses the buttons on the safe. His hand is shaking. It takes two tries for the safe to open. He takes the money and opens the door. They're standing there already. Waiting for him. There's no point in running or screaming or complaining, no point in yelling or pleading. That's it. He's fucked. He'll be inside for years.

"Can I take a few things?" he asks.

"Yes," one of the cops says while the other one goes inside and stands at the window. Standard procedure. So he doesn't jump out. Sometimes they're so desperate that they think they can fly. And if they can't fly, then at least they'll be in a hospital where the family can visit. Better than jail.

His mind is racing. He tries to remember if there's something he should take, or something he's better off leaving here. There's no escape. He wonders who the snitch is. He has no idea.

He remembers the day he was released from jail the first time. He swore he would never go back in. His father came to get him and gave him a really hard slap. Since then, he's done everything to erase it. To get his father's respect. "No one in our family has ever been in jail," his father told him. "Ever. It's a stain on us. A stain." But he really enjoyed the money he'd given him the last few years. "It's clean?" his father would ask him. "You're clean?" And he would say, "Don't worry, Dad, everything's fine. Maybe a little messy, but don't worry, I didn't cross the line." But on that night, he crossed the line. For months he's been going in that direction. Dragged along by his crew and their drugs and their lack of honor. He'd been so busy trying to keep them with him, to impress them. And how stupid it all looks to him now. "Let it go," Ofra told him this year more than she ever had in their life together. "It's not worth it."

And he asked her, "Let go of what? And what will I do? Go to the welfare office and get charity?"

"It's a long way between the welfare office and what you do." A few years before that, she suggested they open a store. A restaurant. Something. And he did. A store and a restaurant. And like a moron, he kept straddling the line.

"Now be clean," his father told him that night in the hospital. The night his spirit left his weak, disease-ridden body.

"I'll be clean."

"Promise me."

But he didn't keep that promise.

"You're addicted to thrills," the jail social worker told him, and he yelled at her not to play psychologist and fuck with his head. But it stayed with him, what she said. Yes, he needed thrills. To feel life. He used to sit with his brothers and sisters and Ofra's family, hear them trying to survive their daily grind, and he, with his rolls of cash, was the one who gave to her mother, to his mother. But in the end, all the brothers who used to look down on him came to ask him for a loan. Only for a month. For two months. Not a lot. Twenty thousand. And they never paid him back.

The uniformed cop takes out his handcuffs and Shmueli holds out his hands. Now he'll use up all his money on lawyers who will promise him that they can give him hope. And make Ofra believe. And attend all the hearings and appeals as if another six months would change anything. This is it. The end of his life. He'll be a frail old man when he gets out.

❖ ❖ ❖

"Tell me," Nina asks Irina, "would you mind if I go out for a little while tonight?"

"What?! Now that I'm finally here?"

"It's just that I've been closed up here for two weeks already and I'm suffocating . . . The farthest I've gone is the bench and . . ."

"There's a boy. Oh God. You have a boy!"

"Mama!" Nina looks shocked. This mother really knows how to read her.

"There's a boy. Tell me, is this what you called me for? So you can go out in Tel Aviv?! Aren't you ashamed? You scared the life out of me. Almost finished me off. I was so worried that the piece of garbage locked you up in some cellar and who knows what, or threw you into a sewer, and then I finally hear from you after I turn into an old lady like Ida Nudel and this is what you do to me?"

"Like who?"

"Nina. This is not a game. The police are involved here. If he finds you, he'll kill you. You saw what happened?"

"No."

"You can testify about what happened there?"

"No. I didn't see anything."

"Oh my God," Irina says, looking deep into Nina's eyes and understanding. "Oh my God!" she shouts.

Carmela hears the shouting in the living room and asks what happened, and they both say nothing happened. Everything's fine.

Then Irina continues being frightened, but quietly. "You saw it! Oh my God! You saw what they did to him! You were there. Oh my God!"

Nina starts to laugh. So hard that she has to bend over.

"Why are you laughing?" Irina asks.

"You're a lie detector. That's what you are," Nina says. "You look at me and you know everything. So why do you ask me?"

"Nina. You have to be careful. Today you're here with me. You don't move. Tomorrow we'll talk. I'm very worried."

"No one knows I'm here."

"Very good," Irina says, then looks at Nina. "Who does know?"

"Mom!"

"Who does know?"

"Eitan."

Irina wrings her hands in desperation. "*Yob tvoyu mat*, Nina. Really?"

"But he doesn't know who I am and what I saw."

"Good."

"And I want to see him," Nina says.

"Tomorrow. Today you're with your mama. And you'll tell me everything."

"I don't want to."

"Okay. Only tell me what I need to know."

"Let me go out for an hour."

"You're so stubborn."

"Yes."

"I'm more stubborn. Today you're here. Carmela will get scared if only I'm here. Come help us to get to know each other. And don't say 'Grandma' anymore, okay?"

"It'll be hard."

❖ ❖ ❖

Eitan's having the hardest day he's had since they met. He can't concentrate in class. Doesn't really sleep either. Yesterday, Nina texted him that Carmela wasn't doing great and a caregiver came who's trying to get used to her. It's tough going and she can't leave her, and they'll meet tomorrow. But he's stressed. He has to talk to her. To warn her. To tell her what his mom said. He looks at the time on his phone and doesn't know how he's going to get through this day. He waited so eagerly for the day they could just be together, and now he wonders what'll happen after he tells her.

The city empties out faster and earlier than usual. It's a shame that the first time they can move from the entrance to Carmela's building comes on the eve of Memorial Day, of all times. It's a special night in the city, everything is closed, all the out-of-towners go back to their suburbs, to their high-quality-of-life neighborhoods or terrible-quality-of-life ones in other cities, and only the locals stay here. And everyone is quiet. Even his mom closes the minimart. But he wants to stroll around the city with her, show her all the places he knows. Spend money on her and not just bring stuff from the minimart shelves. Maybe he'll take her to the square. They sing in the square. It'll impress her. And he wants so much for her to come to his place, even though his mom is home. But she'll make a scene when she sees them together. So maybe not yet. Because he doesn't want Hagit to interfere in their lives. And honestly, he thinks Nina needs time, and it's enough for him just to kiss her and hold her in his arms, even if he dreams about her every night, and his body is on fire, he can't wait anymore. She's driving him crazy. What he loves the most is when she suddenly bursts out laughing. The most unrefined, whole-hearted laughter. As if someone else is laughing. Because she doesn't laugh a lot. And he loves to sink into her sad eyes, which lately have actually been a little less sad, and it makes him happy to think that maybe he's the reason. His dreams about her get mixed into the reality of their meetings on the bench, and all he wants is for them to lie in bed together, to sleep with their arms around each other. They say that guys don't usually want only a hug, and laugh that it's a girl thing, but he's so afraid to cross the line with her. She's so sacred and pure in his eyes that he can barely think of her doing it, and maybe she hasn't even been with a guy yet. Even though she seems to know a few things about life, maybe more than him, and in fact, he's sure she does. Because even though sometimes she's like a princess, other times she seems like an alley cat that's visited all the dumpsters in the city but comes out of them clean and shiny. And he admits to himself that the complex thing called Nina is driving him nuts. Because she has it all and they have to be together. Absolutely have to. And when he hugs her now, he feels how she melts into him and her thorns seem to blunt. But this isn't really a good day to bring her home. Hagit's there and he doesn't feel like dealing with that. Especially because she told him that tomorrow, they would be going with Nina and Carmela, to the cemetery.

And then she dropped the bomb on him. And he has to tell Nina.

"What's her story?" Hagit asked him the previous day.

He didn't say anything.

"What's her story?"

"I don't know."

"I haven't said anything until now. But that's it. I'm giving you two days. I don't want to mess things up before Memorial Day because I feel sorry for Carmela. But we have to tell Itamar. I hope he comes to see for himself and I don't have to be the bad guy, even though I'm sad that it's going to blow up in your girlfriend's face, that little liar. Does she lie to you too?"

"Mom!"

"What? What's not true about what I said? That sad expression of hers doesn't impress me. Watch out for her."

"Did you tell him? Did you speak to him?"

"Not exactly."

"Mom!"

"Do you notice that you're repeating yourself? Yes, I'm your mom and I won't let some little liar steal all Carmela's money and I don't know what from you. Why is she all over you?"

"You called Itamar?"

"No." Hagit averts her glance.

"Mom!" he says, eyes wide.

"I texted him that I think he should come. I'm worried about Carmela. He should come. And if not, he should call me."

"What did he say?"

"He wrote, 'I understand.'"

"What does that mean?"

"I don't know."

Since then, all Eitan can think about is that he has to tell Nina. He tried to write a text message, but it's better to tell her face-to-face. So she won't get panicky and take off. Tonight he'll tell her that Itamar might be coming. That she has to be careful. On the other hand, Carmela can't be left alone. And who is that caregiver? That whole business is suspicious. And it's a problem that his mom hates Nina. She's the girl of his dreams. They'll have to work it all out because he absolutely won't give her up. And yes, she's lying now, but she definitely has a good reason. That much is clear to him.

10

It didn't really make sense, what he did. Maybe it was a childhood dream inspired by a movie that had been sitting in his brain, but instead of taking two flights and being stressed about the connection, he canceled one of them. He rented a red convertible and decided to drive for a few hours to the airport where the flight to Israel would take off. Many thoughts went through his mind during those hours he was alone with himself, and he could have continued that way longer and longer. He should take this kind of week for himself and really get to know America. Like in the movies he saw as a kid, like in Springsteen's songs. Endless roads. Take a car and disappear. He passed through miles of emptiness, surrounded by a sky that was larger and bluer than in the city. And there was nothing on the horizon. He raised the volume of the music, Shlomo Artzi singing in the car and America whizzing by outside his window, infinite sky and land. In Israel, people struggle for a kilometer here or there, and families like his pay the price in blood and pain for what is here in abundance and no one cares about. Marlboro country. In another minute, the man on the horse will pass him. Shlomo Artzi is the best for long drives. He checks Waze, the Israeli GPS, and as always, curses himself for not thinking of the idea before they did. That's what it's like in his terrible, elusive world. When it's right, it looks so simple. But another Israeli invented it before him.

He didn't tell Naama about this car ride, he doesn't really know why. Maybe so she wouldn't worry. For the past few days, he's been flooded with love for her. Something in the endorphins released in all that exercise, along with her enthusiasm about the agreement they recently signed to purchase the house, has restored the energy she once had. That's it. The house will be theirs. Now she'll have to start renovating, the thing she loves to do most, and it's as if she has returned to him, returned to being the person who wanted to devour the world, to experience everything. Now that the Israeli women have taken her into their limited circle, she's a different person. Everyone needs a group to belong to, he once read, and thought that he didn't. He has Naama. That's enough. All he wanted was for her to be content. Not disappointed, not pushy, not a helper, not a manager. Content. And he didn't care whether it was because she was content with herself. And now she is. Even if it's only to make him want to stay. She's happy with the house. With the anchor they've dropped here. Stability, she yearns for stability. He tried to understand how it happened, why the hell she wanted to stay in this nowhere place with its dissolving community, where most of the children assimilate and their parents are fighting the final, desperate battle for a bit of *Yiddishkeit* or Hebrew for their children or grandchildren, who covertly tap their cell phones even on Friday evenings in the temple, and the rabbi ignores it. It's his job to keep them there. Not to push them away but to bring them closer. That's what he's paid for, to show them the beauty of Judaism, so they won't cut ties, so it interests them a little. And it's getting harder every year.

Traffic is slowing down as they approach the city and more and more cars merge onto the road. He honks, even though that's not done here, only because he's stressed about returning the car at the airport. He once had trouble with that in Paris, and he got angry and cursed the French, and when Naama tried to calm him down, he yelled at her, and he's not a person who yells, he was just afraid they'd miss their flight. He knows America better. Parking at the airport in Houston and finding the car return place might be difficult, but he has more than two hours before takeoff. He'll definitely make it, he tells himself. Take it easy.

He'd been going to temple for the last few weeks after Naama explained to him that without community, people are lost. The rabbi was actually interesting. Everyone was a bit too friendly, with their fake smiles and their how-do-you-dos. But he nodded and avoided eye contact, and then ran after Ariel, who acted up while all the American kids sat nicely in their seats, and part of him was proud that Ariel was more Israeli, while at the same time, he knew he wouldn't stay that way. Just like Dana has become a pale imitation of *Beverly Hills 90210*. It's too bad she didn't choose something more interesting, like being Goth or something. But she hasn't reached that age yet. First she has to stop hating him so much. *Yob tvoyu mat*. This isn't how it's supposed to be. They're supposed to be father and daughter, crazy about each other. And they were once. When did it end? And it hurts him. He thinks about how it would be if they were in Israel. Maybe he's losing her here. "Please don't speak Hebrew around my friends!" she told him in English, over and over again.

❖   ❖   ❖

He doesn't understand how he allowed the where-to-live discussion to become part of his life. And he curses the moment he did. He was happy in Israel. He just wanted a little more freedom, to feel what it was like in the rest of the world, in America. And now he does. He's small in this world, and not very important, but it's easy and comfortable to live that way. Not to be everything for them.

For his parents. Not to constantly see the expectation in their faces that he, the remaining child, will fill the place of two. He can't and he won't.

"You can't always give in to him," he once heard Itzik say during an argument with Carmela.

"I will always give in to him. I don't want anything from him. Just for him to be, only to be."

"Do what makes you happy," she told him so many times. "Don't think about me." And now he already sees the signs to the airport. And he doesn't know what makes him happy, and he's not sure that that's all she wants, for him to be happy. He wonders whether he would be happy if he didn't have to carry around this sack of guilt about his mother. Would he be like Naama then, whose entire family is thrilled that a branch has opened in America? At some point, her parents will be old and sick too, but she has enough sisters and it's not the same as it is with him and Carmela, not like that suffocating rock that's sitting in his airway. Or his guilt about being so far away. She deserves more than waiting a whole year to see him. She deserves more than the American grandchildren who don't know her and don't talk to her, except for the stupid short videos they make for her birthday that, in his opinion, she almost never opens. If only she were a little more technological. She needs someone to help her on a regular basis. He has to decide on this visit: Either she comes to America with him or they go back to Israel. This can't go on. It's not fair. That woman deserves grandchildren who will jump on her couch. Who will call her Grams. She deserves one visit a week, not one a year. He puts Rami Fortis on, full volume, in his red car, in a traffic jam on the multilane highway that leads to the Houston airport, where he'll soon board a plane to his mother, to take her to the ceremony at her son's grave on Memorial Day for fallen IDF soldiers.

◆ ◆ ◆

The phone in the apartment rings when Carmela is in the shower. Irina and Nina freeze. It rings and rings. They don't answer. It stops ringing.

"We should probably answer," Irina says. "Otherwise they'll come to see what happened with her. If it rings again, you answer."

"Why me? You answer."

"Me?"

"It makes more sense if someone answers and says she's the care-giver and doesn't speak Hebrew," Nina says. She wants so much to go back to that former role of hers, to be the little girl. She wants Irina to take over the role of the manager who will tell her what to do. Whether she should answer the phone. It's so weird seeing her here, out of her depth. Unsure. Suddenly she realizes how much confidence Irina had. So much confidence that Nina never believed her mom could be so hurt. That she could fall apart. Or be sick. Or just weak. She noticed how people thought her mom was weak and scared and didn't understand. But she understood everything, and it was only when she didn't want to get involved or take responsibility that she started speaking with a heavy accent. And didn't look people in the eye. It was just a game. Because that's what the Israeli women she worked for liked, for their cleaner not to talk back, to know that they were the boss.

The phone rings again.

"Hello," Irina says in a heavy accent.

"Who is this?" the voice on the other end asks.

"Irina."

"Who's Irina?"

"Helper for grandmother."

"Ah, good. Very good. It's about time. How is Carmela?"

"Good. Good."

"Tell her this is Menashe from the taxis. I was at the grave today, made sure everything is clean and neat. I brought flowers. Can you hear me? Do you understand?"

"Flowers, *da*. Grave. Oi. Sad."

"I'll be there tomorrow, nine thirty. Okay. *Khorosho*?"

"*Khorosho*," Irina says, and Nina laughs at her. Irina signals her to stop because she's about to burst out laughing herself.

"Are you going with her? Is Itamar coming?"

"Me *da*, Itamar *nyet*."

"Okay," Menashe says. Then he mutters to himself that his kids better not do that to him. It's a disgrace. If Itzik knew that their son left her alone like that.

"Who is that?" Carmela comes out of the shower and asks with concern, maybe she missed something.

"What you name?" Irina asks, and Nina laughs at the distorted language.

"Menashe Taxi," he says, and she says that to Carmela.

Carmela's eyes open wide and she hurries over to the phone as if the name Menashe Taxi is the secret password that will open Ali Baba's cave.

"Why didn't you tell me it's Menashe Taxi?"

"Menashe says tomorrow nine thirty."

"Tomorrow," Carmela repeats. "Nine thirty. Tomorrow. Nine thirty," and then takes the receiver. "Tomorrow nine thirty."

"Carmela, how are you?"

"Shalom, Menashe. Another year has gone by."

"Yes."

"Dana is coming with me tomorrow."

"Dana? Dana is your caregiver?"

"No. My granddaughter."

He feels that something is off. Maybe he'll call Itamar tonight. For the last few months, Carmela has been calling him every few days to ask if this is the week. And now it's tomorrow and she's surprised. She's getting worse, poor thing. Of course she is, what does she have to get up in the morning for? She has no one. Not Itzik and not Uri. Who are gone. But she doesn't have Itamar either, or her grandchildren. Everyone's there. And she's here with pictures. Pictures of people who left her, and who knows if they'll come back. At least the grave didn't go anywhere. Why are you sticking your nose in it, he says to himself. Still—when he was in the nursery and bought the plants, and went to the cemetery and put them around the grave and cleaned away leaves and washed down the stone with a hose, just like he promised Itzik he would, even though someone from the Defense Ministry or wherever had already been there the day before because everything was spar-kling clean—he thought that it wasn't right. You don't leave an old woman alone like that. And when she's gone, that grave will be alone here. And he swore he would keep coming. He would keep bringing flowers and clean it up once a year. The weatherman said tomorrow would be especially hot. As if the normal heat there isn't bad enough every year. Something awful is happening to Carmela. It's good that at least he got her a caregiver. But what's all that talk about Dana, about her granddaughter?

He'll call Itamar. He has to.

"So tomorrow at nine thirty," he tells her.

"Tomorrow at nine thirty," Carmela repeats. "Tomorrow at nine thirty. Tomorrow at nine thirty," and hangs up without saying goodbye.

"Tea?" Irina asks Carmela.

"Dana, make me some tea," Carmela asks Dana. Ignoring Irina as if she were air.

"Okay, Grandma," Dana says, and Irina looks daggers at her.

"Okay," Nina says to her later in the kitchen, "I won't call her that."

"It's lying."

"Why? You used to call Mrs. Nachmias 'grandma' too."

"That's different. I worked for her and that's what everyone called her."

"Mom." Nina suddenly hugs her. "I'm so happy you're here, so, so happy." And though she doesn't want to, she begins to cry.

"I'm here, my darling, I'm here. And I won't ever leave you, and you won't leave me either, you hear?! You hear?!" And Nina's unwanted tears flow when Irina says, "We only have each other. Do you understand? Men will come and go. And it's just you and me. And if you have a child, it'll be with us. Ours. And this is it. You'll never do this again."

"Okay, Mama," she says, and the word feels so pleasant on her tongue, "Mama. Mama."

"What did he do to you?"

"Let it go. He's a shit. He can go to hell. Amen."

"Amen. *Yob tvoyu mat*. Garbage." She strokes her. "My little girl, what is it? Tell me, what?"

"Never mind, Mama. I'm here. I'm fine. I was stupid, it could have been worse. It's a good thing I ran away. Now you're here. With me. And we're never ever going back there."

"You saw that the police are looking for him?"

"I don't want to talk about him. He's dead. Dead."

"If only," Irina says. "But he's going to pay a big price. He's going to get a terrible punishment."

"Why?"

"Because Michal put a curse on him, even stronger than the curse she put on that woman who looked at her Ronen. You should know that we both put such curses on him that he has no chance. He'll get a terrible punishment."

Nina laughs and her tears of joy blend with her tears of laughter. She laughs at that co-production of Irina and Michal, a sisterhood with the power to destroy men's lives. Women who have a power that no one understands. That no statistics can measure, and none of the shouting feminists on TV can really understand, because those women break ceilings inside their own lives, and they're stronger than any husband they have or who left them or who they ran away from. Women who don't need men. The only reason Michal is with Ronen is because she's really wild about him. Not because she needs him. "He needs me more than I need him," she said when that woman made eyes at him and he blushed, and then she put the curse on her. And that poor woman, she got really, really sick. All her hair fell out. And in the end, she moved to Beersheba. Far from everyone.

◆ ◆ ◆

"I have the right to a phone call," Shmueli says for the hundredth time. He doesn't answer any questions. "I have the right to a phone call. I have the right to a lawyer."

"I have the right, I have the right," the policeman says. "You have no right to anything. Piece of shit. But the law says I have to. You can make one call," he says and hands him the phone, thinking this is a strong guy. They've been with him for hours and hours, and he's like a stone wall. Doesn't say a thing. He lets him make a call because maybe that'll give him a lead. And also because that's it, from now on he might get into trouble if he doesn't let him.

"Hi, baby," he says to Ofra, and she starts yelling and crying.

"Calm down. Tell Moshe to come to Abu Kabir."

"Why, baby, why? Why are you doing this to me?"

"Not now, baby, okay? Tell him to get here fast. Fast. And he should bring that blondie who works for him."

"You promised me," she says.

"Baby, they're recording us here and I didn't call so you could bust my balls. Believe me, I'm the one who should be losing it. I didn't do shit and now they're trying to frame me. Who knows for what. *Yob tvoyu mat.*"

"Don't curse," the policeman says. "*Yalla*, finish up."

"Hugs, baby. Tell Moshe to come, and tomorrow, the day after, I'll be home."

"That's a good one," the policeman says. "Your case is closed. All we need to do is put you in a cell and lock it. We have all the evidence. Everything's in place. The easiest murder case I ever had in my life."

"What murder, what are you talking about? Are you crazy?" Shmueli pretends he doesn't understand. "Bro, it's just a couple of escorts. You're getting carried away."

"You're the one who got carried away, sweetheart."

And he knows that only one person can fuck him up. Nina. If she snitched on him, he's finished. If she keeps her mouth shut, he's home in another two, three years. Five, tops. *Yalla*, Moshe needs to get his ass here now, with that blondie, Yafit. He has to talk to them. To find out if she snitched. If he's fucked. He doesn't know what's happening outside and where she is. The investigators are trying to take advantage of the fact that he's curious and stressed out. So he keeps quiet. But being in jail is hard. None of his guys, the ones who got him all worked up about Leonid, none of those cowards will get rid of her for him. It's too exposed, and the police are sniffing around all the time. Once they would have killed for him, today they're all prima donnas. They just want money. Can't wait for tomorrow. If she didn't sing, then Moshe's blondie will find her and give her everything. So she can hand it over to her mother and they can get the fuck out of his life. Let them go back to Russia, her and her little whore. What a dick I am, he thinks to himself. I work all my life and, in the end, some high school girl can fuck me up. Can finish me off.

◆　◆　◆

The siren on Memorial Day eve begins and Carmela gets up and goes toward the door, shouting, "Menashe! We have to go! Menashe, where are you? Oy, I didn't get dressed. Oy." She stands in the middle of the living room. "Dana! We have to go and I didn't get dressed. Dana!"

Nina comes out of the kitchen to go to her, but Irina stops her. "Let me. She has to get used to me," and then she walks over to Carmela, who is alarmed to see her.

"Carmela," Irina says, "it's nighttime now. You don't have to go anywhere. Everything is fine."

"Who are you?"

"You forgot me again, Carmela? I'm Irina. Irina, who takes care of you. Remember?"

Carmela doesn't know when that woman came here, doesn't know who she is and what her story is, but she does know that this is not the first time they've met here in the house, so she says, "Yes, I remember." Irina smiles and Carmela looks at her and admits that she looks like a good woman, this Irina who's here, she doesn't know how she came to be here.

"Dana," Carmela calls into space, she wants her Dana. "Dana!" she calls, and Nina comes over to her.

"She's Nina," Irina tells her.

"Who?" Carmela says, gaping at her.

"She's not Dana, Carmela. She's Nina. My daughter. You remember?"

Nina gives Irina a murderous look. Why is she doing this? Now Carmela is starting to lose it. It's happening because she feels confused, feels like she doesn't understand, that she's humiliated. Nina pulls Irina aside and whispers, "Why did you tell her that? It just makes her crazy for no reason."

"Because we can't lie anymore. She needs to know the truth."

"Why? How will the truth help her? Make her lonelier? Make her feel that they threw her away like an old rag? You know how filthy this place was when I first came here? Okay, tell everyone who I am, no problem, but leave her alone! Let her think her granddaughter is here. At least until tomorrow. Let's get through tomorrow. So she doesn't fall apart on me."

And the entire time, Carmela is shouting, "Dana! Dana!" and she starts waving her arms and then hits her legs with them, and Irina holds on to Nina and won't let her go, but Nina pushes her away and runs to Carmela and says to her, "Yes, Babushka, I'm here. I'm here," and sits down next to her, takes her hands, and caresses her.

"Who's that? Tell her to go away. Tell her," Carmela says, hugging Nina and pointing at the hallway. "I don't want her in my house."

"She's okay. She's a good woman," Nina says, soothing Carmela. "You remember that yesterday she told you about herself? And she made us such good food, remember? A delicious soup and potatoes with mayonnaise?"

Slowly, Carmela calms down. And remembers.

"It was good."

"Better than what I made for you." Nina laughs. "Don't worry. She's a good woman, a little strict, but we'll loosen her up."

Nina holds Carmela's hands and breathes slowly, deep, audible breaths. And Carmela begins to do the same. Slowly, her body relaxes. Irina looks at them and thinks how much Nina has learned during the time she's been here alone with the old lady, and how much she's grown up.

"Why do you look so nice? You're going out?" Carmela asks Nina.

"Yes, I'm going out for a little while. Okay?"

"She's not throwing you out, right?" Carmela says. "Don't let her throw you out of here. This is your home. It's your home. After I'm gone, it's your home, my little Danushka." Nina hugs her tightly.

Nina glances out the window and sees Eitan waiting for her on the bench. When she leaves, Irina goes over to the window to spy on her.

◆ ◆ ◆

Nina approaches the bench and Eitan gets up but can't decide if he should go to her.

"Wait," he said to Hagit earlier when she and the Eritrean were about to close the heavy grating over the store window, the one they close only twice a year, on the eve of Yom Kippur and Memorial Day. And he took a bouquet of flowers from the pail in front of the minimart.

"Memorial Day today," Hagit told him.

"Some people have birthdays today," he replied.

"It's her birthday?"

"Maybe."

"She cast a spell on him, bewitched him," Hagit told Sisi the silent Eritrean, who locked the grating. "Forget it, Eitan, don't walk in the streets carrying a bouquet today. Bring her chocolate. That's always good."

And Eitan knew she was right.

Nina and Eitan reach each other and hug. He gives her the chocolate and she laughs.

A thin veil of emotion covers Irina's eyes. Suddenly, Nina looks up at the window.

Irina takes a step back, but realizes that Nina has already seen her, and to her surprise, instead of glaring at her, she smiles. Irina waves hello at her, but Nina has already turned around and is starting to walk away. The young couple. Nina's arm around his waist. His arm around her shoulder. Irina sits down and suddenly feels the silence envelop her with softness. After such a long war against Nina and that terrible man, after so much anger and fighting and then so much insane, suffocating worry, after weeks with no rest, alone on the Seder night, afraid that she had lost her daughter forever—suddenly everything is all right. And quiet. And it's here, of all places, in this strange apartment that oddly enough reminds her more than anything of her childhood home in Kyiv with the too-thick rugs and the too-dark pictures, and the embellished porcelain tableware. As if time has stopped here. And the only new things are the lights they turn on at night. LEDs that are too strong.

"Dana'le," Carmela shouts suddenly, "Dana'le, what day is today? What day? Dana!"

Irina comes over and Carmela looks at her in terror. "Who are you?"

"I'm Irina. Your caregiver."

"Where's Dana?"

"Dana went out, but she'll be back."

"Who are you?"

"I'm Irina," Irina says, feeling Carmela's fear intensifying. She remembers Babushka's last week, when she also spoke nonsense. And she goes to Carmela, reaches out and takes her hand in both of hers the way she saw Nina do, and says gently, "I'm Irina, I'm your caregiver, Carmela. I'm here to help. Everything's fine. Sometimes you're a little confused."

"Where is Dana?"

"She went to see her boyfriend."

Those words suddenly brighten Carmela's eyes. "Supermarket?"

"No, boyfriend."

"Boy from the supermarket. A good boy. Madly in love with her," Carmela says and laughs.

Irina laughs with her.

"His mother is the manager," Carmela says. "The owner. Her father was, then he died. Left it to her. Died way before Itzik."

"She deserves a good boy," Irina says, also to herself.

They talked a lot last night, but Nina wouldn't give her details about what happened during those weeks, about Shmueli, about that night she ran away. About why she's afraid of him and why he's looking for her. And why the police are looking for him now. "Let it go," she said, "I'm fine. I'm strong." Irina encouraged her to talk, but Nina said it wasn't a good idea, that she didn't want to go back there. She should let it go.

"What day is today?" Carmela asks.

"Today is Sunday. Memorial Day eve. I don't know where they went. Everything's closed now."

"Today is Memorial Day," Carmela says and jumps up.

"No, tomorrow. Tomorrow."

"Tomorrow? Menashe called?"

"Yes. Menashe called and he'll come tomorrow. I'll wake you up. I'll go with you."

301

"You'll wake me up?"

"Yes. And I'll go with you."

"Dana too. Please, Dana too. I want her to meet my Uri. Please make sure I get up early."

Irina rubs Carmela's shoulder. At first, Carmela flinches, but slowly, Irina senses that she likes it. Better than the words.

"Itamar is coming?" Carmela asks.

"I don't know," Irina says. "I don't know."

◆ ◆ ◆

Irina is very worried about that man who might show up any minute, and although she doesn't usually pray, she keeps begging silently, please don't let him come. Don't let her be forced into giving answers. She told Nina to talk to Eitan today, explained to her that this whole thing will blow up in their face. She can't sleep. There's no one who can tell her whether he'll come or not. Since dawn, she's been going crazy and almost went to talk to that mother in the minimart. She keeps checking to see that the door is locked, rehearsed with Nina a million times what they would say if he suddenly arrived. Nina laughed, although it wasn't the least bit funny. They decided to tell him that Irina came looking for work after the last cleaner left, and then she brought Nina to be with her after she asked Carmela and Carmela agreed. Nina even recorded a few bits of conversation with Carmela so they would have them as evidence in their favor if it went to court. True, Carmela called her Dana in the conversations, but Nina edited them and they had a few videos they could present to any judge.

"He could come any second, that Itamar," Irina told her, "walk right in the door. And he'll call the police, you'll see."

"What do you want? For us to leave her alone? She'll die."

"She lived without you."

"She's much worse now. And we have to take her to a doctor. If she goes out alone again, I'm not sure she'll survive."

Nina even scheduled a doctor's appointment for the day after Memorial Day and Independence Day.

◆ ◆ ◆

Itamar wakes up. Please fasten your seat belts. We're landing. He tries to move and everything hurts him. The long drive and the even longer flight have wrecked his body. What he wants most now is to go straight to the beach and lie on the warm sand. The burning sand. And let it melt away the stiffness. All the preparations for landing have begun, the flight attendants are making noise, slamming drawers, Madam, please sit down, Sir, straighten the back of your seat, please buckle up. Fold up the trays. The back of your seat is not upright, sir, one of the flight attendants rebukes him. As if two degrees would change anything if they crashed. On El Al flights, they used to play the song "I'm Going Home" when landing. Not anymore. Someone chose a different song that he doesn't remember, even though he's landed to its strains for years already. He looks at his watch, which is still not set to Israeli time, and once again calculates the landing time, and once again it comes out too close to the hour the ceremony begins. *Yob tvoyu mat.* He was so pissed at the delay they had that he went to the airline's terminal manager to explain that he's going to Israel only for Memorial Day, only for the ceremony, and now he'll be late and his mom will be alone. I'm sorry, sir, the manager said, it happens. That's how it is. We don't take off if there's a problem with the plane. We have to check it out. I'm sure you wouldn't expect us to act differently. It looks like everything will be okay, but we can't take risks. None of the crew wants to stay here, the manager thinks, all the flight attendants want to be home for Independence Day, to celebrate, and now this guy wants to get home for the ceremony in the cemetery. The manager feels for him. He's thinking about the parents of Gadi, who was killed in a training accident, and about how the years went by so quickly and his buddies from the platoon stopped going when they saw that, from year to year, they had less to say to one another and nothing much in common except for their not very heroic memories. They sat there and saw Gadi's friends from the neighborhood, who all knew one another and the family, and they felt like outsiders. A painful reminder of the fact that Gadi had just happened to be in their platoon, it wasn't a case of that famous comrades-in-arms thing. Far from it. He wonders what would have happened if Gadi hadn't been killed in a training accident and they hadn't been interrogated, but were left with the burden of unproven guilt they felt even though they weren't guilty. None of them was guilty, rather it was the shared guilt of cruel coincidence, the wrong time and a Gadi who stumbled at the wrong time. And an entire family fell apart. He decided that, next year, he would insist on not taking a shift on Memorial Day so he could be in Israel and go to see them after the memorial service. Even if he's the only one from the entire platoon, he'll go. It's his obligation. And he goes over to the angry passenger and says, "Sir, I just want to say that I know how important it is for you to get there in time, and I'm sorry for your loss. And I apologize for the delay, but we really didn't have a choice. I'm sorry," and extends his hand.

Itamar shakes it. He has chills. That Israeli thing, that good thing that connects them all. It's so easy to move away and remember how prickly Israelis can be, and here's a reminder of the togetherness and solidarity. But why is it always at a time of loss, he thinks, and a moment later, he says to himself that that's not true, Israeli brotherhood exists even at good moments. The friends you don't have anywhere else, the holidays, the centrality of family. The sea. The language. Even in America, the Israelis stick together because no one can understand them the way they understand one another. And he fought that, tried not to join those groups of Israelis. Parliaments, they call themselves. He thought that if they're in America, they should be Americans, and for a few years, he managed to avoid that "communitiness," until Naama brought it into their home. She said it would help the kids, help with their Hebrew, and she must have been right, because the other Israeli kids here actually do know Hebrew and go to the Israeli scout meetings and even to temple on Friday nights, in cars, which seems stupid to him, but today he prefers that over nothing. It's probably too late for Dana. She's already American and doesn't want to be with the noisy Israelis, who he thinks are wonderful and she thinks are stupid and gross and clumsy. But in general, she's so anti. He misses his little Dana who used to look at him with large eyes filled with wonder, and her small hand would grasp parts of his face. And she would cling to him and refuse to be put down when he carried her. "That's how they are at that age," Naama told him. "Especially girls." But he has no idea about girls and how they act. He knows only that he has an American daughter he can't reach. And he has to insist on visits to Israel even if Dana says she doesn't want to go because she wants to go to camp with her girlfriends and he shouldn't try to force her because she doesn't want to, she won't go.

The plane hits the ground. No one sings, and only flight attendants speak, reminding them that today's Memorial Day and wishing them a happy Independence Day tomorrow. He looks at his watch: 9:43. It's a good thing he only has a rolling suitcase. He'll drive straight to the cemetery. How can it be that he's late for the ceremony, how?! *Yob tvoyu mat.*

◆ ◆ ◆

Menashe rings from downstairs. "We're coming down," Carmela says. Nina is wearing black. Irina found a white blouse. She doesn't argue with Nina. Let her wear black. Hagit is waiting downstairs. She's holding white flowers. Carmela walks erectly. She cried all night and now her eyes are behind dark glasses. And the boy from the supermarket also hurries over to them. The traveling queen's guard.

"I'll take the bike," he tells Nina as his mom gets into the taxi. And she hopes his mother will give up her seat for him. But no. And they drive to the cemetery in silence.

Carmela wants to tell the woman from the grocery that maybe she should let the nice boy come with them, but she doesn't want to insult her. She has been coming for all these years. As if it's hers, all that mourning. She keeps coming. Not many do. Sometimes people suddenly appear, for reasons of their own. A friend from the neighborhood whose son went into the army and came to tell him. Someone from school who did a project about him. Some of the people who were close to him continued to come for a good few years, but then life, and time, and the children . . .

"Shalom, Carmela," Menashe says when she sits down beside him, with all the women in the back seat. He wants to say, shame on Itamar for not coming. It's not fair. A disgrace. It makes his blood boil. Leaving the old lady like that. Nice to meet you, he says to the new women in the car. Irina introduces herself, Nina says nothing. She understands that Eitan's mom isn't buying their story. She knows she's not Dana. And she knows that now's not the time. They all know. They just have to get through the day. Later, they'll have to find a solution.

◆ ◆ ◆

And now the day has come, Carmela thinks, proud of herself for
not missing it. She woke up so many times terrified that she was
late, that it was over. She thinks that maybe she should have also
gone the day before, alone. Quietly. With Menashe, who goes to
arrange the plants. And now she's here, and again some minister
will make a speech, and again a newly bereaved parent will faint.
And she understands that that's it, Itamar isn't coming. For the first
time in her life, she's angry at him. Really angry. She doesn't accept his excuses anymore. And that anger is like a sharp pain, and
now she wants so much for that fog to come. For it to shroud her,
take away the pain. Why today, of all days, is everything so clear
and why does his absence hurt so much? The absence of both of
them. No, she won't leave Israel, she won't go to live in a house with
a garden in America. She won't leave Uri. It won't happen. And
she thinks about what will happen after she's gone. She's horrified
at the thought that on Memorial Day, at the ceremony, she won't be
there. And that day is not so far off. No one will be there. No one
will come. All the other families will be there, and only her Uri will
be alone. There will be no one standing beside him. She looks at
Irina and at Dana in the back seat. And it's as if her heart has been
struck a blow because the clear truth strikes her. Come back, dear
fog, she pleads silently. Come back and let me not feel such pain.
Pain because Uri is not here. Because Itamar is not here. And because it is not Dana who came to be with me. She doesn't want to
remember that the girl isn't Dana. It's so nice with her. She wants so
much for such a granddaughter to be with her, to hug her, to caress
her. So her home won't be empty. And that Irina is okay too. She
should be easier on her. It's not clear who sent her and it doesn't re-

ally matter, the main thing is that she's here. Yesterday she fixed the shower head that fell, and also changed two burned-out light bulbs.

"She's a bereaved mother," Menashe says to the guard at the barrier. "It's hard for her to walk. I'll let her out and leave."

"You'll leave right away, okay?"

"Okay."

Menashe already knows that he has to drop Carmela off as close as possible to the grave. Hagit gets out first and goes over to Carmela. Carmela looks at her and remembers. "Hagit," she says.

"Yes, Carmela," Hagit says and offers her arm for her to lean on. "Dana," Carmela says, "Dana'le," and Nina goes over and Carmela leans on her. Hagit and Irina walk behind Carmela and Nina.

◆　◆　◆

Eitan ties his bike to the fence and runs over to join them. Nina smiles at him and Hagit sees the smile and she wants to scream. It's a terrible lie. Terrible. How can you lie in a cemetery? But she also sees their love and knows that nothing she says will help. He's blind now. Head over heels in love.

She heard them yesterday when they came in from the square, the first time that girl had been in their home, and she fought herself not to listen to them, and kept watching those Memorial Day eve movies and crying. She thought about Uri and their relationship, and she cursed him for breaking her heart. And then silently asked for his forgiveness. And she thought about Itamar and smiled, remembering the moment they almost became too close. After one of the memorial services. He had just been discharged from the army, she had gone through the breakup and was already the mother of a baby. And they went down to the beach. And they understood and knew so much about each other. And the embrace was so comforting for both of them. A few days later, he said, "I don't want someone to be with me because I'm the one who's left," and she explained to him that it wasn't like that. And at that moment, she really believed it wasn't like that. She told him that Uri was like a storm and he was like home. And he hugged her and laughed. "Like slippers. I'm like a comfortable pair of slippers. And you're a princess. You need high heels, but then you'll be taller than me," he said, and then he understood. "Or even better, you need running shoes, so you can run away from this place. Don't stay here."

"People from all over the world come here," she said. "Where would I go? Where is there a place better than Tel Aviv?"

And he said, "There is no place better than Tel Aviv."

◆　◆　◆

They reach the neat and clean grave, which is surrounded by potted pansies. Good job, Menashe, Carmela thinks, and sits down on the plastic chair that is waiting for her, along with the young soldier from the regiment who has been given the job of standing there. And she says hello to Uri's two friends from the neighborhood, who come every year, and to pretty Ronit, whose blond hair is already full of gray, and she thinks how nice it is of them to come. Eitan asks the soldier his name and introduces him to everyone, and Uri's friends say their names and Eitan points at all the rest and says their names, but with Nina, he says, "And this is my girlfriend," because what can he say? And his mom wants to make a scene, but realizes that this isn't the time. And the girl pretending to be Dana says nothing. Tomorrow, tomorrow she'll explode it. That lie.

And at that moment, Irina understands that it has all fallen apart and everyone knows everything. Even Carmela. It's clear to her that today, she's completely lucid. She and Nina look at each other. Nina understands too.

"Come, Dana'le," Carmela says, and Nina goes over to her, kneels down, and puts her head on her lap, and Carmela strokes her. "Here is my Uri. I'd like you to meet him," Carmela says. "And don't leave me, okay? Don't go, whatever happens. Don't let anyone take you away from me, okay? Fight."

Hagit chokes. Irina says nothing. Eitan smiles. And the chief rabbi begins the ceremony. Suddenly, a strange noise, and someone approaches, pulling a rolling suitcase behind him.

People stare at the man who has come to the cemetery with a coat on his arm and a suitcase on wheels. And he walks among the graves to the place that is so familiar, so cursed, a bit of earth around which his entire life has revolved. He could get there with his eyes closed. How many times he came here without anyone knowing, and spoke to Uri, told him what was happening, and also cursed him and shouted at him, how could he leave him alone. How could he just go like that, without thinking about what he was leaving behind. How did he dare to be a hero. But he was a hero and now he's in heaven, and here on earth, Itamar has to take care of everything and everybody. First he sees Hagit and she sees him. And he doesn't believe that she keeps coming. Honestly, she's the best. Bravo, Hagit, for not giving up, for coming every year. She looks good this year, he says to himself. And they both smile sadly. Maybe she was right and they could have been good together. "If I was with Uri, that doesn't mean you can't be with me," she said then. And he said, "I don't want the three of us in bed together. I don't want to sleep with him. To get up with him. I want my own woman. Mine alone. Who doesn't know about all this and doesn't owe anybody anything."

And he found one. And she's happy in America.

◆　◆　◆

He walks over to Carmela and she sees him and smiles at him. A smile that has only a bit of happiness in it and a great deal of sadness, and her eyes fill with tears that silently begin to roll down her cheeks, and her shoulders shake with weeping. He sees a young girl move out of Carmela's embrace, stand up, and walk away. And he wonders who she is. He looks at her. Everyone looks at everyone. This is not the time.

"You came to me, my son. You came," Carmela says.

"Mom," Itamar says. "Mom."

"I'm Itamar," he says to the people he doesn't know.

And from the adjacent grave, they shush him.

He kneels beside Carmela, but instead of putting his head on her lap, he wraps her in a huge embrace. And the cantor chants *El malei rachamim*, the prayer for the soul of the departed. Then there's a siren and everyone stands.

And Eitan whispers urgently to Nina, asking what she plans to do, and Nina says calmly, "Whatever Carmela wants."

That's what she decided earlier, that if Itamar comes one day, she won't say anything. Let Carmela speak. Let Carmela decide. Let them talk to her.

◆　◆　◆

The policemen escort Shmueli into the hearing about extending his remand. Ofra runs toward him, but the policemen push her away. Her eyes are red. She didn't sleep all night. She made food for him, and thought about how stupid it was that the only thing she could do to help him was cook. And soon she'll have to start taking care of everything. It will all be on her. In the morning, her brother came to get her. It was still dark when she left, carrying lots of bags.

311

"Who's even going to let you get close to him?" he said. "Say thank you if they let you talk to him." On the way, he explained to her that it would take a few minutes, and that's it. They extend remand automatically. Even their lawyer explained it to her, and she began to understand how much money he would take from them, so much that in the end, she'd be left with almost nothing, but she couldn't save money on Johnny. She couldn't not give him the best defense. And the lawyer said that, luckily, the police didn't have any witnesses and he was optimistic, and she said, Optimistic? And he said there was a chance he would get off lightly, only if he doesn't break during questioning. And she said that nobody breaks Johnny Shmueli. And he said that in jail, during interrogations and in prison, it's different. But she has to be strong for him. Don't pressure him, believe in him, that'll give him strength.

Suddenly everyone stands. A siren. They all stop and bow their heads, the cops too, and also the judge, who is on his way to his chair, and all the people and the stenographer and lawyers and defendants. They all bow their heads in the face of death. Even the photographers and the other waiting families who, a minute ago, were shouting. Everyone stands, and the siren is so weak and distant. And Shmueli stands there and remembers himself in the army, how Yiftach, his sergeant, made his life miserable but also taught him a lot, and how, on the day he was discharged, he spoke man-to-man to him, saying, "Shmueli, stay in the army. Believe me, this is the place for you. You need action. Like Rambo. Here you can be John Rambo. Here you'll have action." And since then, everyone has been calling Shmueli Johnny Rambo. Later on, he heard that Yiftach had been killed. When he was already a platoon commander. And every Memorial Day since then, he thinks about him. And what would have happened if he had stayed in the army. Maybe he would have become a great commander.

But when Yiftach told him that he should stay in the army, Shmueli burst out laughing. "I'm going to make money. A lot of money." And Yiftach said, "Forget money. You have it, you're a leader. Don't let it go to waste." It's a good thing he can't see him now, his hands cuffed and his feet in chains, sitting in the defendant's chair. Ofra is looking at him, and she surprises him. She's sitting tall and proud, smiling at him, and her eyes, red with crying, are filled with strength, and he realizes how much strength he draws from her. And he's angry at himself, at how he hurt her. What a dick he is. He has to get out of this, he just has to, and never go back to that world again. He needs her with him, why the fuck did he want so much.

The siren fades, the noise returns, and the judge, who has been standing like everyone else, bangs his gavel and says, "This is a special day. Let's respect it." And Ofra thinks it's good that he's in jail because if he wasn't, she would slit his throat now. She would skin him alive, that cheating bastard, who never thought about her and the girls, who didn't give a shit about anyone, how many stories she's heard about that son-of-a-bitch these last two weeks. Let him rot in prison for a while, let him learn his lesson. If he doesn't get out of this, she'll divorce him, that's what she'll do. Not now, but in a year or two. Get him out of her life, the asshole.

And yes, she won't give everything to the lawyer. She'll put a little aside for herself. She deserves it. Fucking bastard.

◆ ◆ ◆

The ceremony ends. Carmela puts her arm on Itamar's, who with his other hand pulls his rolling suitcase as they begin to walk out. Hagit nods to Eitan, who goes over and takes the case. Itamar looks around at the strange bunch of people escorting his mom. Irina looks worriedly at Nina, who, to her surprise, doesn't seem concerned. Nina

313

looks at Carmela, sees her beginning to retreat into the fog. First, Carmela's movements slow down, and then a foolish, vacant smile spreads across her lips. Nina knows it well. Sometimes it's like this, calm, and sometimes it can explode. It's good that it's calm.

"Dana," Carmela suddenly shouts. "Dana'le!"

Itamar doesn't understand.

"Dana," Carmela continues to shout. "Where is Dana?"

"Mom," Itamar tries. "Sshh . . . What Dana?"

"Dana!!!" Carmela yells, and Nina can no longer stand the way the bereaved families are looking at Carmela, whispering among themselves, and the way their own small group is looking at her.

"Dana!!!" Carmela yells, and Itamar tries to calm her down. It's dangerous. It could end in a violent outburst.

Nina goes to Carmela and sees that she is already in another place. "I'm here. Sshh . . . I'm here," she says, stroking her face. "We're in the cemetery. Today is Memorial Day."

"Menashe came?"

"Yes, he came."

Itamar again places Carmela's arm on his, but Carmela sticks close to the stranger who has the same name as his daughter. He tries to catch Hagit's eye, but she avoids his glance.

He goes over to her, confused, and asks, "What's going on here?"

"Your mom is not in great shape," Hagit whispers to him.

"Who are those people?"

"A good question."

"What's going on here? Why didn't you tell me?"

"You didn't ask."

"What?" He doesn't understand.

"Itamar, where have you been? What did you think was happening with her?"

Itamar is silent.

"Let them take care of her. I don't know what their story is, but they are good women. Anyway, my Eitan is in love with her."

"With who?"

"With your daughter."

"She's not . . ."

"Mom . . ." He goes back to Carmela.

"Itamar! What are you doing here? When did you come?" she asks him. "You missed the service. It just ended. It was so beautiful. Uri would have been happy to see you. It's too bad you came late. But never mind. Your Dana is here. She's with me. And she won't leave."

Itamar stares at Nina.

Nina signals for him to take a deep breath. "We'll talk later."

He has a lot of questions, but he looks at Carmela leaning on that young girl's arm, sees the intimacy. The gentleness. The connection. And he knows that everything can wait.

11

He called Hagit after Eitan came to pick up Nina and they went out to celebrate Independence Day and Irina watched them from the window, walking down the boulevard with their arms around each other, and she knew that was it. They would stay here in the city. If not at Carmela's place, then somewhere else. But they weren't going back. They were starting a different life.

"What do you think about those two women?" Itamar asked Hagit. He still wasn't sure what he thought.

"Come down to the bench," she said, and hung up.

He knocked quietly on the door to the room that had been his most of his life.

"Yes?" Irina asked apprehensively through the closed door.

"I'm going out for half an hour," he said.

"Okay," she replied.

He still hadn't decided what to do with them and hoped Hagit would help him. The mother had been so frightened since he arrived that she didn't say anything longer than a word. But the daughter, the liar, wasn't afraid of him at all. That worried him.

"This is what Carmela wanted," the girl told him coolly. "For me to stay with her. Ask her. Whatever she decides, we'll do."

He went down to the bench. Hagit was sitting there with two bottles of beer she had already opened and the boulevard was full of kids celebrating, running around with spray cans, spraying foam on one another, or waving Chinese plastic toys that lit up in colors and spun around loudly. Music coming from nearby houses and roofs blended with the echoes of fireworks from adjacent cities and neighborhoods, the city was vibrant, wrapped in the familiar, happy noise of Independence Day. This was the painful night when Itamar would run away from home and wander the streets alone. This was the night on which Itzik always gave Carmela a sleeping pill, otherwise she would cry without stopping. "How can they be happy? How can they?" she would mutter. Hurt by the fact that all of Israel was celebrating when only now the painful Memorial Day had ended, leaving her broken into pieces. And tonight, before the celebrations began, Itamar gave her a pill.

"She's gotten so old," he said to Hagit.

"She's alone."

"Yes. And confused."

"You have to find out if it can be treated," she said, "the confusion."

"How are you?" he asks, looking into her eyes, and they both remember that night, back then. When they both were alone but the memory of Uri was with them. He knew Uri would always be between them. That was the night Itamar realized that he couldn't do it.

"I'm okay," she tells him, thinking about that word. *Alone.* A harsh, cruel word. And she finds it strange that she doesn't feel that way, even though she's been alone for so many years. Maybe because she has Eitan to take care of. Maybe because she really hasn't let her heart love anymore.

"So what do you think about those two?" Itamar asks.

"The liar and her mother? Honestly, I like them, and believe me, I hate any girl who gets close to my son," she says, and they both laugh,

"But there's something about her. I don't know what the story is or whether we'll ever know it, but why do you care? You're there, they'll be here with her. Maybe it'll help her be less confused."

"I'm not going back. I'm staying. You look good."

"Those things are connected?"

"What?" He's flustered for a moment.

"The fact that you want to stay and that I'm gorgeous?"

Itamar laughs and thinks that this is a more genuine conversation than any he'd had with an American over the last six years. Right here, on the bench on the boulevard. So many people around, couples and groups of people pass by singing and shouting, and he restrains himself from taking her hand and strolling around with her until morning, to go to the beach, to Jaffa, where they can buy pita bread from Aboulafia, to hug and talk about their childhood, and about Uri, or maybe not talk at all. And they look deeply into each other's eyes.

"Is this where we once kissed?" he asks her.

"No, not here, we were afraid Carmela would see us from the window. This is probably where you kissed other girls."

A gang of kids try to hit one another with huge, inflatable plastic hammers and Hagit yells at them, "Hey, take it easy."

"Are you really coming back to Israel?" she asks.

"Yes, I think so. All of us. We'll see how they react," he says, meaning Naama, but not mentioning her name. "But yes. We're coming back. That's it."

"Why?"

"I miss it," he says. "I miss this place. I miss my father. Uri. My mom. These conversations. I miss the quiet of Friday afternoons. The beach," and they both know that he'll keep on missing some of those things forever.

"It'll be good for Carmela if you come back," Hagit says. "But leave those two women with her. They saved her."

She gets up. Before the warm feelings she has for him in her heart begin to stir again.

"Happy holiday," he says, getting up and hugging her, moving her head so it rests on his shoulder, breathing in her scent. It's so nice to be in his arms, but suddenly, she feels old and heavy, and moves away from him. She has to take care of herself. For too long he has been in her heart without even knowing how much she missed him. And if she stays here, that wound will reopen. She'd better stop now.

"Happy holiday," she says as she walks away.

Itamar wants to run to her, to be enfolded once again in the arms of someone who understands him without words. But he knows it would be a mistake.

And he shouts after her, "I hate this fucking holiday."

And he doesn't see that she's crying.

◆ ◆ ◆

On the way to the Jewish Community Center to attend the ceremony marking the end of Memorial Day and the beginning of Independence Day, Ariel is sitting in the back seat of the car, happy after Naama promised him there would be loads of snacks and sweet corn and cotton candy. He didn't really remember what that was, but he understood that it was sweet. Dana, on the other hand, was sitting there looking sullen. She and Naama had been bickering since morning because Dana didn't want to go and certainly didn't want to participate in the ceremony, for which Naama had volunteered her without asking. She hates being onstage. And she tried on tons of clothes, but white shirts always make her look fat.

"It's also in memory of your uncle," Naama said in Hebrew.

"I don't know him," Dana replied in English. "And Dad isn't even here and isn't coming. And I don't understand what they say there in that complicated Hebrew."

"So maybe you really need to start taking Hebrew lessons," Naama threatened.

"Why do I have to go onto the stage? Who even cares?"

"We have to show respect. Your father went to Israel for that ceremony. All you have to do is say his brother's name and light a memorial candle."

"You could have asked me," Dana rebuked Naama, who almost started shouting at her, but she knew it wouldn't help. Dana was just angling for an argument to start so she had a reason not to go.

Now they're silent in the car because Naama is suddenly tired of cajoling her, and she thinks that maybe she and Itamar have to set more boundaries. Dana can be so delightful, but this last year, she has become insufferable. Suddenly the phone rings. It's Itamar. She tenses. It's a strange time for him to be calling. "Hi, sweetie. Everything okay?"

"Yes," Itamar says. "More or less. It was hard with Mom, she's in really bad shape."

"Oi."

"Yes."

"We're on our way to the ceremony. Dana and Ariel are here."

"Naama," Itamar says, then after a brief pause, adds, "I want us to come back."

Naama tries to understand. "What do you mean?"

"I want us to come back here."

"My love. It's a tough day." Naama takes a deep breath. "It was terrible with your mom. So stay with her for a few days and she'll get stronger. This isn't a conversation for the phone. When you get back, we'll sit down and work it out together."

"I don't want to. I want to stay here. And I want you all to come," he replies calmly.

"Honey, what's going on?" Naama is upset, and even Dana understands that it's time to put down her cell and listen.

"We have to be here. We have to," he says.

"Come back and we'll talk."

"I'm not coming back. I'm here, where I belong. I have a mother here who needs me. And there's air here that's mine. And a language that's mine. And even Dana is here," he says with a laugh.

"What?"

"My mom adopted a granddaughter. She was so lonely that she adopted a granddaughter." He smiles, and a bitter laugh escapes him.

"You've lost your mind."

"My mom has lost her mind. She's so happy I came. Every five minutes, she gets excited about it all over again because she doesn't remember that I'm here. She doesn't remember a lot. She's like a sieve. It sounds funny, but it isn't. It's terribly sad. I'm not leaving her."

"You're not coming back to us? I don't understand. We just bought a house."

"I love you, Naama. But that's it. I've had enough there. I want to come home."

"I'm going to kill you! I'm not leaving America. Forget it!" Dana shouts in English.

"Hey, Dana. Luckily, you're not the one who decides," he says in Hebrew.

"What did he say?" Dana asks, shocked, but she understands from Naama's expression that she'd better shut up.

"We have to talk about it. Not like this. Quietly." Naama takes a deep breath.

"Okay, honey. But I'm not changing my mind."

"We're on our way to the ceremony at the JCC."

"Take a picture of the Yizkor, of them saying the prayer of remembrance in English. It always hits me like a punch in the stomach. I imagine that there is no more Israel because everyone has left except for you and me and a handful of old Jews who meet somewhere and try to preserve a memory of the Third Temple we built here, which was also destroyed, not by war but because everyone went to America. And we meet for Yizkor, to remember and not forget."

"You're scaring me."

And he thinks about what scares him. That Dana and Ariel will grow up and go to live who knows where in America, first college, and then to wherever their jobs take them, and they'll marry Americans and do them a favor and come to visit for a few days twice a year, the way grown children in America do. And he and Naama will stay there in the house they just bought on the far side of the world, a place that for millions of people is more central than the hole-in-the-wall called Tel Aviv or Israel, but for him is just another place, and Naama will renovate the house again and again, and they'll always be waiting for their children, and then their grandchildren, and they'll be two old immigrants with Israeli accents and Israeli friends who love their homeland from afar. And then Naama will move him to Miami, because it's warm there. Or because Zipi tells her it's a good deal. He doesn't want that to be his life. And he knows this is the time to come back, because if they don't—that's how it'll be.

"Is he serious?!" Dana whispers to Naama, and Naama shrugs in confusion and then nods, because apparently, he is.

"I love you," Itamar tells Naama. "You don't know how much. And I want us to be here. I want the sea, I want barefoot, I want falafel. It isn't scary. It's wonderful. You haven't been here in so long. Come home, Naama. Come home. It's ours. And my mom needs me. And I'm not leaving her again."

Acknowledgments

A huge thank-you to Ronit Weiss-Berkowitz, my wonderful editor, who fell in love with Carmela and Nina and gave me no rest until I wrote them. Without you there would be no book.

To my Hebrew publisher, Roni Modan, and my amazing agent and friend, Moran Maor, who believed in me and in the book.

To my friend Tamar Amir, who kept asking whether I'd written today, and to Einat Sarouf for her wise advice.

To Shulamit Lapid, my dear mother-in-law, for her invaluable support.

To my mother, Talma Mann, and my sister, Ilil Keren, who are an inseparable part of me. With them, everything is allowed.

To Yair, who built a family with me. Together with him and our children, I learned that family is commitment, but also a great source of strength. I love you all so much.

Here ends Lihi Lapid's
On Her Own.

The first edition of this book was printed
and bound at Lakeside Book Company
in Harrisonburg, Virginia, February 2024.

A NOTE ON THE TYPE

Designed by Robert Slimbach, Warnock Pro is part of the
Adobe Originals type composition family named after John
Warnock, one of the cofounders of Adobe Systems. John
Warnock's son, Chris Warnock, requested the typeface as
a tribute to his father in 1997. The font was later released
commercially to the public by Adobe in 2000 under the
name Warnock Pro. An old-style typeface, Warnock Pro's
design is made of sharp, wedge-shaped serifs for a classic,
elegant look with all the features of a contemporary typeface. The font features Latin, Cyrillic, and Greek character
sets in a variety of weights and optical sizes, including text,
caption, display and subhead versions.

HARPERVIA

An imprint dedicated to publishing international voices,
offering readers a chance to encounter other lives and other
points of view via the language of the imagination.